GIRL WITH A VENGEANCE

BOOK THREE OF DANIELA'S STORY

PETER WOODBRIDGE

BEARWOOD
PUBLISHING

VANCOUVER, CANADA

This is a work of fiction. The names, characters, and incidents portrayed are the work of the author's imagination. The story is set in the context of recent historical events. However, any resemblance to actual persons living or dead is purely coincidental. Locations of certain police and security services buildings have been disguised.

Copyright ©2023 by Peter Woodbridge
All rights reserved.

No part of this publication may be reproduced in any form, or by any means, electronic or mechanical, including photocopying, recording, or any information browsing, storage, or retrieval system, without permission in writing from Bearwood Publishing.

For Inquiries: info@bearwoodpublishing.com

ISBN
978-1-7775735-7-7 (Hardcover)
978-1-7775735-6-0 (Paperback)
978-1-7775735-8-4 (ebook)

FICTION, THRILLERS, ESPIONAGE

Cover Design by Spiffing Covers: www.spiffingcovers.com

Production Services by FriesenPress: www.friesenpress.com

Distributed to the trade by The Ingram Book Company

ALSO BY PETER WOODBRIDGE

The Girl From Barcelona
Book One of Daniela's Story

Girl On The Run
Book Two of Daniela's Story

For more information, visit: peterwoodbridge.com

Follow Peter Woodbridge at:
facebook.com/PeterWoodbridgeAuthor
instagram.com/peterwoodbridgeauthor

Dedication

For Laura, Michael, Claire, and Robert

Principal Characters

Al-Amin	Rashid al-Muhasib, Supreme Commander of al-Qaeda; codename Alpha.
Ahmed	ISIS explosives expert working for al-Qaeda.
Antonio Valls	Detective Inspector, Mossos Homicide Squad in Barcelona.
Aurelia Périgueux	Gold expert working for Spain's TFPU anti-money laundering unit.
Caterina	Bar hostess and student.
Claudia Ramirez	Chief Inspector, Head of Spain's National Police GEO Group 60.
Colonel Scott	CIA chief, Covert Operations Europe; politically ambitious military officer.
Condesa	Widow of Count Carlos; a former government minister in Madrid.
Daniela Balmes	A spy and former officer with Spain's Civil Guard and the Mossos; CIA operative; codename Felix.
Diego Abaya	Moroccan-born Deputy Inspector with GEO Group 60.
Felipe Zavalos	Lawyer to the condesa.
Hasan	Assistant to al-Amin; codename Krystal.
Helen Hunter	CIA Deputy Director, Europe and Middle East Covert Operations.
Jamal Ismet	Former surgeon in Syria; rebel commander linked with al-Qaeda.
Jules Dampierre	Aurelia's brother.
Louis Valois	French aristocrat; Aurelia's friend.
Lord Garwood	British GCHQ officer; senior diplomat in the Middle East.
Luis	Chauffeur and former special aide to neo-fascist General Bastides.
Michael O'Flaherty	US Navy officer; CIA operative and undisclosed other covert roles; codename Fidelity.

Pablo Delgado	Lieutenant Colonel, Civil Guard Intelligence Service (SIGC).
Raphael Robles	GEO 60 Officer, aka Mustapha; head of al-Qaeda in Spain.
The Grandee	Influential Spanish aristocrat; loyal to the Royal Household.
The Russian	Alexei; officer with Russia's Spetsnaz GRU military intelligence in Syria.
Xavi	Detective Sergeant with the Mossos; Antonio's buddy since childhood.
Yussef	Younger brother of Ahmed; an ISIS operative.

Civil Guard	Senior military force for Spain's border security and other policing roles.
CNI	Spain's National Intelligence Centre.
DST	General Directorate of Territorial Surveillance, Morocco.
GEO Group 60	Fictitious counter-terrorism unit within Spain's National Police, Special Operations.
GRU (officially GU)	Russia's military intelligence service, Moscow.
Mossos d'Esquadra	Catalunya's primary police force.
Mukhabarat	Military intelligence service in Syria.
National Police	Spain's civilian federal police, including domestic anti-terrorism units.
NCS	American National Counterintelligence Security service.
PSD	Political Security Directorate; operates detention centres within Syria.
SIGC	An intelligence service within the Spanish Civil Guard.
Spetsnaz	Russian special purpose forces; part of GRU military intelligence.

CHAPTER 1
Recalibration

He sat at the bar for his first three drinks, then moved to the seclusion of a booth at the back.

As long as he was able to pay his bill, thought his waitress, he could sit there all afternoon if he wanted. All night, too, for that matter. It was a pity, she thought. He was cool but in some kind of dark mood. Too morose and locked away in his own personal world of hurts.

She flirted a little with him at first. He was a lot older than she was. Not harmful, she decided. Just another ordinary guy hitting a few speed bumps along the road.

If he gave her any encouragement, she'd be tempted to go home with him, she admitted to the bartender—half in jest. Her colleague was surprised; she wasn't the type to sleep around. But he knew she'd been through her own wars recently. Some really tough breaks.

He switched to hard liquor and was gripping his hands tightly around the glass. He studied the ice cubes, using them as the focal point for his thoughts. From time to time, he would grit his teeth, grinding them in an act of frustration. His eyes never once looked up to scan the room. Romantic opportunities seemed the furthest thing from his mind. She wasn't even sure he was aware she existed. A man consumed by his own thoughts. But an interesting man— intriguing.

"Another round?" she asked. Was that a yes? She placed it on his table anyway.

Her maternal instinct kicked in; she wanted to help him. She was familiar with the signs. Women, if they can't be lovers, revert to being mothers. He hadn't ordered food, so she put a plate of appetizers on his table. He nodded politely. Brief eye contact but no recognition—even less commitment. Whatever magic it was that he held for her, she couldn't keep her eyes off him.

He went to the washroom. By the time he returned, she'd placed several fresh tapas on his table. He ate them, oblivious to her thoughtful gesture.

The evening crowd was drifting in. Other customers needed to be served. From time to time, she found herself glancing over at him—sitting alone at his table. Keeping an eye on him, she needed to make sure he was all right. She had no way to know what he was thinking, his problem. He was so deep.

Unreachable.

Hours later, he was still binge-drinking but seemed in control. The bar had rules. "Are you driving?" she asked.

He looked up at her. "I know what you're asking. No car keys; I left them at the office. I'm all right. Honestly, I am. If I'm in the way, if I'm disturbing anyone, I'll leave."

She shook her head.

An hour later, she ignored his request for another drink, concerned that he was spiralling downwards so fast in freefall that he had to be rescued from himself. "I'm off duty soon. No conditions. You want to come to my place? . . ."

From the cloud of his intoxicated state, he managed a weak smile. He said nothing; his thoughts weren't connecting any longer. He was too far gone.

"You're coming with me," she told him when she checked out from her shift fifteen minutes later. "I'm Caterina."

"Antonio," he announced, as if he were seeing her for the first time.

"What do you do?" she asked.

"Me?" He laughed. "I screw up peoples' lives. Don't mean to." His words were slurred. "Just happens."

Half an hour later, they were in her apartment. "Just sleep if you want to," she said.

"Do you have any wine?" he asked.

She shrugged her shoulders. "Do you want some?"

"Not really," he conceded, managing a smile. "Sorry. Not much use to you. Very sorry, actually. You're nice."

She undressed him and helped him into her bed. He lay face down on the pillows, breathing heavily with the saturated stench of alcohol on his breath. Worried that he might throw up and choke, she rolled him onto his side.

"Night," she said to his prostrate, snoring form. Taking a pillow, she headed for the couch. Whatever burdens he was carrying, she thought, he seemed like a decent guy.

Heaven knows, there are few enough of them around.

Antonio woke up in his underwear. She was sitting on the edge of the bed, offering him an espresso.

"Morning," she said simply.

No fuss. No loaded glances. He felt relieved. "Sorry about last night. Thanks. You rescued me."

"Seemed like it was something you had to get through. Apart from the hangover, are you feeling any better?"

"Give me a few days, and I'll be able to tell you." He grimaced as he leaned forwards, then managed an embarrassed smile. "I wasn't very good company, was I?"

Her eyes flashed a look of disappointment and resignation. "When I served you at the bar, I thought you were nice. You drank a lot. I don't know why; it's none of my business. But I was intrigued. You were really intense. But I knew you just needed to sleep." She took his empty cup from him. Moments later, she was back and stood at his bedside.

She caught his glance at her thin nightdress. It was temptingly short, ending just below the top of her shapely tanned legs. "You're probably wondering. No, we didn't. You were so far gone, you were useless to anyone." He tried to take hold of her hand, but she pulled away from him. "By the way, you snore. I slept on the couch." Making a grimace, she rubbed the back of her shapely neck. Then another smile . . . and a catchy laugh.

Antonio had woken up in these situations before. Usually, he couldn't wait to get out of the door and away from the scene of the crime. This was different. He felt relaxed and unhurried, strangely free in a way—without any responsibilities. Maybe it was the events of the past few days; maybe it was . . . he couldn't recall her name.

He'd resigned from his job, although he knew it was only in his imagination. It had crossed his mind last night that he would resign. He'd been crapped on from a great height. Important people had let him down. They'd deceived him—kept him in the dark. They'd allowed him to pursue a complex investigation that turned out to be completely unnecessary. He'd put his heart and soul into it.

He'd tracked down and arrested Daniela. In the midst of her interrogation, the chief, Diego, and Colonel Scott had entered the room. "She's a CIA officer," they'd told him. "She has been since the beginning." He'd had no idea; they hadn't trusted him enough to share the truth. "Let her go," he'd been ordered.

He'd been made to feel like a fool; that was the worst part.

Fuck them.

"Another coffee?" she called from the kitchen. Her voice was young and clear.

He looked at his watch and saw that it was past eight. Picking up his trousers, he retrieved his phone—still on mute. Lots of unread texts and messages. He slipped it back into his pocket and decided to ignore the world. His resentment was still raw.

She returned with a glass of water. "Rehydrate." Her voice was kind.

"Thanks . . ." he said, feeling embarrassed.

"Caterina," she supplied, sensing his discomfort. "You're Antonio."

He nodded.

"You don't look like a breakfast guy. In case you're hungry, I have some things on the table. Help yourself. You didn't eat much last night. I have to get dressed. I have classes," she announced.

"You're a student?"

"Sure." She laughed. "Working in a bar isn't how I see my life unfolding."

Her tone was light-hearted, he thought. She wasn't being intrusive, not asking for any explanations. Most of all, she wasn't trying to lay claim. She'd looked after him last night—at a time when he was not very safe with himself. He'd been lucky. She was probably the least complicated and most undemanding female encounter he could have made.

Reaching out, he pulled her towards him.

She came easily and sat on top of him, pushing his strong shoulders back into the pillows. Leaning over him, her long auburn hair covered his face and head. Then she leaned back and pulled off her top—arching her shoulders, baring her firm breasts. She invited his hands to sweep upwards over them, squeezing them together.

"Last night in the bar . . ." he began to say.

"Yes," she replied with a laugh. "They look different, don't they?" Jumping off the bed, she returned carrying her push-up bra. "If I hadn't worn this to work, I wouldn't have got the job. But they're mine, and they're both real."

Her words were smothered as he pulled her down on top of him, his mouth swallowing each of her breasts in turn, moving his tongue in circular motions around her nipples. She gasped, and he felt her buttocks draw closely together. Seconds later, she split her legs apart and began to grind her clitoris into his lower abdomen, pinning his shoulders back onto the bed. He watched, mesmerised, as she closed her eyes and threw back her head and long mane of hair. It fell back in a cascade between her narrow shoulders. The pulsating motion of her body as she thrust herself into him kept him spellbound.

Her lids opened, and he saw her eyes lift upwards, almost disappearing, in a state of absolute ecstasy.

Antonio continued to watch in fascination. He wondered, had he not been there, if she would have derived the same pleasure from another man's body. Evidently, it was not him that she wanted; it was the opportunity for arousal. It was the stimulation of her fevered imagination and her lust . . . the sensations that her uninhibited exploitation of his undeniably muscular and masculine frame could deliver. Her fantasy.

Again, she was working herself up into a fever pitch. Thrusting . . . it was a grinding rhythmic vibration. Antonio had never experienced a woman who was so self-centred, so intent on her own sensual pleasure. She became wild, groaning ecstatically. Her nails dug into his shoulders—so deeply that they cut into him. Still she continued . . . on and on and on. He heard a scream as her rapture reached and then surpassed its peak, her body pulsating with uninhibited female pleasure. The overwhelming ecstasy of her release. The pure, joyful gasp of happiness that escaped from her mouth was almost inhuman.

Her climax seemed to liberate a beast trapped within her.

She pushed away from him and rolled across the bed—her body continuing to shudder as she twisted and groaned. Wrapping her arms around her knees, she drew into a foetal position. Moments passed. Slowly, she rose to her knees and crawled back on top of him. Thrusting her mouth over his, she forced his lips apart, stretching him, searching every crevice with her stiffened tongue. Digging deeper.

Until now, Antonio had been involved merely as a fascinated bystander. No woman he'd ever known had performed such gymnastics using his body, treating him solely as a secondary object of her desires. Released temporarily from the sexual incarceration that had trapped her passions, she proceeded to repeat her slow movements, rubbing her limbs against his muscles. This time, however, it was obvious she was intent solely on his pleasure.

He was ready.

Slipping his hand between her knees, he forced her legs apart, delighted to feel her moisture—the lust, the wanting, the wetness that enticed him upwards to invade her. To possess her, just as she had taken command of his body and dominated him moments earlier.

Her body gave a cartilaginous click as the sacral column of her lower spine thrust upwards to meet him. Hardwired to satiate her demanding hormones and yield to his male desires, she arched her backbone towards him to facilitate his entry inside her. As they met in a unison of pure passion, her legs wrapped around his back, controlling his body so that he had no ability to escape or do anything that was not part of their shared craving to consummate an act of procreation. It was mutual lust, an animalistic determination. A concentration of pent-up energy passionately liberated in pursuit of a single purpose.

He was spent.

Suddenly, her eyes widened. Grasping his hands, she squeezed them tightly in hers—not letting go. It was an act of possession. Instinctively, she wanted to keep him inside—to prolong the moment. But she knew it was much more than that. Despite the disregard for commitment that she had claimed, something physically within her had evolved.

They lay alongside each other, heads on pillows—staring without focus at the ceiling. Still breathless but content. Set free.

Relaxed and happy.

―⌒―

Antonio woke up in work mode. He examined his watch.

Scrolling through his messages, he breathed out heavily in exasperation. A meeting was scheduled with the chief for early afternoon, and Xavi had called him numerous times. There were about a dozen more texts that could be answered later; the chief couldn't be kept waiting.

He uttered a Catalan expletive.

"You have to go," said Caterina.

He nodded. "I'm sorry."

"Don't be. I feel wonderful."

"So do I." He grinned and meant it.

Getting dressed, he heard her shower, the heavy splashes of water and soap on the tiles as she washed away their lovemaking. Wrapped in a towel, she looked young and fresh.

"No recriminations," she said, handing him a slip of paper. "My address . . . if you want to call a taxi. Around here, it's easier than trying to flag one on the street. We don't owe each other anything, you know," she added, sensing his discomfort.

"It's complicated," Antonio said.

She rolled her index finger across his lips to seal them and shook her head. Her smile said that no further explanation was necessary.

His phone rang. "I'd better take this," he apologised.

She nodded and headed back to the kitchen, picking up and bundling several text books on her way.

"Where the heck have you been, Toni?" shouted his squad partner and long-time friend. "We found out you'd been at a local bar. Nobody knew anything else until one of the day-shift employees arrived. She told us you'd gone off with your waitress. We got her home address; I was about to send a squad car around to see if you're okay. Are you?"

"Long story," said Antonio. "I could do with a ride."

"I'll be there in ten," said Xavi.

Antonio walked into the kitchen and put his arm around Caterina. "My partner will be here shortly; I can wait on the street."

She looked puzzled. "Partner? You're a cop?"

He nodded. "Mossos. Homicide detective." He saw her face go pale. "Are you okay? Did I say something wrong?"

"Nothing. Just a bit of a surprise, that's all." She pulled away.

Antonio frowned. He didn't have time for a long conversation. Not right now. He spun her around. She looked hurt. Her mood had changed and he wasn't sure why. "Caterina, we can talk later."

She shrugged. The magic had evaporated.

"I need the washroom before I leave," he said, trying to sound light-hearted. He'd been puzzled by her reaction to the news that he was a cop. His police instincts kicked in. Was there something she was hiding? Antonio soon found himself enveloped in the steam still lingering from her hot shower. Her scent smelled fresh and inviting. Rapidly, he noted that her possessions filled all the available spaces. He hadn't considered it before; now he was wondering if there was a man in her life. His thought was accompanied by a pang of jealousy, or was it just male possessiveness?

While he'd been asleep, she'd have had plenty of time to remove telltale belongings from the bathroom if she'd wanted. He didn't think she had. Smiling at his own insecurity, he checked the medicine cabinet anyway. Nothing there. It didn't seem that she was living with anyone. Still, he was puzzled by her sudden change in mood. Returning to her living room, he saw that she was clutching a framed photograph. She looked sad, approaching tears.

"Just so you know," she said, handing him the photo frame, "it's my brother. It's a long story and you don't have time. Not now. The police were involved. That's why I reacted. It surprised me when you said you're with the Mossos. I wasn't expecting it."

He hugged her. "Sorry, it's none of my business." Looking into her eyes, he added, "Yesterday was a bit of a disaster for me, but this morning with you was wonderful. I want you to know that."

"Last night, you needed me; this morning, I needed you," she replied. "No commitment, okay?" Thrusting a fresh bottle of water into his hands, she added, "You need to rehydrate, Antonio. You must look after yourself."

Smiling at her thoughtfulness, he kissed her.

His phone buzzed a text. "That's my ride. I'll call you."

"I promise."

⁓

"You look like shit," confirmed Xavi several minutes later, after clicking open the passenger door for Antonio. "Better drop by your apartment. You need a shower and some clean clothes, my friend." He wrinkled his nose and sniffed the air.

"Not a word to Pilar, amigo." Antonio shot a severe look at his friend. "I don't want this getting back to Maria."

"No chance," replied Xavi with a grin that heralded an announcement. "By the way, Pilar is pregnant again."

"Amigo! Congratulations!" Antonio gave Xavi such a heavy shoulder slap that he almost lost control of the wheel. "We have to celebrate—when I'm dried out. Another pregnancy? Fantastic! You know what's causing it, don't you?" He laughed.

Feeling more human after a steaming hot shower at his apartment, Antonio rubbed his temples vigorously.

His eyes were bloodshot and his mouth felt like a dried-out dishcloth. If he could have taken the day off, he would. No such luck; the chief had texted him again: "A reminder . . . my office after lunch." He knew exactly what it would be about. He hadn't talked to his boss since Colonel Scott's visit and Daniela's release from custody. Reaching for the bottle of water that Caterina had given him, he drank the rest of it. "Thanks again for the ride, amigo," he said to Xavi. "That was quite a night."

Under other circumstances, Xavi probably would have grinned at his situation, thought Antonio. Over the years, they'd had plenty of nights out together that had gone over the top. This wasn't the same. Last night had been a binge. Self-punishment.

"You'd better get something to eat," said Xavi. "The chief will know what's caused your bloodshot eyes."

Xavi was worried about him, thought Antonio. He knew his friend was concerned—aware that nothing much had gone right for him since he'd met Daniela. She'd jinxed his life, professionally and socially.

"Caterina . . . the girl last night," said Antonio, rationalising his actions to Xavi. "She's really nice."

But he knew it had been a one-night stand: an exorcism.

To dispossess himself of the demon.

The chief was sympathetic and consoling. "You handled the Montserrat raid professionally, Antonio. You're a credit to the force. Madrid was impressed too. Chief Inspector Claudia Ramirez was very complimentary. If you want to take some leave after this Daniela Balmes business, everyone will understand."

Antonio shook his head. "I'm fine, sir. Thank you." His tone made it clear that it wasn't an issue for debate.

"You know we have to close our files on Daniela, and seal them?" asked the chief. "They've sent us a direct order. We're instructed to have nothing more to do with the case—they want all our files and records, everything we've got. They aren't messing around, Toni. A senior Civil Guard officer is on his way here. We have to give him all copies—and wipe our e-storage records clean. Nothing to indicate who she is: phones, laptops, daybooks, our database. The lot."

"Are they taking Diego's outfit off the case as well?"

"The National Police are no longer involved. Claudia's hopping mad. I talked to her this morning." The chief looked at him sternly. "I know it's frustrating after all you've been through, but it's out of our hands. I want you back on regular duties. Homicide. Forget that you ever heard of Daniela."

"Yes, sir. Got it," said Antonio without enthusiasm. "The Civil Guard can have all my files.

The chief beamed. "Fantastic," he said, coming around his desk to pat Antonio on the shoulder. "You're a pro, Toni. I knew you'd take it well. That girl, Daniela, deserves the best veil of secrecy we can provide. From what I understand, she's going to need it."

The heavy wood and metal front door of his apartment building in the Sarrià neighbourhood of Barcelona swung shut behind him.

Standing on the step with his back touching the door, Antonio paused—listening for the click as the locks engaged. Last night was the best sleep he'd had for a week. The effects of his hangover had finally been cleansed from his system. It was a nice day, and he needed a good walk.

His alert green eyes glanced straight ahead, then both ways—searching. Satisfied with what he saw, he stepped onto the sidewalk and set out on his stroll to the Catalan police headquarters. Sights and sounds can play tricks, but Antonio had seen something that confirmed what he'd already observed from his apartment window. Someone was waiting for him. It was still early, just past sunrise. Traffic on the residential street was sparse. A man's footfall started up behind him; the crisp tread of leather shoes on the dry late-autumn ground was unmistakable.

An amateur, thought Antonio. Professionals would never give themselves away so obviously. Besides, he'd observed the man earlier—drinking a cup of coffee at a table at the corner café.

His follower presented no danger, Antonio knew. But it annoyed him. The man was imposing on his personal space, being intrusive. By meddling in Antonio's private life, he was colluding with people who wanted to drag him back to the past—to a life that Antonio had resolved to forget. He needed to leave his mistakes behind. Make a fresh start.

The CIA's revelations about Daniela had hit to his core. He'd been duped, not just by her but by a conspiracy of silence. He'd been excluded, rejected as undeserving of his colleagues' trust. They hadn't believed in him, and she'd made a fool of him again. Professionally and personally, she'd played him convincingly, he had to admit. It didn't help that she'd fooled a lot of people. She had deceived *him*. He hated the feeling, yet there was almost nothing he could do about it. Except move on.

Deception and betrayal hurt. For Antonio, they were particularly bitter and hard to accept. He'd worked incredibly hard to do the right thing. His investigative skills had been outstanding; his deductive powers awesome. None of it, in the end, had counted for anything. He'd been a pawn in a much larger game: an ongoing global covert operation mired in stealth and secrecy. Despite his security classification, he'd been kept far out of the loop—his integrity disregarded and his loyalty abused. As a career officer, the rejection was hard for him to accept. He felt gutted. His normally strong motivation had been battered; he'd been deceived and he didn't care a damn if he never dated another woman again. After he'd found out, it had taken him days of disciplined effort to clear his mind. Now, this morning, the ghosts of his past seemed determined to come back and haunt him.

Seeing his opportunity, Antonio darted down a narrow side street, withdrawing from sight in a café doorway. Seconds later, the footsteps—now almost running—rounded the corner in pursuit. As the man passed the doorway, Antonio stepped out, blocking his path. Grabbing his pursuer, he used the man's momentum to swing him hard against the stone wall. Just as he'd guessed, it was Maria's former husband. "Following me, Sergio?" he demanded. He was taller than his pursuer by several centimetres. The man's breath smelled harshly of coffee and stale cigarettes. Antonio shook him hard.

"Nothing happened, Antonio," he said. "When you saw Maria coming out of my hotel, I agree it must have looked bad, but it wasn't. She wanted to explain it to you; you wouldn't listen. Nothing was going on between us. I swear to you, Antonio. You have to believe me."

"I don't have to do anything," snarled Antonio. He drew his SIG P226 and placed the barrel flat against Sergio's face. "Don't follow me! Understand?"

"Nothing happened," he continued to protest. "She loves *you*. It's only you. But you won't answer her calls. She's desperately unhappy." He stopped talking as Antonio turned his gun ninety degrees so that the barrel was pushing into Sergio's left nostril.

"What did I just tell you?" demanded Antonio. This time much louder.

The man's eyes widened—dark with fear. Slowly, he raised his hands, sliding them upwards against the wall until they were above his head. "Okay," he said. "I'm just trying to help."

Antonio holstered his gun with one hand and pushed Sergio with the other, intentionally banging the man's head hard against the wall.

Abruptly, he turned and strode back in the direction of his apartment. "Damn it," he mouthed as he approached the underground garage, taking out his car keys. Keying in his access code, he swung open the entrance door and clambered down the badly lit steps to his car. Exhaling deeply, he pressed the remote. "Damn it! The asshole just spoiled a nice walk."

Antonio started his vehicle, shifted into reverse, and turned his head to back up. He didn't see her face but was aware that a woman was standing behind—preventing his manoeuvre. Her beige jacket was the same she'd worn in the interrogation room several days earlier.

Daniela!

She didn't move, and for a moment, he was uncertain what to do. He hated the few seconds it took to switch off the engine, get out of the driver's seat, and walk back to confront her. All that time, she was once again in charge of the situation—making the first move, waiting for him to respond. Her assertive action accurately summed up their relationship, thought Antonio. She initiates; I react.

For months, long before her recent arrest, his resentment of her had moved beyond the point of bitterness. It had shifted into a deep loathing and ill-tempered animosity. He'd learned to hate her. Now he stood silently only a metre from her in the underground car park. He had not anticipated that she might have followed him into the garage—he'd been completely unaware of her presence. That annoyed him too. Still thinking of Maria and about Sergio's words, Antonio knew he had let down his guard. He hadn't been at his most alert.

Glaring at Daniela, he said nothing. He had no energy left for her.

"I tried to tell you," she said, her voice soft; her tone contrite. Her eyes revealed that she was close to tears. "I'm sorry, Antonio. I couldn't say anything; neither could Diego."

Drained of emotion, he couldn't rustle up enough residual energy to participate any longer in her far-too-clever games. "What do you want?" he asked eventually, his voice flat and disinterested.

A slight smile crossed her lips. "That would be asking too much; I wouldn't deserve it."

He shrugged his shoulders and half-turned to go back to his car. Changing his mind, he turned back to confront her. Surprising himself, he slapped her hard across her face. The action was so violent, it made her spin and stumble. Falling to the ground, her legs bundled over as she fell heavily onto the concrete. She sat, looking up at him, holding the edge of her bleeding mouth with her free hand, astonished by what had happened.

Antonio returned to his car and was already in the process of reversing.

Daniela had to scramble like a wounded crab across the dusty garage floor out of the way of his vehicle—to avoid being whacked a second time.

CHAPTER 2
Barcelona: US Consulate

Colonel Scott paced the floor.

"I've told you before, I'm not in favour of these covert operations."

O'Flaherty recognised grandstanding when he saw it.

"Invariably, they end up in a mess." The colonel clasped his hands behind his back—General Patton style. "Well-planned conventional military campaigns are far more effective. I don't like amateurs being involved, despite how successful she's been up until now. Anyway, it's not up to me. Langley makes the decisions, and their instructions are for Felix to proceed with her mission.

"She was stupid, becoming involved in a widely broadcast street demonstration," he added. "It was unforgiveable, even if she rescued a young child in danger. Anyway, nothing much has changed in the assumptions supporting Project Catalyst." He paused, as if mentally turning over a page in a well-rehearsed script. "You've been involved since the beginning, Lieutenant Commander. In many ways, it's your creation. The objective is to locate and capture Alpha."

"The thing is, sir, we need her," reasoned O'Flaherty. "We don't have a photo of him or a reliable description. We're relying on Jamal to identify the target—and to lead her to him. As you say, sir, nothing has changed in that regard. Jamal is the key. Where we've had a bit of luck this time is knowing that the al-Qaeda Council is being pressured to move out of Pakistan. There's support in the country for them—among the people, I mean. It puts the government in a difficult position; it's still collaborating with us—but only just. If we carry out another raid like Abbottabad, our friends in the government could be ousted. Fortunately for us, Pakistan is refusing to play host to al-Qaeda any longer. It's a departure from the cosy and collaborative relationship those two have enjoyed unofficially for decades.

"We can't expect the same favourable circumstances that gifted us the Abbottabad raid," he continued. "We were lucky to locate and capture Osama bin Laden. After that, the top people in al-Qaeda knew they were being targeted with a level of scrutiny they hadn't experienced before. Alpha is no different, except that we don't have a good handle on him. We need a face-to-face, absolutely affirmative and secure ID on him. That's going to be her task. No one else—nobody that we know of—can do it."

"Events have made her job a lot easier, Lieutenant Commander!" admonished the colonel. He seemed to resent the superstar status being attributed to Daniela. "Don't forget that we have dependable intel facilities on the ground—a team of effective field agents. We have reliable information that Alpha and his Inner Council will be relocating to Syria. Of course," he continued, "that's a prelude to a lot more violence in the region, so they have to be stopped. It's going to take a lot more than just a peasant girl from Catalunya to achieve that."

O'Flaherty had been on the stinging end of the colonel's invective before. He had to keep his mouth shut and let the man spit out his vitriol. Aware of the colonel's shallow military record and his lofty ambitions in Washington, he knew that Daniela didn't deserve such criticism. She had frontline field experience and, in his view, more natural flair for espionage in her little finger than existed in the colonel's whole body. But that argument could be postponed for another day.

"And"—the colonel paused—"we have new intel. I'm authorised to share it with you. How much you share with the girl is your decision; my advice is to disclose as little as possible. We don't have a time and place. Not yet. But we do know that Alpha is en route to his new location. It's being kept very quiet for good reason. Our informants have reported preparations to depart from Peshawar. We regard the intel as reliable. Not definitive but reliable. So, we have to be ready. Al-Qaeda is tricky. We can expect they'll have decoy operations underway to deceive us. Make us chase the wrong target. Then there are the Russians. They don't trust us, and we don't trust them. Who knows what underhanded schemes they've dreamed up? No offence, Lieutenant Commander, but frankly, I wish we had just one Navy SEAL Team Six unit already involved on the ground. Then, I'd feel confident and in command.

"I'm not even sure about the Brits. Generally, they can be trusted, but their operations have always been full of leaks, double agents, and treachery."

Daniela thought that Colonel Scott seemed less confrontational than at their last meeting.

It helped, of course, that she had a specially assigned GEO 60 officer from Madrid alongside her. Deputy Inspector Diego Abaya was an enigma, she thought. At their last meeting, he'd proved surprisingly supportive—able to handle the bullying Colonel Scott. She'd been grateful for his intervention. Afterwards, during her few days of rest, she'd heard whisperings that the Civil Guard had objected to his appointment as her liaison officer. After all, espionage operations on foreign soil traditionally had been *their* exclusive mandate. Apparently, Diego's boss, Claudia, had convinced the interior minister that this was an exception. In addition, the prime minister seemed willing to follow up on his pledge to shake up and reorganise Spain's security services.

As soon as they were escorted into his office, a far more indulging Colonel Scott offered coffee. "You look rested." He smiled at Daniela.

His cordiality didn't last long. "You will continue with your mission," he announced. "Langley's orders. I'll come to the point. I think your chances of success aren't impressive. I'm concerned in particular about how you're going make a positive ID of Alpha. We have a name—Rashid al-Muhasib—and a nickname, al-Amin, but we don't know if that's just another alias. I mean, these people change their names all the time. We don't know what this person looks like. Or much about his background. Our profiles are incomplete. For once, our intel is failing us. In my opinion, we're not pursuing a man—we're chasing a shadow." The colonel glanced at Daniela, whose face remained politely impassive. "I'm familiar with your plan to confirm his ID, but I'm not convinced it will work. Too many variables we can't control."

"Begging your pardon, sir. I'm confident it will work," she said simply.

The colonel shot a hostile glance at O'Flaherty. Clearly, he didn't like his assessment being questioned.

"Actually, we know a great deal about him, sir," she said. "Not directly, but by inference. We can tell various things from his actions and by what he doesn't do, or hasn't done. We can estimate his age and predict some aspects of his character. Physically, we can presume some important aspects of what he looks like. Behaviourally, some actions and responses are predictable too. His temperament isn't hard to determine. Not surprisingly, given his profession, we know that he has immense capacity for detail; he's a data freak. We know that he likes to give the final commands prior to al-Qaeda's terror attacks. He enjoys seeing the results of his work, gloating over the morbid details."

"We've done extensive profiling at Langley and it's not at all complete," challenged Scott.

"Our profiling people followed standard procedures, sir," intervened O'Flaherty, trying to head off a confrontation that Daniela could never win. "Fortunately, the Saudis have first-class record-keeping. So, we have access to their data. They have excellent statistical databases."

"We're talking about the people who gave Europe the alphabet—and a system of numbers, including zero, that they were using five thousand years ago," Daniela added.

"I don't need to be lectured on ancient history," snapped the colonel, glaring at her.

"Sorry, sir, we simply meant that—from their intelligence sources, we have been able to confirm basic stuff—such as that Alpha doesn't have siblings, or an identical twin or anything like that," she replied. "Our problem is that almost all official records of him seem to have been expunged. In today's day and age, the void of intel and photographic records is highly unusual. There's not even a passport photo—that's missing too. It's evident that they've made huge efforts to hide his identity—to keep him under the radar. So, I didn't waste any time trying to find his real name, sir. That's proved fruitless. What we do know is that reliable intel confirms he's referred to within al-Qaeda senior networks as al-Amin, meaning the trusted one. But, trusted by whom—and why? Well, while I was in Spain, I had access to some Saudi intel files. The CIA has them too. I studied the background and career of Osama bin Laden and his cronies. The timelines of OBL's education, and where he lived, are enlightening. It's reliable intel and confirmed by the agency's country specialists, that OBL was strongly influenced by the Saudi crackdown against the Shia population. He became concerned about the surge in popularity of Shia Islam after the Iranian Revolution. During the 1980s, he had extremist sympathies, and reports suggest that the Shia revival pushed him to become a hard-line Sunni."

She continued, "He spent a lot of time with his al-Qaeda co-founder Abdullah Yusuf Azzam, who was his teacher and mentor—the man who championed the cause of the Afghan mujahideen fighting the Soviets. From there, it wasn't difficult to develop a profile of a boy—let's use the name Rashid al-Muhasib—who would be younger in years than OBL, and almost certainly a protégé. To be influenced by OBL in that way, and under those circumstances, the boy would be impressionable—probably in his early teens and most likely a close Saudi family friend.

"OBL was twenty-two when he went to the Afghan front, organising al-Qaeda from its base in Peshawar," she added. "He was listened to and respected by the others because he brought Saudi money into the group. A lot of it. That's not unlike the situation facing our target, Rashid al-Muhasib, today. Through Mustapha, and more recently my role as a hawala courier, we've delivered significant amounts of money to them. Recently, we've been dangling in front of him the prospect of enough financing to ensure that al-Qaeda can recover its momentum and expand its influence substantially in the region. Enough to expand across Africa and Asia."

O'Flaherty nodded in agreement. "We know from our profiling at Langley, sir, that he's ambitious but painfully retiring and cautious. He does everything through middle men. Always men, never women. That's a unique aspect of Project Catalyst—they won't be expecting a woman, especially a female infidel jihadi, to get anywhere close to him."

"Why did OBL repeatedly refer to him as 'the trusted one'?" asked Daniela, then quickly answered her own question. "There was confirmation of his name from the computer files captured at Abbottabad. It had been confirmed also during the US interrogation of OBL. That was back in 2011. His name implies that for most of his career he's had a backroom position, not a fighting role. That's been corroborated since, from captured combat records.

"He's cerebral and seems mathematically gifted. I'm guessing he may have been passed over for a combat role because of a physical limitation. OBL trusted him, so did Azzam—and later, Ayman al-Zawahiri relied on him. Most likely, the boy became indispensable to them. He'd been living in Jeddah. We can speculate that there was family resistance to allowing a young Saudi boy, especially one with a physical handicap, to go to the front in Afghanistan. The circumstances also suggest that he may have been Syrian originally—or, like OBL, he may have come from a family with Syrian roots. We also know that his existence was not mentioned in our intel reports until the late 1980s. He would be around sixteen at the time. It was when we think he was finally allowed to join OBL in Peshawar.

"So, already, sir, we can project a profile of a person who today is in his early fifties. It's probable that he looks much older—he's sedentary and remains in hiding most of the time. That means he has to exercise regularly to avoid becoming overweight. OBL was tall, almost lanky. Our intel says that al-Amin isn't. At most, we can put him at 1.70 metres in height—about five six. Bearded, of course. Glasses, too, because of long hours of bookwork and computer use."

Scott's body language suggested he was unimpressed by her analysis. His reply sounded harsh. "That sounds to me like an awful lot of guesswork. Do you have any confirming evidence?"

"I spent a long time with Jamal in Latakia, sir. As you know, I've just come back from there. I had various reasons to stay at the Russian airbase, helping nurse him back to health. I was careful to avoid asking him any questions about al-Amin. That would have given me away, for sure. From time to time, Jamal would let things slip, just little things. They helped me fine-tune my profile of our target. One day, for example, Jamal stumbled and fell—banging his head just above his left eyebrow on the edge of a door. It was nothing, really, but Jamal mimicked a squint eye and said that now he would look like al-Amin. He told me that al-Amin has a medical condition called esotropia. It affects his left eye, apparently. Jamal is a surgeon; he would know. It's in my field report, sir. You may not have had a chance to read it."

O'Flaherty had been watching the colonel carefully and saw him frown. Daniela saw it, too, and knew her guess was right. He hadn't read her report. Instead, he was grasping to find other faults in her plan.

"Circumstantial and inconclusive," said Scott. He seemed to be thinking that Daniela's assessment was full of risky assumptions: the thinking of an amateur. "You're relying on Jamal to take you to him? Completely relying on Jamal?" he asked.

"Yes, sir."

"What if something happens to him?"

"I don't have a Plan B, sir, because nothing compares with what we have already in place. Plan C would be to rely on Yussef and his brother, Ahmed. I'd prefer not to—I would consider them only if Jamal weren't operational for some reason."

"What about the money?" Scott continued relentlessly. "How do you propose to get it to al-Qaeda?"

"That's as much their headache as mine, sir. To them, I'm a jihadist. I'm not pretending to be a logistics expert. What I did was to steal the contents of Aladdin's Cave for the benefit of the cause. I tried to make contact with an al-Qaeda cell near Barcelona, to ask for help. But my efforts weren't successful. They know that. So, I took the precaution of making sure Yussef knows the location of the gold—if anything should happen to me. That should add to my credibility. They don't know that the Mossos subsequently discovered the gold. That's why, when I'm asked by al-Qaeda about the gold, I can't have all the answers. I plan to throw the task back at them. The bearer bonds in Cyprus? Well, they're much easier to recover when the time comes. They're readily accessible.

"What I'm saying, sir, is that if we make it too easy for them, they'll suspect something. It would be unexpected and absurd for a young jihadi woman, no matter how savvy, to have figured a way to transport the gold. Make them work for it. If they really want it—which they do—they'll find a way.

"After all, they have plans to dominate the world, don't they?"

Daniela and Diego had left his office.

Colonel Scott looked sternly at O'Flaherty. "Your candid assessment, Lieutenant Commander. Can she pull it off?"

"The odds are against her, sir. We are talking about one of the most inaccessible and heavily protected men in the world. The only reason we are even discussing the possibility of getting face-to-face with him is that he needs something we have—the money. Without that, we wouldn't be having this conversation. My opinion is that if there's anyone who can get close to him, she's that person. This operation has been almost three years in the making. We are in the final phase, and she is the only reason we've achieved so much and gotten this far. She has an uncanny feel for the operation, almost a sixth sense."

"She's a rookie, Lieutenant Commander," moaned the colonel. He looked and sounded resentful.

"Felix *is* a rookie, sir. However, she brings a lot of skills to the table that most other officers do not. She's proven herself in the field—beyond our expectations. Most importantly, she's able to think the same way as they do. She and our target have a lot in common—their intense personal discipline for attaining a single objective. Her ability to put herself in his place and think like he does is unnervingly prescient. Those insights make it easier for us to predict his next moves," he added, noting that the colonel still seemed dubious. At least, thought O'Flaherty, that was the colonel's external face. He guessed that the man almost certainly wasn't worrying about Daniela's well-being. He was thinking about his next career move—constantly assessing the odds and plotting his most favourable positioning.

"We have lots of people who are capable of thinking the same way as their targets, Lieutenant Commander," the colonel snapped. "They're trained to do so. I need something more—a compelling reason why we should support her. Something that will satisfy Langley."

O'Flaherty looked thoughtful for a moment, using the silence to good effect. "Being trained to think like your target, sir, is one thing. It's quite different to have an intuitive, natural flair. Unlike most people working at Langley, she's an instinctive field operative. She doesn't clock off at the end of the day. She doesn't have weekends off to visit the Smithsonian or head out to dance somewhere along the U-Street Corridor. She lives her mission 24/7, every day of the year. She's intensely motivated. She sees the big picture and is good at following orders. Maybe a little unpredictable at times, but she never takes her eyes off the objective."

"Hmmm," grunted the colonel. "That's another thing too. I'm not at all happy about handing that much money over to terrorists like al-Qaeda. The equivalent of nearly a billion euros."

O'Flaherty nodded. "It is a lot of money, sir; you're right. However, there are two things we should keep in mind. The money is essential bait for her to get close to al-Amin. Number two, there's very little risk that they will actually get their hands on it. As she says, al-Qaeda has to figure a way to take the gold from the cottage and then monetise it."

"What happened there?" asked the colonel, seeming to recall something that had been worrying him. "She wasn't able to link up with her al-Qaeda contact—to transfer the gold to North Africa."

Inwardly, O'Flaherty groaned. He knew that, once again, the colonel hadn't read Daniela's field report. Despite his senior rank, he was a sloppy officer. "While she was in Syria, sir, Jamal instructed her to find a way to arrange the transfer. When she got back to Barcelona, she needed to be seen to connect with her al-Qaeda contact—but for obvious reasons didn't want to make the actual transfer."

"Why not?"

"Well, once the gold is in the hands of al-Qaeda, we'd lose control. She wants to keep it where it is so that when the time comes, she'll have more leverage—more to offer al-Amin. Thus, giving him more reasons to allow her to get near him. She's being smart, sir. To make it look believable, our people in Morocco staged a traffic accident—nothing fatal but hospitalising her al-Qaeda contact and his deputy.

Temporarily, we managed to cut their lines of command. She was able to report to Jamal that she had tried—but not succeeded—in carrying out his orders to make the transfer. The ruse shifted the focus of blame away from her."

"Let's hope it works," said the colonel.

"The bearer bonds at the bank in Cyprus are more liquid and easier to transport," continued O'Flaherty. He was aware that they were wasting time. He wanted to strangle the colonel for his negativity. "The Cyprus funds can be used to buy explosives and weapons. Of course, they can. Ultimately, they have to be cleared by Nicolas's bank in Spain, and we still control the timing of that process."

"Well, you know my reservations, Lieutenant Commander," said the colonel, his mouth turned down in disapproval. "You've made a strong case in her favour—and I respect that. You have credibility within the service." He turned and performed his quarterback walkabout for a moment—feigning a dummy QB pass.

"Okay, but I want to be kept informed every step of the way. I'll hold you personally responsible if it goes wrong." He strode out of the room.

"But you'll take full credit if it succeeds," muttered O'Flaherty.

―◦―

An hour later, the colonel sent an encrypted message to an obscure email address in Vermont. From there, it was inserted into a document summarising the quarterly results of tree harvesting operations in the state, and delivered a few moments later to his superior officer at Langley. It was rapidly decrypted.

In it, the colonel parroted O'Flaherty's assessment of Daniela's suitability, presenting it as his own work. He stressed her uniqueness for the mission. Crediting her detailed profiling of al-Amin to himself, he added a note of caution that read ambiguously. The odds against the field officer's success were long, he said, but the rewards from a

27

"mission accomplished" result were overwhelming attractive. The big risk, his conclusion emphasised, was not being able to obtain a prior affirmative on the target's ID. He'd been assured by his field operatives they'd be able to do that.

His message said that, with reservations, he had initiated the next steps of the mission. With the green light regarding her participation already received from Langley, preparations were well underway to get the officers into the field as soon as possible. The precise timing depended on when the target was confirmed to have arrived on Syrian soil. That was the big unknown.

In the meantime, the colonel assured his superiors, he and his team would remain at full alert—on standby and ready at a moment's notice to close in on their objective.

Cyprus Boot Camp

Outside the log cabin, a sparse forest of drought-stunted pine trees provided them with an ideal hiding place. It was a safe house. A secluded, uninhabited area. From here, they could observe the movement of vehicles and anyone approaching on foot. It helped, thought O'Flaherty, that the Brits had wired and alarmed the surrounding area. Above the fireplace, a console of video-screens—unobservable from outside—supplied the occupants with 24-hour surveillance. No one could get near without being spotted.

In the kitchen, he was preparing an undressed salad. It would go well with the freshly fried kalamari that Daniela was spooning onto plates for their lunch. On the wood table, a bowlful of fresh lemons was set alongside a dish of olives and Syrian flatbread, baked from an imported pre-mix by O'Flaherty—who joked that the Brits had stocked the larder so full, they could hold out there for months.

Neither of them expected that their mobilisation orders would take very long. It was a question of waiting. They would be behind enemy lines soon enough. Preparations were happening around them.

A massive and well-coordinated effort of surveillance, interpretations, evaluations, decision-making, logistics, and clandestine operational support was underway. A well-oiled machine was humming with activity. They were the stars of the show.

Game on? Game off? They'd be informed. If it was confirmed, they'd get the green light.

They'd had combat area drops before, of course. War zones were their theatre of choice—their profession. Both of them knew that being sent in was different each time. Like actors practising their lines, they were constantly thinking about the events about to unfold; living half in the present, their minds concentrating almost constantly on the future. Tonight's big meal would be their last, they'd agreed—a break from the boot camp routine they'd imposed on themselves. O'Flaherty's appearance had been changing for weeks. She'd noticed it when they'd reconnected at the border crossing in Turkey. He'd been transitioning even then, she thought, admiring his single-minded focus. Already, his clothes seemed to hang off his body. He would eat less and less each day, training himself to living rough in the harsh Syrian Desert. He tanned each day in the warm Cyprus sun, wearing a full robe exposing only his face, hands, and feet. "Just getting them seasoned," he wisecracked to her in Arabic. "I have to look and smell right, to play the part."

She thought he looked handsome, despite his unruly disguise. Her preparations were not dissimilar. Their daily routines were demanding. In an adjoining room, a full gymnasium facilitated the arduous workouts they imposed on themselves several times each day. For O'Flaherty, it wasn't enough. The success of their mission relied on their abilities to assimilate without attracting attention—to look commonplace. Each day, carrying a weighted backpack, he would sprint to the ridge of a hill several kilometres away, and then back down. On several nights, he'd left their cabin and practised his commando manoeuvres, creeping stealthily, then crawling, to the barbed wire fence over the other side of the hill where he knew the British sentries were keeping guard over them. Last night, undetected, he'd come to within several metres of where a young squaddie was standing—well camouflaged. O'Flaherty had enjoyed the experience, and had retreated without revealing his presence. He needed to be match fit, he said. Their lives depended on it.

It was their sixth day. Still waiting.

"Michael, you and I know a lot more about al-Amin than we revealed to the colonel," said Daniela.

"I thought you were smart not to get into a deep discussion with him," he acknowledged. "We're both students of the Arab world; he isn't. No need to give him any more ammunition to shut down our operation than he has already. But I agree with you," he continued. "Al-Amin exhibits predictable patterns that can help us get closer to him. He follows routines that reinforce our profiling. He's guided by what he believes to be his divinely ordained destiny—but we haven't been able to use that information to predict when and where al-Qaeda will hit its next big target."

"On this mission, that's not our focus, is it?" said Daniela. "The purpose of our profiling and our indirect communications with him—through Jamal for instance—is to understand him, to get closer to him. I need to engage him. He's a student of mathematics, a very smart one. In some ways, he's an elitist too—an intellectual snob. That's what I'm relying on, to get his attention. Make him willing to meet me."

"Well, he is a fanatic on details," agreed O'Flaherty. "We know he favours numbers like five and seven that have special significance to Islam. Our backroom teams have confirmed that he avoids numbers, like twelve, that are especially important to Shia Islam. Yet, he's also acutely aware of the need to cover his tracks to ensure that he doesn't become predictable. He knows that would be fatal—we'd be onto him. But I'm intrigued about how you're planning to get his attention."

"It's about respect, really," she replied. "The 9/11 bombings didn't have al-Amin's signature. The attack was the brainchild of al-Zawahiri and Khalid Sheikh Mohammed. Al-Amin's operations were distinct, especially the ones delegated to him by OBL. You and I both know that the precise time lapse between September 11th and the Atocha train bombings was nine hundred and eleven days—exactly nine-one-one. That's a prime number. Like Fibonacci sequences, it's the basis for simple mathematical patterns we all learned as kids." She chuckled. "Undoubtedly, as well, he will recognise digital roots and vortex patterns."

O'Flaherty grinned. "Nicola Tesla's fascination with the 3 6 9 code and keys to the universe!"

"All of them too simple in isolation to hold his attention—unless we can appeal to his sense of neatness and tradition," she continued. "I'm hoping that his belief in destiny, and perhaps self-identification with his namesake in the golden age of Arab mathematics—Harun al-Rashid—will work in our favour. Aware of his fascination with patterns, I've been building in a few teasers as we've been going along." She looked at him keenly. "Knowing you, Michael, you've probably picked up on them already."

He smiled. "Well, I have noticed a few, but you probably have more. I saw that you recorded the actual count of gold bars from Aladdin's Cave at seven hundred and ninety-seven, a prime number. That wasn't an accurate count, but it serves your purpose. I thought that using prime numbers was clever. Al-Amin won't miss the significance. But why do you think he'll bite?"

"The trail of discovery I've laid has a lot more embedded number patterns than that," said Daniela. "I'm guessing he's confident enough about his superior intellect to play a bit of a game with me—knowing from Jamal that I'm a proven jihadist and recognising a fellow numbers nut. He's superstitious. For him, it will be a good omen. None of his regular al-Qaeda henchmen will pick up on the maths, so I'm anticipating he'll want to interrogate me personally. Especially because Jamal will have told him there's more money available; more than the billion euros we're promising to deliver. A lot more."

"Speaking of gold," said O'Flaherty after a pause. "I've been thinking. Our profiling suggests that he isn't normally a tactile person. He's an accountant, a numbers guy. He may be socially awkward, avoiding excessive direct contact with people, but what about physical things?"

"The *feel* of the gold, you mean?" she asked with rising excitement in her voice. "I hadn't considered that. You're saying that, in this case, touching one of the gold bars from Aladdin's Cave may evoke special symbolism for him? I think it's brilliant. If you can arrange it, I'll carry the gold bar with me." She returned his smile. Daniela was thinking that O'Flaherty would make a convincing screen actor. He constantly rehearsed his scenes and lived through how they might play out. She was impressed, yet again, by his professionalism. Attention to detail. It certainly made her life easier—and a lot safer.

"There's another thing too. Al-Amin will be intrigued by what Mustapha has told him—about me, I mean. For al-Amin, Spain has personal significance. Under his watch, he will want to implement his plans to regain al-Andalus. It's a long-term strategic project of theirs. Spain is special; it has huge significance for Muslims. The final stages of the 9/11 attacks were completed by one of the pilots, Mohammed Atta, along with Ramzi bin al-Shibh. They lived for a time in Barcelona—actually, we found out later, not far from my neighbourhood." She paused. "He's going to want get his hands on the money. The thing is, I'm just the courier—the pack horse. He will extract everything he can from me. I'm an infidel. Once he's got what he wants, I'm dispensable. Even so, he might just be willing to play cat to the mouse that I'm offering."

O'Flaherty looked concerned. "You don't have to go through with this, Daniela. You know that, don't you? Chances are that our air attack forces might get lucky. If they get an opportunity, high command might decide to take him out with a lethal Hellfire missile strike. If the odds against our mission become overwhelming, it would be crazy for you to risk your neck."

Daniela was not expecting him to be so protective of her. She was touched by it. At that moment, he seemed more like an older sibling than a fellow officer on a dangerous covert mission. She breathed in heavily and deflected his concern. "Without positive identification of the target, how are they going to do that?" She shook her head. "The only way we can achieve certainty is the way we're doing it, Michael.

"But thank you."

She gave his hands a grateful squeeze.

They had a visit from a British Army major.

He was alone, out of uniform, and drove an older model four-wheel drive loaded with neatly chopped bundles of firewood. He saluted them with characteristic British stiffness. "A gift from the colonel, sir," he said with a disarming grin as he handed over the gold ingot. Daniela thought he looked very much like a well-bred public-school boy. Not nearly as tall as O'Flaherty, she noted, although his lean, athletic build was quite similar. Major Sandy MacDonald would have looked at home playing squash in a private country club, she imagined, or equally in a combat zone, somewhere in the world where the Brits still had influence.

Addressing them, he stood stiffly to attention—shoulders square, his feet planted wide astride, and his hands clasped behind his back. "When the time comes, we'll deploy you quickly into the field—flying you firstly to the US military and Coalition forces base at al-Tanf as a staging ground." He studied Daniela for a few seconds. "It's a drop-off there for you, ma'am. Bit of a delay before you see any action, I'm afraid. Until we know for certain that al-Amin is in Syria, we have to keep you on ice—ready to go into action at short notice. When we get the signal from our American colleagues, we'll arrange a flight delivering you very close to where we believe the target is heading. You'll receive further briefings and regular updates at al-Tanf." He twisted the strands of his boyish moustache, as if considering what to say next. "I should mention there's a risk of you being spotted by Syrian rebel soldiers—possibly by agents of the regime, ma'am. Generally, they're safe. But our people on the ground will make sure no one observes your arrival or departure. You'll be confined to close quarters, I'm afraid. For your own safety," he added redundantly.

"The lieutenant commander will travel by the same aircraft directly to north-east Syria, where he will link up with the remnants of Jamal's platoon." He turned to O'Flaherty. "Sir, can I confirm that you are still able to get a coded message through to your contacts?" He referred to some notes on his cell phone. "How soon can you activate that, sir? We need Nazih and Mohammed to organise their men and rendezvous with Jamal. Regarding IDs, it's your usual, sir," he continued. "And I see that you're already well into the disguise stage." He pointed to O'Flaherty's unkempt flaming red beard and hair. "Jolly good. I'd like to spend an hour or two with both of you to go through the operational details." He examined their faces. "Q and As. Then we'll leave you alone until the balloon goes up."

Daniela looked puzzled. She glanced sideways at O'Flaherty at the major's obscure reference, receiving a quick touch under the table by his foot on her leg. It said, "I'll explain later."

The major stood to attention and saluted. "Right ho! From here on in, we'll try not to disturb you."

"Until the balloon goes up," said O'Flaherty without any hint of a smile.

Girl With a Vengeance

O'Flaherty received a coded text message. "We're operational, Daniela!" he exclaimed.

Then he frowned. "Damn. We've been switched to RAF Akrotiri." He sounded annoyed, she thought. "Something's going on at Dhekelia; they're not telling me what. The changeover means we lose ninety minutes." He looked hard at his watch. "We'd better get going. Our aircraft will be warming up by the time we arrive. Don't forget your gold ingot."

She was already at the door. "You want to drive?" she asked unnecessarily, aware that the GPS-disabled pool car was set up for him. The driver's seat had been pushed back to its maximum to accommodate his tall frame.

Driving fast down the mountain dirt road, he opened his window and allowed the wind to dishevel his already long and unkempt hair. "Got to look the part." He grinned. "Our people know we're coming," he shouted over the road noise. "An escort will pick us up en route and guide us in."

O'Flaherty was right. Joining the A5, speeding west, their escort vehicle caught up and went ahead of them, its emergency lights warning vehicles ahead to give way. They pulled into RAF Akrotiri after a breathlessly fast ride. Within minutes, they'd parked their vehicle and were striding across the tarmac towards the aircraft.

"MV22 Osprey," O'Flaherty shouted to Daniela, over the engine noise. "Did my basic training on one of these babies." Strapping himself into the twenty-four-seater, he returned the salutes of two gunnery officers manning the doors. If needed, when they entered Syrian airspace, they'd operate the 0.50 calibre heavy machine gun. Roaming bands of jihadist guerrillas infiltrating the surrounding deconfliction zone were known to be armed with ground-to-air missiles. American and Coalition personnel stationed at al-Tanf would provide groundcover on their approach.

Ahead of him, the RAF pilot and female co-pilot swivelled in their seats and gave him a brief salute before continuing their preparations for take-off. O'Flaherty was feeling at home. He knew the Brits would be manning the flight with some of the best and most experienced special services operatives. Sitting back, he and Daniela donned their headsets. Minutes later, they taxied down Runway One-East and were airborne. As they levelled out, O'Flaherty made his way forward to talk to the flight crew. Later, approaching the Syrian coast, they diverted over Jordan, re-entering Syrian airspace on a northern approach.

"This is where we say goodbye, Daniela," said O'Flaherty. "We'll drop you off, and as the major said, you'll have to remain incognito at the airbase until it's your time to join the action. After we're airborne again, they'll do a low-level flight across the country and take me close to where I know that Nazih, Mohammed, and the boys will be."

"How will you contact Jamal?" he asked.

She smiled. "The usual. Our drop box on the darknet. Fingers crossed he's still checking it."

"Well, good luck, Daniela." He leaned over and kissed her forehead. "This is where the fun begins."

South Syria: Al-Tanf

The US military base at al-Tanf, known as "the 55 km area," is also home to several Syrian rebel factions who spent years fighting alongside the allies against ISIS. With the British Army major's forewarning, Daniela was not surprised by the elaborate procedures they took to transfer her clandestinely from the aircraft to a high security area at the base.

The quarters she was allocated were sparse but comfortable. Essentially, it was a large room with a bed and functional bathroom but no windows. They had prepared an adjoining room for a lengthy stay, with plentiful exercise equipment and a range of entertainment choices. There was a stack of CDs, which, she noticed, included several disks that would help her rehearse her cover story. And lots of music options.

Daniela understood the requirement for absolute secrecy and the need to wait until it was her time to go behind enemy lines, but she felt deflated. After spending so much time with O'Flaherty, she missed him already. It was also the feeling that he would soon be in action, while she had to bide her time waiting for orders.

"Sorry about the lockdown," said a sergeant in her mid-thirties, wearing RAF desert combat fatigues. "And the cloak-and-dagger procedures. We will make your stay as comfortable as possible, ma'am." Her voice was bright and cheery. "We've been fully briefed by London on your cover story.

"The basics are that you travelled from Spain to Syria through Turkey, as a tourist. During your stay in Turkey, you visited various archaeological sites, including Mount Nemrut in the south. From there, you continued into Syria—again as a legitimate traveller with an entry visa—crossing the border just south of Mardin. You proceeded to al-Hasakah, where you were met by two local men paid to drive you to a drop-off point here." She pointed to a detailed map of northeastern Syria.

"Your instructions are to wait at this destination—it's a cheap but secure hotel. Don't worry, it's one of ours. I'll come back to that in a minute. We couldn't take the risk of letting you make the actual journey, so it will be up to you to become familiar with the details of your routing, as if you'd actually travelled it." She gestured to the CDs and a pile of books and magazines. "These will help, but we did a few extra things to help authenticate your cover story." She glanced at Daniela; it was a defensive look. It seemed to say that they were aware Daniela was a stickler for detail, but please trust them: they'd done this before—and were good at it.

"We've arranged a stand-in for you, ma'am, to make the actual journey through Turkey and Syria. She's Syrian—a deep-cover friendly of ours. She's solid; you can trust her completely. By the way, she's almost your exact double. Don't be startled when you meet her. I've seen photos; she's quite convincing, actually. You'll be doing the switch with her at the hotel. She'll give you a full briefing about her journey from the north. It's all a ruse, of course. I think you'll be impressed by the degree of detail our team has been able to provide. Speaking of which, here's your cell phone—in your real name, as we've been instructed. A good long-life battery and recharger. They will expect you to be carrying it but probably will confiscate it. Here's your password. You're loaded up with bogus emails and texts. Review them, please. We're certain you'll be interrogated intensively before you get anywhere close to the target. He's likely to be very well protected.

"We've also loaded up photos that you would have taken along your way in Turkey. But none in Syria, as you are no longer posing as a tourist. As you'd expect, ma'am, our techies have done all the clever stuff—to authenticate your journey, I mean. The photos were taken in Turkey several days ago by one of our field officers. The techies have even thrown in a few selfies of you at the archaeological sites. They look really authentic.

"Oh, and here's a used boarding pass for your journey from Barcelona to Istanbul, then onto Ankara—and the details of your aircraft. To be additionally convincing, I'd suggest you keep the boarding pass as a bookmark inside this novel you've been reading. It's wallet litter." She smiled. "In terms of timing, it may be just a few days or possibly weeks before we transport you to your hotel for the switch. We've been advised that you're familiar with the drop-off area. I understand, ma'am, that you've been under deep cover several times before, so you know the drill. There's a lot of coordination and security involved, as you're aware. The precise timing will be dictated by Alpha's arrival into the area. We'll schedule you into the field and install you in the hotel before your doppelganger arrives.

"Then it's just a question of waiting. You must be getting used to that by now." She smiled a look of encouragement. "Your instructions will come from Jamal or one of his men. We don't know when, but we'll be monitoring your drop boxes." She pointed to a table next to the military bed. "There's a menu. Order whatever you like, anytime. Mostly Turkish and Syrian dishes, as you'd expect. Also, ma'am, we are not infallible. Please check through your cover story and let us know if there's anything you'd like us to change. Here's a pager: it's old tech and has limited range. We find it's a good way to ensure complete security. Buzz me anytime you like. I'm on duty twenty-four hours for the duration of your stay.

"Again, welcome to al-Tanf, ma'am. To compensate for being locked up in here, just bear in mind that there's absolutely nothing to see out there.

"Just scrub desert.

"And a few jihadis."

CHAPTER 3
Caterina

She'd been kind to him.

He felt he owed Caterina something.

Antònio sighed. You're growing old—becoming soft—he chided himself. Years ago, he wouldn't have thought twice about such overnight encounters. His women friends appreciated him as much as he liked to oblige them. He wasn't out to make conquests; it was always mutual attraction. If sleeping together met their needs, everything was fine.

This was Barcelona, after all, he thought—a city that understands art and passion. Every tiny brushstroke on the coital scale spanning from hurried satiation of carnal lust to unselfish, uncompromising, and everlasting adoring love was here, he rationalised. After more than two thousand years, the city had seen it all. Numerous times.

There was no reason to have any feelings of guilt. He hadn't lied. He hadn't cheated . . . well, not really. No promises had been made in the heat of passion that he'd no intention of keeping. She'd said it herself, and he remembered her words: "Last night, you needed me; this morning, I needed you. No commitment, okay?" Antonio recalled their discussion about her brother. It had been a police matter, she'd said. He thought she'd seemed embarrassed, although not defensive. What had happened to him? Did it involve a crime? Maybe he could help her, he thought. It would be a nice gesture, a kind thing to do. He dismissed the notion that he was trying to compensate—to assuage his vague feeling of responsibility for their night together. He wanted to help. Talking about her brother, even though she'd only hinted at a possible tragedy, seemed to have distressed her deeply.

One thing he didn't need, not yet anyway, was another relationship. He'd had enough of them recently and each had developed significant complications—Daniela, in particular.

Mossos Homicide Division had been running smoothly during Antonio's absence from regular duties.

Except for his brief involvement in the raid at la Garriga, the squad had learned to do without him. They'd adapted. It didn't worry him. The idea of having a light workload for a change appealed immensely. Besides, he wanted to find a way to pursue some pressing items on his personal agenda. Officially, the Mossos had been taken off the case, but Antonio reasoned that the Civil Guard's hands-off instructions didn't extend to investigating unsolved attempted homicide cases. In Catalunya, at least, those were still within Mossos jurisdiction.

He resented some things about Daniela's behaviour but couldn't ignore his job. Top of the list: he was determined to look deeper into her claim about the sniper attack. If that happened to link back to her undercover assignment, he reasoned, it was just a coincidence. He wouldn't be disobeying any direct orders.

Xavi had worked hard following up on Daniela's sniper claim. He'd assigned a keen young recruit, Officer Francisca Diaz, to investigate the incident. His luck was in: she'd done a great job, Xavi said in the handwritten note he'd pinned to a file for Antonio to read. *"Didn't think you'd want this traceable online, amigo,"* his note said. *"So, paper only."*

Turning the pages, Antonio saw that numerous reports of shootings in the region had been filed over the past year. Amazingly, the rookie officer had pursued each one. She'd categorised them into solved and unsolved cases, and then into levels of low and high potential interest to Xavi's enquiry. She had dismissed a report of a Renfe train hit by an object fired from a pellet gun. It had caused no significant damage and the youth involved had been punished by his parents. A farmer in rural Catalunya had shot two barrels from his farmhouse window at thieves trying to steal chickens. There were no reports of injuries, and the chickens were fine. Antonio chuckled at the detail.

In the more serious cases, Officer Diaz had found that around the time of the separatist referendum vote, several federal officials had been fired upon at a number of locations. Her investigations showed that the shooter, or shooters, had been apprehended and charged. Twenty-nine mafia-linked or gang-related shootings involved the discharge of multiple rounds of ammunition, her report noted. Most had been linked to known criminal gangs or execution killings. Five were unsolved, though there was a body in each case. During the year, there had been two other instances of rifle or handgun rounds being fired at public vehicles. A Barcelona hop on/hop off bus window had been hit by a single bullet. In a separate instance, an irate truck driver had discharged the contents of his Glock into the cab of an empty semi. The man's explanation was that a rival driver was having an affair with his wife. It had just been a warning, said the assailant. If the bastard went anywhere near his wife again, things might get serious.

Officer Diaz had obtained file pictures of the damage to the Barcelona hop on/hop off bus. Photos and a lab report she'd obtained from ballistics confirmed that the shot most likely had been fired from a low-rise building nearby. Numerous witnesses had heard a loud crack. None of the tourists on the bus had been hurt, and none had an explanation why they might have been a target. Police screening at the time showed that none of them fitted the typical profile of a likely target of a sniper. A compacted bullet had been recovered from inside the reinforced metal sheeting of the bus side. Analysis suggested that, because of its weight, it was 7.62 mm calibre—similar to ammunition used by the military, also favoured by mafia shooters and contract assassins.

The ballistics technician had concluded that either of two explanations were plausible: If a sniper had targeted someone on the bus, the attempt had failed and the intended victim had not waited around. No one reported hearing a second shot. Alternatively, the technician speculated, the shot might have been a stray round—possibly a ricochet—from a shooting attempt on a nearby building. Nearby rooftops had been searched. No such evidence had been found. There was no sign of a killing or an attempt. No telltale signs had been left behind. No shell casing had been located. Because of the angle of attack and corroborating evidence, the technician strongly favoured the first explanation. It had been a targeted shooting—most likely by an experienced professional.

Antonio was astonished. It was a really informative report. The writer had been detailed and comprehensive, and she'd reached a plausible conclusion. There was a footnote that caught Antonio's attention. At the time of the shooting, Mossos officers had interviewed the few bus passengers who'd remained on the bus after the driver had reported the shooting. He was impressed that, despite the gap of over a year since the bus shooting, Officer Diaz had contacted each of the Mossos officers who'd attended the scene. She'd asked them to review their notebooks and reports. Had there been anything that they had forgotten at the time, or remembered since, she'd asked.

One of them, an officer who had since left the force, provided her with a gem of information. He recalled that the bus shooting had occurred the same day as a manhunt had been set up for a terrorist fugitive. She had a Spanish name that he couldn't remember. Yet, he did recall one of the bus passengers, a British resident from Marbella, saying that a young woman had jumped off the bus soon after the shooting. The officer had taken down the woman's name and her phone number. He'd added a recommendation for follow-up by a Mossos desk officer. She'd checked. There had been no follow-up. Thinking it might be important, the young officer had taken the initiative and phoned the British woman in Marbella.

"I'm amazed it took you guys so long to contact me," said the breezy Brit. "I remember the woman very well. Our bus driver had started off; then he just slammed on his brakes. So, most of us were off balance. There was a shot. Someone screamed. I saw a young woman jump off the bus and start running back up the street. The bus driver pulled over, and we all looked at the bullet hole in the bus window."

"Can you remember what she looked like?" the officer had asked her.

"Remember?" The woman had laughed. "There were pictures of her plastered everywhere for weeks afterwards. She's that jihadi terrorist woman you guys were looking for. I guess you arrested her? I figured that was the only reason why none of your lot contacted me to follow up. I hope you locked away the bitch for the rest of her life."

After he'd finished reading the report, Antonio made a mental note to thank Xavi and send a quiet note of congratulations to the rookie officer. Xavi would make sure she said nothing to anyone about her investigations. He'd put a merit note in her file later. Feet up on his desk, Antonio was pleased with the information. Daniela hadn't been lying to him: someone had wanted to kill her.

It was quite possible they still did.

―○―

Moments later, his phone rang.

Aurelia.

He ignored it.

A lot had happened since he'd last seen her. He'd neglected their relationship, half-wondering if, as the chief investigating officer checking into the sniper's attempted assassination of Daniela, he should distance himself from her professionally. The other half of him wanted to give in to his physical desires. She was an incredibly sexy and alluring young woman. And she'd made it clear she was attracted to him too. The echoes of her irresistible French accent, and everything it promised, had tortured his fitful dreams since their first meeting.

Imagining what she might be thinking, he recalled the spontaneous kiss she'd given him while they were examining the hoard of gold discovered in his grandfather's garage. At the time, he'd had no idea that they were being observed from a distant vantage point by Daniela. He flinched, recalling Daniela's sarcastic snub later—after her arrest and interrogation at Mossos Headquarters. "Ask your girlfriend," she'd said, referring to the gold pendant that Aurelia was wearing that day. It was identical to the one she herself had snatched from the sniper, she'd told him. Daniela must have witnessed their affectionate kiss as well, he thought. He'd been stung by her sharp words. It was irrational, in a way, but he also felt a little guilty—as if he was being unfaithful to Daniela. It was part of the reason why he hadn't called Aurelia since.

When, a few minutes later, the caller alert showed up again on his phone, he let it ring before answering. She was inviting him to dinner. On the spur of the moment, he accepted—making an effort to sound like his usual cheerful self. There was no strain, or subtle messaging, in her sultry voice, but he knew she must be wondering why he hadn't been in contact.

It was interesting, he thought later, how his relationship with her had shifted from potentially romantic to one where he'd become suspicious of her. Once again, Daniela had insinuated herself between him and a woman in his life. If it hadn't been for Xavi's report about the sniper, Antonio would have dismissed his concerns as groundless paranoia. Yet, now he had valid doubts. That wasn't necessarily bad: they made him more wary—on the lookout. His senses were on full alert and finely tuned, listening for scraps, signs, and clues. Anything. They chatted idly for a few minutes, then called off. Placing his feet back on top of his desk, he thought he might as well put time to good use—and figure out how to extract the information he needed from Aurelia.

He was certain of one thing.

Aurelia knew a lot more than she'd volunteered so far.

Missing Person

It had been several days since Antonio had spent the night at Caterina's apartment.

He'd been thinking about her.

Dropping by one evening to say hello at the bar where she worked had crossed his mind, but didn't seem like a good idea. It was too casual and would be invading her space, he thought. She might not appreciate it. After all, she'd told him they had no commitment to each other—although he didn't agree completely. He sensed that she wasn't uninterested. Yet, there had to be a better way to meet without rekindling the passions of the morning after.

Besides, he was anxious to find out more about her brother's disappearance. It was a difficult situation, he thought. He had no right to go meddling. Worse, if he built up her hopes that he might still be alive and afterwards their investigations found he wasn't, it would be really cruel. She'd end up hating him and he'd feel even worse about himself than he had over the past several months.

He would talk it over with Xavi.

"Minimally intrusive would be to find out her brother's name and a few other details," said Xavi. "Then we could carry out some background checks. That wouldn't build up her hopes."

"That's what I'm trying to avoid," agreed Antonio. "She's great; I really like her. But I have too much going on in my life already—to start a new relationship, I mean."

"I'm happy to help if you want," said Xavi. "But I can't just call and ask her. That's something you have to do, amigo."

"I'm not that good at handling intimate relationships with women," said Antonio, noting the broad grin that spread across his friend's face.

"That might just qualify as the understatement of the century." Xavi laughed, finally unable to hide his amusement. "Not good? You're absolutely hopeless. You need to get some guidance from your sister. Isabel will tell you how to handle it. My advice? Do it soon. I think she'll tell you to call Caterina and just say hello. It doesn't have to be any more complicated than that."

"I'm not sure . . ." Antonio began to say.

"That's your problem in a nutshell," Xavi shot back. "You can never make up your mind what you want. All your life, women have fallen for your easy-going good looks and charm. You've never had to make any commitments—until Maria came along." Xavi bit his lip. He hadn't intended to raise the subject. Immediately, he wished he hadn't.

"That's another reason not to get involved," Antonio snapped back.

"Pick up the phone and call Caterina," said Xavi firmly. "If you can't do that, ask Isabel for advice. Just don't let it drag on without talking to the poor girl. Calling her up and saying it was great but you don't want to get into a relationship is far better than trying to spare her feelings and not saying anything at all."

"I'm not good at that, amigo," said Antonio.

"Well, you'll hurt her more by ignoring it. Besides, she did you a big favour and took care of you on a night when you got completely wasted and could have hurt yourself. You owe her a call and some sincere thanks. It's not like the first time you've been in this situation, Toni. You've turned down lots of women before."

"Yes, but somehow this is different. I can't put my finger on it."

"Pick up the bloody phone, Toni, and just say hello to her. The rest will be fine."

Caterina's voice sounded wonderful, he thought.

There wasn't a hint of censure; quite the opposite—she sounded light-hearted and happy.

She giggled when he finally got around to suggesting lunch. "You're not interviewing me for a job, Detective. We've already broken the ice—and I've already told you there's no commitment. So, I'm going to cook dinner for you at my apartment, and you can tell me all your deep dark secrets." Her youthful light-heartedness made him feel old. "Then we can shake hands and you can go home." She laughed. "You'll feel a lot better than you did before you called me." She paused. "Antonio, you do have other women friends, don't you? I was beginning to wonder." She giggled again.

"You're a policeman, so you probably remember my address. If you don't, it's on that piece of paper I gave you with my phone number on it."

Antonio and Isabel headed off for lunch.

"So, tell me about the new girlfriend," she asked, giving him a searching look. "Does Maria know about her?"

"I told you she's not my new girlfriend, and I don't care if Maria knows or not," he replied huffily. "Well, I do . . . but I don't. I don't want to hurt her; we'll always be friends. Anyway, how's your life working out? Tell me about this new adventure into politics."

Isabel laughed. "Okay, I can see you don't want to talk, brother—not now . . . but next time, I want all the lurid details. If no one else is looking after you, I will." She held up her hand as he started to protest. "You'll be pleased to hear that I'm giving up my present occupation. Politics doesn't pay much—at least not at this level—but Julia has insisted on it, and she earns enough to support us both. I have a couple more clients coming into town. After that, I'll become an honest woman again—if you ignore the inherent dishonesty of politicians . . . and assuming I get elected."

"You're well-known and popular; you'll get elected easily." He smiled proudly. "What issues are you running on, apart from the medieval rental laws in the Old City? Are you going to stay away from the separatist minefield?"

"Hard to, in this town," she scowled. "Too many diehards. It's become so emotional too. Tell me, Toni, what's your advice? I'm trying to give voters a taste of what we could do with a little less regulation in the rentals market and start bringing back some of the businesses we lost in the region—I mean, after the referendum and the economic downturn and other stuff. Too many people are without secure jobs. Protect the people and make sure they have jobs. What do you think?"

Antonio looked across the table at his sister. She'd kept most of her youthful good looks and was in great shape physically. She sounded mature and reasonable, he thought. "Well, you're up against the hotel lobby. The more short-term tourist rentals they can shut down, the happier they'll be."

"And richer," she shot back.

"Anyway, it's the developers you're trying to regulate, isn't it?" he asked. "I'm talking about the hedge funds buying up blocks of rental units—renovating them as boutique hotels and high-rent apartments. You're fighting developers; you'll have natural allies within the hotel industry lobby group, won't you?"

"Getting into bed with Satan." She winced. "I've done that a few times. Besides, I'm not against all developers; they help improve the housing inventory. A lot of residents are getting older. They need elevators and health services, not five floors of three-hundred-year-old narrow steps to climb every time they drag their groceries home."

"Give priority to developers who also offer affordable housing units," suggested Antonio. "That's what you've always told me is the future for the downtown barrios. Meet the needs of several groups of constituents . . . living side by side, more or less civilly."

Isabel unzipped the bag she'd been carrying and produced a heavy document. "This is the proposed community plan. If it goes ahead without any revisions, it will force a lot of the small businesses out. You know how Catalans feel about American-style big-box companies moving in, don't you! We can't let that happen to Barcelona; it's such a beautiful city with so much history and magnificent buildings. We've already lost a lot of our heritage."

He grinned. "I think you just made your first campaign speech. Now you need a platform to launch it. Tell me about your plan to get elected."

"What can I do to help?"

Students don't always impress as masters of outstanding cuisine and healthy eating, Antonio was thinking as Caterina buzzed him up to her apartment, leaving the door ajar for him. The fantastic aromas that greeted him forced him to revise his critical opinion. Something smelled very good—and it wasn't delivery.

"I'm in the kitchen," she called out. "Help yourself to wine."

Maria was a brilliant chef. So, too, was Aurelia. Now, it seemed, this young student earning a living as a part-time hostess in a bar was also able to rustle up a delicious meal. He'd thought through his lines several times that day—resolving to be firm. He also needed to find out more about her brother, without being intrusive or building up her hopes. Now she was making it hard for him to remain firm. "What are you cooking?" he asked. "It smells fabulous."

"Nothing special. A surprise. Amuse yourself until it's ready? About ten minutes."

"Is that fresh bread I smell?" he asked, opening the bottle and pouring himself a generous serving of a very palatable Rioja.

"Yes, my brother taught me. Hope you're not too weight-conscious, are you?"

"Not tonight, I'm not," he answered happily.

She met him at the kitchen door and wiped her hands on her apron. Giving him a quick kiss, she pushed him back out. On his previous visit, Antonio's lack of sobriety had dulled his normally sharp senses. He remembered the photos of her brother, yet had no recall of how tastefully her apartment was furnished. Quite elegantly, he thought.

"Ready," she called. "We're eating in the kitchen tonight. Do you mind?"

He carried the wine bottle and sat down. "You're not drinking?" he asked. The food was delicious, he quickly conceded. She had an amazing flair for the subtlety of spices. The quantities she served were small but incredibly tasty. "Wow, you could be a professional," he said effusively, meaning every word of it. "Is that what you're training for?"

"Business administration degree, actually. Cooking is just a hobby. Do you know how many exceptional chefs there are already in this city? I like to go out to eat, don't you?"

Several hours later, as they finished their coffees, she looked at him. "Your mood is changing," she observed. "I know what you want to tell me—that you're not ready for a commitment. Well, that's fine, Antonio. I enjoy your company. Call me whenever you want. I just ask one thing: When we're together, let's be honest with each other. Let's have fun. I'm not looking for a serious relationship. I'm the independent type. Have I guessed right?"

As she spoke, he felt a huge weight being lifted off his shoulders. There was little else he could do but posture an apologetic look—and agree with her. It had been a conversation he'd been dreading and now she'd made it so easy for him. "You're fantastic," he said.

"I know." She laughed. "So are you."

"Salud," he toasted.

The evening had flown by. She was making another espresso, and he'd already announced that he'd have to leave soon. They carried them into the main room. "That side table is his," she said, pointing to a beautifully crafted piece of furniture. "My brother . . . he made it."

"He's talented." Antonio ran his fingertips gently over the highly polished wood. "This marquetry is magnificent. It's really intricate."

"His hallmark," she said simply. "He loves detail."

"There was an accident?" asked Antonio, no longer wanting to remain impartial.

She shook her head. "Not that we know about."

Antonio sensed that if he said nothing she'd continue talking—that she wanted to talk about it. He remained silent.

"He was out in the district of lakes. He had his own kayak and a tent," she said. "He wanted to get a break from the city—a bit of mental therapy. We always asked him to take a buddy along, but he was such a loner. It would have been safer had he listened. He just laughed at us. Lorenzo was such a free spirit." Her eyes wandered back to the photographs. "When he didn't return home, we called the police. We figured he might have capsized and maybe hit his head. We refused to think he might have drowned. After a few days, he was still missing and we begged the police to search the lakes. There are several of them, you know." She looked at Antonio, but her mind was elsewhere—probably recalling a mental picture of the area, he thought.

Her voice was flat, almost a monotone—as if she was describing something detached and abstract. Antonio guessed she was still suffering from the trauma and had built a protective barrier around herself. Her self-control was palpable, as she described the setting. Yet, he knew that her nerves probably were still raw. "The police dragged every square metre of the larger lakes. They had special equipment—sonar, I think—that they used for the search. They found nothing."

"Not even his kayak?" asked Antonio, his instincts as a detective already at work.

She shook her head. "No."

"Did the police tell you that they think he . . . your brother, Lorenzo . . . did they think he'd drowned?"

"They said there was no evidence of that. They viewed him as a missing person. Much earlier, before they'd agreed to search the lakes, we were asked to think of any other places he might have gone. Visiting friends or relatives, that kind of thing. But we didn't think it was likely because his car was still parked where he'd left it. It was locked, but the police opened and searched it. Finally, they towed it to a holding area."

"When was this?"

"Five months and nearly a week ago," she replied without hesitation. "We went around the area appealing to anyone who might have seen him. The police were helpful, but after a time, they admitted that there was little more they could do to help. It's still classified as an open case. Officially, he's a missing person. His credit cards haven't been used. There's no evidence of a crime having been committed."

She got up and went to her desk, handing a business card to Antonio. "This police officer was on the case. She was very helpful. They'd called all the hospitals. She's phoned me several times since to find out how I am—even though the authorities have no further information about his disappearance."

"They didn't find his kayak or his tent or any of his belongings?" Antonio asked. He felt sorry that such an awful thing had happened to her. She looked so lost; it dismayed him. He'd surprised himself a few moments earlier, knowing that he'd become quickly involved. He realised that he felt protective of her. "Nothing at all?" he probed.

"His tent and some other things were found," she answered. "Not his kayak. It's a popular area. The policewoman said that someone might have taken a liking to it. It was an expensive one—a performance racing type. Custom-made, sleek, and quite distinctive; the paddle too—also custom made. Probably too much temptation for someone to resist if they found them lying there. The police were very kind. They posted information notices around the area—with his photo. Another poster offered a reward if anyone found his kayak or provided information about him. There were a few responses, but nothing helpful. Part of the problem, she said, is that tourists frequent the area. There's a lot of traffic in and out."

"I'm sorry to ask this, Caterina. It won't be the first time the police have asked you: Were there any reasons he might have wanted to disappear—on purpose? Was he having any problems that you know of? Job? Financial? Was there anyone who might have wanted to see him out of the way?" he asked, avoiding the implication of a possible drug deal connection.

She shook her head. "We've been through all of that. You're right; it's what the other investigators asked too. He didn't really have a job; he sold some of his carpentry. No money troubles; I know that for sure. There's nothing. Nothing that would explain it. Besides, Lorenzo loved his life. He was always laughing. I've never known anyone who was so uncomplicated and who cared for everyone and everything. Honestly, I don't think there's any criminal activity or foul play involved."

"Does he have a workshop, somewhere where he did his carving?" asked Antonio.

"Just a small space he rented. It's locked up, and he hasn't been back there. I keep checking. I'm still paying the rent, just in case. It's stupid of me, I suppose."

Antonio pointed to an elegantly inlaid wood table. "That's a lovely piece. Your brother really is very talented."

She gave him a wonderful smile. "Thank you!" she said, taking his hand. It was a natural gesture.

He was aware that she was grateful to him for continuing to speak about her brother in the present tense. It seemed less final, yet it didn't raise false hopes about Lorenzo. To Antonio, it didn't seem likely that he was still alive—not after all this time. Yet, nothing could be ruled out. He felt sorry for her. It was so evident that she desperately wanted to remain optimistic. "Is there anywhere he might go, somewhere you haven't discussed with the police?" he asked. He wanted to leave her with something—some kind of tangible action to show that he cared.

She shrugged. "The female officer asked me the same thing. Our family comes from Italy, originally. From a woodworking region. I think that's where his carpentry talent comes in. We've checked with relatives. No one has seen or heard from him."

Antonio gave her a hug. "No promises, but we will look into it. Is that okay?"

Walking him to her front door, she hesitated.

Seeing the look that she gave him, he leaned over, one arm balanced against the wall, and kissed her. He sensed rather than heard her moan of pleasure. Pulling away from his embrace, she dropped to her knees and pulled him towards her. He shook his head and pulled her back up, standing.

"We shouldn't," he said, breathing heavily.

"Of course, we should—if we want to," she answered.

Against all his instincts, Antonio shook his head. He wanted to say to her, "Let me try to find your brother first." Taking advantage of her vulnerability didn't sit well with him. They kissed for a time. Breaking away, he hugged her.

Climbing the stairs down to the street, Antonio hailed a passing cab.

He felt old, deflated—and completely wretched.

Xavi

He nodded his understanding.

"I'll start with the female officer who was handling their investigation. She may know more than she's told Caterina. If I can, I'll arrange for the case file to be transferred to our department. There's no real reason to have it moved from Missing Persons to Homicide, and foul play isn't suspected, but they're usually glad of our help. With so many cases to handle, they'll be happy if we take one off their plate."

Antonio nodded in agreement, yet looked troubled. "It's been nearly a half year," he said. "I'm okay with taking over the investigation, Xavi. But I'm not convinced that merely reviewing the files will get us very far. I want to believe that her brother is still alive. Don't worry," he added quickly, seeing the concern on his partner's face. "I haven't said anything to her. Without any evidence, that would be cruel.

"You know my way of thinking by now," he continued. "Too many of our drawn-out and unsolved investigations start off with the scene of the crime, or maybe the scene of the incident in this case. We think outwards from there. Then our lines of enquiry run out of leads. Instead, let's put ourselves in her brother's position. He's paddling away out on the lake in his kayak, which he's adept at, when something happens. There weren't any weather events; our police reports confirmed that. So how does a skilled and apparently level-headed kayaker suddenly become a missing person? His kayak wasn't found, and searches to date suggest that the chances of it being at the bottom of one of those lakes are remote. They looked thoroughly. My guess is that it was taken by someone. On the lake? That's doubtful. Probably much later. Maybe after he'd got back to his tent, his camp. Let's assume he was okay until then.

"So, what happened at his camp? And at what time of day or night? There were no obvious signs of violence or an accident. His tent flap was unzipped, as if he'd left hurriedly and intended to go back inside. Maybe he was disturbed by something or someone. His car was found where he parked it. No clues there. No indications of a robbery attempt or attack of any kind. Insurance money isn't involved. He wasn't suicidal and he wasn't the type to intentionally cause a lot of stress for his family."

"With those factors eliminated, you're asking me what might have happened?" asked Xavi. "Well, the possible explanations are that it was a planned, premeditated disappearance. Or an abduction or an accident of some kind. You've said you don't believe it was premeditated. So that leaves a random abduction, possibly with a fatality, or an accident."

"When you talk to the female officer, review the incident report with her," said Antonio. "Find out if there's anything that can support what we're thinking. The missing kayak is a possible lead. Maybe it's the smoking gun. If it was stolen, it doesn't sound like another kayaker would have taken it. There's a code of honour between those outdoor types, after all. I'm thinking it's an amateur. Someone who took a liking to Lorenzo's shiny sleek new kayak. Maybe he was caught in the act. Possibly there was a confrontation—not necessarily at the camp but where he left it. It could have been at the lakeside.

"A sneak thief might have stolen and kept it for a time, then either lost interest, panicked and dumped it—or sold it," he continued. "Not locally, somewhere else. A visiting tourist perhaps. The question is this: If someone tried to sell it, who would have bought it and where is it now? You don't paint fiberglass kayaks to disguise them. So, we need a big push of enquiries at kayak clubs, and see if we can identify it somewhere. Not just in Spain either. Let's do a really wide circulation of a photo—via Interpol if necessary. One other thing. William is a sleuth when it comes to security video footage. Let's get all the tapes we can for the lakes area around the time that Lorenzo went missing. See if he can spot anything. Ask him to look for a car or truck carrying a kayak with that description. Then perhaps we can find out if we have a murder on our hands, or something else.

"Let's just hope, for Caterina's sake, this doesn't have a bad ending."

Aurelia

As soon as she opened her front door, Antonio's heart skipped a beat. His passion for her had been building for months. Tonight, she was exquisite, he thought. Poised, elegant, and sophisticated.

A silver sequined narrow-slit evening gown hugged Aurelia's elongated fashion model's body. It fitted her so perfectly that he knew the outfit must have been tailor-made by a highly skilled modiste. Low heels magnified the impact. His eyes sparkled with admiration; hers returned the compliment. Her smile challenged him, just as it had when they'd met in Ramon's office months earlier.

"Wow," he said, speaking his thoughts aloud.

Her dark hair was pinned away from her neck, allowing a single thick tress to cascade over her right shoulder. She said nothing as she opened the door. Her elegant movements communicated everything with a serene command of time and space—and attitude. He didn't think he'd ever seen a more alluring woman.

With an almost imperceptible movement of her head, she invited him in. As he floated past, he caught the faint whisper of a fragrance that immediately disabled any lingering physical resistance. He felt her reach out and take his hand, guiding him inside. He couldn't recall what she said to him; he simply found himself following headily behind her as she glided sensuously into her dining room.

"These are my friends," she said. "Louis Valois and, of course . . . Phoebe." She seemed to have difficulty remembering her female guest's name. "This is Antonio." She awarded him another irresistible flash of her eyes and squeezed his hand. "He's an absolutely brilliant detective.

"Phoebe is from here—from Barcelona!" she continued with a stunning smile. "Louis lives in Madrid; he's visiting for a few days. Antonio, why don't you take care of the wine? Get to know each other. I have to get back to the kitchen."

Aurelia's friends remained seated. They smiled up at him politely.

"Antonio Valls," he said, offering a handshake to Louis and was disappointed to find the man's response was limp-wristed. His face, in contrast, was politely animated, and he made strong eye-contact. It was a searching look. "Ah, the policeman." He raised his eyebrows. The tone of his voice was measured. Not dismissive, thought Antonio, not even indifferent. Not haughty, aloof, or condescending. Rather, there was an absence of interest—an insouciance, for which Antonio had only a limited frame of reference. It was the attitude of a person who knew himself to be superior—an old-time, finely bred aristocrat.

If Louis had intended to make him feel inferior, he had done so very effectively, thought Antonio. Yet, even to attribute such a motive to Louis seemed to exaggerate the man's level of interest in their brief exchange. His expressionless eyes, having settled on Antonio, remained set at the same distance—then switched off like a doused flashlight. It was a weird, unsettling encounter, Antonio thought. There wasn't enough in their initial conversation for him to conclude very much. Not enough to take a liking to the man, or even a dislike. It wasn't a testosterone-driven competitive male thing, he thought afterwards. Louis was not challenging him in any way. Antonio's impression was that Louis simply had no interest in conversing with him beyond the trivial and superficial.

Feeling his competitive instincts flare, Antonio turned to Phoebe. Reaching forward, he kissed the back of the short and stubby pink hand she offered. "Phoebe!" he exclaimed breathlessly, gazing into her wide and moist doe eyes. "Such a pleasure. Aurelia told me you're beautiful. *Dios mio*! You are stunning. I think it's unfair that a woman so alluring as you should have such power to captivate and control we poor, mortal men." Hearing his exaggerated words tumbling out, he noted the flattering effect they had on her. Phoebe's already heavily lacquered eyelids widened and then fluttered. He heard her gasp in deeply, then sigh—face flushing with pleasure.

"Antonio! You're just a flirt. You don't mean it. Not really." She giggled.

Looking away, Antonio glanced at Louis. He had returned to his own world. There was no reaction from him, except for a brief motion as the indifferent aristocrat brushed a speck of imagined dust from the cuff of his shirt.

"Up yours, Louis," said Antonio under his breath, walking to a side cabinet where an array of wine bottles was on display. He was impressed. A Rothschild Puillac 1970 had already been opened. Its companions were another Bordeaux, a vintage Chateau Margaux, and a single bottle of a poor cousin—a 2017 Alter Ego. Ignoring the opened bottle, Antonio uncorked the Margaux. Selecting four fresh glasses, he poured each a measure. "Less rough, don't you think," he commented, handing a glass first to Phoebe and then one to Louis. He caught a flash of recognition that confirmed he'd struck a chord. "What do you think, Phoebe?" he asked, ignoring Louis.

She giggled.

Aurelia returned from the kitchen. "About ten minutes, I think," she announced. "I see you've met each other." She sniffed her glass of wine. "Mmmm, I like this. Clever you, Antonio—guessing what I'm about to serve. What do you think, Louis?" she asked, walking around the table and placing her free hand on his shoulder while studying Antonio—who was fairly sure that she wasn't asking Louis his opinion of the wine.

"What's it like to be a policeman?" gushed Phoebe, allowing Antonio to embark on a series of entertaining anecdotes. Antonio wanted to amuse Aurelia rather than impress her lacklustre friends. Glancing at Louis, it seemed unlikely that the diffident nobleman would make any effort to elevate their conversation in any way. He was wrong.

They were seated, eating their main course of exquisitely prepared duck, when Louis spoke at last. "Do you spend much time in the country, Antonio? In the rest of Spain, I mean."

His question didn't offer enough of a clue for Antonio to guess which direction Louis intended to take the conversation. So, he played it down the middle and answered the question with a question. "By the rest of Spain, do you mean the region outside Catalunya, Louis? Or the rest of Spain outside Madrid?"

He thought he caught a brief smile from Aurelia.

"If you're asking about my profession," Antonio continued, "most of my time is spent in populated areas, where the bulk of crimes are committed—although I will admit that Spain's rural areas are not devoid of their excitement and, in most cases, are just as involved in criminal activities."

"I think Louis is asking on a personal basis, not about your work," said Aurelia. She seemed to be sensing the onset of a clash between the two men.

Antonio smiled at her and winked. "Well, as a student, I spent two summers working in the vineyards of la Rioja. I lived with a family in Logroño. It was slave labour really. Anyway, I learned a few things about making wine." He raised his glass to Aurelia. "Then I was in Zaragoza for a year, studying at an academy."

"Academy?" asked Louis, his eyebrows raised inquisitively.

"Yes, the Academy," said Antonio. "I trained initially at the Academia General Militar." It meant nothing to Phoebe, but Louis exchanged glances with Aurelia.

"You mean you're a graduate of AGM?" he asked with undisguised astonishment—tinged with a new tone of respect.

"First year graduate only," said Antonio. "After that, I didn't see the army as my future, or the Civil Guard. I transferred to Arabic Studies at Rabat."

"That's an unusual career route for a Mossos homicide detective," continued Louis, his voice showing sudden life and now giving Antonio his full attention. "Most Catalans planning on entering the Mossos don't seek such a broadly based international education—if any at all." From years of breeding, his mouth reverted downwards. It was a natural and derisive response, yet held little real vehemence. In fencing parlance, it was a parry, not a lunge.

Antonio met his gaze and overreacted to the put-down. "I thought that the new Spain would be more relevant than the old." He smiled patronisingly and enjoyed seeing the aristocrat's discomfort. "How about you? Were you at the Academy?"

"Prior to the Sorbonne, yes," Louis replied, speaking slowly. "Maybe we have more in common than I'd thought."

"We both appreciate fine wines and beautiful women," replied Antonio. "That's usually a good start, isn't it?" He had noted Aurelia's close attention to what they'd been saying. Trying to determine the connection between her and Louis, he figured that he could run a search through the national database later. For now, he was a guest at her dinner table and ought to act like one, he reminded himself. Still, if he could pry out some information about Louis, it might be helpful.

Aurelia was quick to anticipate his thinking. "You'll have to forgive Louis," she said with a disarming smile. "He's never quite got over the disappointment that he's not a king, or a prince of the realm. I keep telling him he was born two hundred years too late for that. He has links to the Borbóns."

Thinking that Aurelia was not just beautiful but incredibly smart, Antonio knew that she was supplying him with information that he'd soon be able to discover for himself. Doing so enhanced her credibility, he conceded. It was clever. "I thought he looked a bit like Louis the First," joked Antonio, making them all laugh—except Phoebe, who giggled, looking anxiously from face to face trying to understand the joke. "That's quite a cross to bear, isn't it, Louis?" he continued. "I can't imagine that you're much a fan of the European Union."

"Well, I'm not exactly rushing to have myself elected as a member of that assembly," said Louis. "You shouldn't forget, however, that my ancestors tried for centuries to unify Europe."

"Yes," drawled Antonio, stretching out the word. "I understand that's true. But it was still Europe under the control of the monarchy, wasn't it? Hundreds of years of control by the same family—kings and queens. Too much nepotism, for me."

"I understand that the Mossos hasn't been entirely free of a little nepotism," Louis shot back.

Antonio was taken aback. So, they knew that his father was the former Mossos chief. "Touché!" he conceded. "You have me at a disadvantage." He wondered how much Aurelia had told Louis about him.

"Le dessert?" she announced hastily. "Perhaps a little sweetness would go over very well."

"Oh, I love dessert," said Phoebe, missing the point and causing them to smile.

―――

"What news do you have, amigo?" asked Antonio, looking up from his desk.

"Maybe a breakthrough." Xavi smiled. "You were right about the kayak. Eagle-eyed William checked the CCTV tapes. He narrowed the prospects and came up with several possibilities—including a real gem."

Antonio looked impressed. "A gem?"

"Security video footage shows an older model sedan driving away from the lakes area—with a kayak roped across its roof. That's the giveaway: outdoor enthusiasts have a metal roof rack or other safe way of carrying their loads. He got the licence plate too. It's registered to a Frenchman living in Perpignan. I had a word with the local gendarmerie, who gave him a visit. They took photos of the kayak," Xavi offered his phone to Antonio. "It fits the description of the one we're looking for. He claims to have found it—concealed among some bushes by the roadside. So, he took it home. The Frenchman wasn't trying to deny anything. He's given a sworn statement. They're asking how you want to proceed."

"What's your sense, Xavi?" asked Antonio.

"I don't think he's lying. The paddle was missing. The gendarmes thought he had been an opportunist. He found the kayak but didn't wait at the scene to find out if it belonged to anyone. Probably not much more underhand than that. The roadside spot was several kilometres away from where Lorenzo had pitched his tent. The gendarmes said the kayak looked like it had been dragged along the gravel. My guess? Someone else took it from his camp and abandoned it when it became too hard, or too risky, to move any further."

"There might have been a confrontation between Lorenzo and whoever stole it. That would make sense if it was stolen at night. What did our female officer say?" asked Antonio.

"I gave her an update. She didn't seem surprised. She still thinks he's a missing person and doesn't suspect foul play. Her main concern is the emotional toll on Caterina; she and her brother were very close, apparently."

"This new information brings us back closer to the scene," said Antonio, combing his fingers back through his streaked blonde hair. He'd been growing it out again—much to the delight of the girls in the office. "Apart from anyone living in or near the woods, you'd need some kind of transportation to get in and out of the area. Do we have any footage of car parks near the scene? Have the locals been interviewed?"

"They did that, actually," said Xavi. "The officer was quite thorough. She wrote up detailed notes. It might be worthwhile revisiting."

"Good," said Antonio. "If we raise the stakes and pass the word about it being a possible homicide enquiry, that might spook someone, but we don't want to upset Caterina if the news gets out. Can you contact her and let her know what we're doing? Explain it to her."

Xavi looked at Antonio, his face revealing his confusion. "Isn't that something you'd want to do? I'm saying it would mean a lot to Caterina if you spoke to her yourself."

Antonio shook his head. "I'd like to distance myself for the time being."

Xavi shrugged and left the room.

He didn't look impressed.

Surprise Call

"Detective Inspector Valls?"

The caller introduced himself as a senior metallurgist. "I didn't know who to send our report to, but your name is mentioned on the file." He provided a reference number. "We have the test results on the piece of gold jewellery you sent us some time ago. Our apologies for the delay; we've been working with quite a backlog."

For a moment, the call mystified Antonio—until he remembered the gold pendant he'd sent to forensics for analysis. It had been returned to him after they'd taken a core sample. The Civil Guard had seized the pendant along with all their files and records relating to Daniela.

"We're an independent laboratory, sir," continued the caller, who seemed to realise that the detective inspector required further explanation. "It was sent to us for spectrometry testing."

"Ah yes," said Antonio. "I remember it now. Can you brief me over the phone?"

"It's an unusual sample," began the caller. "Very old gold. In fact, throughout my career, I've only seen one other sample similar to it in composition. It has a high pure gold content. Exceptional fineness.

However, the trace levels of charcoal impurities introduced during the refining process are not something we see much of these days. I'll be sending a complete report, of course, along with returning the sample. Undoubtedly, its origin is European. Probably over a thousand years old. We believe it may have been melted down comparatively recently from a much older object, probably also a significant piece of jewellery. It happens quite often, although this is a rare example. Unique, in fact. I would imagine the original piece had an impressive provenance."

For several minutes after the call, Antonio typed notes into his private file. Reaching for his phone, he scrolled through his photo library. Eventually, he found the images of the gold pendant he'd taken from among Daniela's belongings at the time of her arrest. The metallurgist's comment about the age of the gold sample had caught his attention. With the exposure that the investigation had given him to the topic of gold, Antonio had become intrigued by the precious metal. He recalled, too, that Aurelia had cautioned him of its alluring powers when they'd first met at Ramon's office.

Scrolling through his photos, he wondered again what significance the number seventy-nine had for his investigation. It was the atomic number of the precious metal, of course, but the scientific classification of elements had been developed only comparatively recently—fewer than a hundred years ago. The gold sample predated that by many centuries. He was aware that the number seventy-nine is culturally significant in several European countries. Maybe Aurelia would have some answers. It wasn't a question he wanted to ask her—not until he knew more about it.

The pendant had been created later and might simply be an attractive and expensive piece of jewellery. After all, she was involved in a profession with direct ties to the gold bullion business. Somehow, he doubted the explanation was that simple. Xavi had investigated Aurelia's past after Antonio had visited her office. She had no priors. Her distant connection to the Borbón royal family had been declared.

She wasn't trying to make a secret of it, and she certainly wasn't attempting to leverage the connection for her own benefit.

Was the pendant a linkage to the monarchy, perhaps? Was the sniper involved too? Once again, he had more questions than answers. Somehow it was related to his investigation. How was it all connected to Daniela? he asked himself. They were fascinating questions, but frustrating.

On an impulse, Antonio sent a copy of his photos to Diego. Maybe GEO 60 could shed some light on the significance of the gold pendant.

Perhaps they could help explain why Aurelia and the sniper both wore one around their necks.

And what the seventy-nine meant.

The Grandee

Only one key existed.

It fitted the lock of the secure filing cabinet and safe bolted to the floor of the grandee's private office. Under normal circumstances, the key hung alongside a gold pendant on a leather thong worn permanently around his neck. From the safe, he had extracted a file that was now lying open on his desk. Alongside the file was a handwritten note that had arrived by courier that morning.

The grandee recognised the penmanship—written cryptically in Old Latin by a scholarly grammarian, clearly of considerable distinction. The message provided no names or traceable details, merely confirming for the grandee's eyes only that the intensive course of medical treatment administered to an injured officer of the Royal Guard over the past year had been completed successfully—physically, at least. He knew that the officer had served the Crown well. Regrettably, the severe hand injuries the officer had sustained during the discharge of his duties meant that he was no longer able to pursue his former profession as a skilled marksman. Moreover, there were veiled questions about the officer's mental health.

Still active and able, the grandee himself was well past the normal age of retirement. He was closely familiar with the contents of the young officer's file, as indeed he should. He was its sole custodian—its guardian. Refreshing his memory of the events a year earlier, the grandee perused several other confidential documents in the file. One, in particular, caught his attention. It was a report submitted outside the normal chain of command by the marksman's commanding officer. He had confirmed that the injured officer had followed standard procedures throughout his assignment. There was just a hint that, had instructions been given to him just a few seconds earlier, his mission most likely would have been successful. An affirmative kill.

No reproach of the officer was necessary, said the commanding officer's report. A vicious psychopathic terrorist had attacked him after his failed assassination attempt. She was still being sought by the police and would be dealt with suitably. Breaking the fingers of both hands, and one thumb, indicated the mind of a pathologically vicious criminal, he'd added. Regrettably, the marksman's military career was over, the commanding officer had concluded. His recommendation, supported by several other senior officers in the Royal Guard, was that the officer should be retained as a reserve within the service. He hinted that the former marksman's skills might be suitable to an occasional non-combat role.

The grandee knew that the commanding officer was unaware of the special credentials held by the young man. It was obvious to him that he had spent a considerable amount of time writing and fine-tuning his report before sending it by personal courier to the grandee. It was also evident to the grandee that the senior man very much respected his junior officer and admired his impressive record of combat service. Few in the Royal Household, or in the Royal Guard, were aware of young officer's pedigree. None were inclined to regard the young and highly decorated officer as anything but loyal to His Majesty. Nor were they inclined towards recriminations: he had been doing his duty—serving his country.

Like his sister, the young officer was a descendent of the Borbón throne. The grandee was one of the few who knew that, although a distant relative and far removed from the line of succession to the Spanish throne, the young man was family. "*Blood is thicker than water*"—he was mindful of the saying. He could not share all his thoughts—and actions—with the monarch. Indeed, it was prudent to prevent the king from learning about certain things which, on his behalf, were better performed in the shadows. He could trust the young officer implicitly in that regard, the grandee was certain of that. There would be no objections to the special treatment the grandee was planning for the injured officer. As he prepared himself for his daily attendance at Mass, he reflected on the theme of reciprocity. The Curia of the Holy See had ancient and longstanding obligations to protect the monarchy, and its loyal servants.

An executive-level job, relating vaguely to security, had been created for the officer at a well-known Spanish investment bank in Madrid. Overnight, a human resources file had appeared. It provided a convincing backstory in case of prying eyes. The grandee felt satisfied as he closed the file and returned it to its secure place. In doing so, absent-mindedly, he fingered the heavy gold pendant on its leather thong around his neck. The pendant signified certain responsibilities. The young officer had both hereditary and well-earned professional claims for protection.

He would be well looked after.

CHAPTER 4
North-East Syria: The Parting

For a few hours, there had been a lull in the fighting.

To the ears of the five rebel soldiers fighting against the al-Daser government, the silence was filled with echoes of gunfire. It carried its own unique tone—a phantom echo created by the sudden cessation of repetitive and overwhelming noise. They felt relief from the barrage of Syrian Army shells and missiles that had assaulted their position relentlessly. Through a miracle, they were still alive and uninjured.

It was nearly sunset. They knew the respite wouldn't last.

"It is soon time for *salat*," Farouk reminded the others. He looked at Ali, who would lead the prayer after their wudu. "Then, God willing, we will speak a final word together of the future."

Ali understood the solemnity of the occasion. This would be their last night together, they had decided. Their commander Jamal, and most of their brigade, had been separated from them long ago. They'd heard he'd been killed north of Hama. For months, while they were still a fighting force, their straggling band of survivors had retreated eastwards to relative safety—hiding when they could, fighting skirmishes only when they could not avoid them.

With Russian help, Syrian government troops had recaptured the lands formerly held by the caliphate. ISIS had lost the war—not that Farouk's group of rebels had any regrets. Soldiers of the caliphate had become monsters. Their once-unified fight against al-Daser had revealed deep schisms—not in their fundamentalist beliefs, not in the jihad, but in their very different methods of waging war.

The rebels considered theirs to be a holy cause. It was a fight against al-Daser's atrocities and the relentless pursuit of the time-honoured calling to get rid of all foreign infidels. To them, ISIS had waged an unholy war. It had been too focused on establishing the caliphate and elevating a powerful emir. ISIS was indifferent to the sufferings of millions of ordinary people. It was singularly dedicated to vicious killings and the wanton and unnecessary destruction of precious artifacts belonging to Iraq and Syria.

Farouk's group was among the last of the al-Nusra rebels still fighting. Now it was time for them to disband—to give up the battle, but not the fight. Soon they would fade like evening shadows into the darkness of the night. Not to yield, but to survive. To live and fight another day. Several hours later, each had gathered his scant belongings. For safety, they would travel east together on foot towards the Euphrates. After that, they would abandon their weapons and travel separately to their destinations. Taking shelter during the day, they would travel only at night.

Powerful and intimidating, Farouk insisted they each repeat aloud their commitment to the cause and to each other. A war-weary band of brothers, they did so with renewed fervour—furious and determined. Leaving behind all they could not carry easily, or did not wish to be found in possession of when they were searched, they melted unhurriedly into the night. Behind them, in the distance, the heavy gun barrages from the regime positions soon resumed their assault. Return fire from the semi-automatics of their comrades crackled in retaliation but did little to cheer them.

Resistance to al-Daser soon would be silenced.

For now.

Farouk

He had killed many people.

Now he thought only of the present and the future. For two days, he had walked alone—a refugee looking for someplace to settle. A place of refuge where he hoped the regime soldiers would not find him in their frenzied and bloodthirsty quest for retaliation. He had not eaten in three days and had used the last of his water for his ablutions that morning.

He was fortunate. It was late November, and the rainy season would begin soon. Shivering, because the day was unusually cold, he pulled his gown closer to his scrawny body. His lips were cracked from razor-sharp desert sand blown into his face. His leather boots, taken from a dead soldier, were cracked and worn. Feeling every stone on his path, he'd started to limp. Luckily, he'd found a stout weather-beaten pole that now served as a walking stick. Ahead, he saw several emaciated goats and a low brick building. A child with long hair, perhaps a young girl, caught sight of his dusty, stumbling figure in the distance. Leaving the animals to fend for themselves, she ran for shelter. It was a desolate place, he thought, as he watched the child slide hurriedly over a low brick wall and disappear inside.

There wouldn't be many travellers along this way, he judged. Perhaps they had food he could take. Not *take* any longer, he realised; those days were over. Without a weapon, he was just another refugee—and a fugitive. Get used to an even more modest station in life, he reminded himself. He would beg them for a few scraps. As for water, the place must have a well. They might allow him to drink.

He approached cautiously.

Living this far away from a village or town, the herdsman almost certainly would have a gun—but most likely an old shotgun handed down through the generations. Perhaps something more modern, a captured weapon maybe. He had no wish to provoke any hostility. Taking a low-value banknote from the purse secured inside his clothing, he placed it flapping on a rock in sight of one of the windows. He made a sign of peace and retreated to a safe distance.

He waited. No one emerged, so he retreated further.

Soon a young boy, not much older than his sister, came out. Moving hesitatingly, the boy kept his body below the tops of the grey stone walls that penned in the animals. He carried a metal cup of water, which he placed on the bare rock. From his belt, the boy took a small flask—a gift of fresh water for the traveller's journey and a piece of dried goat meat. He scurried back inside.

Farouk observed the proceedings with interest. He noted that the boy had not taken the money. In the towns, they would do so. But out here, the ancient dictates of the Koran—generosity to all travellers—were still upheld, despite the distrust and hardships created by the wars. It was unusual, he thought, for a parent to expose a child to such a risk. But his need for water was considerable and he shuffled towards it with a show of humility. Drinking from the cup, he noted the water was cold. There must be well water here, he deduced. Perhaps spring water from the rock outcrop behind the homestead. There could be no other reason for people to settle here. The grazing was sparse and mean.

Replacing the metal cup on the rock, Farouk stuffed the gift of the water flask and dried meat into his pocket. Crouching, he lingered long enough to take a good look at the building. From its construction, it had been there for many generations. The leaf-and-timber thatched roof was overlaid with sheets of rusted corrugated iron that rattled in the wind. An outbuilding of a height suitable only for small animals stood deserted. Stretching across the outside enclosure, a metal wire used for drying clothes was bare and appeared unused. A large flat stone served as an outdoor table. The building had small windows, without glass but with wood shutters of a design that could be pulled closed to protect its inhabitants from dust and the weather. Apart from the goats, there were no other animals that he could see.

Nor any adults.

Still considering his course of action, Farouk gave thanks to Allah and waved a brief farewell at the empty windows, shuffling away to continue his journey. Some giveaway markings on the ground and two mounds at the edge of a field helped him decide his next action. Continuing for some time, he glanced occasionally behind him until he was out of their sight. Withdrawing behind some rocks, he waited.

The boy could move silently, yet he did not have the finely tuned hearing of a combat soldier. Nor was he observant of the tracks that would have told him Farouk had doubled back and was hiding, waiting for him. Grabbing the boy by the collar of his robe, he stepped back to avoid the wild kick aimed at his legs. The boy was no match for Farouk and eventually gave up the struggle, but not his yelling.

"Why are you following me?" Farouk demanded.

The boy looked at him resentfully. "We need medicine. Our sister is ill. You have money; I thought I would ask for some."

Not long ago, Farouk would have clipped the boy's ear with his hand for his impertinence. Instead, he let go of him, taking the risk he would run away. "You thought you would steal my money, didn't you?" he shouted. "I know more than you think. How long has your sister been ill? Since before they came and killed your father?"

The boy looked at him in surprise.

"Or was it your mother they killed, and afterwards you buried her next to your father?"

"It was my mother they killed," answered the boy. "Then, afterwards, they shot my father."

"I saw their graves," said Farouk, observing the boy's eyes widen, "after you gave me water. You did not take the money. Why not? You need medicine."

"The Koran," said the boy with a puzzled look. "Allah teaches us to be generous and to look after strangers. It is His command to us."

Farouk nodded his approval.

"Tell me about her illness," he instructed. "Everything you can remember. How old is she? That can make a difference. Then I need to hear what ails her. Tell me all."

After the boy had finished, Farouk nodded. They made their way back to the homestead. "Do you know about medicines?" the boy asked along the route. "Are you a doctor?"

"A soldier," answered Farouk. "Just a common soldier."

"Too many soldiers; not many doctors," the boy said sadly. He ran ahead, saying nothing else until they arrived.

"You are right. She needs a doctor," said Farouk after he had looked at the young woman. "It is as you said; she has a bad fever. Also, a rash."

"I have heard there is a doctor at al-Sumaya. It is a day's walk," said the boy. He turned and conferred with his younger sister, the child that Farouk had seen earlier. "She says that there is also a hospital. It is a two-day walk—maybe more with her." He pointed to his older sister lying on the bed. "How can we move her?"

Farouk thought that weeks ago, the logistics of moving the sick young woman would have been easy. His platoon had commandeered an almost new pickup truck. It seemed like a long time ago. Now he felt helpless. "This doctor," he asked, "in which direction?"

The children pointed north.

"The hospital?" he asked, hoping for an answer that would not take him back the way he came."

They pointed east.

That was more acceptable to him. "Can you walk that far?" he asked, and they nodded.

"For her, of course," the boy said with a frown.

"We will go tonight," said Farouk. "First, I will need your help to build a stretcher."

Two hours later, they had fashioned a durable A-frame wood structure that he could drag behind him. Farouk spent some time making sure it was solid and would not fall apart on their journey to the town. The boy was innovative; he took down the clothes wire from outside and helped bind it tightly to the wood. With the mattress lashed to the top, it made a serviceable carrier. Slow but sure.

As he lifted the young woman onto the stretcher, she reached out and gripped Farouk's arm. "Thank you," she mouthed, giving him a grateful smile.

Noticing a small container with a red paste, he asked the children, "What treatment is this?"

"It is a remedy my mother made from plants outside," said the boy quietly. "Is it good?"

Farouk shrugged his shoulders and pocketed it. "It looks like peganum; it might be helpful."

The young girl approached Farouk with a pair of stout leather sandals.

"Your father's?" he asked, looking down at her from his considerable height.

She pointed at his boots. "You look like a soldier. They will know what you are."

Farouk said nothing as he accepted them; he tousled her unruly head of hair.

"What about our goats?" pleaded the boy.

"Bring them, if you can take care of them." He shrugged.

―❀―

They had walked through the night.

Farouk's shoulder strap, with a blanket as padding, helped ease the weight of the loaded stretcher. It was awkward, but years of combat had hardened and toned his muscles to a fine pitch. Keeping to the compacted desert ground across the flat valleys, they made good progress.

Several times he stopped to ask the children if they wished to rest. He was astonished by their endurance. When asked, they simply said, "Our sister," and carried on walking—herding their few goats ahead. He stopped several times to check on the condition of the young woman, encouraging her to drink water even when she selflessly refused it. Her fever was still high. By daybreak, as the sun rose and blinded their faces, an early morning wind picked up—blowing stinging grains of sand into their eyes even though their faces were covered.

It was the boy who heard the sound first. "A truck is coming," he warned.

Farouk knew there was no time to drag the stretcher to a hiding place. Soon he saw the vehicle on the horizon. His heart sank. Maybe it was a Syrian Democratic Forces convoy, he thought. Or possibly a regime patrol, armed and filled with fresh-faced, gun-happy young Syrian Army soldiers seeking out the last remnants of ISIS fighters. There must be a garrison nearby, he guessed.

Laying the stretcher on the ground, he took out the container from his pocket. Using his finger, he rubbed the red paste in a series of spots on the young woman's face. He called over the children and did the same. He had just enough time to add red spots to his face, and continue dragging the stretcher forwards, when the fast-moving regime patrol came to a dusty stop a short distance from them. Farouk had been correct in anticipating their combative zeal.

Pointing his semi-automatic at the group, the commander ordered them to stop and raise their arms.

"*As-salamu alaykum*," called Farouk. "We have a sick woman. We are taking her to hospital," he addressed the young commander.

The soldiers smirked as they looked at the makeshift stretcher. The commander jumped down from the vehicle and approached the travellers. "Your papers!" he ordered. Suddenly, he stopped when he saw the red spots on their faces. "What is that?" he demanded.

"She has a fever, sir," said Farouk, gesturing to the young woman in the stretcher. "Maybe some disease."

The commander recoiled and took a few steps back. He was joined by several of his platoon, who covered their noses. They stared in revulsion at the straggling group. "Then we will arrest the goats," he exclaimed, and turned to his men, who laughed and muttered their approval.

All of them wore new uniforms, and Farouk guessed they had not yet had much combat experience. Mostly just a bunch of rookies, he thought. He calculated his odds of killing all of them. The commander would be easy; he was no more than two metres away. Farouk could snatch his semi-automatic and turn it quickly on the others. There were four standing in the back of the truck—they would be slow to react. Another two, including the driver, remained in the cab. They would be more difficult. His main concern was the hardened-looking soldier manning the M16 assault rifle mounted on the cab. It was aimed directly at the children. Maybe the commander would order them all to be killed.

"Sir, the fever," said Farouk, dropping to his knees. He threw his hands in the air as if to plead for their lives. He pointed with both arms to the stretcher. "God willing, she will survive. The children too."

"Collect the goats," ordered the commander, not wishing to lose face.

"Maybe they, too, carry the disease, sir," pleaded Farouk. "Their meat will be infected. We are just a poor family. Please let us pass."

The commander stopped in his tracks.

"The hospital. There they will cure us, Allah willing," Farouk pleaded.

The commander stood uncertainly for a moment, then turned back to his vehicle. "Do not touch anything. Let us leave the disease to these lepers and their wretched livestock. Let's go!" he ordered.

The group watched as the patrol vehicle speeded away, and its dust swirl settled back onto the desert. When it disappeared beyond the horizon, the two young children jumped up and down with joy. They skipped in a happy circle around Farouk. "You are our hero." They laughed. They rubbed their hands on their faces, removing the red dye. They caught a goat and plastered the animal's face. "See!" They doubled over with laughter. "It has the red disease too."

Farouk checked on the young woman; she smiled weakly at him. She was beautiful, he thought. Her perfect teeth showing through her full lips. He placed his hand on her forehead. "You still have a fever," he told her. "But no disease, I think. The doctor will know."

Exhilarated by Farouk's ingenious handling of their encounter with the government troops, the children quickened their pace. The group reached a village several hours later. A sympathetic shopkeeper left his wife in charge of their store and, for the price of two goats, drove them in a beaten-up old truck to the town.

"She needs antibiotics," an overworked medic told Farouk. He pointed to the partially bombed shell of the hospital. "I regret we have none."

"There is always a black market—for those with money," stated Farouk. "Where do I find the dealer?" He returned half an hour later with a package of medicines. "These are for her," he said sternly to a nurse. "You understand? You look after her; then I will buy more for your other patients." He held out the bag. "We will wait here, but please arrange water and food for the children." He handed her some money. "I do not mean to insult you, but she is all they have. Their parents are dead."

He watched as the children devoured the food that was brought to them. He refused to eat or drink. "I must wash and give thanks to God," he said. "It is time." Later, he returned to sit among those waiting for treatment. Exhausted, the two children were fast asleep on a concrete bench. Awkwardly, he lowered his tall frame alongside them. Gently, he brushed the young girl's hair away from her face. Moments later, Farouk felt something. The young girl had found his hand, and had slipped hers inside his. It was the natural gesture of a young child; it was a gesture of complete trust.

He felt his throat tighten, and his eyes welled. It was hard to swallow. He sniffed deeply to stop a dribble, but he was unable to prevent a warm tear from trickling down his cheek. It landed with a splat on the dust of the tiled floor. Quickly, he pulled his robes over the evidence. Since he had split from his comrades, he had been wondering where he could hide. Somewhere, he'd thought, there must be a place where the SDF and the regime's revenge troops would not find him. Quite by accident, he had stumbled on the perfect new set-up to conceal his real identity.

Yet, looking down on the little girl, he realised that he had found something much more valuable than his personal safety, something more precious—something he had known long ago. During the long wars, they were things he'd thought had gone from his life altogether.

Silently, he again gave thanks for this day.

For this blessing from God.

Yasser and Mahmood

It had taken them almost a week, frequently remaining in hiding to avoid skirmishes with government forces. Finally, they arrived at al-Mayadin.

Yasser had a cousin living in the town, but he did not know if the man was still alive. He recalled that many years earlier someone had said that his cousin owned a truck business. Perhaps he and Mahmood could get a job, maybe help a little and earn some money, he thought. Yasser was proud of Mahmood's skills—he had been the mechanic for their platoon. He could fix anything.

They had spent a few days in al-Mayadin during the fighting several years ago. Their platoon had helped capture the town for the anti-government rebel forces. He regretted some of the things that had happened. There had been some executions. Some of the town's elders—regime collaborators—had been killed. His men had not participated directly, but Yasser knew there was blood on his hands. Government soldiers would be hunting for former ISIS operatives, and for rebels. They would offer rewards to informants. Yasser knew he'd have to be very careful. There would still be many anti-government supporters in the town, but also citizens who would be overjoyed to denounce them. He didn't know on which side his cousin's loyalties lay. There was no way of knowing if his relative would turn them over to the retribution police. It was a risk he'd have to take.

They found his cousin's garage after a short search and a few cautious enquiries. It was not much of a place, just a single building in the industrial area near the river close to the sewage treatment plant. It was surrounded by other small businesses where many structures had been destroyed during the fighting. They could see only one truck in the yard, and clearly it was not functional. The vehicle's engine had been stripped down, and men were crowded around some oily parts lying on the ground. There was a lot of talk but, apparently, not much progress.

Mahmood, who was always happy with the prospect of working on anything mechanical, was keen to see if he could help. Yasser was reluctant. He held Mahmood back and they did not immediately enter the yard. He wanted to assess the situation before enquiring about his cousin. They walked past casually and did not stop. One time, he had to pull Mahmood into the shadows as a regime patrol vehicle drove slowly down the street.

They had not eaten for several days and the smell of fresh flatbread from the oven of a nearby bakery compelled their attention. It was irresistible. They drifted towards the entrance. Mahmood had little concept of money, and Yasser kept control of what they had. Recent times had been tough. It was not like the old days when soldiers of all sides could steal and pillage at will. Yasser knew he'd have to be prudent with the meagre savings they had between them. Approaching the bakery door, he was shocked. At that very moment, his cousin emerged—carrying several fresh pitas. They recognised each other at once. Surprised, neither knew what to say.

"Feras," blurted Yasser, breaking the silence. "What are you doing here?" He thought his voice sounded shrill and nervous.

His cousin looked at him with narrowed eyes. Eventually, Feras remembered his manners. "*As-salamu alaykum*," he replied. "Are you travelling?"

"We are looking for a job," replied Yasser, pointing to Mahmood, who was staring wide-eyed at the fresh pastries in the bakery.

"A job here?" asked Feras, with a voice of suspicion. He examined Yasser and Mahmood in turn. "Have you eaten?" he added.

"We were walking past and just about to buy breakfast. May I invite you?" insisted Yasser.

Feras's pride was at stake. His manner revealed that he did not wish to be humiliated by his cousin from Homs. Slowly, his face lost its frown. "Please, I insist. Come and join us. Your friend too; he also is our guest." He gestured in the direction of his garage.

Feras and Yasser went inside to his office while Mahmood remained outside in the yard, watching from a distance as the men tried to fix the truck. Venturing closer, he examined the parts they'd removed from the engine.

"What have you been doing?" Feras asked Yasser. In the office, they shared flatbread with hummus and tea. "How did you end up here? Why not in Homs?"

"Things have changed there," said Yasser—stating what everyone knew. "How are your parents?" he asked, anxious to change the subject.

Feras shook his head. "It has been difficult here too. Especially for them. But they are still alive, thanks to God. Their house near the river, it was damaged several times. Now they have no money left to fix it. No one has any money," he added, in a poorly disguised message to Yasser.

"And the farm?" asked Yasser.

"It has been impossible to grow any crops," his cousin replied. "Maybe things will get better now that the war is coming to an end." He looked at Yasser. "What have you been doing during the war?"

Yasser studied him, pausing before giving his answer. He watched carefully for Feras's response. "Soldier," he replied simply.

"I guessed as much," said Feras. "I would like to help you, but I am struggling too. Stay tonight if you wish, but you will be better off in the big cities where there is more work."

Outside in the yard, there was a loud noise of the truck being started up. The engine spluttered to life and then backfired several times. A large cloud of thick blue smoke was emitted from its exhaust. There was a chorus of cheers from the men working on the vehicle, and much laughter. Then the engine failed.

Feras glanced over his cousin's shoulder through the window. "It's amazing they got it going at all. They have been trying for three days."

Yasser was grateful that Feras had offered hospitality for the night, but he and Mahmood needed somewhere permanent to hide. He wondered how he could persuade his cousin into extending his invitation. Their families had never been really close, so talking about their relatives would be like throwing old seed on barren ground. He would have to think of some other way to convince Feras. "How is your truck business?" he feigned interest.

Feras shrugged his shoulders. "Now that the government troops are clearing out the ISIS stragglers, things may settle down. Maybe

I can do some business; maybe not." It was obvious to Yasser that his cousin really did not want to encourage him to stay in the town.

"There must be black-market activities?" said Yasser, probing. "I have a little expertise in that area."

He saw Feras's eyes narrow. It was illegal to carry out profiteering, and the government was handing out harsh punishments to those who participated. Yasser guessed that Feras was wondering about him—assessing if he could be trusted. Maybe his cousin suspected that he and Mahmood had been anti-government soldiers. There would be a reward for informing the authorities. It was not large, and he guessed that Feras did not want to attract too much attention to his little operation. They might discover more than he wanted them to find. "I do not approve of these black-market activities," he heard Feras say, although neither of them believed his claim.

There was more noise in the yard, as the truck was restarted. This time, there were no backfires from the engine. Instead, it sounded sweet and balanced. There were loud cheers from his workers. "What the hell are they doing out there?" Feras sprang to his feet. "It sounds like my boys have fixed it. This is really good news. Now we can transport some freight."

Yasser hurried outside after him. The driver was leaning out of the broken cab window, pumping his fist in the air as Feras approached. "It's going, boss," the man shouted with delight.

"What was wrong?" demanded Feras.

The men shrugged their shoulders. "Don't know. Ask him." They pointed to the oil-smeared, smiling face of Mahmood, who, at that moment, was clambering out from beneath the truck. "He fixed it."

Yasser smiled.

Things might get better.

They were allowed to sleep at the back of Feras's garage for several more nights. It seemed that Mahmood could turn his hand to anything needing repair. He shunned the praise heaped on him and settled down quietly to do what he wanted to do—fix things.

A day or two later, looking for scrap metal for a repair, he searched among the rubble of the bombed-out building next door. He found an electrical cable, which, although mostly buried under the ruins of the building, was still connected to a live source of power. He spliced it into the power supply for the garage. The town's generators worked only intermittently, but for several hours each day, Mahmood was able use the free power supply. He salvaged a charger and began to repair discarded lead-acid batteries, which Feras then sold for a profit. At night, he would recharge flat batteries for a small fee.

Yasser was proud of his companion's achievements. Feras was vaguely resentful but liked the money that Mahmood earned for him. His guests proved to be scrupulously honest in their dealings. He began to trust them with additional tasks. There was no further mention of how long they were permitted to stay. Soon they ventured into restoring some of the homes that had been less badly damaged during the fighting. With help, Feras was able to repair most of the damage at his mother's house. He sowed seeds at their farm. Mahmood's gravity-fed irrigation design, pulling water from the Euphrates, proved to be ingenious. The crops thrived. Yet, Feras was prudent. As he grew richer, he invested wisely in further repairs and renovations. It seemed there was nothing to which Mahmood was unable to turn his talents. The willing little fix-it man asked for almost nothing in return. Yasser, too, proved to have skills in finding and transporting black-market goods. He located several wrecked vehicles that Mahmood and the other workers were able to restore to working condition.

Their soldiering backgrounds were never mentioned. When the authorities routinely checked, there were numerous people in the town who vouched for the legitimate activities of the two men during the war—working on behalf of the community. In turn, the two men were content with the arrangement. When they were together, they reminded each other of their commitment to the cause. They spoke quietly of the pledge they had made on the night they had disbanded. When called again for the jihad, they would be willing and prepared.

They were delighted when they received word from the others in their platoon. Farouk, they had heard, had settled down. News reached them that Ali was completing his studies and soon would become an imam. Of Nazih, they had no news. As a former ISIS fighter, he'd always had a vicious streak. They hoped he had not fallen foul of the retribution police. That would be a concern for them. If captured alive, he would be tortured. Under duress, despite his physical and mental strength, it was almost certain they would force him to reveal the identities of the others in his platoon. In the meantime, they were content to bide their time. They'd found a rewarding way to burrow themselves deeply inside the woodwork of the dark economy. At least for now, they were protected.

Biding their time, they awaited word of their recall.

Nazih

Unlike the others, Nazih had kept his gun. It had been such a vital part of his identity for so long that he couldn't bear to be without it. He knew every part of it. He loved the sensual feel of its smooth dark barrel and its killing power. Throughout the prolonged years of the civil war, and even before that, he had kept the same weapon. He could take it apart and reassemble it in his sleep. Every day, he oiled the moving parts. It was a ceremony that was almost as regular for him as his *salat*. As a soldier of the jihad, he considered these things inseparable.

After his platoon had disbanded, Nazih had chosen not to go home. For years, he had not sent any word of himself to his family in Eastern Ghouta. He thought they would assume he'd been killed.

If not earlier, then certainly when the government troops supported by the Russians had begun their final rout of rebel forces. He knew only that he was still very much alive—and contented himself in the knowledge that his assumed death would make him a martyr within his family. He imagined his presumed demise would inspire his brothers and sister to pursue the jihad—to dedicate their lives, as he had, to the expulsion of all kafirs.

Nazih had been an accomplished foot soldier for al-Qaeda in Syria when it had been known as al-Nusra Front, and later, as Jabhat Fateh al-Sham. He had fought alongside the great al-Julani, their emir. Al-Julani had split his group from al-Qaeda, pursuing the sole objective of defeating the al-Daser regime. Al-Nusra spurned global ambitions. When it had re-emerged, stronger and more potently, as Hay'at Tahrir al-Sham, the emir had created a formidable new force in northern Syria. Nazih's rebel group and the HTS had fought alongside each other in several campaigns.

During his lifetime, Nazih had seen many things. He'd fought many difficult operations. His hatred of the Western powers was so intense that he could barely hide his contempt for its peoples and its corrupt and immoral governments. He ridiculed the whole concept of democracy, adamant that it was a Western ploy to undermine his country and obstruct the global spread of Islam.

He could never settle back to a life where the holy war took a secondary role. A world in which his peoples' traditional doctrines did not drive the future of the world was unacceptable. His role, he fervently believed, was to help wage the violent jihad that would force out the infidels and direct all Muslims along the path to true Salafist beliefs.

Recently, his journey away from the last remaining conflict areas had taken him south, then east. He regretted his platoon's shared decision to disband, yet he acknowledged the common sense of it. Live to fight another day, they had decided. That meant they had to retreat, for now. Keep out of sight, yet always alert and prepared. Above all things, Nazih was determined to continue the fight; he would not permit al-Daser to be victorious. The regime had been on its knees, almost defeated, when the Russians had intervened. He would never forgive them.

Nazih had been thinking about al-Julani. He saw two choices for his own future—he could rejoin the emir and focus on the defeat of al-Daser, or he could pursue al-Qaeda's more global ambitions.

He wondered why he couldn't do both things.

Ali

His mother was convinced he'd been killed.

She could not believe it when he walked through the door. He looked so deeply tanned and weather-beaten, she thought. He had trimmed his beard, and despite his hardships, she thought he hardly looked his twenty-five years of age. She had planned to celebrate his upcoming birthday in a week's time—alone and in a quiet and respectful way.

Fussing and bustling around him, she continued with such intensity that he had to plead with her to stop. It was to little avail. Hearing of his safe return, throngs of relatives and friends arrived at their home. Their presence served only to magnify the commotion. Clamouring for his attention, they kissed and hugged him constantly, throwing out questions in such rapid succession that he had no chance to organise his thoughts. Already exhausted from his long journey, the swarm of attention became too much for him and he fell asleep in the middle of the impromptu party to honour his homecoming. It mattered little to those who rejoiced in his safe deliverance. They continued to celebrate. There was plenty of time for him to tell his story, they reasoned. Now they just wanted to express their thanks to God for the homecoming of their favourite son.

Ali awoke early the next day in the comfort of his bedroom. Nothing had changed. His mother had kept all his things exactly as he had left them. Like a shrine. Preparing for his morning prayers, he reminded himself there was much for which to be thankful.

Several hours later, his mother knocked on his door and entered. "I heard you awaken earlier," she said, sitting comfortably on the edge of his bed. "You will stay this time, I pray. It has been a terrible war. There is no need for you to continue. Besides, there are many things for which we need you," she said. "I have lost you once," she pleaded. "Please, my son, do not leave me again."

It was painful for Ali to see his mother in such distress. He wished he could spare her the pain. "Mother," he began, "I have been spared by God for a purpose. Please try to understand. Whatever happens in this world, we will be reunited in the next life—with Him."

She had heard him say these things before and knew it was pointless to argue. He was determined. It was difficult not to be proud of such a fine young man, she conceded. Yet, she loved him so much that she wanted to be selfish with him. To keep him close to her. For herself.

"I will complete my religious studies," Ali informed her a few minutes later. "It is my calling. Maybe fight too; that also is my duty."

She understood, yet she was immensely sad. Saying nothing more, she left his room.

He reached his hand over his left shoulder and gave the still sensitive region a brief massage. Two years earlier, he had received the bullet wound. A surgeon had removed most of the fragments. Residual shards still remained, causing pain that was disproportional to their size—like slivers of wood deeply lodged under a fingernail. The pain was a constant reminder to him of his obligations to God. He had been given a responsibility; it was not his place to decline. Setting his street clothes to one side in a neat pile, he put on his robe. Minutes later, he left his home. Heeding the call to prayer, he walked briskly to the mosque.

A single thought drove him.

When he was called, he would return to fight for the jihad.

Western Syria: Latakia

The Russian guard glared at the skinny middle-aged Syrian orderly nervously carrying food from the canteen to Jamal's cell.

It was a routine delivery, happening three times a day. Yet, each time, the prospect terrified the orderly. The Russian guards seemed increasingly more suspicious. He'd become so intimidated that he wouldn't dare add even a single speck of salt to the prescribed diet without authorisation. Today, he was even more nervous. His family had been threatened by one of their own people; the terrified orderly had been coerced in the name of the jihad. He knew that the price of his failure would be high.

Shouting out orders to a colleague, the Russian guard waved the orderly to stand facing the wall. One of them would perform a complete body search; the other would check the tray and examine the food being served to the prisoner. The guard was reading his favourite novel—*Anna Karenina*—so his colleague received the less savoury task. Putting on latex gloves with a scowl, the colleague did not spare the orderly any pain. Seemingly absorbed by his reading of one of Veslovsky's flirtations, the Russian guard used a fork to separate the food on the tray. There was nothing. He checked under each plate, deliberately ignoring the note written in Arabic carefully attached under the paper cloth.

The orderly was astonished when he was waved through to Jamal's cell, accompanied by a junior guard. He could not believe they had not tumbled to his rudimentary deception. That morning at home, he had left a brief note addressed to his wife apologising for being a poor husband and worthless father. Now, thanks be to Allah, he might not be beaten by the Russian overlords, escaping punishment for his subterfuge. He remained cautious. His task was far from over. He would have to wait outside and collect the empty dishes, accounting for every item taken into the cell. Desperately wishing away the minutes, he prayed that the prisoner would find the note. The people threatening his family were expecting a reply—they had instructed him to wait for Jamal's orders in response to the escape being planned for him.

The orderly's instructions to wait were routine. Yet, knowing the vital nature of his assignment, he sweated profusely. Keeping his eyes cast to the floor, he tried not to look up—terrified about drawing attention to himself. A loud growl from his stomach, and a fart, caught the attention of the Russian guard still reading his book.

"What's wrong with you?" The Russian was now standing over him. He sniffed at the air and held his nose. "That's disgusting," he yelled. "You pig. Take him to the washroom," he shouted to the second guard. "Make sure he cleans his hands properly too. He'll give us all typhoid."

In the orderly's absence, the Russian carefully examined the tray. In his pocket was a high precision camera—its lens much more powerful than that of a regular cell phone. As instructed, he took numerous photos of Jamal's handwritten reply and replaced the items exactly as they had been. He would deliver the photos shortly afterwards to the Spetsnaz officer who'd given him his orders.

Unaware of the guard's discovery, the orderly removed the tray. Within the hour, he had passed along Jamal's message to his contact. When he finally reached home that night, he gathered his family together. They would never know about his assignment. He had rescued the note he'd written to his wife and burned it before she could see it. Later, he attended the mosque for *Salat al-'isha*, offering several additional devout prayers of thanks.

Saad

The man who'd befriended Saad had been introduced by a mutual friend.

For the first several months of their affiliation, he'd been given modest assignments. They were testing his loyalty. He knew it and carried out his tasks willingly and well. Mohammed introduced himself using his first name. That was all that was necessary for Saad to know, he'd been told. "It is better this way. God willing, our mission will succeed," said Mohammed. "It is a simple act of sabotage. Yet, it is vital to our task."

Saad understood perfectly. "I am not afraid," he said confidently.

"It is not your fear that we are concerned about," snapped Mohammed with undisguised derision. "If you fail, our operation will be doomed."

"Can I know my assignment?"

"It is not yet. You will be told when. In the meantime, you can continue to help us with other tasks."

Ahmed

Nightmares still haunted him.

Ahmed worried constantly about his little brother and cursed himself for not taking better care of him. After the Catalan police raid on his apartment in Barcelona, when he had been lucky to evade being captured, he had searched for Yussef. He'd gone to the store where he knew Yussef liked to go, but his little brother was no longer there.

Fleeing the police barricades, Ahmed made his escape as far as Greece. There, he was caught up in a police raid on a refugee encampment. "Did he want to apply for asylum?" a social services interpreter had asked him. Ahmed was using a false name and didn't want anything to do with the asylum process; he wanted to get back to Syria. That was where Yussef would go, if he were still alive.

Trusting no one, he'd eventually arrived back in Syria. It had taken months of furtive travels avoiding the authorities, always bypassing the official borders. It had taken luck. Several times, he'd nearly been apprehended. He found that conditions in his country had changed dramatically since his departure. The once-formidable ISIS had been defeated as an organised fighting force. Government troops were entrenched confidently and triumphantly throughout the country. His career as an ISIS bombing expert was over, he realised. At least for now. His priority was to survive, not to get caught and be tortured by the regime. If he failed, bled dry of information, his only option would be to hope his death would be merciful and quick. He doubted it.

Returning to his hometown of Homs, he located a sympathetic school friend whom he knew would never stoop to being a government informant. Ahmed now had a roof over his head. Cautiously, he made enquiries about Yussef. His little brother had not been seen for a long time. As far as anyone knew, he was another tragic casualty of the wars. Every family had been affected. There was an active trade in information about missing persons, with multiples sources and millions of desperate seekers. So many refugees and displaced persons trying to become reunited. He shunned the well-meaning international agencies. He avoided the regime websites set up to connect missing persons—knowing they were monitored by the secret police and that he would be high on their most wanted list. He shunned cafes frequented by the hopefuls who posted messages for loved ones on their walls—for they, too, were a trap.

To no avail, he scanned old copies of *al-Naba*, the online weekly newsletter of ISIS, which, astonishingly, was still being published. He sought the coded messages he knew would be embedded within its pages—aware that even innocent online searches would be pounced upon swiftly by the regime. He remained in the shadows . . . and never gave up hope.

Venturing out one day to the local market to buy food for an evening meal, Ahmed sensed that someone was observing him. It was not obvious—just the animal instinct of being watched. Paying quickly for his scant handful of vegetables, he decided to return to his shared apartment by a circuitous route. There were several places where he could throw off an unwelcome pursuer.

He was in luck. News of fresh vegetable supplies had circulated quickly. Local residents took to the streets in droves quickly buying up all that was available—and what they could afford. In the aftermath of the civil war, it would take decades for the city to get back to normal. At least things were better than they had been. He despised the ever-present phalanx of meagrely paid spies, eager to outdo each other and please their masters. Today, despite his diversionary tactics, he could not shake off the feeling he was being followed. It was strange, he thought. They could easily have arrested him already. After that, a session or two of torture would have yielded all the information they wanted. His school friend would be arrested too.

"Ahmed," he heard his name called. It was more like a muffled call than a shout. He hurried on without stopping. His pursuer was persistent. Soon afterwards, this time closer, he heard his name again. His pursuer was almost upon him. The man grabbed his arm and pulled him into the shadows.

Not immediately recognising him, Ahmed tried to pull away. The man had an iron grip. "Mohammed," his pursuer persisted, supplying his name. Slowly, realisation came over Ahmed. This was one of the soldiers of the al-Nusra brigade who had made a pact with Ahmed's demolition squad. He was one of the negotiators of the deal that had resulted in him and his little brother being sent to work for Mustapha in Spain.

Ahmed's protective guard was on full alert. It must be a trick, he thought. Mohammed was now a government informant sent to betray him. They would arrest him. Anything he said would be turned back onto him. They would find ways to twist his words, intimidating him at his weakest point of resistance. He should know: he'd done it himself many times to captive regime soldiers. The torture would not stop, even when the prisoner succumbed. He would be dismembered—his bloodied severed head hoisted on display in some public place. Desperately, he looked for a way to escape.

"Your brother, Yussef," said Mohammed, his mouth close to Ahmed's ear. "I know where he is."

Ahmed's face revealed his shock. His pursuer's words cycled several times through his brain. He smelled Mohammed's stale breath and wondered again if this was some kind of trick. Yet, the words had been hopeful. Mohammed had not said that he knew where Yussef's body was; he'd said that he knew where his little brother was—right now. Here? Was it possible?

"Where?" he heard himself ask. It came out as a pitiful whine.

Mohammed glanced behind him. "He's alive. Not injured, but he's a prisoner. He did not know if you were dead, Ahmed. He feared so, but Jamal sent a message for me to find you so that we would know for sure."

"Jamal? Your commander?" said Ahmed, not wanting to voice the words al-Nusra.

Mohammed nodded. "We need your help." He waited until his words sank in. "We will help you if you want to be reunited with Yussef."

Ahmed almost cried at that moment. Praise Allah! Yussef is still alive. He felt his legs weaken. His little brother—all that remained of their immediate family.

Mohammed, a seasoned veteran, recognised the signs of elation. He shook Ahmed's gown and looked angrily at him. "We need your help. This is no time to be a woman, weeping with emotion. Do you want to see your brother?" he demanded. Not waiting for a reply, he tugged Ahmed back along the street.

The vegetables that Ahmed had so carefully selected were left behind.

They remained there for several hours. Respectful that a neighbour may have left the precious food behind accidentally, many saw them, but no one took them.

As beaten, starving and humiliated as they were, the people still had honour—and dignity.

CHAPTER 5
The Condesa

She had been thinking about the lodge.

Thinking of selling it.

It had been empty for over a year—since Carlos died.

During the police investigation, she'd given her set of keys to the National Police in Madrid. They'd returned them several months later. Hortensia set them aside safely, knowing the condesa's intense dislike of the place and the terror she'd experienced there. Awful memories: the general, the sinister chauffeur, Old Spain cronies . . . the place where Carlos had suffered a massive heart attack.

Maybe it was her remorse over Carlos, her guilt. Each time the condesa had thought about the lodge, she'd quickly dismissed it from her mind. It was an evil place. Yet, she knew she must move on with her life. Her agent advertised the property. Not wanting to give it away, she had priced it above market—a reflection of its unique qualities as a hunting lodge. It had history. Not just her own, but also of Spain. The generalissimo himself had stayed there. He'd hunted among its grouse hills. Possibly, he'd enjoyed the coolness of the lake during Madrid's scorching hot summers.

The condesa had no tolerance for the caudillo's politics. He represented all that she detested about Old Spain. Yet, she felt reluctant to sell the place to the most likely type of buyer—a young, brash, "new money" person who'd made a fortune on la Bolsa or in the technology sector. If she sold it, the lodge most likely would be torn down, replaced by an ultra-modern edifice, destroying with it a part of history—erasing one of the enduring, and still precious memories she had of Carlos.

On an impulse, she called her agent. "I want to take it off the market. Thank you for your service. Send me a bill for your fees. No, nothing wrong—just a change of heart. It's a unique place and should be preserved as such. It has value to the nation."

Her next call was to the prime minister. She apologised for disturbing him. "Regrets are completely unnecessary, my dear Condesa," he protested, and listened as she spoke. "What a wonderful idea," he said moments later. "Also, very generous of you. Donating the lodge and its grounds to the nation in Count Carlos's name is a wonderful gesture," gushed the PM. "He did so much good for our country. On behalf of a grateful nation, I gladly accept your offer, Condesa. Also, your idea of dedicating it to young people as an outdoors training centre is a stroke of genius.

"I will instruct the director of the heritage foundation accordingly. Tell me, dear Condesa, are you acquainted with the Duke of Valladolid? He was, I believe, a friend of your late husband. Like him, a grandee of Spain."

Hortensia was delighted with the news the condesa had just shared with her. The loyal housekeeper was almost in tears. "Señor Carlos was a wonderful gentleman. *Excelentísimo*," she said, a lump rising in her throat. "A great man."

The condesa was heartened to witness such unreserved endorsement, mirroring almost exactly her own view of him.

"If you would prefer not to visit the lodge, señora," the housekeeper began, "I can box up his things . . . until . . . until you are ready to deal with them?"

The condesa shook her head. "No, but thank you, Hortensia. It's my responsibility.

"I must lay my demons to rest."

Days later, the condesa retraced the journey she'd made more than a year earlier, up the A6 to the lodge. Now it seemed like a lifetime ago. She tried not to think back on those times, Wisely, she'd chosen a sunny day with a lot of daylight still remaining.

Hearing of her plans, Felipe had called. "Surely it is not necessary for you to revisit the lodge, Condesa?" He sounded concerned. "As your lawyer, I can prepare all the legal documents necessary to transfer the property. I'm anxious that you do not put yourself through unnecessary stress. Those terrible memories."

Determined to go, she'd finally agreed to let him come but insisted on driving. Felipe had stood by her at her most difficult times after Carlos's death. He had been resolute in defending her against several abrasive and insensitive police officers. She appreciated his loyalty and held him in immense regard for his steadfast defence of Carlos. At the worst of her times of grief, she'd been unaware of the extent to which Felipe had defended her husband's reputation. As she recovered from her self-imposed isolation after Carlos's death, friends whispered to her that Felipe had been among her most stalwart champions. Always low-key, he declined any fuss, shunning any praise—always there as her devoted counsellor and friend.

He was an attractive man too. She enjoyed his company, but their relationship had always been strictly platonic. The condesa recently had lamented as much to a girlfriend. "Why is it," she asked, "that when a woman discovers an almost perfect man, invariably he is gay?"

They arrived at the lodge gate. The tall wrought-iron structure was intimidating and the condesa shivered involuntarily. She recalled having clambered over the stone wall and making her way down the long gravel drive to eavesdrop on Carlos's meeting with the general and his fellow plotters. It was only through luck that she had not been discovered and most probably killed by the evil chauffeur. She breathed in deeply and exhaled twice before she could summon the courage to press the remote. Slowly, almost begrudgingly, it opened.

Felipe reached over and gave her arm an encouraging squeeze. "We've come this far," he said.

She nodded. Reaching over, she clasped his hand in hers—just for an instant. Then she revved the engine and drove with determination along the gravel driveway leading to the lodge. Above the doorway, the mounted head of the giant antlered ibex stared back at her.

"Are you all right, Teresa?" asked Felipe gently.

"I'm not sure the children of the next generation are going to appreciate that thing," she replied, pointing at the gruesome trophy. "Maybe we should remove it before we transfer the property?"

Felipe shrugged. "Political correctness, señora. Maybe it is better, when they visit here, if our young people learn the realities of those times. I doubt they will share its values."

The condesa gazed again at the head of the ibex. "Maybe you are right, Felipe. Perhaps in death, it may serve an even more valuable purpose."

She planned to remove from the lodge all the personal things that Carlos had left behind. Then Hortensia would arrange for a commercial firm to clean out and donate the furnishings to charity. But now that she was here, the condesa could not force from her mind the terrible memories of that night. She couldn't breathe properly—and felt claustrophobic.

Felipe was so supportive and helpful, she reflected. She was immensely grateful to him. He'd had the foresight to bring along several suitcases into which he was now neatly—almost reverently—packing Carlos's clothes. In a separate suitcase, he placed the personal items. Within thirty minutes, he was standing by the door with the luggage, waiting for her to finish. "It will do no good to linger here any longer, Condesa," he said gently. "These are difficult emotions.

All his belongings are packed. Please allow me to drive you home so that you may calm your nerves."

It was as though she had not heard him; she seemed transfixed by the place. It had a morbid fascination and gripped her in its power, not allowing her to leave. She couldn't seem to drag herself away. Since their arrival, while he'd packed, she had wandered aimlessly from room to room—recalling scenes from the past and evoking memories that probably would still haunt her for years to come.

Felipe saw the signs and tried to coax her away. Nodding vaguely, she acknowledged the wisdom of his advice, yet the past seemed unwilling to release her. Something seemed not to want to let her go. A force she couldn't define. "This is where Carlos had his heart attack . . . where he and the general and their friends plotted against the state," she whispered.

She knew the reasons why Felipe had advised against this journey—not to come to this evil place. He was looking at his watch anxiously. There was still enough daylight time remaining; they could avoid the night-time hazards of the narrow mountain tracks and reach the safety of the paved roads. The condesa wandered back into the main room. The past was too strong; it still clung to her. Flashes of memory of her visit to warn Carlos kept returning. She recalled standing in front of the roaring woodfire, warming herself after her drive from Madrid into the cold mountains—still dressed in the lightweight clothes she'd been wearing earlier in her parliamentary office at the Cortes.

She recalled how, in her pocket, she'd had a copy of Father Damien's letter written just before he'd been murdered. She'd intended to show it to Carlos, to convince him to go to the police and explain that his involvement with General Bastides was just a harmless friendship with an old comrade. Then she'd found out the truth. Only then did she realise how much her life had been in danger. Not from Carlos—he loved her and would never harm her. But the creepy chauffeur was evil; she had seen the malevolence in his eyes. She'd overheard him talking to the general. They were plotting to eliminate her. She stood in their way. They were determined not to allow her to talk to Carlos. They would kill her, and Carlos would have been powerless to do anything about it.

Standing in front of the fireplace that had not been lit for over a year, the condesa glanced at the painting that still hung over the heavy wood mantlepiece. It was a pastoral scene of no consequence, yet it triggered a thought in her mind. "I suppose they emptied the safes?" she asked, reaching up and tugging one side of the painting. She knew it was hinged and concealed a safe where Carlos had kept his valuables. Swinging the hinged frame to one side, she reached up and pulled it open.

It was unlocked. And empty.

"The police will have cleaned everything out, Condesa," said Felipe's voice behind her. "Is there something you are looking for? Something personal?"

She shook her head. "It's such an obvious hiding place. Carlos never left anything of much value in it. As you say, the police will have taken the contents."

Felipe's face looked inquisitive. His intellect was razor sharp. "You said 'safes,' Condesa. Is there another?"

She shrugged. "I'm sure they found the other one too. It's probably empty." She reached forward with difficulty into the cavity—searching with her fingers. "Carlos told me that the other hiding place was for his private papers. Can you help me, Felipe? There's a hidden bolt here, where it's screwed into the stones above the fireplace. I had to put things in here a few times. There's a latch on the other side too. Try to feel along the felt lining for a slight depression—then press hard."

Felipe did as she instructed, searching with his fingers until they heard a click.

"Carlos told me that it's an old-fashioned spring mechanism," said the condesa. "It's ancient, but it works. It releases a wood panel on the side of the fireplace. Behind it is a small safe—just enough to hold a few papers and valuables. It's located low down so that Carlos could reach it. Over here," she added, kneeling and pulling at a narrow wood panel. "Carlos told me the combination. He made it easy for me—the four numbers of my birth year. Not very sophisticated, I'll admit, but easy to remember." She spun the dial four times. It swung open to reveal several documents and an oblong leather box. "Now that's interesting," she said in surprise, looking at Felipe. "It seems that the police didn't find it."

"Condesa," said Felipe, his tone full of caution. He had been thinking rapidly, anticipating the implications. "Before we touch anything, we should think our actions through a little, don't you agree? I mean, what we find inside might be important to the authorities. If they had done their job properly, they would have found this second safe during their investigations. But they didn't. I don't know how they overlooked it. Still, that's not the point."

"Let's take a look inside first, shall we?" suggested the condesa. "It may be nothing important." Her voice trailed off, and she looked again at Felipe. "No, you're right. If those documents are in Carlos's private safe, they are likely to be significant. What should we do? We can't just leave them here."

"Speaking as your lawyer, Teresa, my concern is for you. I don't think it's a good idea for you to touch them. If there's anything significant inside to do with . . . well, to do with their investigation, we must inform the police. What I'm saying is that if there's anything in there that might come back to affect you in some adverse way, you shouldn't put yourself in a potentially incriminating position. It's probably nothing, but let the police decide. Let me take a quick look," he continued. "As an abogado, I'm under oath. If they are merely personal things belonging to him, we don't need to inform the police. You can take them home along with his other things."

"Very well." The condesa nodded. "I won't touch anything. You look instead and tell me what you think. Go ahead, look if you wish. I'll just sit over here on the couch, out of the way." She seemed annoyed by Felipe's overcautious procedures. "In fact, I'll take a walk. I could do with some fresh air and get away from this place."

She huffed, threw back her head, and went outside.

Felipe photographed the safe before he touched any of its contents.

Reaching inside for the oblong leather box, he placed it on a nearby table. As he'd expected, it was quite heavy. Removing a bulky item that looked like a well-used accounting ledger, he saw underneath a document tied with a red ribbon that he immediately recognised as a will. Sitting down, he looked at each of the objects more closely—beginning with the heavy leather box. It contained a piece of jewellery that he recognised—a gold pendant tied with a leather thong. The gold piece was intertwined, but two letters stood out: a seven and a nine. Knowing its origins and its importance, he sighed and took a photo before reclosing the clasp.

He hadn't seen the accounting ledger before. As he scanned quickly through its pages, it was immediately obvious that his advice to the condesa had been prudent. The entries stretched over a considerable span of time—over ten years. Next to a series of initials, Carlos had entered in his neat handwriting various financial amounts. Felipe frowned. The amounts were huge. The initials undoubtedly were of well known and influential people. He wasn't slow to understand the ledger's significance. It was a complete set of accounts of the money that had flowed into Aladdin's Cave. Carlos's handwriting was evident in the document; nobody else's. It was incredible. There was no way that Felipe was willing to permit this highly incriminating document to fall into the hands of the police. It would ruin everything.

His eyes moved over to the will.

With a feeling of impending dread, he picked it up and began to read. Within a few minutes, the blood drained from his face. From its date, it was clearly Carlos's last will and testament. As he absorbed the details, his head started to throb. He recognised the signature as being Carlos's. He'd seen it numerous times, and there was no doubt it was genuine. The writing was a little shaky, perhaps, but bona fide. He saw that the will was dated the day that Carlos had died. That, in itself, could be regarded as suspicious, he thought. Otherwise, the will looked legitimate. Carlos's dying wishes had been laid out succinctly. There was no evidence he'd been coerced into signing it—but there was one glaring anomaly. The witness who'd attested to Carlos's signature was Luis, the chauffeur. That didn't necessarily make it invalid, Felipe knew. Yet, it raised a lot of questions.

He continued reading.

It was unbelievable. Felipe had no way to explain it. On the final day of his life, Carlos apparently had signed a new will. He had left to his wife, Teresa, their villa in La Moraleja. In addition, he'd left her a modest annuity. However, the vast bulk of Carlos's considerable fortune had been gifted to the Society of Seventy-Nine. Felipe knew the name well, of course. Even so, it was astonishing. Nothing had been said about the existence of this final will and testament when Carlos's estate had been probated a year earlier. As Carlos's executor, he would have been told about it. Yet, no one had come forward to make a claim.

Under his previous will, Carlos had left everything to the condesa. She was a fabulously rich woman. Or at least she had been—until now.

Under this new will, she had been left virtually nothing.

Felipe knew he had some significant problems to solve.

He mustn't allow the condesa to find out about the documents. Worried that she might come back into the room anytime, he reopened one of the suitcases he'd packed with Carlos's clothes, his sterling silver cufflinks, and some personal belongings. Extracting a collection of unimportant regimental papers that he'd found earlier in Carlos's desk, he placed them inside the safe—and quickly secured the accounting ledger and will inside the suitcase. Taking some quick photos of the regimental papers with the leather box inside the safe, he replaced the bags by the front door. He took several deep breaths. Making his way through the open back door, he saw that the condesa had walked down to the lake.

Sitting on a wood plank bench near the water, she looked up as he approached. "Well, Felipe?"

"No need to call the police, I think. Merely some regimental papers from Carlos's army days. There's only one item of any importance." He handed her the leather case. "This looks valuable. Are you familiar with it, Condesa?"

She examined it and shook her head.

"I've seen it before," said Felipe. "Carlos belonged to a little-known society linked to the monarchy. The pendant is worn by a few select members—an elite of sorts. It's a harmless organisation really. Certainly not illegal, and they pay taxes on their investment income, he once told me. They're mainly involved in good works: educational scholarships and that type of thing."

"And full restoration of the monarchy, I suppose?" she scoffed.

"Precisely," he acknowledged. "Fairly innocuous, as I said. Full restoration or anything like it is never going to happen. As part of Carlos's estate, I'm sure the pendant belongs to you now, Condesa. As a precaution, I will inform the authorities of our find. It probably means nothing to them. I took photos of the contents of the safe, to make sure we have a record on file."

He looked up at the darkening sky. "Daylight is short this time of year. We're finished here. I recommend we lock up and get going.

"Let's get back to Madrid while there's still some light remaining."

Connecting Dots

His phone buzzed.

Diego spent no time over pleasantries. "What do you know about the gold pendant?" he asked brusquely. Antonio was surprised by his tone but gave him the facts. Diego's rapid-fire follow-up questions surprised and intrigued him.

"You gave it to the Civil Guard officer?"

"Yes."

"Did he have any questions about it?"

"No."

"Any follow-up from him?"

"No."

"Is there anything else you can tell me, Antonio?"

"Well, I can tell you that the pendant is identical to one that Madame Aurelia Périgueux was wearing several weeks ago. She works for the government's money-laundering prevention agency—the TFPU. She's their bullion expert."

"You're sure it was the same?"

"I saw it, several times," said Antonio.

"Anything else?"

"The Civil Guard officer didn't ask me anything about the pendant. I just handed it over," replied Antonio. "If he had asked me, I would have told him what I'm telling you now. Daniela claims that a sniper tried to kill her—it was over a year ago, she said. At Mossos Headquarters, after we had arrested her, she told me about the incident. She said that the sniper was wearing it. She snatched it from him after the shooting, thinking it might help her identify who he was. Then you and Colonel Scott, and my chief, came in and ordered her to be released from custody. It was among her possessions when we arrested her. They went into the usual safekeeping lockup in the Evidence Room. It remained there until the Civil Guard officer arrived and took everything.

"The sample of gold we'd sent for analysis was one thing I'd forgotten in the commotion, Diego. I'd sent the pendant to forensics. I thought they might be able to lift some DNA samples from it. Unknown to me at the time, they sent out a sample of the gold to a metallurgist, to test its origins. The Civil Guard officer took the gold pendant, but the metallurgy exam was still work in progress. Its existence was overlooked. I got the results about an hour before I sent you the photos. Does it mean anything to you?"

"There are at least two pendants, as far as you're aware?" asked Diego, avoiding his question. His tone seemed to be softening. "Antonio, would it surprise you to know that a third one has been found—last week, in fact. Actually, the condesa found it when she was emptying out Carlos's personal items from the lodge. By the way, she's donating the place to the state as a wilderness retreat. She said she'd never seen the pendant before, but her lawyer Felipe recognised it. It's a ceremonial thing worn by members of an obscure charitable foundation linked to the Spanish aristocracy—to the monarchy, actually. Have you heard of the Society of Seventy-Nine? Based here in Madrid. It ties together a number of interesting people. But tell me more about this Madame Périgueux. Do you have her under investigation relating to the sniper?"

"Just under observation at this time," said Antonio. "I haven't questioned her about it yet. I've been waiting to see if she leads me to the sniper who tried to kill Daniela. Why are you interested in the pendant, Diego?"

"I can't say just yet. I can tell you something, though—off the record," said Diego. "The Civil Guard officer who picked up Daniela's files is being remarkably coy. At GEO 60, we didn't even know about the sniper's pendant until you emailed me that photo."

"Diego," said Antonio. "There's something else that might help you. Ramon has been leaving me messages to call him; I haven't responded. My hunch is that he's trying to find out what I know. He's fishing for information. Maybe he's working for someone."

"Thanks, Antonio," said Diego. "Keep this between us, please."

His conversation with Diego got Antonio thinking.

The gold pendant suddenly had taken on special significance. Diego wouldn't say why. There wasn't much point speculating on his colleague's reasons for not sharing the intel. Mentally, Antonio shrugged his shoulders. By now, he was used to being kept in the dark. He sat at his desk and reviewed what he did know. Aurelia was involved; that much was evident. The Society of Seventy-Nine was relevant too—and somehow it connected Aurelia and her friend Louis to the sniper.

Switching off his phones, Antonio propped his feet up on his desk. The need to identify the sniper was foremost in his mind. He knew that in any military organisation, or quasi-military group, there would be a chain of command. If the sniper was part of the armed forces, or with the special forces, the feds would have found out by now—unless, of course, the information had been deliberately expunged from the official records. Maybe the feds just didn't want to reveal the truth. Antonio had already checked discreetly among his contacts; his enquiries had come back with nothing. The existence of the sniper was not being admitted by anyone in the regular security forces. He could be a vigilante—but working for whom?

Normally, Daniela didn't miss an opportunity. If she'd had a chance, he was sure she would have photographed the sniper. It was a question that nagged at him. Antonio had asked her the question during her interrogation. He hadn't received an answer—they'd been interrupted by the arrival of Colonel Scott, the chief, and Diego.

It left him with nothing to go on. The investigations carried out by Francisca Diaz, the Mossos rookie officer for Xavi, had confirmed that Daniela had not been lying—the sniper did exist and the shooting had occurred. Effectively, the only clue he could use for follow-up was the gold pendant, and Diego had just quashed that line of enquiry. Still, there was one avenue of investigation remaining. He wouldn't normally proceed this way, he reminded himself, but events were forcing his hand. He would meet Aurelia and ask her about the gold pendant.

It would be a perfectly natural question to ask.

⁓

"Louis was interesting," said Antonio, his left eyebrow arched high.

"I thought you got along well with Phoebe," Aurelia responded with a sly laugh. "Apparently, she hasn't been able to stop talking about you since. Louis says he's quite jealous."

It was Antonio's turn to laugh. "I doubt it. But he is an interesting guy."

"You're asking if we're involved together?" she asked, flashing him a flirtatious look over the wine bottle set squarely in the middle of the lunch table.

He moved it to one side after replenishing their glasses. "None of my business," he answered. He took the opportunity to glance at the gold pendant that—quite by chance—she was wearing around her neck. If she was trying to keep any secrets about it, she was doing a poor job, he thought. "That pendant is beautiful," he said, returning her smile. "I first saw you wearing it at Ramon's office. Seventy-nine is the atomic number of gold, isn't it?"

Aurelia nodded and gently took hold of the gold pendant, toying with it. "I shouldn't wear it as often as I do. The thing is, Antonio, it's extremely precious. Unique—in its provenance, at least!"

"You mean no one else has one?" He feigned surprise.

"Well, very few people anyway," she replied. "There's a bit of a story involved, if you'd like to hear about it?"

He nodded. She probably knew the names of the others who were owners of the same pendant, he thought. He would just let her talk. Questions later.

"I'm an orphan," she began. "I don't remember my parents, but I do know something about them. You know about European history, of course, and that the monarchies of Spain and France are closely connected."

"The House of Borbón?" he offered, and she nodded.

"You asked about the pendant," said Aurelia. "History tells us that after the 1789 French Revolution, in the turbulent years that followed, powerful republicans and numerous street gangs of revolutionaries seized the vast riches of the French monarchy. Among them, they pillaged crowns and coronets that had been handed down through the centuries. They were quickly melted down. Crown jewels were sold to help pay the new republic's expenses and others were diverted for personal enrichment.

"Here's where it gets interesting." Her voice was bubbling with excitement. "Some of the many aristocrats who'd survived, and who later helped organise the Bourbon Restoration, regained possession of some of the former monarchs' most prized possessions. There was one in particular—and it's highly symbolic. The coronet of Charlemagne had survived since the eighth century. Scholars believe that it was still intact in 1879—almost a hundred years after the French Revolution began. Then it disappeared again. The coronet was a powerful symbol of attempts to restore the monarchy in France. Folklore has it that it was sent to Spain for safekeeping—the House of Borbón connection again. Certain aristocrats are believed to have regained possession of the coronet and kept its existence secret for decades, up until modern times. There were always rumours about it being held in secret by the Spanish Borbóns, yet nothing was ever substantiated. That's where the pendants come in." Her face was now alive with excitement.

"Just before the Spanish Civil War, during the Second Republic, the future of the Spanish monarchy looked bleak. General Franco was one of several powerful military men at the time. He became the all-powerful caudillo later. It's said that a certain Spanish aristocratic family, which by then had possession of Charlemagne's coronet, sold off its jewels and melted down the gold. You can guess the rest, Antonio."

"I think you're telling me that each of those pendants is made from the gold melted down from Charlemagne's coronet? That's amazing," he agreed. "I'm guessing that probably means that the owners of those pendants—including you—are sworn to safeguard Charlemagne's legacy. So, if the Borbón title to the throne of France were ever restored, a skilled goldsmith would use them to recreate the coronet, using the gold from the original. That's ingenious! And the Society of Seventy-Nine is the official custodian, shall we say?"

From her animated reaction, he knew that his assessment was correct. "Well, obviously, you're somewhere in the line of succession. Who else is a member of the society?" he continued. "I mean, it's got to be a very small, exclusive group, hasn't it?"

"I'm not sure I know everyone, but I know a few," she replied. "We don't have meetings or anything like that. There are no get-togethers. Its purpose is charitable works, and I was a beneficiary—while I was still very young, and, later, as a teenager."

Antonio was tempted to ask her for some names, but thought he'd throw in a few other questions first. To start with, a few diversionary tactics. "Are you really that close to the Borbón bloodline?" His tone stopped just short of gushing.

She seemed relaxed. "It's a custodian role. We take care of the gold that one day, we hope, will be restored to Charlemagne's coronet. I'm a long way down the line of succession, so I don't even begin to compare with Louis. But I take my role seriously. I think you would, too, if you were in my position."

"Do you have any brothers or sisters ahead of you in the line of succession?" he asked.

"That's an interesting question, Antonio." She looked at him quizzically. "Why do you ask?"

Confrontation time, thought Antonio. "Because about a year ago, a sniper tried to kill someone. He missed. But we know he was wearing a gold pendant just like yours." He took out his phone and scrolled through his gallery. "This is a photo of it. Do you recognise it?"

Her face had gone pale, almost a colourless white. She said nothing.

Watching her carefully, he thought that she didn't seem to be scrambling for a plausible explanation. Nor was there any attempt to deny it. Just a sadness. "Where did you get that?" she asked eventually.

"I'm sorry, but you need to answer my question," replied Antonio.

"It looks like one that belonged to my brother," she said, looking scared. "They're all fairly similar. I can't tell, but he told me that he lost his—under similar circumstances to the one you just described. You have to understand, Antonio, that I only found out about him recently. My brother's name is Jules Dampierre. We were both adopted as young kids and sent to separate foster homes. It's a long story."

"I need to know the exact truth, Aurelia—and all of it. It's very important."

"I'm telling you the exact truth." She bristled.

"Where is he now?" he asked.

"I don't know," she answered. "A few nights ago, he had dinner at my place. I invited him after I'd found out that we are related. Is he wanted by the police?"

"We need to talk to him," replied Antonio. "Urgently. And it's important that you don't call to alert him. Right now, he's on one side of the law—the wrong side. We need you to cooperate with us, Aurelia, so that we can bring him in for questioning."

She had put down her knife and fork; her elegant fingers were balanced on the side of the table. Antonio thought she looked hurt and confused. "I wasn't expecting our lunch together to end up like this," she said. "Of course, I will cooperate. I have nothing to hide. But I don't know where he is. Honestly, I don't."

"Do you know who he works for—anything about his whereabouts?"

"Well, he was in the army, serving in Afghanistan, as I said. He mentioned something about being in a special role within the Royal Guard at the palace. But he was discharged because of an injury. He showed me where his hands had been broken—very badly. He had several scars. I don't know any more than that."

Antonio thought it was time he lightened the conversation. He believed what she was saying, and she was beginning to look terrified. He'd seen innocent witnesses freeze up when they were scared, and sometimes, they became dysfunctional to the point of not being able to converse any longer. "That's what I need to know, Aurelia. Finding a brother you didn't know you had must have been be a hugely emotional experience. I don't think you're in any danger from him—I don't know if anyone is—but I want to make sure that you're not. So, thank you for answering my questions. As I say, all we need at this time is to talk to him, to help us with our enquiries. So, if you can help us locate him, I'd really appreciate it. Do you have his phone number?"

She shook her head. "He told me that he'd just arrived back into the country and isn't settled in yet. He was a bit mysterious about that, but I was so excited to be reunited with him that it didn't seem to matter. He'd phoned me from a call box. After the dinner we had together, we agreed to get together again soon. Where and when have yet to be arranged."

"So, he could call anytime?" asked Antonio. "In that case, we need to rehearse how you should handle it. I'd like to get the call box number from your log—would you mind?"

"Sure," she replied, handing over her phone. "I think I can do better than that, Antonio. At dinner, we took some photos of each other and of us together; I can send them to you if you like."

Antonio was thinking that Aurelia was being cooperative and helpful. He hoped there wasn't a dark side to her. He didn't think so, but he had to make sure. This was the first real breakthrough he'd had since they'd started searching for the sniper. With the photos from Aurelia now arriving on his phone and her brother's name, they could issue a warrant for his arrest in connection with the attempted homicide—the attempt on Daniela's life—over a year ago. He didn't intend to issue the warrant, or do any follow-up. Not just yet. The feds were in the middle of this situation, and he wanted to talk to Diego first. There might be national security implications he hadn't been told about. He was determined not to place Daniela in any greater danger than she was already.

In addition, he'd have to make sure that Aurelia spoke to no one.

Out of her sight, he messaged Xavi: *"Urgently need eyes-on surveillance of Aurelia Périgueux from the TFPU. She's sitting opposite me at el Restaurante Mar Azul. Confirm when units are in position."* Moments later, he received an acknowledgement from his partner. Then, ten minutes later, an affirmative: *"Units in position."*

"Well, I seem to have put a dampener on our lunch, Aurelia. I apologise; I really do. Hopefully, you can understand the urgency. Before you leave, let's have coffee.

"I'd like to go over what you should say if Jules calls."

⁂

When he got back to his office, Antonio called Diego's private phone.

"Is there any reason why we shouldn't proceed?" he asked point-blank. "I plan to issue a nationwide warrant for the arrest of Jules Dampierre, wanted for questioning in relation to the attempted homicide of Daniela Balmes over a year ago."

"You can," replied Diego without hesitation. "I was about to call you, Antonio. The Civil Guard has just issued a federal warrant for him. Without our knowledge, by the way.

"They've had him under surveillance for some time.

"But they lost track of him an hour ago."

⁂

"That's three agencies—all separately pursuing one suspect, sir," said Antonio to the chief.

"No wonder we have jurisdictional problems in Spain." The chief shook his head. "Did the Civil Guard say what they want Jules Dampierre for? Is it to do with the attempted homicide of Daniela Balmes?"

Antonio held up his hands.

He had no explanation.

Claudia

Diego knocked on the glass door of Claudia's office and was waved in immediately. She put a finger to her lips to silence him. "Join me for a walk?" she invited, picking up her jacket.

"It comes to something, Diego, when we have to resort to passing old-fashioned handwritten notes between us," she said as they walked along the busy street. "These days, I'm not sure who I can trust. You're not included in that statement, by the way."

Ten minutes later, they sat down on a park bench, take-out coffees in hand. "I'm giving you a new assignment. As of this morning, I'm under the orders of a senior officer whose credentials are impeccable. We can trust him, Diego."

"A Civil Guard covert operation?" he asked.

She looked at him with close attention. "He's an SIGC career officer. Very powerful . . . and influential."

Diego looked troubled. "Civil Guard Intelligence Service? That *is* powerful."

"Lieutenant Colonel Pablo Delgado," she continued. "It's a temporary posting: top secret. He's been given the job of rooting out the terrorist architect. Despite the arrest of Robles and the others, we suspect that someone from inside our senior ranks is still actively coordinating al-Qaeda networks throughout Spain. The CNI and the Civil Guard think that, so far, we've only scratched the surface in our investigations and arrests. Pablo's mandate can't be acknowledged because it's possible the mastermind is a senior officer within our federal security services. But it's also possibly a civilian who is being protected by some powerful people. We have our suspicions, but we simply don't know.

"Confidentially, I can tell you that the prime minister is under pressure from the CIA," she continued. "They are determined to see Project Catalyst through—and that means Daniela has to be protected above all else. To combat the enemy agents inside our security forces, we have assembled a small multi-agency special team to cut through the crap. Let's face it, Diego, despite having Raphael Robles in custody, our attempts at GEO 60 to infiltrate al-Qaeda cells here in Spain have been mostly unproductive so far. The DST in Rabat has been cooperating with us on intelligence matters for years. They've identified several Moroccan nationals living in Spain who we suspect are key members of al-Qaeda cells. After the Las Ramblas attack in Barcelona, we thought they were working as isolated groups—headed by fanatics like the now deceased Es Satty—smuggling Schedule 1 drugs into Spain and operating meth labs to fund their activities. We were wrong. The money from those sources is just small stuff."

Claudia glanced around and let several walkers pass by before continuing. "Recently, we've discovered that al-Qaeda cells here in Spain are being supplied with sizeable funds, which means they are able to concentrate on their destructive holy war. The CNI and Civil Guard are convinced there's a centralised command module coordinating and directing targeted attacks." Claudia paused for a moment. "We thought we'd captured the terrorist mastermind—Robles. Maybe he was one of the main plotters behind the bombings, but we are now convinced that there's someone else. Whoever he or she is, they are still working their evil. Our job, Diego, is to find them. We must obtain the intel needed for our people to break up the terrorist structure—dismantling it from the top down.

"You and I have been selected for the assignment because our investigations are already closing in on some of the people involved. Pablo wants a big push to finish the job and, as I've said, make sure that we protect Daniela's mission in the process. You're going to like this next bit." She smiled. "I've received permission for you to include Antonio in your investigating team—if you want to. It's your call, of course."

Diego nodded but said nothing; he appeared to be thinking through his next steps.

"I'm going to be passing along to you some highly classified national intelligence files," she continued. "You'll have full access to the relevant profiles and a wide mandate. You will continue to report to me, and I'll help open some doors for you. If you run up against resistance from the old boys' network, I'll deal with it. We're fighting to protect modern Spain. Not everyone's on our side, but we do have the support of a legitimately elected government."

Diego spoke. "I appreciate your trust, ma'am. I'm flattered. I won't let you down. I have a few questions, though, as you might expect. Some can wait until I've read the file. I'm intrigued about one thing; maybe you have the answer? We're looking for whoever is providing funding to the terrorists. Those gold pendants and the society—the Society of Seventy-Nine—do they have terrorist links?"

"That's something we don't know, and you'll have to find out," said Claudia. "I do have an important piece of information for you. We know that a certain grandee—the Duke of Valladolid—was closely associated with Carlos. He may have been involved in helping accumulate the money siphoned into Aladdin's Cave."

Diego looked puzzled. "In that case, can we trust the condesa?"

Claudia nodded. "I'm confident that we can. We're sure she knew nothing about General Bastides's attempted coup. In fact, she was instrumental in revealing it—to you. Also, we are reasonably convinced that she has no knowledge of the Society of Seventy-Nine or her late husband's involvement. She's credible. You can trust her, Diego. Even though the plotters' coup failed, there are people in powerful positions who are determined to undermine and ultimately destroy democratic Spain, and restore a dictator.

"We have to weed them out."

The prime minister was as good as his word.

Not long after he and the condesa had talked, she received a call from his personal assistant. The woman sounded enthusiastic, almost excited. Yes, the grandee has been contacted. He'd been surprised at first about the condesa's offer of gifting Carlos's lodge and grounds to the state—but grateful for her generosity, she confided. Yes, he would be delighted to meet with the condesa at any time convenient to her. Would a meeting at his office at the Royal Palace be suitable?

The condesa called Felipe. "Come for lunch," she invited. "We can talk about the endowment. I'm sure there are tax consequences which you'll want to tell me about. There's no reason not to take advantage of those, is there?" She sounded happy.

The Grandee

Informed by the prime minister's office of the purpose of the condesa's visit, the grandee was well-prepared.

He'd never liked the woman.

He thought that his friend Carlos could have done much better. Had Carlos chosen instead to marry more selectively, even from the lower ranks of Spain's aristocracy, it would have reinforced their numbers. Perhaps such a marriage, earlier in the count's life, might have provided his line of succession.

She was an intelligent woman, he was quick to concede. Something of an opportunist, according to things he'd heard. Successful in a modern way, with some influence in a few quarters of little real consequence. As a former minister in the national government, she had some contacts. When Carlos died, she'd been having an affair with a Russian immigrant. He had good looks, yet little else of any lasting merit. When the truth became known about her role in precipitating a police raid on the lodge, and the subsequent collapse of General Bastides's attempted coup, it had been a simple matter for the grandee to restore Carlos's honour—and arrange the Russian's disappearance. He'd been permanently dispatched by the general's man, Luis—the trustworthy chauffeur who'd also taken care of the troublesome journalist Francisco Rioja.

It was the condesa's fault that their plans had fallen apart in such a dramatic and spectacular manner. Therefore, there was a debt to be collected against her. So far, he had not decided how it would be arranged, or when. Besides, his hands were tied in that respect. There was a higher authority—the society's elusive grandmaster. He would have to authorise her killing, and so far, he'd vehemently forbidden it.

He'd never met the grandmaster. No one in the society had. Undoubtedly, he was a powerful figure. The grandee had speculated on his identity. He'd wondered if he might be a member of the Royal Household but doubted it. With the exception of their majesties the king and queen and their young daughters, most members of the Household weren't that clever.

Even Carlos had not known the identity of the grandmaster, in spite of his influential position as custodian of the society's treasury and his supervision of the riches of Aladdin's Cave. At one time, the grandee had been convinced that Raphael Robles was the grandmaster. After Robles had been arrested, he'd concluded that it wasn't likely after all. It couldn't have been Robles, he reasoned: there had been virtually no break in command. The grandmaster had continued to operate as normal.

The grandee was an expert on the issue of succession. After all, he'd advised the Royal Household on such matters for generations. For the monarchy, the line of succession was established beyond doubt. He worried deeply, however, that no clear line of succession had been defined for the society itself. He'd wondered over the years if the grandmaster had a bloodline that would ensure a natural succession—one that would be announced at the appropriate time. He imagined it would be a regal link. The grandmaster's successor might be part of the Borbón line—even if he came from outside the Household.

That would be eminently satisfactory, he thought. For himself, the grandee had no pretentions to accede to the role, even if it were offered. By his nature and temperament, he preferred the role of a loyal guiding hand behind the scenes. However, he'd thought it prudent to put in place a secondary line of succession, should the first become unworkable. He'd taken it into his own hands to groom several protégés. Among them the splendid young Louis Valois and the former Royal Guard officer Jules Dampierre and his sister, Aurelia Périgueux. Several others too. He'd made it his business to ensure the creation of a veritable stable of suitable bloodline candidates. Of course, they were completely unaware of his secret plan. It would not serve any purpose to have them compete with each other to be first in line. He would make his choice known to the grandmaster at the appropriate time.

It needed money, of course—lots of it. After the failed coup, he'd worked hard trying to divert the riches of Aladdin's Cave into the society's vaults. So far without success. Knowing of Carlos's weak heart, the grandee had prepared—weeks before his friend's death—a will that named the society as his primary beneficiary. At first, Carlos had refused to sign it. The grandee could see that his friend was still far too emotionally involved with his wife—the adulterous condesa. Days earlier, she had confessed her infidelity to him, pleading that it was just a one-time fling, Carlos had told him in strict confidence.

Reluctantly, the grandee had shown his friend a fresh set of photographs. They'd proved that she'd been deceiving Carlos for years. Several affairs had taken place. Already in deteriorating health, the dispirited Carlos had relented under the pressure. At the lodge, he'd signed the new will. Luis, the chauffeur, had eagerly witnessed it. As a beneficiary, the grandee avoided doing so. Carlos had insisted on keeping the original but had agreed to let the grandee photograph each page. The photographed pages still lay in his safe, but Carlos's original had never been found. The grandee knew that his actions, and the chauffeur's, had been predatory. He'd been anxious at the time to ensure that enough money was available within the society to support his succession plan. He had thought it prudent not to inform the grandmaster. That could be done later.

A sharp rap on his office door brought the grandee back to the business at hand. "Come," he called out, and immediately adopted the face of a person delighted to be greeting such an illustrious guest. "My dear Condesa," he purred, striding towards her—holding out both hands to clasp hers.

"A refreshment?"

―∽―

Her host was charming but seemed to take a combative tone as soon as the initial pleasantries had been dispensed.

The grandee appeared unimpressed by her offer to donate the lodge and its grounds—which the condesa found surprising. It wasn't that he was resistant, she thought. Just not as positive as she'd expected him to be. Polite and grateful, to a degree, yet with a hint of dismissiveness. Their meeting seemed to deteriorate from there, she thought. Soon she found herself at a disadvantage, without knowing why.

The grandee's tone became imperious, which she began to resent. Their discussion became awkward and unproductive. His attitude fell just short of being rude, she thought, mystified by the turn of events. Smiling sweetly in return, she resolved to be more than equally annoying—by appearing obtuse.

Their conversation had gone back and forth, like two boxers throwing dummy punches to test and rile their opponent. "The grounds of Count Carlos's lodge certainly are magnificent and full of history. Such a bequest to the nation is indeed generous, Condesa."

"An endowment perhaps, Your Excellency. Clearly not a bequest, which would have to wait for my death—which I'm sure both of us would not be anxious to see."

"Exactly as you say, my dear Condesa. An unfortunate slip of the tongue."

"You have visited the lodge?" she asked.

"I'm not the hunting type," he conceded. "My duties are rather closer at home—here, serving the Royal Household. It's a rather demanding task, taking into consideration the socialist hoards who would sweep away all our traditions in the name of political correctness. You must have witnessed some of that ghastly phenomenon during your time as an elected official, Condesa?"

"I witnessed many things during my time in office, Your Excellency. Many things that were illegal and some of which still remain unpunished. But, to my purpose here today. On the recommendation of the prime minister"—she paused to clarify—"with the support of the first minister of the party legally elected by the people of Spain, I am here to arrange the transfer of the lodge and grounds to your stewardship. Is that something you are able to handle?

"Oh, there is one other item on which I beg Your Excellency's opinion," she added, pressing her temporary advantage. From her handbag, she withdrew the leather case and extracted the gold pendant found at the lodge. "This was among my husband's possessions. I was unaware of its existence and I have no idea of its meaning. Ceremonial, perhaps?"

The grandee was unable to hide his surprise. His eyes widened, and he reached forward to take it, just as the condesa drew it back into her possession. "I have no idea, Condesa," he said, recovering quickly. "Most certainly, it is magnificent. In fact, we have several heraldic experts here at the palace. I would be happy to take it and ascertain its significance. If you wish to leave it with me, of course."

"Actually, I've become somewhat attached to it," said the condesa, putting it back inside her handbag. "Sentimental value, you understand? It must have meant something to Carlos. Obviously, it has no significance to you. Thank you, Your Excellency," she said, getting up. "I'm sure its meaning—the number seventy-nine—will emerge eventually.

"I'm so grateful for your time . . . and kind hospitality."

His face flushed with anger, the grandee conceded that the condesa had got the better of him. He'd been surprised to see the gold pendant and hadn't been quick enough to hide his reactions. Helping himself to a large measure of Luis Felipe Gran Reserva, he admitted that events were not unfolding as planned. The pendant had belonged to Carlos. It had been missing for some time. They'd searched for it, to no avail, immediately after Carlos's fatal heart attack.

Later, under the guise of being a National Police detective, one of his men had searched the condesa's house at La Moraleja. His efforts had been hampered by the dissuasive efforts of her housekeeper. The fierce woman had stood over the man and watched his every move. Until now, the pendant's whereabouts had remained unknown. Now the condesa had it, and she had refused to part with it. The gold had inestimable value. He knew he must recover it. A sacred duty.

It was only one of the difficult tasks currently facing him. He conceded that some of his duties recently had become burdensome. Months ago, the prospect of locating—and seizing—the riches of Aladdin's Cave had seemed within reach. Society members were well-positioned to step in and divert the fortune to their own safekeeping. With their connections, they could move the money back into circulation. It would be expensive; commissions would have to be paid. Even so, the net proceeds would ensure the survival of the society for many generations to come. The future of the monarchy.

Examining his manicured fingernails, the grandee knew that desperate measures had become necessary. Thanks to an informant, they now knew the location of the gold bars—stored at a rural cottage not far from Barcelona. However, his sources had informed him it was heavily guarded by federal security forces. So far, his agents had been unable to locate the bearer bonds. They knew about them, of course. Pro-monarchy spies were everywhere. Even with their help, the grandee couldn't trace the location of the bonds.

He'd been distressed to hear from the prime minister's office that the lodge was now likely to change hands—especially as its new owner would be the state itself. Around the lodge, there were secrets from the past that were best kept hidden. Distrusting modern phones, the grandee sat down at his ornate desk and composed a coded message in Latin. Reading it over, he signed and sealed it. It would be delivered by a trusted courier to an intermediary. Then hand-delivered to the grandmaster. Within the hour.

Felipe

He was worried.

Felipe had been agonising about it ever since his visit to the lodge with the condesa.

Only through a stroke of luck had she remembered about the second safe. If she had found the accounting ledger and Carlos's will, or if the police had, the outcomes would have been vastly different.

On the drive back to Madrid, they'd chatted amiably. She was glad they'd made the journey, she told him. It helped her close off that difficult chapter of her life. Once they were out of the mountains, she'd spoken in animated terms about the good that could come from giving Carlos's lodge to the state. She was intrigued too about the gold pendant and grilled him about his knowledge of the society—which wasn't much, he claimed.

He was glad she was doing the talking. His mind was preoccupied with how to deal with the two documents. The accounting ledger was dangerous. It would expose a lot of powerful and rich people to criminal prosecution. He wondered why Carlos had allowed such a damning written record of financial contributions to continue to exist.

Felipe's first instinct was to destroy the ledger—and the will. Then he wondered if they had been placed there as a police trap. A trick to find out what he and the condesa would do about the evidence—to see if, as the condesa's lawyer, he would declare them to the authorities. Or if he would destroy them. Perhaps in setting a trap, they'd already made a copy. If it was a police trap—set up to ensnare him—destroying the evidence would prove his guilt. On the other hand, if he kept hold of documents for a time, which logically he might do as the condesa's lawyer, he might be able to avoid prosecution. There were risks either way. Finally, he made his decision. Within hours, he had incinerated the accounting ledger. Now it was ashes—which he ground to a powder and scattered widely.

The will, however, was another matter. It indicated that the grandee had his own agenda. He was acting independently. It was an agenda that was totally unacceptable to Felipe.

There would be consequences.

Xavi

Antonio had been spending more time in Madrid—on the special assignment he couldn't discuss with anyone. Inevitably, responsibility for the investigation into the disappearance of Caterina's brother fell into Xavi's lap.

He wasn't unhappy about it. He thought she was a nice young woman and admired her positive attitude. Having been involved in missing person cases before, he knew how exhausting not knowing about the fate of loved ones could be—physically draining and mentally taxing. Talking to Pilar about her, his wife's reaction had been predictable. Caterina doesn't have any family nearby. Let's invite her over for dinner, she enthused. She'd be wonderful with the kids.

Xavi wasn't so sure. Mixing police work with family was something he tried to avoid. He knew that Caterina was very much in love with Antonio. It seemed such a pity that his friend didn't reciprocate. Long absences on special assignments didn't help Antonio's already poor communication skills when it came to romance. He hadn't been calling her—and Caterina was too independent and proud to keep chasing him.

Pilar came up with an idea. The bishop was visiting their church to celebrate Easter. Her church group was having a neighbourhood fair. "She's a young girl," Pilar reminded him. "She needs to get out more and meet new people." Xavi scoffed at the thought that attractive young women needed encouragement to get out and socialise, but Pilar prevailed. He had learned to respect her judgement.

Caterina was delighted. She would love to attend, she said, and join them for mass too. She'd heard about the personable young bishop and the ways he wanted to reform the church. If she was given the opportunity, she'd be honoured to meet him. Pilar smiled at Xavi; she would arrange it.

In his office, Xavi leafed through the case file on Caterina's brother. He wished he had some news for her, but nothing had resulted from their reinvigorated investigation. Then he received a break. House-to-house enquiries, led by the female officer from Missing Persons, had identified a promising lead. A boy in his mid-teens had caught the attention of a perceptive interviewing officer. Attendance records indicated that he was missing school frequently. A quick search of his parent's garden revealed a stack of stolen bikes hidden in a shed. The boy claimed to be repairing them for extra spending money, but the officer wasn't fooled.

A second interview was conducted with a youth services officer and a social worker, with the parents of the boy present. Xavi guessed that the pressure on the lad must have been too much. He quickly admitted to several other minor thefts—including the missing kayak, claiming not to have profited from the incident. He'd observed the camper's tent and the almost new kayak near his home, and had crept back at night to steal it, he admitted. Things had gone wrong. He'd located the kayak and was dragging it away when the owner, a man maybe in his late-twenties, gave chase through the woods. The teenage boy had run and dropped the kayak. He'd almost been caught, but in the dark, the man had tripped over something and hit his head.

Realising he was no longer being pursued, the boy had carefully retraced his steps. He'd found the kayak and the dazed man—his forehead bleeding. He was sitting with his back against a tree, said the boy, and didn't seem to know what was going on. He'd spoken to the man, but his reply had made no sense. The boy had left him there, taking the kayak—dragging it along a trail leading to the road. He told the officer that he'd become scared. He'd realised that the kayak would be hard to conceal. Besides, he thought the man might recover and come looking for him. Taking fright, he'd abandoned it near the road.

The interviewing officer had checked the consistency of the boy's story and was satisfied he was telling the truth. They'd gone back to where the boy thought he'd last seen the man. His explanation of events seemed believable. It was not far from where they'd found the missing kayaker's abandoned tent and his car nearby. Months had gone by since the incident. Despite a new search of the area, there was no trace of Lorenzo. There were no clues where he'd gone.

Antonio was still out of town and hard to contact. Feeling that he shouldn't conceal the new developments from Caterina, Xavi consulted with Pilar. They decided to tell her after Easter Sunday dinner.

They'd had a wonderful day, and the kids had really taken to their young guest. Caterina seemed to have a natural way with them; she had them laughing constantly. After dinner, she'd read them bedtime stories.

When Xavi told her, cautioning her not to get her hopes up just yet, Caterina became animated. She seemed relieved by the news. Hopeful but not overconfident. "What happens next?" she asked.

He knew the question was coming and was prepared for it. Instructions had already been issued to his team of Mossos officers to develop a search plan. They intended to issue a fresh missing person advisory and circulate it to several nearby countries. Statistically, he knew, the prospects were not encouraging. They were dealing with breadcrumbs at this stage of Lorenzo's disappearance. Caterina understood. She told Xavi that she was grateful to him and Antonio for re-energising the search.

Pilar's praise of the young woman was unrestrained. "She's so level-headed, Xavi. I can't understand why Toni doesn't see it. He's not getting any younger, and she'd make a wonderful mother."

Xavi was more sceptical. He simply shrugged his shoulders. If Antonio wanted to remain single all his life, he'd miss out on some wonderful years as a father.

"Try telling him that," he said.

CHAPTER 6
Saad

Mohammed had summoned him, and Saad obeyed.

"It is time for Jamal's escape," said Mohammed, examining him critically. "Next to where you work, inside the Russian compound, is a transformer. As a civilian worker, you walk past it every day. You remember? You have a security pass that allows you to proceed through the area to get to your work station."

Saad nodded. He knew it well. There was a constant buzz of electromagnetic radiation from it.

"You will carry an iron pipe," instructed Mohammed. "Strap it to the crossbar of your bicycle. You must sabotage the transformer by throwing it across the unprotected live terminals. Can you do that?"

"Surely that alone will not disable the Russian base?" Saad asked, and heard Mohammed's guttural laugh in reply.

"Of course not. That is not our intention. We wish only to interrupt the power to the electric fence nearby. The wire surrounding the prisoners' exercise area must be cut so that Jamal can escape." Mohammed scrutinised him carefully. "Do nothing that will give away our plan. Take careful note of the security fence that surrounds the transformer, yet do not attract their attention. You must plan how to achieve what we ask. Think carefully about it. On the other side of the base, our colleagues will create a diversion. A large explosion. When you hear it, you will have only thirty seconds to do your work.

"Dr. Jamal Ismet saved your life, and your mother's, when you were born," he continued. "His skill then was far greater than the task we are asking of you now. This is your chance to help save his life," said Mohammed gravely. "And, if necessary, you must sacrifice yours for the jihad."

The Russian

The tall, thin officer stood next to the widescreen projector, waiting for his Spetsnaz superior and colleagues to settle into their seats. Within a few seconds, he received a nod to proceed.

"The first set of images is of the prisoner, Jamal Ismet. Also shown are the al-Qaeda spies who are helping him," he began. "In the second set, I will show you how we propose to assist their escape—and how our people will enable Jamal and the teenage boy Yussef to join the convoy travelling empty to Syria's northern border with Iraq. American intelligence has informed us that the prisoners have a rendezvous in two days' time with an al-Qaeda terrorist cell. We don't know where yet. Either the Americans are being cagey, or the people on the other side haven't yet tipped their hand about the location."

He pressed the remote to show a close-up photo of Jamal Ismet. "He's been our prisoner for eight months. Most of that time was essential for his physical recovery; he was badly injured. Sometime later, we were able to apprehend the Spanish spy, Daniela Balmes. It was luck, really. She and the boy entered the country illegally, and we were tipped off.

"She's the link to the money that al-Qaeda is expecting from Spain. Also, she was instrumental in helping Jamal to recuperate. She has cooperated fully with us. We released her back to the Americans at the border with Turkey—that was a month ago. As soon as they receive confirmation that al-Amin has departed from Pakistan and is on his way to Syria, she will be put back into the field. Our American source tells us their plan is to arrange for al-Amin to meet up with Jamal at an al-Qaeda stronghold. Somewhere south of his initial rendezvous point on the M4 highway at al-Yarubiyah.

"It's here on the map." He tapped on the screen. "That's the overall plan, sir. With your permission, I'll present the details." He received another nod.

"We have to be convincing in facilitating Jamal's escape," he continued. "He mustn't suspect anything. Fortunately for us in this instance, there are al-Qaeda cells here on the base that we've been monitoring for some time. We'll be using three of their agents in the escape. One is a civilian employee working here on the base. His name is Saad. He knows nothing about our plan; we will simply allow our security to lapse at critical times so that he can assist Jamal's escape. He's a family friend of Jamal, from Homs, and completely loyal to him. There's no risk of leakage there. We will also be using two double agents who are under our control." Noting that his superior officer had raised an eyebrow, he knew he must address the issue without delay.

He stood aside to allow a confident-looking major to report to the group. Although small in stature, the officer's appearance was intimidating. The man seemed to be built in a series of triangles. His boxer's cauliflower ears seemed to be set inside the bulging muscles at the base of his neck. Still relatively young, he was prematurely bald; his forehead slanted back at an acute angle to a sharp point at the peak of his head. Two narrow slits of eyes saw everything but gave nothing away. His triangulation was matched by his overdeveloped chest and wide shoulders that dropped away to what, for any male, was an unnaturally narrow waist. His upper legs, swollen with steroid-assisted muscle mass, slimmed rapidly below his knees to narrow ankles reminiscent of the tendons of a racehorse. Even his uniform could not disguise his awkward shape. He was known within the Spetsnaz as the Torture Machine.

Smiling confidently at the group, he projected a look which seemed to say that all was well in his hands. "The other two are relatively new in our employ," he began, speaking coarsely through a set of ferocious-looking teeth. "They remain trusted members of their respective cells." He paused for effect and stared at his audience, almost daring them to contradict him. "They've been carefully vetted." He grinned a foul look. "Also, their families are housed as guests at two of our military facilities. We will release them, of course, at a suitable time after the operation has been successfully completed. I'm confident the men will deliver. To make sure, we carried out a bogus operation a month ago—to test their loyalty to us. They both passed."

"How crucial are their roles, major?" asked the senior Spetsnaz officer.

"One is a tanker truck driver who works for the state oil company, sir. His truck has been adapted with a hidden compartment for the escapees. He's vital to our plan." He crunched his knuckles, as if to demonstrate the fate that would befall the driver if he failed. "The other is a local taxi driver who will ensure that Jamal and Yussef are transported from the escape point here at the base to join the empty tanker convoy coming up from Homs. They will join the main convoy here, sir." He pointed at the map, using his stubby forefinger to indicate the town of Saraqib.

"There's a meeting point here, on the M4," he continued. "It's where the two convoys will converge and consolidate. Our people will make sure the escapees board the truck without being detected. I'll be there to ensure the transfer takes place as planned," he added with a reassuring smile. He stood stiffly to attention, then stepped away from the projector, allowing the tall thin officer to continue.

"It's a two-hour drive in the taxi, sir. Our roadside patrols will allow them through with minimum fuss. Then they'll travel about eight hours in the tanker truck to the drop-off point near the Iraqi border. The prisoner, Jamal, is unable to move about very much because of his injuries. That's why we have chosen this route and means of getting him there. His escape is being arranged by two al-Qaeda cells working in collaboration. We are making sure it's allowed to happen without them getting any hint we know about it."

"Why such an elaborate operation?" queried the senior man.

"We got lucky, sir," responded the tall thin officer. "Ten days ago, the Kirkuk to Baniyas oil pipeline was sabotaged again. Later, there was a fire at the Homs refinery. The Syrian government immediately asked for Russian help to escort a large convoy of empty tanker trucks to the Iraqi oilfields and bring back the crude they need to keep the refineries operating. Our military police escort is heavily armed and will fly the Russian flag to prevent attack by local militants. There will also be Syrian Army escort vehicles and a total of twenty-five empty tanker trucks. We'll advise the Turkish military in advance, to make sure they don't interfere. They'll be aware of potential retaliation from our air escort capabilities.

"We agreed to the convoy with Damascus a week ago," he continued. "Of course, they know nothing about the escape plan—they'd stop us if they did. The convoy will be a regular feature for several months—until the pipeline becomes operational again. It's a normal and predictable way for us to cooperate with our allies. Just another aspect of our post-war economic development with President al-Daser, sir. As you know, Moscow has instructed us to support our companies, including Stroytransgaz, to assist in reconstruction and infrastructure. To answer your question specifically, sir, we saw the opportunity to include our enterprise using the cover of the convoy's mission. It's a simple and uncomplicated way to transport the escapees. We believe it's safe and secure. Just needing your approval to proceed."

"No one suspects us?"

"We've taken every precaution, sir," said the tall thin officer. "It's a tightly managed operation."

The Spetsnaz senior officer had given final approval. He was sitting in his office at the airbase, massaging his forehead, when the tall thin officer knocked and entered. "Let's take a walk, Alexei," he said, getting up from his desk. "I could do with a breath of fresh air."

"You might want to bring a jacket, sir. It's a lot cooler today, and the wind has picked up." Alexei stood aside as the senior man headed to the door. "Although not as cool as at home this time of year," he added. His face mimicked the pained look of a man recalling Moscow's harsh winters and cold, arctic winds.

The senior officer dismissed their security guard and was at the wheel of the Viking all-terrain vehicle. It had highly polished Russian military police markings, and its tricolour Russian national flag flapped noisily in the wind. Seated in the passenger seat, Alexei seemed impressed with its high-tech dashboard screens. They drove to a hilltop overlooking the base and got out to walk.

"Our man, the Torture Machine. You don't trust him any more than I do, Alexei," said the senior officer, lighting a Turkish cigarette. The blue-grey smoke he exhaled swirled and quickly disappeared downwind. "In the meeting, you didn't tell us how you plan to track the prisoners. You were keeping that information to yourself. I think you know exactly where and when the prisoners' rendezvous will be with al-Qaeda. So, please inform me now."

Alexei stopped walking. Even though there was no one nearby, he was cautious about being overheard. He moved closer and cupped his hand over his mouth. "The red-haired American—as you know, he keeps us informed. It is part of Moscow's agreement with Washington. It's rare for us to cooperate in this way, but for once, we have the same objectives—to apprehend al-Amin and to defeat al-Qaeda in this region.

"That is why—under Moscow's instructions—we captured Jamal and kept him alive," he continued. "It is why we have allowed the Spanish girl, Daniela Balmes, to help him recover. And it is why we will help Jamal escape and lead the Americans to where al-Amin will be—his new location."

"Yes, yes, Alexei, I know all that. My question is about the American agent with red hair. Can we trust him to keep us informed? After all, it is a dangerous game we play."

"Can we ever trust the Americans, sir?" scoffed Alexei. "Especially when it comes to the money in the Cyprus bank. It is a fortune."

"And a big temptation for Moscow," added the senior man, drawing in a full breath of tobacco smoke into his lungs. "Our orders are to inform Moscow before al-Qaeda has the opportunity to collect it. They intend to intervene. Wagner will carry out the retrieval operation, and I do not trust them. We are left exposed, you and I. Sacrificial mutton—if anything goes wrong. We might want to have a backup plan. I want this to work, Alexei," he continued. "Despite its winters, I miss living in Moscow, but I don't want to be forced to go back there for early retirement if the operation fails. Living on basic pension in a spartan GRU apartment in a Moscow suburb would not be fun. Are you confident we can pull this off? Al-Qaeda is a deceitful group of terrorists, you know that."

"Our orders come from our section chief in Moscow, sir," replied Alexei. "Just the same, I know what you mean." They continued walking in silence for a time. The wind, already strong, had picked up strength from the north-east. Both men shivered.

"We were in Afghanistan together, Alexei," said the senior man. "We fought against the Taliban and al-Qaeda. That campaign wasn't a military success for Russia. We can't afford to screw up here; we have to stay on the good side of the president."

"And his rich and powerful friends, sir." Alexei nodded. "They're just starting to enjoy the commercial rewards of our intervention here. They wouldn't be happy if a couple of old-school Spetsnaz officers screwed things up for them."

New Orders

Their rendezvous would be in two days.

Farouk knew the town of Yarubiyah well. At least he would not have far to travel. His surprise at being summoned at such short notice was matched only by the good news that Jamal was still alive. *Alhamdulillah*! It had not seemed possible. The abrupt manner in which they were being mobilised left no doubt in his mind: Jamal's timetable was urgent. Something very important must be about to happen.

During the time that Farouk had been living at the remote small-holding, he'd trained the boy and his sisters to defend themselves. The older one had recovered from her illness, and her strength had returned. She was naturally resourceful and produced nutritious meals, almost from nothing it seemed. At first, she'd kept her distance, regarding Farouk as a father figure—as a guardian. Yet, as the weeks passed, her formality gave way to familiarity. The sly looks she gave him and the affectionate messages in her eyes suggested that she would welcome his attentions. However, Farouk was conservative and traditional. If Allah willed it, then it would happen. For now, there were practical things that they must learn to be able to fend for themselves. He had shown the boy and his younger sister how to divert water from the well to a pit he'd dug inside the home. It was primitive, but they'd lined the base of the pit. Farouk had shown the young girl how to allow it to drain out. It worked superbly. The water was clear and fresh. "Enough for several weeks," he told them. "In case you cannot go outside."

The boy seemed resentful of the attention Farouk was giving to his little sister, but the soldier knew this—and had planned it deliberately. When Farouk and he went to forage for food and to collect a store of firewood, he knew that the boy would want to prove his manhood. He showed the boy how to set traplines for small animals and was impressed with how quickly he caught on. Within a few days, they had several months of winter firewood stored inside the house.

There were smiles in the household now, and laughter became more frequent. Regular meals appeared on the table. The family felt less threatened by the outside world and seemed more hopeful of the future. Farouk thought that the older sister was beautiful. Yet, he remained respectful. He knew he must leave soon, to reach the rendezvous in time. His final act was to create an escape route at the back of the house that would allow them to crawl to safety. For hours, they piled stones high onto a wall. He demonstrated how to do the military crawl, as if they were soldiers.

They knew he must go, but he promised to return. On their last night together, after prayers, the mood was subdued. Before dawn the next day, Farouk left the meagre homestead. He had not travelled far when he heard the sound of running. The older sister thrust a cloth containing food into his hands and the metal flask of water left for him by the boy, months earlier, when he'd first arrived. In a moment that felt to Farouk like hours, their eyes made contact. An understanding was made without a word being spoken. She leaned forward and kissed him.

Then he was gone.

Yasser and Mahmood were living in rooms in al-Mayadin, above the repair shop belonging to Feras.

Business had continued to thrive, and already Feras was planning new ventures. When Yasser informed him they would be leaving soon, he knew better than to question their decision—and certainly not ask where his guests were going or for what purpose.

By now, Feras had a small fleet of trucks. They looked like wrecks but were surprisingly functional. Mahmood had worked with the crew to repair them all. Together, they'd done an amazing job. Feras had secured a contract with a farmer's cooperative to bring in seed and fertilizer—a bulk purchase they'd made. When the crops were ready for harvest, Feras would have the contract to distribute them to several regional markets. The regional economy had continued to recover, and times were getting better.

"The driver can give you a ride as far as the city," Feras offered. He pulled out a small bundle of banknotes. "Here. It's not much. You may need some food and other supplies." He gestured to the rooms they occupied above the repair shop. "I'll keep them empty for your return—if you'd like?" He went to a cupboard and took out three handguns. "Only one has ammunition. But they may be useful." Early next morning, the two joined in the household's morning prayers. Carrying neatly wrapped food parcels, they climbed into the cab of the truck and sat alongside the driver. The night had been cold, but the early morning sun was already warming the ground. Springtime was arriving.

The truck ride would save them several hundred kilometres of walking. Yasser guessed they would arrive early at the rendezvous point. During the journey, he whispered to Mahmood, "It will give us a chance to check out the neighbourhood. Watch for government spies." He patted one of the handguns hidden under his robe.

Mahmood grinned.

If Yasser said so, it was fine with him.

─────

It was exactly what Nazih had been waiting for—the opportunity to get back into action with his comrades. To pursue the holy war. He rejoiced hearing the news that Jamal was still alive.

Yet, he had a problem. The rendezvous was in two days' time. He and the Western jihadi with flaming red hair and beard had planned a raid on a government warehouse. They had reliable information that it contained a cache of Russian-supplied armaments. The place was heavily guarded, but they had a clever plan. It was the jihadi who'd already figured a way to break into the building—at night, through the roof. The man was a genius, Nazih acknowledged. He had some kind of sixth sense. For several years, they had worked alongside each other—raiding places of value, seizing money from regime-supported banks, looting artifacts from museums, stealing precious national treasures, and selling them on the black market to provide funds for ISIS. The jihadi seemed to gain particular pleasure taking prisoners and selling them for ransom. He had sold many women prisoners of ISIS to the Turks, or to rich old men in Kuwait.

During the early years of the caliphate, the red-haired infidel had proved his value in Iraq. He had organised the repair of damaged refinery facilities at Kirkuk, captured from the Iraqi Army. Soon he was selling oil to their enemy al-Daser, filling the coffers of ISIS with much-needed cash. But he was a wild man too. He forced his men to endure great hardships. Sometimes, he disappeared for many months at a time—often returning triumphantly with new spoils of war.

There had been many changes as the civil war had progressed. When two competing brigades of Syrian rebels had merged, Nazih had chosen to join Jamal's group. The red-haired infidel had preferred to remain apart—acting as a mercenary, although they stayed closely in contact. Several times, Jamal's platoon had called on his procurement skills. The jihadi could locate and steal almost anything, and did so willingly. He seemed more interested in the process of the theft itself, and selling on the black market, than about enriching himself. The red-haired infidel was an old-style brigand. Nazih had said so to Mohammed and Jamal. "He can help us," he declared triumphantly.

The red-haired infidel had returned recently from raids across the Turkish border. He had sold a truckload of stolen ammunition to the Syrian Free Army and the Kurds. Handing over the cash proceeds to Nazih for safekeeping, as he always did, he'd described the government warehouse opportunity to his friend. They'd spent days together planning the raid. He would not be pleased with the news that Nazih had to leave.

"Why can't it wait, Nazih?" O'Flaherty asked. "Our raid will be in a few days. I don't want to bring in someone new to replace you—someone I would not be able to trust with our plan, possibly risk my life."

"It matters not," stated Nazih emphatically. "Instead, you must come with me." He was annoyed that the jihadi was not grasping the significance of the summons he'd received from Jamal. He'd been met with an indifferent shrug of the man's shoulders.

"It is not my fight," he'd said. His independent spirit had been a longstanding source of contention between them. The jihadi operated on his own. He refused to be included among the fighting forces of ISIS, al-Qaeda, or the rebels. Both men bitterly opposed al-Daser's regime, but their ways were different. The red-haired infidel was respected for his special talents; as a result, he was tolerated and widely admired. His procurement skills had become legendary—even though his independence was distrusted by some of the more hard-line troops.

"It *is* your fight." Nazih yelled at him. "It is our fight, together."

The red-haired infidel seemed surprised at his friend's outburst. "Nazih," he reasoned, "we have talked about this before. You are a soldier for our cause. My purpose is to make sure you are supplied with weapons and food. I am able to steal from our enemies. Surely, it is the same thing in the end, the same result? Let us first take these guns from the government warehouse. We can sell them for money and provide ammunition to our comrades. It is too good an opportunity for us to miss. When we have finished, surely then you can go to meet Jamal?"

Nazih shook his head. The red-haired infidel's words made sense, but Jamal's orders were uncompromising. They no longer had time for the raid on the government warehouse. "Why not tonight?" he asked. "Why don't we do it tonight? Why wait? Surely it makes no difference?"

His friend looked annoyed. "In a few days, Nazih, they change the guard. You know that. We must carry out our raid on the last night—when the regime troops are weary and anxious to get back to their barracks and their families. After their tour of duty, they will not want to sacrifice their lives if, by chance, they stumble across a handful of local thieves trying to steal a few boxes of guns and ammunition. Even if they discover us, which they will not, they will look the other way." He placed his hands on his friend's shoulders and implored him. "Trust me, Nazih. We will steal many new-model guns the Russians are now supplying to the regime. You know the plan. The rest will be destroyed—when we detonate the warehouse. By then, we will be far gone. The citizens will know that our fight for the jihad is still alive. We must keep up their faith in us." His fervent eyes burned into Nazih's.

There was no doubt in Nazih's mind that his friend was a vehement fighter for the cause. He was uncompromising and relentless. Yet, on this occasion, he was wrong. Nazih did not know precisely what Jamal wanted, or why he'd chosen to remobilise his old platoon. It mattered little. Jamal's orders must supersede the opportunity to raid the government warehouse. Jamal's orders were supreme.

"We must carry out the raid tonight," he insisted, and watched as the red-haired infidel's features darkened. Nazih had killed many people; he was not easily intimidated. But his friend scared him—especially at moments like this. He saw the man's eyes narrow into impenetrable slits and stared in terror as his brow furrowed. The savage twist of his mouth seemed to prelude a violent outburst. The silence that followed created a tension that was unbearable. He could even hear his watch ticking. Slowly, the red-haired infidel breathed out heavily.

"All right, we will do it tonight, Nazih. Frankly, I do not know why I allow you to persuade me—but you are my friend. Tonight, we will be able to assemble just a few of our men. We will have to leave much of the merchandise behind. If it is what Allah wills, so be it. Afterwards, I will dynamite the warehouse so that the regime will not have the new Russian guns to fight us.

"Then I will follow you—and the orders of Jamal."

Ali had been spending nearly all his time at the mosque and teaching at the madrassa. His mother was content. At least now she knew where her son was—close by, as she dearly wished—and that he was safe.

Later that night, she was reminded that such happiness is fleeting. Ali announced that he had orders to rejoin his platoon. She pleaded with him, arguing that the war was nearly over. Al-Daser's regime troops had won; his troops occupied all the major cities and nearly all the towns. Except for a few pockets of resistance, there was now almost no opposition to his reign of terror.

"There are more of us than you think, Mother," Ali assured her, confident in the righteousness of their cause. "The jihad calls. I must go."

He set out on the long and perilous journey to rejoin his comrades—and obey the orders of Jamal.

The evening before, Mohammed had been particularly edgy. His black eyes darted everywhere, anxiously seeking early signs of danger. He was unaware that his right foot constantly tapped the ground—it was a nervous habit.

His unease showed through in several ways, thought Saad. It was unnecessary, in his view, to keep practising each step of the escape plan, as Mohammed kept insisting. He already knew it by heart.

"Repeat them," his handler ordered.

"On my way into work," Saad began, "as I approach the transformer station at 6:55 am, there will be a loud explosion on the far side of the base, followed by a lot of black smoke. It will look as though a plane or helicopter has crashed." He stopped and studied Mohammed, receiving no response, just an impatient frown. "By then, I will have already passed through the security gate on my normal schedule. No one will take any notice of me. When I hear the explosion, I will stop—like everyone else. It is likely that the guards will look in that direction too.

"That will give me time to detach the long iron bar I will be carrying on the crossbar of my bicycle. I will throw it across the two exposed bare wires of the transformer infeed. There will be a small explosion, as it causes a short circuit in the electrical system. I will shout to get the guards' attention and point to the transformer. Jamal will be out in the yard already—doing his daily exercises near the perimeter fence. From that position, he will be hidden from the sight of the guards. I will go to the fence. I will pick up the wire cutters left there for me. I will proceed to cut a hole—of sufficient size for the commander to make his escape. I am to remember that last year the commander sustained severe injuries fighting; the hole must be big enough for him to crawl through without difficulty. There will be a man and a car waiting for him on the other side. To help the commander escape without being detected, to divert the guards' attention, I am to run to the opposite side of the exercise compound and rattle the fence and shout as loudly as I can." He stopped and waited for Mohammed's approval of his rehearsal, just as he had done numerous times before.

"There is one change," announced Mohammed. "For the past week, Jamal has been joined in his exercises by a young man—Yussef. You have seen him, perhaps?" He handed Saad a photograph.

Saad nodded. "Yes, I have seen him a few times. I have not spoken to him. He is a prisoner, too, I think."

"He and Jamal will escape together," said Mohammed. "You understand?"

Saad nodded, but inwardly, he was angry. He wanted to ask why he could not assist the commander in his escape outside the fence. After all, he could speak many languages—and could assist the great man much better that any peasant boy.

Mohammed's scowl in his direction made it clear that he should not entertain such thoughts. The plan was set in stone.

Even so, Saad felt resentful.

The Convoy

The escape plan worked. For several hours, Jamal had been sitting cramped inside the confined space of the compartment hidden at the back of the cab of the oil tanker truck. He knew that despite travelling empty and able to make good speed to the oilfields at Kirkuk, there were at least eight more driving hours before they could leave the convoy at the Iraqi border.

Someone had installed a strip of high-density foam, cut from an old mattress, to cover the hard metal bench. With the soreness in his leg getting worse, Jamal was grateful for it. Darkness and monotony were making their travelling conditions difficult. Yet, he was happy at last to have escaped from Russian confinement at Latakia. Yussef had curled himself into a ball and was sleeping soundly. His younger, more flexible body seemed to render his journey not dissimilar to an uncomfortable bus ride, thought Jamal. He wasn't sure how well the boy was breathing. An airpipe had been fitted. It channelled fresh air into their hiding place, but the air was contaminated with diesel fumes. Carbon monoxide entering their space was a real concern. At times, the engine fumes became unbearable. Yet, it was the holes and craters in the road surface that Jamal dreaded the most. Unable to see outside, there was no way he could prepare himself for the jolts inflicted upon his already pain-wracked body. He tried to focus his thinking on the task ahead. He did not know if his hand-couriered coded letters had reached the men from his platoon. Their help was vital if he was to reach his ultimate destination and join up with al-Amin, the trusted one. Jamal had been incredibly cautious. All his men, except Mohammed, were completely unaware that the great man was the focus of their journey. Almost no one knew of the new leader's imminent arrival in Syria.

If the rendezvous did not come together as planned, Jamal knew he would be powerless to influence events. Even if things went well, he and his men had a demanding task ahead—fraught with risks. Their success, or not, depended on the will of Allah.

There were noises outside. The convoy seemed to be coming to a halt. Their driver knocked hard twice on the bulkhead—a pre-arranged signal instructing them to remain silent. Jamal could hear voices—some of them Turkish. It must be a border region patrol, he thought, even though they were still in northern Syria—probably somewhere around Manbij. In a way, the delay was a welcome relief; he massaged his leg and hoped there would be no searches of the vehicles. Yussef had woken, and Jamal motioned for the disorientated boy to remain silent. The boy was trying to stifle a cough, which increased the danger of being discovered. Jamal quickly passed the water bottle to him and his coughing soon stopped. Jamal squeezed the boy's shoulder reassuringly with his hand. He was a natural leader and knew how important it was to impart confidence into his men. The boy grinned a grateful smile in return.

Jamal took note that their driver had remained in his seat—and hadn't been ordered out. That was a good sign. He was aware they depended on the man completely for their safety. He was one of the group's best local operatives, Mohammed had reassured him. "You don't have to worry about him," his trusted lieutenant had told him in the escaping taxi. Immediately afterwards, as they were being driven at fast speed to where they would join the convoy, Mohammed and Jamal had talked in hushed whispers. There had been much to discuss, and they would have liked more time together. Mohammed told him that he would not travel with the convoy. There was an alternative route—away from the main roads. It was a wise move, agreed Jamal. By separating, there was a better chance that at least one of them would reach the rendezvous point safely. If Jamal didn't make it, his lieutenant would assume command. Their commitment to the new leader would be met.

Hearing loud sounds outside in the distance, Jamal knew what they meant. The Turkish patrol was verifying that the oil tankers were travelling empty. Soldiers with metal bars were moving from vehicle to vehicle, hitting them hard. The sounds echoed increasingly loudly as they came alongside. Yussef followed Jamal's lead and covered his ears. He did not expect trouble. After all, it was an official Syrian government convoy—protected by Russian troops. The Turks had no jurisdiction in this area. But it was a time of war. Most likely, they were only flexing their muscles—local contingents provocatively demonstrating that they controlled the roads in the area. Thankfully, Ankara kept a tight lid on the behaviour of its frontline troops—unless they were looking for prisoners of war. If they knew about him, Jamal was aware he would be a significant prize for the Turks. His continued freedom depended on the will of Allah.

The sound of engines starting up reached them. Their driver did the same. Shortly after, just before the truck lurched forward to restart its journey, they heard his all-clear signal. Jamal dreaded the prospect of many more hours of jarring vibrations as the truck hit potholes, but he knew now that they were moving away from the active conflict area. As much as he could, he would start to focus his attention on their next steps.

The worst was over . . . for now.

Hours later, they heard a signal from their driver. They had arrived in al-Yarubiyah; they were close to the border with Iraq. It was time for Jamal and Yussef to leave the convoy.

Their driver grimaced as he saw Jamal struggling to extricate himself from the confined space, and he bowed several times in apology for their difficult journey. He smiled effusively when Jamal—the peoples' hero—offered his heartfelt thanks. They were able to leave the convoy without attracting any attention. A small, covered truck drove them to a walled compound surrounded by thick groves of palm trees, at the edge of the city. At first sight, it seemed an unimpressive place, but Jamal saw that it was closely guarded. Groups of armed rebels patrolled the grounds of the compound. They would be safe here.

Jamal was grateful for the opportunity to be able to exercise his limbs. The journey seemed not to have affected Yussef. The boy was staring upwards—clearly enthralled by the trillions of stars in the clear desert sky. For both of them, it was a very different place than on the coast, where they'd been subjected to months of Russian confinement. Without a word being passed, they both acknowledged that the desert was where they felt happiest. It was their country—not an imperialistic possession of the infidels who had occupied their lands for so many centuries.

There was time for a quiet moment of reflection. The solitude, with only the sounds of night-time insects disturbing the peacefulness, appeared to rejuvenate the travellers. They lingered, not wanting it to end. Breathing in the cold night air, Jamal said, "Come, Yussef, we should wash and get ready for prayers. Let us give thanks to Allah. Indeed, we have been blessed. We will go and meet the others.

"There is much work for us to do."

Rendezvous

Inside the main building within the compound, the others were assembled. They sat in a loose circle around the room—talking, mostly preoccupied with their own distractions. Mohammed had not yet arrived.

As Jamal entered, they looked up in surprise and arose almost in unison, spontaneously cheering—waving their arms in the air and rushing towards their leader. He had not been killed in battle after all.

Soon he was surrounded and could not enter further into the room. Such was their joy that they continued to mob him as he padded his hands downwards to quieten their celebration—yet smiling happily. They continued to swarm him, calling out their questions—asking how he had survived. Praise be to Allah!

The throng gradually fell silent when Jamal said that he wanted to address them. There were more of his men assembled than he'd anticipated. And something totally unexpected: the red-haired infidel was standing alongside Nazih. Jamal knew the two were close friends and acknowledged that his own relationship with the Western jihadi had always been a good one. Yet, his presence here was still a surprise.

Moments later, Jamal was delivering an impromptu impassioned speech—reminding them of their past times together and speaking of their gathering today. With his words, spoken in the way that only gifted leaders and natural orators can, Jamal pulled each one of them more tightly into their collective resolve. He made only vague references to their task ahead—alluding to a vital mission they had been called upon to carry out. They would succeed, he said, if it was the will of Allah. He would have more details for them soon, he told them. For now, he admitted that he was humbled by their dedication to the holy war. He thanked them for the journeys they'd already made—and once again were about to make together.

The time for Isha, the evening prayer, was near. He asked that they should pray together—for the special work that lay ahead.

Sometime later, Nazih took Jamal aside. He needed to explain why he had brought his friend the red-haired infidel with him. To his surprise, the commander accepted the reality of the jihadi's presence at their compound. "We don't have much time, Nazih. He can help us procure the equipment and supplies we need. He has been useful for that purpose in the past.

"Nazih, we have fought a long time together," he continued. "He is your friend, but you and I are blood brothers. I have something very important to tell you about the purpose of our mission here. You will be one of only a few who know. It means that we cannot trust infidels being too close to us. Your friend must not make the final steps of our journey with us. You will see to it, Nazih," said Jamal, staring at him with undisguised meaning.

"While he is still useful to us, he is a welcome addition to our band of brothers.

"But he must not be allowed to threaten the success of the jihad."

O'Flaherty sensed that he should not push his luck.

The American had achieved his goal: to re-establish himself within Jamal's camp. He was content with the outcome of several local raids he'd organised over the past several days. They'd stolen trucks full of weapons from a regime-held local garrison. It had gone better than he'd expected and provided a morale boost to Jamal's troops. His popularity among the frontline fighters had been enhanced, and Nazih had shared the glory. It was widely known they had always been a formidable combination working together. But, to follow the group into the desert might be seen by Jamal as seeking too much familiarity, he concluded. O'Flaherty didn't want them to suspect he knew about their plan to join up with al-Amin. It was time to leave.

Observing the hurried preparations being made, he concluded that Jamal's rebel group would be departing soon from the compound at al-Yarubiyah. Now that he knew their approximate whereabouts, he had other ways to pursue his primary objective—in support of Daniela and the capture of al-Amin. Besides, it was important to report the most recent intel to his base as soon as possible. The rendezvous at al-Yarubiyah had confirmed what they had suspected. It was vital up-to-date information. He was certain now that Jamal and his group were working with al-Qaeda to link up with the new leader.

Al-Qaeda in Syria was about to be reborn—in ancient Mesopotamia.

It would be Daniela's job to confirm the target's identity—and his precise location. Then the long-planned, intricately managed preparations in the West would be set into motion.

Their mission . . . locate and capture al-Qaeda's new supreme leader, al-Amin.

At Jamal's compound, O'Flaherty was packing the few possessions he carried with him. "My work here is done," he said without looking up at Nazih.

His friend had been thinking about his instructions from Jamal. It posed a problem. He'd developed a strong bond with the Western jihadi over the years. Despite the wars, they'd had many good times together. Yet, Jamal had been adamant; his orders must be obeyed. Now his friend's announcement of his imminent departure would solve the problem.

"I'm in the military supply business, Nazih." The American grinned, as he zipped up a small holdall. "The government is presenting me with many opportunities to steal their weapons."

"Where will you go, my friend?" asked Nazih.

O'Flaherty shrugged. "Where the guns are, of course. You will need more of them—if we are to overthrow the tyrant al-Daser. I fear it will be a long fight. Our raids have been fun, Nazih. But they will inflame his wrath. The government will become more determined. Do not worry, I will bring you more weapons when you need them, my brother," he promised. "Many more. That is what I do best."

Nazih laughed. It was a typical response from the red-haired infidel. Then he frowned. "I have your money. It is not here but hidden—near my home."

"It is *Zakat*," said O'Flaherty. "It is for the poor and those most in need. You know what the Sunnah tells us." His tall frame loomed over Nazih as he gave him a parting embrace. "We will see each other again. One of these days, I will become old. Too old any longer to run faster than the government troops. Then I will need a quiet place to sit and talk with you over coffee—to reminisce about our good times together."

"You can stay if you wish," protested Nazih. He was aware it was a lie but wanted him to feel welcome.

"It is better this way. Take care, old friend," said O'Flaherty as he started to leave. He gave Nazih a final embrace. "*As-salamu alaykum.*"

Nazih felt the sadness of parting in a way he had not experienced with his friend before. He had learned many things from him. Yet, he was aware that if it had been necessary to carry out Jamal's orders, he would have shot him—despite the fraternal bonds between them. "*Wa alaykumu as-salam,*" he responded without any energy in his voice. War brings people together and it separates them, he reminded himself after his friend had left.

He walked to the building where he knew the boy Yussef could be found and saw him cleaning the gun he'd been given. Taking money from his purse, he gave it to the boy. "Follow the red-haired infidel," he ordered. "Be careful. He is an experienced soldier. I want to know where he is going and what he does."

Minutes later, Nazih reported to Mohammed. "The infidel has left us. The boy Yussef will follow him and keep us informed."

Mohammed nodded his approval. "It is for the best. He has been useful. Now we must not take any risks. He must not be allowed to know our purpose here. We must not permit him to come anywhere close to al-Amin."

Band of Brothers

Nazih met with Farouk. It was not long after O'Flaherty had left the compound.

He described how he'd had to act quickly and had sent the boy Yussef to track the Western jihadi. "The infidel is my friend, but Jamal has warned us not to take chances. Mohammed has approved of my actions. To be honest, Farouk, I am not even sure that we can rely on Yussef. Jamal seems to trust him, but he and the boy were imprisoned for many months by the Russians. It is possible they have become soft. Their judgement may be weak. So, I have sent one of our trusted fighters to follow Yussef and the infidel. Our man is a wily old fox. We can rely on him; he will act as our eyes and ears. We will soon find out if we can trust the boy Yussef."

Pleased with Nazih's quick instincts, Farouk summoned the remainder of the band of brothers. Yasser and Mahmood arrived promptly. Ali joined them soon afterwards. "We must talk and agree how we will proceed," Farouk told them. "To do that, I must tell you what Mohammed has confided to me and to Nazih. On pain of death, no one must breathe a word of it . . . to anyone. Before we came here, our purpose was to protect Jamal and advance our struggle for the jihad. After what I am about to tell you, brothers, you will understand that now we have an even greater task.

"It is one to which we must again dedicate our lives. There is nothing more important. Nothing!

"*Inshallah*, we will be successful."

CHAPTER 7
Peshawar, Pakistan: One Month Earlier

Rashid al-Muhasib scanned the room for a final time. He turned and started to leave the building—not without emotion. It had been his principal place of operation for over thirty years.

The journey he was about to undertake would be as momentous as the one he'd made many decades earlier—orchestrated by his mentor. He had been thirteen years of age when Osama bin Laden had graduated from the University of Jeddah in 1981. They were linked through their families—both part of the "Syrian Group," whose matriarch was bin Laden's mother, the eleventh wife of Osama's Yemini-Saudi father. By a twist of fate, Rashid was born on the exact day that his mentor's father, Mohammed bin Laden, had died in a plane crash. Osama had been ten years old at the time.

Rashid excelled at school. He was poor at sports, due to his eye defect. But he had a gifted brain for mathematics—a quality that did not escape the attention of the increasingly fanatical bin Laden. Osama was devoted to his mother and the Syrian Group. By that time, his branch was long estranged from the mainstream of his father's extended family. Osama took a personal interest in Rashid—who, in turn, was enthralled by his mentor and by the teachings of Osama's university lecturer and friend, Abdullah Yusuf Azzam.

Mindful of his responsibilities to the boy's mother, bin Laden considered him too young to travel to Afghanistan and fight with the mujahideen. Besides, Rashid had become useful to him. The boy's memory was photographic. Wary of the close political bonds between the House of Saud and major Western powers, Osama bin Laden had chosen a policy of committing little to paper. He realised that the boy's active brain was an ideal and secure repository for his network of contacts. The youngster was able to keep mental track of Osama's extensive financial contributions to the fight in Afghanistan. Despite his youth, the boy became increasingly vital to the future co-founder of al-Qaeda.

Taking him aside one dull cloudy day in Jeddah, bin Laden had told the boy about his plan for the future of the global holy war. Rashid could hardly contain his passion and enthusiasm. He wanted to accompany Osama to Peshawar, travel through the Khyber Pass, and join the mujahideen to kill the Russian imperialist infidels. "We will rid the land of all non-believers," he promised his mentor.

Still mindful of his mother's wishes and his responsibilities to the Syrian Group, Osama bin Laden was concerned about the boy's age and his eye defect. He would be handicapped as a soldier. Osama understood the realities. Soon he convinced the young boy that the holy war required soldiers of many talents. The future emir and leader of al-Qaeda cooled the boy's fighting passion. He painted, instead, a vision for the impassioned youngster that would lead the boy in a different direction. "Allah has given you these gifts for a purpose, Rashid," bin Laden had told him. "The path He has chosen for you is not that of a foot soldier. You have been chosen by Him instead to guide us along the cerebral path. Use your head, Rashid, not your trigger finger. If you do, our holy war will succeed much earlier and more effectively."

Inspired by his mentor's eloquence and by Azzam's supportive words, the young boy acquiesced. Osama convinced his co-founder that to protect the boy, the youngster should have a low profile in the conflicts. He could work easily in the background, argued Osama. Later, when he journeyed to Peshawar, the boy was rarely identified by name. There was little need for it. The focus, and the fight, was on

155

the front lines with the mujahideen—not in the dusty back rooms of the office.

The teenage boy grew up.

Over many decades, he'd worked tirelessly on behalf of al-Qaeda. His agile brain helped Osama raise and manage vital funding for the holy war—especially among the rich Saudi dreamers who felt alienated by their Western-biased relatives controlling the House of Saud. He had been able to make secret visits and spend time with bin Laden at Abbottabad, yet he'd never appeared on the radar screen of Pakistan's security forces or Western surveillance. Many years later, Rashid had been pleased when a defecting Western spy made a comment to the succeeding leader of al-Qaeda, Ayman al-Zawahiri: the turncoat spy had never heard of the dull bookkeeper. Throughout his time there, he had remained virtually unknown to the CIA and Europe's antiterrorism forces. Rashid relished his anonymity—his invisibility. Over the years, he had carefully protected his concealed identity—blending into the background as an amorphous seemingly low-key member of al-Qaeda's central command. Yet, he was aware of his significant contributions to the cause—and was determined to do much more.

In the event, it was a shift in the power struggles in the Middle East that would determine his future. One day, many years later, he was summoned to a meeting of al-Qaeda's Inner Council. He knew its supremacy and power. Before Osama bin Laden had been captured at Abbottabad, he'd spoken respectfully of it to Rashid. The Council comprised a small hand-picked group from within the larger Shura gathering. Now, the elders invited Rashid's views—testing the strength of the protégé's religious convictions, his resolve, his tactical knowledge, and his strategic sense.

They were impressed. Most importantly, in their deliberations, they wanted to hear details of the plans he had just outlined to them—a bold plan to finance a reinvigorated global expansion of al-Qaeda.

Rashid remained patient over the next several days while the Inner Council deliberated. When called back into their meeting, he was told they had a new role for him. A change of structure and tactics had been decided. His receptive brain retained every piece of information they gave him; he memorised every detail of his new instructions. Rashid had been promoted leader of an elite group—answering directly to Ayman al-Zawahiri, the aging operational head of al-Qaeda. He was being groomed to replace him. For the jihad, it was timely and pre-emptive. Pakistan was under financial pressure from the United States, which was threatening to withdraw its sizeable development aid. Under pressure, Islamabad began a lukewarm crackdown on al-Qaeda operatives sheltering in their country.

Al-Qaeda's central command made a strategic decision to move location. As a base, Pakistan was no longer safe. Afghanistan was unstable, despite the assurances of al-Qaeda's close allies, the Taliban. Within al-Qaeda's leadership, the question was where to go next. As it had done years earlier, moving from its birthplace in Saudi Arabia to northern Pakistan in order to be close to the conflict areas of Afghanistan, al-Qaeda's central command ordered another migration.

This time, its move would be even more ambitious—and risky. Just as Israel had in 1948—but, in the Jewish state's case, with Western support—al-Qaeda's central command, its Shura, decided that it would occupy the void left by defeated ISIS forces in northern Syria and Iraq. That would be the only comparison with the hated enemy that the Shura would tolerate. Violent removal of the Zionist state from Arab lands was seared deeply into their psyche.

They decided that the epicentre of the new global jihad would be the Fertile Crescent—the original cradle of civilisation.

Mesopotamia.

A trusted courier reported to al-Amin.

News of the media and public outcry in Spain over the theft of the riches of Aladdin's Cave was conveyed to him. He knew, from Jamal, about the splendid hoard of riches that existed. In fact, he had given his personal consent for the arrangement made between al-Qaeda cells in Spain and Jamal. He'd supported Jamal's contract-for-terrorism services with the Spanish neo-fascist group led by a retired general.

He had a cynical view of money that originated from there. Even the jihadist diaspora could not be trusted; there were spies everywhere. Yet, the substantial initial payments that al-Qaeda had received a year earlier—via hawala transfers—had been delivered as planned. A young Spanish jihadist had been the courier from the al-Qaeda network in Spain, Jamal had told him. It had been a clean transfer that had caught his attention. The commander had informed him that much more money was available.

Spanish media stories confirmed the existence of the laundered funds, and Jamal could be relied upon to arrange its transfer. Al-Amin considered the former surgeon from Homs among his most trusted counsellors. There had been reports he'd been badly injured in the fighting in western Syria. Orders from the Ayman al-Zawahiri to Jamal, instructing him to relinquish command of his troops and report immediately to the Inner Council, had not been acknowledged. No one had heard from Jamal. It was believed he was dead. Then, good news. There were reports that Jamal was still alive—but captured and in Russian hands in Latakia.

The prospect of additional funds coming from Spain intrigued him. Jamal had been his only conduit to the money—and recently, the supply had dried up. Reading again through the Spanish media story, he felt a renewed sense of opportunity. One billion euros could finance a large part of al-Qaeda's global operational program. He had reported the opportunity to the Council, preaching caution. Yet, they all knew that in seizing the initiative from the decline of ISIS, they would have to take some risks. With news that Jamal was alive, access to the Spanish funds had again become possible. Al-Amin had ordered al-Qaeda's network to organise Jamal's escape. In recent months, it had become one of his highest priorities.

Besides, al-Andalus occupied a special place in his heart. His family had not forgotten that, five hundred years earlier, the invading Christian regents Ferdinand and Isabella had driven his ancestors from the land they had occupied continuously for almost eight hundred years. The return of Spain to Islam was high on his personal agenda—and that of al-Qaeda.

As a youth, he had tried to convince Osama bin Laden to launch a series of terrorist attacks within al-Andalus. After 9/11, Osama bin Laden became a fugitive—sought after almost fanatically by the US and the West. But he'd listened to his protégé. Rashid's recommendations for another massive attack had been prepared in exacting detail. Osama had been impressed. The high command had listened and swiftly agreed. In 2004, al-Qaeda cells carried out the backpack bombings at Atocha train station in Madrid, killing at the scene one hundred and ninety-three men, women, and children, and injuring over two thousand. His protégé's first experience of managing a campaign had been a resounding success for al-Qaeda.

Several years later, Spanish al-Qaeda operatives organised additional terrorist attacks within the country. Political instability within Spain was endemic. But Rashid wanted something big. Now was the ideal time for another major attack, he was convinced. His immediate priority, however, must be to secure al-Qaeda operations within Mesopotamia. They must recapture the hearts and minds of devout brethren, rebuilding and consolidating al-Qaeda's base of power. The prospect of an influx of freshly laundered funds coming from Spain seemed entirely appropriate to him. He would personally lead efforts to secure them. It would be a pleasurable irony to relieve the Spanish infidels of their riches.

He had the authority of the Inner Council. More importantly, he had a divine calling: the jihad. As the newly chosen supreme leader, he must ensure that the plans he'd presented to the Inner Council would be implemented. For that, he needed Jamal.

And the Spanish money.

All of it.

Northern Syria: Al-Yarubiyah

The arrival of their revered commander, whom they had thought was dead, and a successful raid on the government base at al-Yarubiyah had injected fresh optimism and confidence into Jamal's men.

Jamal, too, seemed to relish his new task. Despite the pain in his leg, he moved around with the energy of a twenty-five-year-old, looking much more like his former self than he had under Russian captivity. His self-assurance and determination inspired his men to even greater efforts. Mohammed had taken up his former role in the platoon and stayed close to his revered commander at all times.

As soon as he was able to tell the rest of his men about the impending arrival of al-Amin, Jamal knew they'd be overjoyed. Until then, it had to remain a tight secret from all except an essential few. Yesterday, he'd heard that al-Amin had already left Pakistan and was on his way. Now, the vision and dreams for Mesopotamia they'd discussed as younger men were a step closer to reality. Yet, Jamal fretted that dreams sometimes can become nightmares. His most important task and responsibility was to protect the new leader's life. He had to make sure that al-Amin remained safe—and able to guide their shared journey through the uncertain times ahead.

Towards the end of his incarceration in Latakia, Jamal had plenty of time to plan for the new leader's arrival. Since his escape, consulting at length with Mohammed, he'd already given orders to reorganise their platoon—assigning experienced teams to essential roles. To one, he assigned the task of contacting and mobilising the remaining foot soldiers who'd gone to ground after the rebel forces had dispersed.

Farouk and his squad were ordered to take charge of the company's logistics. One of their special tasks, as an advance guard, was to ensure the secrecy and security of hideouts that would be used as alternating bases by al-Amin.

Yasser and Mahmood were assigned to supervise the vehicle pool and fuel sources. Nazih was placed in charge of procurement—which gave him latitude to requisition or steal anything in the name of the jihad. Ali, who spoke numerous languages and who at one time had worked on the dark web producing the ISIS news magazine *Dabiq*, took charge of communications and propaganda.

Jamal focused his mind on obtaining the money. He was confident that Daniela would be able to deliver it. She would keep her solemn promise. Mohammed had told him about international news reports of the manhunt still underway for her in Spain. If she was still free, Jamal knew she would find a way to journey back to Syria—to be with him. He had one nagging fear. If she was imprisoned or dead—if their financial scheme was doomed—he would have to inform al-Amin. With so much money almost within al-Qaeda's reach, it was not a prospect that he relished. He didn't fear the new leader's wrath; Rashid rarely lost his temper—he was far too cerebral. Nevertheless, he would be angry. It would be a huge setback. The money coming from Spain was absolutely vital for the rebuilding that al-Amin planned for the region. Daniela simply must succeed.

Al-Qaeda's sworn enemies—al-Daser's Syria, as well as Iraq, Iran, and the Hezbollah of Lebanon—posed seemingly insuperable threats to its closely held secret plan to become re-established in Mesopotamia. Yet, among many people here, al-Qaeda retained a deep spiritual foothold. It was a solid foundation for the future. Jamal, as a student of the region, knew that the new leader of al-Qaeda was well versed in the history of Palestine. He knew how the usurper State of Israel had been established illegally on Muslim lands, aided by the despised infidels of the West. Now, within the Islamic world, here in this region, the same type of struggle was being fought—this time between orthodox forces, extremes of Sunni and Shia pitched head-to-head against each other, driven by the overwhelming desire of millions of the faithful to return to conservative spiritual values, to finally reject the ways of the corrupt and decaying West and cast out the foreign infidels forever.

In his mind, Jamal was sure that in a hundred years' time, history books would talk of an almighty battle between the two sects—and, more specifically, between their most ardent conservative factions. He knew that many people in Syria adhered closely to Sunni beliefs. Many were embracing the Salafist desire to return to religious fundamentals. Jamal knew that the power struggles taking place could not be explained alone by tensions between the two main sects—or even by religion itself. There were global power plays. Regionally, there were long-standing ethnic and tribal aspirations. Deep schisms existed. Despite the sage advice received from their experts, the world-governing infidels of the West and Far East understood little about these deep divisions—and cared for them even less. Muslims, Jamal was confident, could sort out their internal differences—even if it took a hundred years, or a thousand.

He was interrupted from his thoughts as Mohammed entered the room. His faithful lieutenant placed a finger on his mouth to stop him from speaking. Both of them feared spies of the regime. Seconds later, Mohammed whispered in his ear.

Jamal's eyes brightened with unrestrained excitement. "He's arrived?" he whispered, unable to contain his joy. "It is the beginning. Remain here, Mohammed. I must go and welcome him.

"Praise be to Allah."

Mohammed had given Jamal the name of the village where he would find al-Amin. It was south of where they were located and, in more normal times, a short journey by road. Now it was patrolled by their enemies—the government, American forces and the Western coalition, and freedom fighters from the north.

Jamal remembered the place. Several years earlier, his company had fought a skirmish there against the fragmented remnants of a retreating regime platoon. His men had not taken any prisoners. His thoughts returned to the last time he'd seen al-Amin—now the most powerful man within al-Qaeda high command. He recalled that they had met in Baghdad prior to the heyday of the caliphate. Al-Amin had not yet been elevated to supreme power, and Jamal's al-Nusra was strong. It represented al-Qaeda in the Levant.

Subsequently, their influence had been dwarfed, as ISIS gained dominance. With the caliphate's subsequent demise, al-Qaeda could now re-establish itself. Jamal knew it would not be easy. He was worried about his leg and nervous about his ability to serve their new leader. His wounds had been causing pain since the beginning of the convoy journey; they were an increasing distraction. Alone in the room, Jamal reached into his jacket, extracting a plastic bag containing the last of the tramadol. He'd brought it with him when he'd escaped from the Russian base. He chewed and then swallowed his last tablet—the full 50 mg. Usually he took eight at a time.

Bidding farewell to Mohammed, Jamal left their camp soon after dusk. He planned to arrive at the village in the early morning. Explaining his concerns to his driver, Salman, a young fighter from his unit, he cautioned the youngster. Americans and the Russians constantly patrolled the skies, he reminded him. Their tracking technicians used sophisticated, high precision, night-vision equipment. "Let's not give them a pattern they can follow," he urged.

Jamal was pleased with his driver's caution—first travelling north-east, before turning south. Measured directly, the drive to the village where they would find al-Amin was less than a hundred kilometres. Using deserted and unlit dirt roads, and taking diversionary tactics, the drive would take more than six hours—assuming they did not encounter any regime patrols. For the next several hours, they made frequent stops to conceal their trail. Towards midnight, Jamal directed his driver towards a group of isolated farm buildings. "I know this place," he said.

As they approached, several shadowy figures wearing balaclavas emerged from almost nowhere. Semi-automatics were trained on their now stationary vehicle. Jamal wound down the passenger window and spoke to one of the masked men. He heard the crackling of a hand-held radio, a pause, then some more talk. Finally, they were allowed to restart the vehicle and drive slowly to a farmhouse. Under close guard, Jamal was escorted inside. After the warmth of their car, he found the desert air chilling; his leg was now throbbing with pain. "Get some sleep, Salman," he called confidently. "We will leave for our destination in four hours."

Surprised by the unexpected turn of events, the young driver dutifully curled up into his seat. Sometime later, music blared from the farmhouse. Loud voices and laughing told him that Jamal was indeed a welcome visitor.

Jamal had exchanged animated greetings with an old friend. Ibrahim had been one of his best officers, a platoon lieutenant before he'd returned to his former profession—farming. His father had cultivated this land for wheat, even though the crop yields had always been poor. Ibrahim had found it more lucrative to grow hashish. Now he was the undisputed drug lord over an extensive area. His motley collection of former ISIS and rebel soldiers ensured that he remained uncontested by any rivals. Clearly, he was proud of his stature in the region.

Ibrahim beckoned Jamal to follow him to the rear of the buildings. There, a wide camouflaged netting was spread over a sleek black five-seater helicopter secured down to a green-painted concrete landing pad. "From the sky, it looks like a pile of hay." He laughed. Feeling no pain from the fresh supply of drugs provided by his host, Jamal slapped his former lieutenant on the back and roared with delight.

"Let's take it out for a spin," suggested his host, to which Jamal waved his arm in protest.

"No, really, I want to show it to you," said the man, pretending hurt feelings. "It is easy to fly."

Jamal knew that his former officer had lost the sight of one eye in the battle for Homs. There was no way in the world he was going to get into the aircraft with him as pilot. His host grumbled amiably and tapped his watch. "It is only 2 am. We have the sky to ourselves." He laughed again. "But if you insist, Commander." He put his arm drunkenly around Jamal's shoulder, and they made their way back inside.

Several hours later, fully refreshed—and feeling like the top of the world—Jamal shook the sleeping Salman's shoulder, instructing him to continue their journey. Bidding a fond farewell to Ibrahim, Jamal patted his inside pocket. He had replenished his stock of tramadol, courtesy of his platoon lieutenant. Plus, he'd accepted a large bag of Captogon—jihadi pills that, out of sight, he would distribute discreetly to his platoon.

Guided for several kilometres in the direction of their destination by a heavily armed group of Ibrahim's henchmen, Jamal reflected that the government would always have a tough battle to win support in the north-east. Al-Daser and his father had milked the area of its wealth to feed the citizens of Damascus and keep them warm in winter. In the civil war, they'd been vicious and cruel to civilians and opposition forces alike. The surviving inhabitants had long memories—they would not forget.

It was indeed a fertile foundation for the renaissance of al-Qaeda in the Levant.

Al-Amin had chosen well.

Jamal arrived at the village.

He was expected.

In one of the buildings, al-Amin had assembled a small gathering where they embraced, drank tea, and discussed matters of little consequence. Beckoning for the gathering to leave, he motioned for Jamal to stay. Two well-armed bodyguards remained, as was their rule. With impassive faces, they stared into the mid-distance. They came from different tribes and trusted each other as they might trust an enemy; al-Amin had cleverly ensured there would be no collusion between them. He was safe. But, needing to speak privately with Jamal, he instructed the guards to wait outside the room. "You, too, Hasan," he said to his young assistant. "Jamal is an old friend. Give us some time together."

Moments later, Jamal spoke. "You wish to remain in this place, Emir?" he asked, glancing with concern at the unfortified walls of the farmhouse. "We have arranged somewhere much safer for you." Pointing to the sky, his meaning was obvious. "Their drones . . ."

"Fear not." Al-Amin smiled. "I will be here for a few days only. Then I will need the help of you and your men—in the city."

Jamal nodded his approval. He knew that the new leader would be much safer in a more densely populated area—where he could move easily between safe houses, staying several steps ahead of enemies seeking to find him. The list of pursuers was formidable. Foremost were al-Daser's infamous secret police units—the Mukhabarat. Equally dangerous was Iran's Quds Force. Then the Americans. Others too. In Jamal's view, the city of al-Hasakah was a better choice than Raqqah, which had been occupied as the capital of the short-lived caliphate. It was smaller but still sizeable, and Jamal had backup plans.

"Your safety . . ." he began to say.

Al-Amin waved away his concern—saying, "*Inshallah*. We should talk about the money coming from Spain."

Jamal briefed the new leader. "Emir," he summarised, "the money from Spain—soon we will receive it, as I have told you. I ask for just a small part of it. Not for myself, of course. My proposal is to use it to help the people, to treat their wounds and feed their families. While we are in the process of advancing our vision, pursuing the holy war, it will be important for us also to be seen to be a *just* governate. Able to reinforce the resolve of the people."

Al-Amin's eyes narrowed as he studied his friend. "You speak of the need for a kind and generous governate, Jamal. Describe to me your thinking, please."

"Supreme Commander, you know the minds of the people of the north. Always, it is the rich families and merchants of the south—and governments in Damascus even before al-Daser—who control the farmland in the north-east and its oil resources too. They invest only so that they can extract the wealth and line their own pockets. For decades, little of that money has gone to the local people. The Damascus government—always, it has kept farm prices low—to provide cheap food for its supporters.

"We know that Russia and Iran will continue to seek control of the north-east for its resources," Jamal continued. "To them also, the local people do not matter; they are expendable. Western governments and NGOs are mere lackeys. Even with Russia's considerable influence over al-Daser, Westerners will offer money to help the regime—seeking to regain some influence in the region."

"Surely, the peoples' lives are better than you suggest?" said al-Amin. He seemed to be testing Jamal. "Industry here has been modernised; it is recovering after the wars."

Jamal knew that he was under the leader's scrutiny and on dangerous ground. Disregarding the personal risks, he proceeded to say what was on his mind. "The people hate the government, Emir; yet many of them remain attracted to the materialism of the West, despite its evils. They listen as well to those from Asia who promise them a better life. False prophets. If, instead, we speak to the people about true land reform—under our governance, it will do much to help our cause. The coming growing season, with its rains, is an opportunity. If we provide seed to every farmer, it will quickly result in support for us. After the wars, much of the land is barren and yields nothing. That is how we can use some of the Spanish money. Invest first in pesticides and fertilisers. After that, modern irrigation and productive farming can follow.

"Under your leadership, our holy war can continue on several fronts." Jamal's passionate excitement was now overcoming the pain in his leg. "Foremost, of course, we must remain a military force—but as you have said, as guerrillas. For us, that is the easy part. Also, our young people are well-versed in cyberterrorism—the battleground of the future. Our imams continue to preach the Salafist way. But surely part of our purpose is to unify the people behind us?" He fell silent, realising that he must not push too far. As he waited, he heard the new leader crack the knuckles of his hands—systematically one joint and cartilage after the other. It was an eerie sound, loud in the otherwise silent room, amplified by the silence outside.

"I am impressed by your passion," al-Amin said finally. "Clearly, you are not just an outstanding military leader—with a vital role in creating our future. In fact, I was intending to talk to you about taking up that command. Now, you have caused me to think of other priorities that face us. Guerrilla tactics worked for us in Afghanistan," he continued. "There, the mountainous terrain was our ally. It afforded a means of escape and the ability to hide. The people survived because they grew poppies for opium. I do not approve, but these drugs weaken the infidels' resolve. Here, in this land, there is little of the same type of protection. We must learn to adapt. For that, we must build on the military lessons we have learned in the past. But come, old friend, let us continue later," said al-Amin, getting to his feet. "Give me time to think about what you have proposed. After your journey, you are welcome to retire to the room I have set aside for your stay. You will want to rest." He smiled knowingly. "And take the medication for your pain."

Satisfied that Jamal was now out of earshot, al-Amin leaned over his desk and retrieved a miniature tape recorder. It was unobtrusive, and he used it often in private conversations.

Calling for his assistant, he indicated for him to be seated. "Hasan, listen and tell me what you think."

Hasan sat back in his chair, his hand frequently stroking through his coarse black beard. "This is the former commander of al-Nusra?" he queried when the tape was finished. "Our comrade to whom you intend to entrust the command of our military forces here in Mesopotamia?"

"I did intend to do so," al-Amin shot back. "Now it is clear to me that our formerly valiant and dedicated commander is not the man I once knew. He was badly injured in battle—and evidently has been brainwashed by the Russians during his time in captivity. We shall have to rethink who should command our military.

"Yet, we still need him," he continued. "He is our link to the Spanish girl who brings us the money."

The Switch

The low-level flight to the north-east from al-Tanf had been arranged. The British sergeant had described the aircraft to Daniela as a high-powered crop duster. "Don't be fooled by it." She smiled. "Single engine and one pilot—but he's one of the best. Besides, it's equipped with a full set of eyes and ears. No armaments, but you won't need them. Extra fuel on board. You'll fly under the radar all the way.

"It's a seven-hundred-kilometre ride, including the diversions you're going to be taking to avoid traffic and Syrian military installations," she added. "It's a modified M600 actually—retrofitted with stealth deflectors. The engine is a turboprop specially designed for dusty, low-flying desert conditions—about a two-hour journey, depending on the precise route taken by your pilot.

"You speak Arabic, so you can listen in on local news channels in flight. Your destination touchdown is remote. A farmer's pickup truck will be waiting for you. You'll be hidden in the back of the cab, so your arrival in the city won't be observed. As I've mentioned, ma'am, our people control the hotel. If you need anything ask Aliye at the front desk." She handed a photo for Daniela to memorise and a slip of paper. "In emergencies, call this number; the codeword is your middle name.

"Oh, you'll be flying at night, no lights.

Drop off ETA 0700 hours."

The flight had been a dream, and Daniela—practising her role—was now sitting in the cab of a vintage pickup that had seen better days. An hour later, her driver pulled into the covered courtyard of her hotel. Sipping a fresh coffee sent up to her room, she sat on her bed and fired up the sanitised laptop they'd supplied her. Around midday, there was a knock on her door.

She'd been prepared for a shock, but the reality still surprised her. It was completely unsettling—the woman was her exact double. Daniela knew that she herself was attractive; she knew the effect she had on men . . . and women. Yet, she'd always lived with an internalised self-image of herself. The woman standing in front of her took her breath away. She was captivating. Mouth gaping, Daniela forgot her manners and stared at the woman—who became embarrassed and, in modesty, lowered her eyes to the floor.

"*Ahlan biki,*" Daniela managed to say finally. "Welcome."

Silently, the woman brushed past her—gently and with confidence, not rudely. She was a woman sure of herself and mindful of the instructions she'd received. Walking across the room, she pulled shut the cords controlling the venetian blinds. In the subdued light of the room, she began to undress. Garment by garment, she disrobed without any hint of self-consciousness or embarrassment.

"It is necessary they are not washed. My orders, you understand? I have been told it, yet I am ashamed. This you will forgive?" She smiled with embarrassment. From a bag, she took out a replacement set of clothes for herself. Handing Daniela a small bar of wrapped soap, she explained that it had been taken the day before from a resting place along her route. She had a few other items that a Western female masquerading as an Arab woman might accumulate along her journey.

They'd help authenticate her cover story, thought Daniela—grateful for the woman's intelligence and foresight. She knew that the woman would have no knowledge of her mission; the purpose of the changeover would have been kept from her. Yet, the woman had sensed the importance of her role; she had paid attention to details.

"Two days ago, we set out from a small settlement south-east of al-Hasakah," the woman said. "There has been much fighting in the city, but the regime is isolated at the centre of town. The second-floor apartment where you stayed is near a mosque that has been destroyed by the war. Electricity supply is sporadic. There are some stores nearby; they are where you shopped for food."

Daniela nodded gratefully. She listened with close attention as the woman described the places, her journey, and her experiences along the route. She learned the names of the two men who had driven the pickup truck. From the woman, she learned their habits, where they had stopped, and what they had eaten. Yesterday, they had been delayed, said the woman. The driver had needed to change a tyre. The older of the two had been in a bad temper: he'd yelled at her when she'd asked for a rest break. They had stopped regularly for prayers, and one time she was late in climbing back into the vehicle. The older driver had scolded her again. Otherwise, said the woman, they had ignored her. They'd smoked incessantly. From their conversations together, they were paid mercenaries, she assumed. They had been instructed to deliver her to a final destination, several blocks from the hotel.

"I was not followed, I made sure of that. Now I must go," she said quietly. Glancing at Daniela, she made direct eye contact. There was a warmth in her eyes.

"I wish you well."

CHAPTER 8
A Setback

Jamal was annoyed about his meeting with al-Amin.

He'd left the room frustrated—aware that their conversation hadn't gone the way he'd anticipated. He sensed that al-Amin was disappointed in him. The new leader had been almost patronising towards the end of the meeting. He'd appeared to attribute little importance to what Jamal had recommended.

Jamal dismissed the notion that he'd gone soft. He conceded that his time as a prisoner of the Russians in Latakia hadn't involved the same stresses as fighting on the front lines. He'd been treated well, at times like an honoured guest. But he hadn't lost his passion to continue the fight. As a soldier, he'd been responsible for many extreme acts of violence inflicted on combatants and civilians alike. He'd witnessed the pain and suffering of his countrymen. The cruelty of it was hard to comprehend. Convinced that what he'd recommended to al-Amin wasn't wrong, he knew the bombings of innocent people had to stop. He believed fervently in the jihad, yet he felt a deep compassion for ordinary civilians. They couldn't continue to suffer like this.

It seemed that the new leader was listening to people who were preaching an escalation of the violence. Now he, Jamal Ismet, was about to facilitate more killings. He was a vital cog in an elaborate plan to funnel essential funding from Spain to al-Qaeda—to the tune of a billion euros.

He swallowed five more tramodols and waited for the hit.

Days after the switch with her doppelganger, Daniela was sitting in her bedroom at the hotel, still waiting to hear from Jamal.

She was becoming concerned and wondered if he had been checking their drop box hidden in a crevice on the darknet. At the hotel, she'd used her time going over the details of her cover story—her explanation of how she'd fled back into Syria while on the run from the Spanish police. She'd rehearsed her story so many times, she was exhausted from boredom. Without contact, she had no way of knowing what was going on around her. It was the eye of the storm, she knew. It didn't help. She needed to get into action, and soon. Complete her assignment—do what she'd come here to do.

The last bit would be unplanned. She'd have to innovate and decide on the spur of the moment how to get close to al-Amin. Before that, she needed Jamal to identify him for her. She had to be sure he was the man they wanted. The Navy SEALs were relying on her positive ID. Capture him alive, Colonel Scott had ordered.

Looking in the narrow mirror in the cramped bathroom, Daniela thought she looked older. There were fatigue lines around her eyes. It might have been the food, but she didn't feel great either. Lying on the lumpy sagging mattress, she tried yet again to get some sleep. She sighed.

Waiting was always the worst.

Yussef returned late at night and reported immediately to Nazih. "The infidel travelled as far as Deir ez-Zor. I followed him. There I lost him in the crowds—I am sorry, master."

Nazih did not seem unduly surprised. His man had returned already and had reported Yussef's movements to him. He observed that the boy was covered in road dust: his shirt was dirty and his denim jeans were creased from hours of riding a motorcycle. Nevertheless, he was suspicious. "Where did you lose sight of him?" he enquired; his eyebrows arched.

"In the city."

"Yes, I understand. Which part of the city, Yussef?" He saw the boy colour slightly, although his eyes were defiant.

"In the suburbs. He had been travelling by bus; it travelled south. I followed on a motorbike that I'd stolen. It is outside. Come, you can see."

"Then what did you do?" Nazih asked. He wasn't interested in seeing the vehicle. "Perhaps you followed him for a time, but then you grew fearful? There are many regime soldiers, especially near the city. No one could blame you for being scared—not wanting to go back to jail. Maybe getting shot or tortured for being a rebel?"

"No, no, it was not like that, sir. I swear on my family's honour. I did my best, but there were too many people. Too many soldiers. Mukhabarat spies also—I saw them. Despite the danger, I did my best."

Nazih dismissed the boy and went to see Mohammed. "It seems that red-haired infidel went in the direction of the city—as he stated was his intention. We cannot rely on the boy; he lied to me. He's scared. It is true that he has been on a journey, but I do not think he went very close to the city. He lost track of him. Our man confirms it. Maybe there is nothing for us to be concerned about. For now, the Westerner is out of the way, as Jamal ordered."

Mohammed agreed. "The emir is becoming restless. Increasingly, he is anxious to move to the safety of the north-east, where he can be better protected." He paused. "We must get the money soon, Nazih. Jamal has promised that the girl will bring it. He trusts her, yet there is no word from her. No one has seen her. The emir wishes to know more about this girl; he wants to know if we can trust her. I myself do not, as you know. I did not trust her when she first came to our camp near Aleppo. It is my instinct. *Alhamdulillah*. Bring the boy Yussef to me. We will take him to our leader. Between us, we will tell him everything we know about her. Jamal, too, should come; he knows her well. If the emir does not believe she is a loyal jihadi Westerner, we should break camp and take him to the safe place without delay.

"The money, it is important.

"The safety of the emir and our jihad is even more vital."

―◦―

Yussef repeated his account of the escape from Barcelona—hiding out at the farm and the rented cottage with Daniela. He described their journey by ship to Cyprus and through Beirut to Latakia. Al-Amin listened intently, without interrupting. He seemed interested in the details of the escape of Jamal and Yussef from the Russian military base.

"This much, Jamal has told me before," he said at last. "Mohammed too. Certainly, she is very clever, this young woman. If it is a trick, it is an elaborate one. Yet, she also has delivered many millions of euros to us already. The infidel Mustapha has proven himself loyal to our cause many times."

"She is Mustapha's messenger," Yussef offered. "Yet, it is he who was arrested by the Spanish police. I do not trust her."

"Explain to me again why you think she is a spy," Hasan instructed. He listened as the boy told him that he did not trust women to do the work of men. The boy said that Daniela was so clever, she must have received help. No women could do what she had achieved—not without assistance.

"There are specific things that indicated to you she is a spy?" Hasan pressed. He seemed doubtful of the boy's explanations. Yussef stumbled several times in his recollection of the events and, at times, contradicted himself. He was flustered—made nervous by Hasan's aggressive questioning. Al-Amin sat back and listened, trusting Hasan to coax out the truth. At the end of the quizzing, al-Amin dismissed the gathering—except for Mohammed, Jamal, and Hasan.

"Mohammed?" he invited when the room was emptied.

"I believe she is a spy; I have thought so since the beginning, Emir. Jamal and I have discussed it." His face was hard and determined. He swirled his robes in a gesture of protection—of resolute certainty.

Al-Amin looked at Jamal. "What do you think?" His good eye searched Jamal's face for clues. Aware they'd known each other for decades, his tone confirmed that Jamal's loyalty was not in question. They all knew that he'd sacrificed himself for the jihad many times, and somehow survived. There was no doubt in anyone's mind that the former commander of al-Nusra was dedicated to the central pillars of Salafist and al-Qaeda beliefs—complete and permanent expulsion of foreign infidels.

When it came, Jamal's response was delivered in a low voice; his tone confident and unequivocal. "We must proceed with caution. Undoubtedly, it is a trap. All the signs point to it."

"Yet?" asked al-Amin.

"Emir, sometimes we must deal with the devil," answered Jamal. "Traps and spies are all around us. It is nothing new. In truth, it is the normal condition of things. In the end result, it is not the presence of enemy spies that will end our lives; it will be our inability to outwit them. To do so, we must first secure the money. From that stroke of good fortune, others things will quickly flow.

"*Inshallah*, then we can deal with them.

"The traitors and spies . . . on both sides."

Jamal was livid with himself.

He couldn't understand why he hadn't thought of it before; it must be the side effects of his medication. The lockbox online, of course! They'd used it many times when she had brought him the hawala money—and later too. But in Latakia, in the early days of being a prisoner of the Russians, he had trained his mind not to think of many things—to block them from his memory. He'd been determined not to reveal any secrets. Ironically, he'd disconnected so successfully from parts of his past life that he'd forgotten about the darknet lockbox. Moreover, he could barely recall their shared online procedure. He told Mohammed and asked to use his laptop. The glance he received from his trusted friend was a caution, a warning to use only the darknet for such communications.

Minutes later, Jamal read Daniela's message aloud. "I know where she is. She has been waiting for us—for several days," he exclaimed, making no effort to hide his frustration. Seeing the concern on Mohammed's face, he asked, "What is it?"

"If it is a trap, it's better that I go," said Mohammed. "Our leader expects to keep his commander alongside him . . ." He didn't finish his sentence.

Jamal saw the wisdom of the advice. He was aware that al-Amin knew of his close personal relationship with Daniela. He'd never attempted to hide it. Yet, he knew that Mohammed was being prudent. It would be wrong for him to rush to her. His responsibility was to the jihad—not a personal relationship. "You are right, of course." He clasped Mohammed's arm. "For a moment, my emotions were driving my brain. It may be a trap, although I think not. There are several phrases and words that she and I share to alert each other to danger. But your point is rooted in wisdom and concern for me. *Alhamdulillah!* Thanks to God you are at my side.

"I will remain here—as a commander should, at our leader's side," Jamal continued. "She will not be expecting you. It is a clever idea. Please go, hurry."

"Take good care, my friend."

Camel Train

It was midday.

Mohammed had collected Daniela from the hotel. They'd recognised each other immediately, but there had been no joy in their reunion. He seemed hostile, she thought. Even more filled with hatred towards her than when they'd first met at Jamal's camp, long ago. Gruffly, he'd ordered her to bring her bag and follow him. He didn't search her—which was surprising, she thought.

"I have brought something from Spain," she said, holding back . . . hesitating.

His dark eyes narrowed. More mistrust.

Reaching under the bed, she pulled out a heavy bundle wrapped in cloth. It took both her slender hands to lift it. Unwrapping it, she offered the gold ingot to him.

Mohammed glanced at the bundle but didn't accept it. Yet, he seemed to understand. "Bring it," he ordered.

As she climbed down the concrete stairs leading through the almost deserted lobby to a narrow alley outside, a wave of dry heat hit her face. After weeks of waiting in Cyprus and the stuffy seclusion of her hotel room for the past several days, the smells of the north-eastern Syrian city and street noises were refreshing. They were a welcome sign that important events at last were beginning to unfold.

If things went well, it would lead her to al-Amin. Continuing to play the part she'd been thinking about for years—and training for—would be the culmination of her mission. Beyond that, she'd given little thought. She was mindful that field operatives, at least those assigned to deep covert operations, rarely allow themselves such luxuries. There was only one priority: the target. First, she had to get there.

Following Mohammed along the street, she was aware they would regard her as a Western spy. They would assume she was part of an infidel trap. She would be taken somewhere; searched intrusively, without regard to any sensibilities. Interrogations would follow. They would play mind games with her—intimidating, disorientating tricks and tests. She understood and anticipated it—knowing that al-Qaeda would be resolutely determined to protect its new leader.

Behind her, she'd heard footsteps. Walking alongside a van with its engine running, she was suddenly pushed inside. Within seconds, the man who'd climbed in behind her thrust a thick sackcloth hood over her head. Her travel bag and the heavy gold ingot were snatched from her possession. She'd had just enough time to see Mohammed climb into the passenger seat and nod to the driver. It was all done so quickly. None of her captors had uttered a word. In a way, she felt reassured: she still had value. If she hadn't, Mohammed surely would have killed her in the hotel room. Driving quickly, they took her somewhere within the city. It turned out to be a disused warehouse. After searching her intimately, they scanned for embedded chips. Mohammed didn't take part, and she didn't see him again until later. She was entirely at their mercy. Soon the questioning began.

Her initial interrogation focused on her journey from Barcelona to Syria. Daniela was grateful once again for the authentic details of her cover story that her double had supplied—the clothing, the bar of soap, and her encounters with the men who'd driven her to the city. She remained hooded and seated, her hands roughly tied behind a chair. Answering their questions, she provided them with almost identical explanations each time. She knew that, under rapid fire questioning, perfectly consistent explanations made interrogators nervous. A convincing spy would never be perfect in her recall. Under pressure, it was important to remember details you'd forgotten to mention earlier. Nothing must appear staged. Daniela's inconsistencies were minor and inconsequential—like a person's normal memory in life. She had no doubt they'd be verifying her story. Despite the interrogations, she was well-treated. Water was provided and, later that day, food—hummus and basturma. It was consistent, she concluded, with her status as a potentially valuable Western jihadist. She was given the opportunity to pray.

Over the next several hours, her captors moved her several times. She had the impression that they had found no fault with her account of her journey into Syria and were now concerned mostly about not being discovered and tracked by their enemies. It was a normal state of mind for them. They had elaborate systems of procedures to throw off any pursuers—whether human or technological. They were patient, but she thought they'd be under orders to expedite her travel to al-Amin's encampment. That was where Jamal would be, and she had no doubt that Mohammed would ensure her safe delivery to him. He'd be under orders to do so. After that, she would be able to deploy her own skills and instincts.

Play the game that she wanted.

It was early next morning, still dark—long before dawn.

Woken by Mohammed, she was taken to a large black SUV. As they approached, sparks flew as their driver, wearing a shemagh, stubbed his cigarette into the concrete roadway with the toe of his sandal. Instructions were given. He pulled the same sackcloth hood roughly over her head and pushed her into the rear of the vehicle. A closing door confirmed that Mohammed had climbed into the passenger side. Wrists and feet bound, lying across the back seat, she had little opportunity to observe their route. That wasn't critical, Daniela consoled herself. Exact positioning of their destination was more important. Yet, she regarded it as a professional challenge to glean as much intelligence about the journey as possible. After days in the hotel, she must get her brain working actively again.

Driving out of the city, she listened carefully for giveaway sounds. In the front seat, their voices were muffled—inaudible over the engine noise. The stop-start of the back streets gave way to a rhythmic bump as the vehicle's tyres speeded over stretches of asphalt highway. She doubted they'd travel north; it would take them back into the oilfields—strategic territory where the regime had been making gains. There were frequent stops and diversions, as the driver was forced around damaged areas onto side roads. Mentally, she estimated the length of each distinguishable part of the journey. If nothing else, it forced her to remain alert. Being mentally sharp for what lay ahead was vital.

Dawn broke and the morning chill transitioned quickly to warmth. The thick sackcloth hood began to suffocate her. It was bound tightly and felt coarse against her face, its fibres scratching her skin. With her salty sweat and condensation from her breath, it soon became irritating. It smelled earthy and was stifling. She was partially in the dark, but soon determined where the natural light source was brightest—the rising sun. Now they were travelling east, towards the Iraq border. It wasn't the direction she'd expected.

The driver changed course several times. Lying across the back seat, Daniela struggled to remain oriented. She could hear Mohammed on his radio phone—receiving information about the location of enemy patrols, she guessed. One time, he ordered his driver to shelter the vehicle under the shade of a thick grove of olive trees. She could smell them and hear their leaves rustling in the wind. The trees provided shade. They offered relief from the increasingly intense sun. She was allowed to walk a short distance for exercise and basic ablutions—although still blindfolded. They waited over an hour until whatever danger they feared had passed. Most likely, Russian or regime fighter jet aerial reconnaissance, she imagined. Possibly a Syrian Democratic Forces patrol. Either way, Mohammed was being cautious, taking a circuitous route to their destination. Evidently, he had no wish to draw attention to their presence—or provide a pattern of travel that could be tracked by the ever-watching drones.

Eventually, their journey resumed. Then the terrain changed. Noise from the tyres and occasional sharp jolts from uneven ground indicated they were travelling fast across scrub desert. From time to time, the driver would engage a lower gear and the SUV laboured—climbing inclines where clearly there were no roads. Through pores in the sackcloth, she could taste the fine dust of the desert thrown up by the wheels. Her throat was dry, and her eyes stung from the driver's acrid cigarette smoke. It was imported Turkish tobacco. Unusual in a country that has a plentiful output of its own varieties, she thought, despite the disruptions of the wars. Contraband, possibly, or stolen on a raid up north.

Without warning, the vehicle skidded to an abrupt stop. Mohammed ordered the driver to pull her out of the vehicle. Thrown roughly to the stony ground, she wondered—for a moment—if they were going to shoot her and dispose of her body deep in the desert. But somehow it didn't seem likely: if they'd wanted to, they could have disposed of her hours ago. Moments later, the hot and heavy tyres of the SUV gouged deeply into the dry gravelly surface as its driver accelerated away.

She smelled and heard them before she saw them—camels, a train of dromedaries. The putrid stink of their urine permeated the air. Baying and moaning, they complained and bitched incessantly. She'd always hated them. She detested their hostile attitude and feared their bite—Daniela was terrified of their teeth. Sheets of tough uncompromising brown-stained bone protruding forward from their fat-lipped mouths like ugly flat scoops, just as capable of ripping a human's flesh as wrenching their diet of vegetation from the ground. She was grateful for the protection of her long robes. When the hood was removed from her head, she confirmed the worst. She and Mohammed were joining a Bedouin camel train. Only five beasts. It seemed that he planned to travel the rest of the way using traditional methods of transport. Her heart sank. Security around al-Amin really was at a paranoid level.

Shading her eyes from the harsh glare of the midday sun, Daniela squinted. For hours, her head had been covered. Now, free from the rough sackcloth, her eyes watered. Eventually, they adjusted and she was able to examine the vast expanse that lay before them—the Syrian

Desert, an arid, barren wilderness made worse by the droughts and bush fires that, for years, had plagued the region.

The Bedouin camel drivers appeared ready to move off as soon as instructed. Their beasts were laden and seemed restless to get going, she thought. Mohammed, too, seemed impatient. They'd lost valuable time hiding from an unseen enemy. Now, he was anxious to get underway. They'd assumed that she had the skills necessary to guide her animal, thought Daniela. From experience, she knew that at a walking pace the animals were easy—once you got used to the camel's pitch and sway, like a boat upon the high seas. The thought of galloping scared the living daylights out of her. It was not a part of her mission that she'd anticipated, or relished. Yet, it confirmed an important fact: the extreme security precautions being taken for his protection could mean only one thing.

Al-Amin was not far away.

That evening they stopped to camp. Before the journey, Daniela had expected her body would be wracked by sore muscles and legs fatigued from hours of strenuous riding. She surprised herself and was thankful for the extreme exercises she and O'Flaherty had practised in Cyprus. With ease, she adapted to sitting cross-legged, moving with the camel's motions. Apart from some soreness in her tailbone, she felt fine. Of course, she reminded herself, it was like riding a horse—the pain of stiff muscles might not appear until the next day.

Other more important worries were foremost in her mind—how much freedom she would be allowed when they arrived at al-Amin's encampment. For now, she wasn't being restricted. The Bedouin camel master and his two tribesmen largely ignored her. Mohammed was in control, and no doubt he'd given them precise instructions. Thankfully, they were older men. It was the virulent, predatory younger warriors she feared most. Later, she was given food. When they prepared for prayers, she moved a discreet distance away and performed hers alone. Sleep came to Daniela almost immediately as she laid down on the rough bedding she was provided.

Several times during the night, she awoke—disturbed by the baying of the camels. She slept fitfully, her broken dreams punctuated by terrifying images of being attacked by great armies of camel spiders. It was a nightmare for naught. Burying themselves into the stony sand, as they always did, they'd developed better ways to survive the rigours of the cold desert night. She emerged unscathed.

Before dawn next morning, the drivers were up early feeding and watering the camels. Daniela knew they were clean animals, almost fastidious in their habits. But she didn't look forward to another day of riding. Her hands were already feeling weak from constantly gripping the saddle post. The previous day, they had travelled due south and had covered a considerable distance—although she still had no clue about where they were going. Most likely, they would stay close to the Iraqi border where no man's land still held strong.

It seemed like a very elaborate journey—when using the roads would have been much faster. She kept reminding herself that their paranoia over al-Amin's security was a good sign.

The Village

They'd left the camel train.

The Bedouins had continued their journey, leaving Mohammed and Daniela to shelter from the sun in the only shade available—the wreckage of a burned-out Syrian Army tank. They'd been there several hours already, carrying only the luggage she'd brought from her hotel. When he wasn't looking, she checked her luggage—fearing the gold ingot may have been slyly replaced with a heavy rock by one of the tribesmen. No cause for concern: it was still there.

Mohammed spoke little, ignoring her infrequent attempts at conversation. His resentment of her was as unmistakable and intense as on the first day they'd met. She didn't fear him because she knew he was under Jamal's orders—she'd be safe for now. Yet, as the hours passed, she grew tired. Sitting in the shade against the metal treads of the weather-beaten tank—its wrecked gun turret lying upside down on the ground nearby—she was tiring of the stench of old diesel that had seeped over time into the stony ground. His distrust was so deep that he would not even allow her to get up and exercise. Eventually, they saw a vehicle in the distance. As it got closer, he motioned to her. They took shelter, and he trained his rifle on the approaching pickup. When its swirl of dust settled, Mohammed spoke to the driver. "Get in," he ordered.

To most observers, the village appeared sleepy and deserted. In the hot sun, it seemed unusually quiet, she thought. Just the buzz of insects and acrid smell of woodsmoke. Without children on the streets, there was little obvious evidence of its inhabitants—although she could tell that, somewhere, midday meals were being cooked—the aroma of lentils, onions, and aromatic mujaddara. Keeping her head and face downcast, she observed several men who looked like farm workers—yet their AK-47s were close at hand. They were eyeing her with a vicious hostility. She shuddered. Recognising Mohammed, they looked away and continued their vigilance.

"Follow me," he ordered, leading her away from the street through a series of corrugated iron and straw-lattice-shaded passageways to an open courtyard. To her practised eyes, it looked very much like the kind of obscure place where al-Amin was likely to sojourn. The insurgents had done a thorough job of sanitising the village, she noted. Probably without any need for bloodshed. Years earlier, ISIS had been effective in weeding out regime supporters and enemy agents in the region. The few remaining villagers, pastoral people raising sheep and goats, would be compliant.

Mohammed had gone ahead, calling to his men. Nazih emerged from a doorway, bringing the youthful, now heavily bearded, Yussef with him. "You see," said Mohammed, turning to Daniela with a sneer. "We confront you with your past. Now you cannot lie to us."

Yussef and she looked at each other in surprise. She recovered more quickly than the boy. "Yussef." She smiled and went forward to embrace him. "You have escaped the Russians. Do you have news of Jamal?" She hugged him, wrapping her arms around his waist—not wanting to let go. It was a very Western gesture, and he pulled away in a mix of embarrassment and resentment.

"You will see Jamal soon enough," said Mohammed. He grabbed her elbow and pushed her in the direction of a thick-walled brick building, leaving her in the care of three local women and two male guards. He kept hold of her travel bag—including the gold ingot.

She'd been lucky to meet Yussef, she thought, although not surprised. She'd anticipated it. By now, they would know the full story of Barcelona from him. It would authenticate everything she'd told them—especially about the money. She wasn't worried about the negative things he'd say about her. He'd been convinced long ago that she couldn't be trusted. The information that she was "clean" would have been provided to Jamal and al-Amin. For now, seeing Jamal was all she wanted. How he responded to her arrival would tell her a lot about the kind of reception she would receive. His behaviour would be a vital indicator.

The women took her to a room where a bath had been prepared. It seemed incongruous in its rough rural setting—almost like a spa. Too luxurious, actually. A lot of effort had been expended and she wondered why. Obviously, it was for her. Was she about to meet al-Amin, she wondered? Did he have a fetish about cleanliness? She was glad to get out of the travelling clothes that her double had provided. They smelled of camel, and diesel from the wrecked tank. As she bathed in the pleasant water, scented with jasmine and other aromatic fragrances, she felt like a concubine being prepared for her first encounter with her master. The water released her tension; she rehearsed in her mind the events she thought might unfold.

Dressing, her fresh clothes felt good. They were traditional and local—making sure she would fit in easily among the village women. She'd wondered about them. In Pakistan, bin Laden had often worn Saudi clothes and perhaps al-Amin now favoured them too. Yet, if al-Amin dressed the same way, it might seem to the local people like an uncompromising stamp of imperialism—the uniform of the Saudi Kingdom's ruling class reinforcing their dominance over the region. She wondered momentarily how the villagers felt about it.

Taken to a separate room, she saw that it was unfurnished and resembled a reception area. Its windows were shuttered, but the sun shone strongly, providing abundant natural light. Soon, she heard footsteps and the sound of a metal cane outside. Jamal stood in the doorway.

His smile told her everything she needed to know. She knew at that instant that her cover had not been blown. He was alone. Even so, she was cautious and traditional in her greeting. Bowing down and partly uncovering her face, she returned his smile. She'd immediately understood that he required a formal encounter. His words might not be affectionate, she thought, but the warmth in his eyes betrayed his joy.

"How was your journey?" he asked politely, his eyes sparkling with goodwill and humour.

She shrugged and placed her hand over her heart. "*As-salamu alaykum*. You look younger, Jamal. I hope the world is treating you well."

"He wants to see you," said Jamal to her surprise. "It is a great honour." His eyes swept over her, as if vetting her for an audience. "Yes, you look good." He paused. "There is one thing." He touched the side of his left eye. "Since childhood, he has had esotropia. Ignore it. Look only at his right eye, please; it will be less uncomfortable for him."

There was a scuffle of footsteps, and a formally dressed young man entered the room. Thrust inside a thick belt wrapped around his robe, he had a Longslide Glock. Jamal made the introductions. "This is Hasan," he said simply; his voice was edged with caution.

"I, myself, was at the Sorbonne," said Hasan, ignoring Jamal. "INSEAD," he added, obviously anxious to impress.

"An excellent school," she said, injecting as much admiration as she could into her voice.

"I have visited Barcelona several times, in fact," he continued. "Gaudi, for me, was difficult. I could not understand why he would permit such an extended period of construction at the Sagrada Familia."

Daniela had little interest in his small talk. From Jamal's introduction, she sensed that this young man—perhaps just a few years older than she—was influential with al-Amin. Instinctively, she doubted he would ever become an ally, but she certainly did not wish to make an enemy of him. He seemed attracted to her. She caught his lewd look—noting the information and thinking it might be useful later. With the image of her doppelganger at the hotel still strongly in her consciousness, she mimicked some of the woman's impressive haughtiness—edging it with subtle flirtation. Just a momentary flash of her eyes, certainly nothing that Jamal could observe. An insurance policy, just in case.

Breathing in sharply, she cast her eyes towards to the floor and obediently followed them along a narrow path until they reached a cinder-block building. It was guarded by several heavily armed wild-looking men. Glaring at her, they did not disguise their disapproval and loathing. One stopped her and searched her. He was clumsy and intrusive.

Her heart rate increased as she stepped inside the building; she could feel her chest pumping. She hadn't expected this. Not so soon. Yet, it was the moment she'd thought about for so long—her first sight of al-Amin, the new leader of al-Qaeda. She had to peer hard into the darkened room to see him. He sat on a chair behind a makeshift table, not looking up as they entered. It gave a hierarchical feeling to what was about to unfold, she thought. Keeping her head bowed low, she was able to scrutinise him. He, too, was dressed as a villager. Her overwhelming thought was that she must confirm his identity. Was he al-Amin . . . or an imposter? A stand-in surrogate with orders to converse with the infidel jihadi? Was it a test, a trick? Was this really Rashid al-Muhasib . . . al-Amin . . . the Accountant?

Rapidly, she ran through her profiling: Early fifties—yes, that seemed about right, although, as she'd expected, his sedentary lifestyle and grey-streaked heavy beard made him look older. Glasses necessary after years in front of a computer? Yes—but many at his age wore them. Despite her confident reassurances to Colonel Scott, their profiling hadn't actually yielded much that could help her. The man behind the desk had left-eye esotropia. It confirmed what Jamal had told her months ago in Latakia. She couldn't confirm the height of the seated figure, but he didn't appear tall. There were other ways to authenticate his identity. If this was an act—an elaborate ruse being staged for her benefit—the attitudes and behaviour of his men towards him could reveal a lot. One of the CIA's profiling conclusions had caught her attention and impressed her—a stand-in actor would never command the same respect or deference as the real person.

Daniela thought that, ultimately, his physical characteristics were of limited help in identifying him. She'd only be able to confirm that he was their target by playing mental games—evoking a response that would reveal his fascination with numbers. Nearly everything depended on that. Without validation, she could not be certain that the man sitting behind the desk was whom Jamal was claiming. She would have to watch carefully. Mental games would intrigue him and help corroborate his identity. Would al-Qaeda be that clever—deceitful enough to play such an elaborate game? Yes, they would, she'd concluded without hesitation. Al-Amin had spent his whole adult life covering his tracks, giving away no clues to his identity—providing nothing that would allow him to be tracked. Absolutely nothing.

At that moment, he looked up and stared directly at her. In front of him, on the table, was the gold ingot that Mohammed had confiscated when they reached the village. Al-Amin spoke. His voice was low: unmistakably cultured and calm. His attitude to her was surprisingly courteous, enquiring after her health and asking if she was tired after her long journey—traditional Middle-Eastern courtesy to travellers, she noted. She recognised his accent as that of a well-educated Saudi, but it contained other linguistic nuances at which she could only guess. Perhaps a little Urdu, from his time in Pakistan?

At that moment, he clapped his hands, calling for tea. She knew he would not speak of business matters until afterwards. As a woman, she would be expected to remain silent until spoken to. Sneaking a glance at his two bodyguards, she noted their alertness. Five other people were in the room, each heavily armed, and several additional guards outside.

Minutes later, there was a shuffling of sandalled feet at the door. A young boy in threadbare attire, evidently the child of a villager, was permitted into the room. Unsteadily, he carried his tray of tea. He was short and had an awkward gait, almost bowlegged, she observed. He stopped, and Jamal indicated with his metal cane where the boy should first serve the tea. Grinning a vacant smile, blissfully unaware of established protocols, the village boy first served the leader. With shaking hands, he placed tea in front of the others. Standing with his empty tray, he waited to collect the empty glasses. Discreetly, Jamal whispered his thanks, pointing to the door.

They drank in silence.

"You have brought us the money?" asked Hasan eventually.

She nodded. "Yes, sir." She paused. "There are two parts to the transfer. The bearer bonds are secured in a safety deposit box in Cyprus—at a bank in Nicosia. They can be recovered at any time. I will provide the passcode. The gold remains hidden in Spain. I will need assistance to move it. The Cyprus bank authorities have no idea of the contents of the safety deposit box, or the value of the bonds," she continued confidently. "I opened the account posing as a tourist. There is only one other item there of any interest."

This caught Hasan's attention, and she described the cheap street painting she'd bought—ostensibly for her father. Although she relayed the story in detail to Hasan, her eyes watched keenly for a reaction from al-Amin. If he was impressed by her resourcefulness, he didn't reveal it.

Hasan had several questions about how she had been able to convert the banknotes stolen from the general and chauffeur. She noticed that al-Amin was paying close attention—especially to the deal she had done with the Bank of Tarragona—laundering the funds. Hasan grilled her several times about Yussef. "He was with you in Cyprus. You did not tell him about this safety deposit box?" he asked. "Did you share the passcode with him—as a precaution—in case you were killed?"

"Would you trust a young boy with such information?" she protested, allowing her voice to rise. "The money belongs to the jihad, not to a mere teenager. Besides, I do not completely trust him." She didn't care about Yussef. She thought she saw a flicker of respect cross al-Amin's face . . . or was it just imagined?

"But in Latakia you were reunited with Jamal," pursued Hasan. "You trust him. Why did you not give *him* the passcode? Why have you waited until now to deliver it to us?"

"Jamal and I were captives of the Russians," said Daniela. "He was a prisoner of war—a highly prized detainee. In the fighting—before he was captured—their soldiers tried to kill him many times. I was there with him, at his camps and in al-Raqqah. In Russian hands, Jamal did not know what fate awaited him. I told him about the money, how much it was, and where it was being hidden. Jamal knew the importance of complete secrecy. He instructed me to arrange delivery to the jihad."

"But you had given Jamal the hawala passcodes before—as a courier from Mustapha. Did you not trust him any longer? Is there some other reason why you have waited until now—until you have a chance to be in the presence of the emir?" provoked Hasan. His face was etched in mockery, his mouth distorted in contempt.

Daniela reply was confident and clear. "Sir, we are no longer dealing with small hawala transfers. The money I stole is a fortune, and I am a trusted courier. I ask you: If you had the opportunity to deliver it personally to the cause—to pledge your allegiance to those who will strike at the heart of the corrupted West, would you not do so? This much I have said many times already to Jamal. I wish to serve the holy jihad. Whatever small talents I have, I offer them to the service of God."

Hasan was now standing behind the desk, speaking quietly in his master's ear. Then he looked up at Daniela. "He wants you to describe the bearer bonds."

She gave a slight bow to the leader. "They are drawn in euros on the Bank of Tarragona—a reputable bank in Spain. I have each of the series numbers memorised. Their face value is six hundred and fifty-three million euros."

"So, about six hundred and fifty million," interrupted Hasan impatiently. Clearly, he was anxious to continue his questioning.

"No!" snapped Daniela. "Six hundred and fifty-three million." Her raised voice startled some of the men in the room. "Exactly that amount," she added more softly, observing that Hasan was angry at her contradiction. Going through her head was the thought that if the man behind the table really was al-Amin, he would not have missed the significance. "I thought it was a good omen," she added.

Hasan glanced at the leader, as if for guidance. She was encouraged to see the slight circling motion of al-Amin's fingers—instructing his young assistant to keep pressing the point.

"A good omen?" Hasan asked uncertainly.

"Yes, the date of the transaction was important too. I wanted it to be supportive of the jihad. Good numbers, not unlucky ones," she said with confidence. "Six hundred and fifty-three," she repeated.

As Hasan looked again for guidance, she saw the leader frown at him impatiently.

"It's a prime number," explained Daniela with feigned exasperation. "Everything we do, *inshallah*, has a purpose to it." Her voice rose with the conviction of a zealot. "The times we pray each day, the dates of our religious observances, the days we choose to strike into the hearts of the foreign infidels—they are proclaimed for us. Yes, I thought the value of the bearer bonds was a good omen." She looked at al-Amin. "Emir, any sequence of numbers that does not form a prime number, you will see immediately that they are fake. They must work together to create a prime number. Here is the safety deposit passcode." She took a step forward, offering a folded piece of paper to him.

Hasan strode forward to take it.

"Give it to me," said al-Amin, accepting it from her and immediately placing it inside his robe.

In mid-stride, Hasan stopped.

He looked uncertainly at the leader, and Daniela could see fear in his eyes. The man behind the desk had spoken with the absolute authority of a battle commander. She was certain now. There was no doubt that he was the supreme leader: Rashid al-Muhasib . . . al-Amin.

Tension in the room had risen. It was not only Hasan who was terrified. Daniela could sense their collective fear. It seemed to seep through the pores of every man in the room. Hardly daring to breathe, they awaited al-Amin's next command. Daniela lowered her head to avoid the searing heat of Hasan's resentful glare. She knew she had made a mortal enemy. Hasan had been humiliated; she knew he would never forgive her.

Moments later, al-Amin called Hasan to his side and they consulted briefly. "He wants to know more about the gold," said Hasan, almost spitting his words at her.

Taking a deep breath, she described in detail how she and Yussef had stolen the stash and why they kept the banknotes separate from the gold. In detail, she told Hasan how they'd transported the bullion to the cottage and hidden it in the old man's garage. After a few questions from Hasan, al-Amin seemed to be satisfied with her explanation. Daniela knew that everything she had told them would have been confirmed earlier by Yussef.

"Before leaving Spain on my recent journey," she continued, "I tried to contact the people whose names Jamal had given me to contact. There was a manhunt underway for me, and maybe for them too. Despite my efforts, they failed to reply. I have been worried that we might have been betrayed—that is why I have not trusted many people. About the gold, you need not worry. The boy Yussef knows where it is hidden; he can guide you to it. But do not trust him alone, Emir."

Dreading Hasan's next question, Daniela became aware of a sudden pause in the proceedings and the shuffling of feet. She had lost track of time. It was the call to prayers. It meant that the meeting would be postponed until later. Hasan shouted out his orders.

Under triple guard, Daniela was pushed from the building like a common criminal.

Noor and Sattam

Thirty, or maybe closer to forty, Noor was plump and no longer regarded as pretty. It was hard to guess her age from the heavy clothing she wore inside the house to keep warm on cold desert nights. A yashmak constantly hid her face.

Among the few relatives of her husband's family with whom she begrudgingly was still permitted to meet, her presence was regarded as gloomy; her dark eyes, brooding; her body odour, dank and unpleasant. Only rarely did she take off her headwear, even to sleep. It was as if she wanted to repulse any approaches, to repel any attempts at close friendship—wishing, instead, to be inconsequential, pious, and penitent. Yet, she was a prudent housekeeper and fiercely loyal to her family. She loved her husband and their two sons.

Omar was pleased that his wife was reverent, never missing prayers—not once. He was content that she was abstemious, contrite, and humble; that she often chose to go without food, voluntarily fasting for days on end. A fighter and an expert marksman for the jihad, Omar was used to deprivation; it was their way of life. Their older son had followed in his footsteps, but they hadn't heard any news of him for many months. He was at Idlib, fighting near the Turkish border.

When she was seventeen, Noor was married to Omar. It was an arranged marriage. He was the son of her uncle; he was also her cousin.

Unlike Noor, their younger son, Sattam, was outgoing and loved to be in the company of others. He smiled gregariously; he spoke to everyone. It was mostly nonsense—his brain had not developed normally. He was a teenager but looked half his age.

It was late morning. Sattam trod carefully as he balanced a tray of fresh hot apple tea. His pink tongue stuck out the side of his mouth as he strained with concentration. He knew it was wrong to spill the drinks and was proud of his skill. Arriving at his destination, he saw that the men were speaking loudly to each other—almost arguing. He gritted his teeth, for he was almost at their table. He had done his job. He could be proud; he was one of them.

Most of them ignored him as he offered tea from his tray, one unsteady glass after the other. Al-Amin looked at the boy and felt sympathy. Since his group's arrival several days ago, he had become fond of Sattam. He smiled. Sattam was overjoyed. He understood little of the wars taking place, but he knew that al-Amin was their leader. Al-Amin was a hero. Sattam grinned back at him, but al-Amin had already looked away. Gazing at their semi-automatics propped against the wall, Sattam wished he could have a more important job, like his father.

Lingering by the door, he tried to think. He had served the tea. What next? He had forgotten already. His mother had given him an instruction, if he could just remember. No one in the room was paying any attention to him. His head listing to one side, resting on his shoulder, he tried to think. It was about the tea, he recalled. What was he told? Then he remembered. "Let them drink their tea," she'd told him. "Later, go back for their empty glasses. They are important people; they must have time to talk." Grinning to the men who did not see him, he turned and left the room. He had served them well.

Holding the empty metal tray by its ornate long stem, he shuffled his way back home—to his mother's side.

In her room, Daniela went through the motions of praying. She knew they would be watching—the women attending her would report every detail. The recent pause in questioning brought relief. She was still overcoming her surprise: she had not expected to meet al-Amin so soon after her arrival.

For her, the meeting had been vital to confirm that the man was the new leader. It could have been a set-up. Now she was sure. he was Rashid al-Muhasib—he was al-Amin. Wishing that Jamal would come back to see her, she realised it might not be appropriate. It would be reported and could compromise him. Even so, it would help if they could talk—if only for a few minutes. Deep undercover, out of contact, waiting for morsels of information from other people, had been stressful—even for her. She sat on the carpeted floor and exercised hard for several minutes. Then she repeated the moves, with deep breathing exercises.

There was a tapping sound on the door. The eldest of the three attending women opened it, allowing the tea boy to enter. Nervously, he moved towards Daniela and looked to the older woman for guidance. "On the table, Sattam," the woman instructed kindly. He placed the tea and stood staring at Daniela. He seemed mesmerised by her—spellbound. She was so beautiful.

"Thank you, Sattam." She smiled before the boy was ushered from the room.

Half an hour later, food was served to her by the women. "Rest," they instructed. Her dishes taken away, Daniela decided to take their advice and undressed to sleep.

Moments later, there was a confident knock on the door and it opened slowly. "Jamal," she called excitedly, jumping up to greet him. She stopped in her tracks.

"Hasan!" she exclaimed.

From the look on his face, he clearly was not there with any good intentions. He pushed her back against the wall.

"No," she protested. "Don't do this. I don't want you to." His face was flushed; he seemed determined to take her. "Stop it!" she shouted. Then he hit her. It hurt. She tasted blood in her mouth.

"I want that bank passcode," he hissed in her ear. She refused. "Give it to me," he said, twisting her arm. The pain was unbearable, but again, she refused. "Western jihadis belong to us," he said, beginning to rip off her clothes. "You serve the jihad; you serve us." She tried to knee his testicles, but he anticipated her move and protected himself. Now he had hold of both wrists—his superior strength preventing her from hitting out. His free hand was pulling at her underclothes. Twisting, she tried to gain a tactical advantage, without success. Hoping the noise would attract the attention of the women, she realised there would be no help—they were scared of his status and his power. Nothing would be said.

There was no alternative but to fight dirty. She headbutted him. As he lifted his arm, she bit his wrist. It was a monster of a bite—like the jaws of a shark. He yelled with pain. She kicked out, and he kicked back. Then he got hold of her hair, slamming her head against the brick wall. The impact stunned her and she cried out—searching with her free hand, attempting to claw her fingers into his eyes. His masculine determination was difficult to overcome, but she could try to even the odds.

Daniela was losing the battle. Hasan's strong fingers were around her neck, choking the breath from her body. Feeling lightheaded, she began to drift away. Her brain was not receiving the oxygen it so desperately needed. Her muscles relaxed, and she could no longer resist. One by one, her systems were shutting down: all with one final last-gasp objective—to keep her brain alive. There was no longer any pain. She felt relaxed and ready to go. It was over.

She moved in and out of the death zone. She didn't know it, but the assault had stopped. Blood oozing from her mouth and her lungs gasping for breath, she saw that Hasan was lying on the floor. Over him crouched Jamal, his eyes black with fury—handgun pressed hard into the young man's forehead. He was yelling words she had never heard before. Hasan was on his back. Like a trapped crab, his legs were clawing desperately to get away—begging for his life.

"No, Jamal!" she tried to shout, but there was no sound. She watched him stagger backwards. His left leg—no longer supported by his metal cane—finally gave out. Other people were entering the room. She felt herself being dragged from the floor by the guards. Slammed against the wall, her arms were pinioned behind her. There was a loud bang. Al-Amin was standing in the doorway, his gun pointing at her. He had shot over her head; it was a warning.

"So, this is the evil you bring to us?" he barked at her. "Lock her up," he ordered the guards.

"You two." He glared at Hasan and Jamal.

"Come with me."

Daniela wasn't locked up.

She was imprisoned in her room. With ferocious-looking armed guards posted at the door and others outside the window, no cell of confinement could have been more secure at that moment. She knew that if she took a single false step, they would gladly shoot her.

Sometime later, one of the guards opened the door. Jamal was standing there, looking tired and defeated, she thought. Entering the room, he looked with concern at her bloodied and bruised mouth and swollen neck. "Tell me where you are hurt," he said gently, placing several bandages on the table. Glancing past him, Daniela could see that the guard was standing feet astride across the open doorway, his semi-automatic pointing directly at Jamal and her.

"Thank you," she said politely to Jamal, hurriedly covering her face. "I think I've twisted my ankle too. It is difficult to walk."

Examining her foot, he asked where it hurt. "Possibly a muscle strain, nothing broken," he said brusquely—for the benefit of the guard. "Exercise it. That is the best way."

"It hurts, though," she said, wincing. "Could you leave that bandage for me, please—in case it gets worse?" Her eyes darted repeatedly over at the table. It was a signal to him.

"No, you do not need it," Jamal said harshly—again for the benefit of the guard. But as he collected his supplies, she felt him press the cotton roll into her lap. He stood up, his face stiff and resolute. "They want to kill you, Daniela," he said loudly. "The passcode you gave al-Amin for the money in Cyprus—if they do not receive it, they will execute you. I am sorry, but it is the way of our country."

He paused and took a laboured breath. "I can guarantee nothing any longer—both of us are being denounced as spies. Hasan is evil. *Inshallah*, the bank passcode you gave us is not a trick you are playing, Daniela."

"Hasan has the fury of the devil."

Latakia, Syria

At the Khmeimim Air Base, Alexei was deep in conversation with his senior officer.

Hours earlier, on Moscow's instructions, a series of high-resolution aerial photos had been taken by a latest generation VKS-controlled military satellite and relayed to its Russian Aerospace Forces' Tu-214R reconnaissance aircraft flying over the eastern area. Its flight path had been revised at the last minute. The photos and linked ground stations' intel were not shared with Syrian authorities.

"Our ground-tracking confirms the arrival of al-Amin at a location here," said Alexei, pointing to a village in north-east Syria. "Meanwhile, the American Navy SEALs are assembling here." He tapped sharply at al-Tanf on the three-dimensional relief map spread across the desk. In addition, they have an aircraft carrier on manoeuvres in the Gulf, just here."

"Their raid is imminent?" asked the superior office, rhetorically.

"No orders yet from Moscow?" asked Alexei. He was met by a shrug. "Our ground forces can send in a low-level drone," he continued. "It will give us more detail of the village."

"Without authorisation from Moscow?" asked the senior man. "It's too risky, yet I think you're right, comrade. Very well, I will authorise it. My instinct tells me that sitting on the sidelines at this time would be a big mistake. If they fail to intercept the courier, Moscow will not be pleased.

"Inform Control immediately that we believe the transfer of the Cyprus money is already in play."

Cyprus

It was a fortunate coincidence that the young manager of the Cyprus bank, who many months earlier had opened the account for Daniela, was working that day.

A middle-aged female teller nervously approached his desk. Would he be available to talk to a customer and her husband? she asked politely. She hadn't worked at the bank for long and was struggling to master English. She'd been hired to deal with the recent influx of new customers from Syria. Most were impoverished refugees, but several had departed the country with substantial amounts of wealth. The bank did not want to turn away their business.

"What does she want?" he snapped, his authoritative tone reinforcing his senior status.

"She wants to have access to a safety deposit box," replied the teller meekly.

"So?"

"She and her husband have the correct information." The teller handed him a letter. "It mentions your name, sir."

He examined it. The teller was right; it was addressed to the bank and it did mention his name. It also named the friend and gave the bank permission to allow her access to the safety deposit box. Would he facilitate that, please? The letter was signed Susan Garcia.

He recognised the customer's name at once. He remembered her coming into the bank and opening an account. She was very good-looking young woman; quite stunning, in fact. He'd thought about her several times since, but she hadn't returned to the branch. Her parents were American, he recalled. She was paying extra fees each month for a premium safety deposit box. He recalled being amused when she'd shown him the cheap street painting she'd wanted to keep in it.

He also knew that an attempt had been made that morning to obtain access to her safety deposit box. A man, who was not a customer of the bank, had presented what appeared to be adequate documentation to the teller. But he'd had the wrong passcode. For months, the account had been flagged by the authorities. Internal alarms were triggered. The police had been called—but the man had already left the building and disappeared. Within minutes, the bank was filled with British Army Special Forces. They had seized the video tapes from the bank's security system, and the manager had been told to resume normal business—and warn his staff to stay alert for another withdrawal attempt.

"I'll handle the customer," the young manager instructed the teller.

"How can I help?" he asked the young female, forcing her to explain her request again. She was about the same age as Susan Garcia, he noted—and, by extraction, probably also Spanish. Her husband smiled and nodded an excessively reassuring greeting. The woman spoke English well and her explanation for requesting access to the safety deposit box seemed plausible. Her friend Susan had returned to the States; she needed some papers to be sent to her.

"You wish to draw money from the deposit account—to withdraw cash?" he probed.

The young woman shook her head vigorously. No, she assured him. Susan just needed some papers from the safety deposit box to be sent back to her. It was all explained in the letter she'd signed. And Susan had attached a photocopy of her driver's licence and passport for identification purposes. The young manager glanced at her husband. Despite his wide-eyed collegial smile, the man seemed nervous, he thought. He'd noticed, too, that when she'd finished speaking, the young woman had looked again at the man, as if for confirmation.

"I'll just have to check this against the signature and identification we have on record." He smiled expansively at the couple. "Please take a seat. Would you care for coffee? I'll just be a few minutes." Leaving a seasoned clerk to look after them, he went immediately to the senior manager's office. The senior manager alerted the British authorities. Connecting quickly with an operator, he explained his concerns.

He was kept on the line for less than twenty-seconds before a cultured English voice identified himself as a member of the security services. "Thank you for your initiative in calling us, sir. The transaction is perfectly legitimate. Please allow them access to the safety deposit box. We'd prefer you didn't delay the couple any longer. Here's my phone number if the bank requires a record of the authorisation."

Ten minutes later, the couple left the bank with a compact leather travel bag containing the bearer bonds that Daniela had deposited many months earlier. They were worth six hundred and fifty-three million euros, payable on a reliable and well-established bank in Spain—convertible into cash anywhere in the world, in any currency.

The couple knew they were being tailed by their al-Qaeda handler. They'd been ordered to carry out a "brush past" handover to him at a prearranged place near the central bus station. The nervous handler was under surveillance from his own people—and by several MI6 officers already at the scene. The Brits had been given a terse instruction by Langley: "Follow and observe: do not intercept."

It was a well-planned and executed operation, by both sides. For the Brits, physical recovery of the bearer bonds could come later. Much more vital was the destination of the coded signal sent soon afterwards by the couples' handler—to north-east Syria. It was tracked by Langley's eyes in the sky. Now they had a precise fix on the village, and al-Amin's location.

Not long later, al-Amin would be informed that the withdrawal in Cyprus had been made successfully.

Daniela had kept her word.

Separately, in the midday shadows, at a café not far from the bank, another interested party had been observing events.

For weeks, the man—dressed as a tour guide—had been monitoring activities at the bank. His orders were to wait for a phone call from a bank employee alerting him to a withdrawal from a particular safety deposit box. Nearby, his well-trained snatch squad was ready to carry out a diversionary tactic and retrieve the package. After no action for weeks, it had been an eventful day. Earlier, he'd received a warning call and minutes later witnessed the arrival of a unit of heavily armed British Army Special Forces. He'd ordered his squad to stand down—but remain in position. They didn't have long to wait.

He received a second call with a description of the couple who, at that moment, were exiting the bank. His experienced eye confirmed that they were being followed. He decided that his snatch attempt was a no go and ordered immediate dispersal of his squad. It was regrettable, but in Moscow, his naturally cautious nature had kept him out of trouble many times. Satisfied that he had followed his orders to the letter, the man picked up his shopping bags and pulled his wide-brimmed straw hat down to shelter his eyes from the glare of the midday Cyprus sun.

At a leisurely pace, he walked away from the area.

Inside the bank, the meek middle-aged immigrant teller had overheard the conversation between the couple and the manager. Momentarily closing her service window, she hovered in the vicinity and scribbled some notes of the withdrawal. Hurrying home at the end of her shift, she informed her husband. For most of the time, the lazy, do-nothing man lounged about their low-rent apartment, constantly drinking. After their escape as refugees from Syria, he'd come to enjoy his new life. The money his wife earned was far more than he'd ever been able to provide or had any desire to contribute to the household.

"They told us to report everything about that safety deposit-box account," his wife protested after he'd told her to forget the incident. The man wouldn't listen. "What have I told you, woman?" he yelled. "Stay away from these things; they can only bring trouble."

Undeterred, she glanced again at the names and information she'd written down. They might mean nothing. Perhaps her husband was right. The recent memory of the wars in Syria were still foremost in her mind. She didn't want to go back there—not until a lasting peace had been achieved. Europe was their home, for now. Yet, with close family in Syria, she was terrified what the vengeful regime might do to them. Clearing away the dishes from their meal, she saw that her intoxicated husband had already fallen asleep. Leaving their apartment, she walked to an address not far away. They'd been given it, along with certain instructions, not long after they'd arrived from Damascus. The woman answering the door admitted her to a small side room. Ten minutes later, a man arrived and was ushered in immediately.

She sounded apologetic as she explained what had happened. "They told us to report everything," she explained, handing over the information. The man shrugged and asked several other questions. He seemed indifferent; yet he, too, knew better than to ignore it.

The intelligence was transmitted later that evening along with several other routine reports generated that day by his network of refugee informants across Cyprus. When it arrived at the Idarat al-Mukhabarat al-Amma—the General Intelligence Directorate in Damascus—it was routinely run through a keyword screening process. The name Susan Garcia immediately sounded an alarm. A night clerk alerted his superior.

There were people in Damascus who were far from indifferent about the information that had been received from Cyprus. Within hours, an agent woke up the bank teller and her hungover husband. She was subjected to an intense grilling before the agent was satisfied. "I told her she had to report it," said her husband as he shuffled behind the departing agent. "I had a feeling it was important, sir."

Hesitating at the still closed apartment door, the agent took a handgun from an inside pocket and brandished it in the man's face. "Say anything about this to anyone, and you're both dead. Understand?" The husband's terrified eyes told him he need not worry. Glancing down, the agent saw confirmation on the man's trousers.

The panic-stricken man had wetted himself.

The Spy

Hasan summoned her.

There was no indication on his face of their previous encounter. "Come, Daniela," he said in a reassuring cosmopolitan voice. "There is something I want you to see. We have caught a spy of the regime—a Mukhabarat agent. The villagers reported him to us. He has been tried. Let us go and learn his fate."

The guards pushed her roughly towards the central square, where she saw the convicted man. He had lost all hope and showed no resistance. His life was already over, except for the terror of the execution. Several chairs had been set out for spectators. Hasan directed her to the front row, seating her next to him. Jamal, leaning awkwardly on his walking stick, was already seated on the other side of her. Behind them, the villagers occupied the next best seats. Less than a metre away, the spy knelt on the ground—hands tied roughly behind his back. His robe was peeled back from his neck, as if he were about to receive a long overdue haircut.

Above him, his stern-faced executioner stood feet astride.

"Sharia Law," said Hasan into her ear. "He has been given a trial and found guilty. The verdict for a spy is death. You understand, Daniela? Do you understand?" he repeated.

She nodded.

"We have not yet received confirmation that the Cyprus money has been received," he lied. "Is there anything you wish to tell us?"

Her face was white, and she was trembling—but she managed a brave reply. "The money is there. You will receive it, I promise."

"I hope so."

Hasan nodded to the executioner.

Daniela wanted to close her eyes, but Hasan leaned over and squeezed her neck between his fingers until it hurt. She witnessed the executioner acknowledge Hasan's signal. Slowly, as if in an elaborately choreographed ceremony, the butcher grasped hold of the prisoner's scalp and pulled it backwards. With a sweep of his arm, the long-curved blade sliced easily and deeply across the man's throat—through his neck muscles to his spinal column, severing head from body. The executioner held the blood-dripping head high—for all to see.

As the headless corpse fell forwards, she heard a dull thump as it hit the ground. A splatter of warm blood splashed her face. Mouth open wide, her eyes in a daze, she was aware that the spy's body was being dragged away. It would be buried quickly—before the flies and the regime troops found it. Blood on the ground would be washed away by villagers. They did not want the evidence of a traitor to stain their land.

"It is his warning to us all," Jamal whispered hoarsely in her ear. "Hasan wants to demonstrate al-Amin's power—to show that he controls us."

Escorted back to her quarters, Daniela grabbed a metal basin and threw up.

CHAPTER 9
O'Flaherty

News that al-Amin's agents in Cyprus had collected the bearer bonds from the bank quickly reached O'Flaherty.

It was incredibly vital information and confirmed some essential operational details. Most importantly, the bait had been swallowed. Daniela was their only field agent in a position to identify al-Amin. No one else had been able to get anywhere close to him. By providing the new supreme leader with the correct password, Daniela was signalling a positive ID.

The American knew it would take at least twelve hours for the bearer bonds to clear the system. Langley had figured that al-Qaeda's agents would use a Dubai financial clearing house to cash the bonds. That didn't give him much time, but at least he now knew exactly where al-Amin was located—and so, too, did Langley's drones. There was just one more step—he had to get to the village and direct the raid from ground zero.

He could be there in two hours.

For several days, the aircraft carrier Abraham Lincoln had been on manoeuvres off the coast of Tel Aviv. Aboard the vessel, Falcon Squadron was poised on high alert. After the withdrawal of the bearer bonds had been confirmed, the squadron was ordered airborne within minutes. Crossing safe Israeli airspace, flying high over the West Bank, they travelled the normal Coalition Forces permitted route to al-Tanf through Jordanian airspace—arousing no suspicions. There, the squadron would await further orders. When O'Flaherty was able to transmit the final encrypted signal, all hell would let loose. The squadron's heavily armed combat Super Hueys would launch rapidly to the target site.

It would be an identical raid to the one at Abbottabad in 2011, but in daylight. Back then, on orders issued from the control centre at the White House, the mission commander had ordered that Osama bin Laden be taken alive. Contrary to US military—and subsequent tabloid—reports of his death at the compound, the al-Qaeda leader actually had been captured alive. He had not been shot dead as was reported to the global media. The body reported as being disposed of later in the Persian Gulf actually was a deception. Langley knew the value of capturing the extremist commander-in-chief alive. The strategic intelligence his interrogation yielded over the following months had priceless value. In the same way, it was predicted, al-Amin's capture and interrogation also would yield vital intel.

The current occupant of the Oval Office regarded himself as the ultimate warrior. Falcon Squadron's orders from the commander-in-chief were unequivocal.

"Bring back al-Amin alive.

"This won't be fake news," he bragged.

The stolen Syrian Army truck that O'Flaherty drove into the village was loaded with goodies. It was a gift for Nazih and his men—although they did not know that, in reality, it was courtesy of a commando raid carried out days earlier by a platoon of British Special Forces.

Sentries on the approach road to the village recognised the red-haired infidel from the daring raids they'd made together at al-Yarubiyah. They grinned as they examined his latest acquisitions for the cause. Adhering to standing orders, they radioed ahead. O'Flaherty was approved to proceed. His safe passage did not last long. Pulling the truck to a stop near the village square, O'Flaherty was met by a hostile cadre of former comrades—led by Hasan. He was taken straight to a building where a sizeable group was assembled. Daniela was already there, sitting on a bench at the side of the room. She didn't look at him.

He saw that Yussef and Ahmed were there and realised that the two brothers had been reunited at last. Hasan was strutting like a victorious overlord, alternately brandishing his long-barrelled Glock, then stuffing it back into the thick belt of his gown. O'Flaherty saw that Hasan seemed to have the full support of a man behind the desk—whom he assumed to be al-Amin. A subtle nod from Daniela confirmed his guess. It was what he needed to know, and he looked away quickly. Scanning the room, he tried to figure out what was taking place. He saw Nazih, but his friend ignored him. That wasn't good, O'Flaherty thought. Hasan seemed to have succeeded in setting the room against him. Then something unexpected happened.

Daniela leapt to her feet. With a face that displayed fanatical hatred, she attacked O'Flaherty—beating her hands against his chest and face. He stepped back in shocked surprise. "He's a spy," she yelled. "He's an American spy." Guards quickly separated them, but she continued her vitriolic verbal attack. "Jamal, don't trust him," she shouted. "He's the one who helped me escape from Kirkuk. He's with the CIA, I'm sure of it."

Several loud arguments broke out around the room. There were some who regarded the red-haired jihadi as a hero, and others, like Hasan, who trusted nobody. Only al-Amin's personal intervention managed to quieten them—achieved by loudly banging the butt of his handgun on the table. Hasan conversed quietly with his boss.

Moments later, reverting to a courtroom lawyer's strut, he went to where the guards still pinned Daniela tightly by her arms. "Why do you accuse him?" he demanded. "How do we know that you are not a spy and denounce him to protect yourself?"

Daniela spat in the direction of O'Flaherty, glaring at him—but said nothing.

O'Flaherty was taken by surprise; he hadn't expected this turn of events. Daniela had planted the seed of doubt in everyone's mind about his loyalty to the cause. He swallowed hard. This was really risky. He realised she was deliberately feeding their imagination—firing up their emotions. Now each of them was mentally processing what they knew about him—questioning if the red-haired jihadist truly was on their side. It was a dangerous game she was playing, he thought; yet he said nothing, offering Hasan no words in his own defence. Tall and muscular, he stood his ground awkwardly—playing to his unscripted new role, glaring back at her with equal hatred.

"The Barcelona bombing—the attempt on the Mossos Headquarters. It failed!" Daniela continued. "The men sent to do the job were cowards." She levelled an accusing finger at Ahmed and Yussef. "They ran away. They took the money." She looked around the room, making eye contact with as many as possible. "Ahmed, the bomb expert who came to us from ISIS. How much money did he have in his possession when he returned to Syria? Lots of euros. You know it! Yussef, his brother"—she pointed at him—"he is working for the Americans too. These brothers want to make money from the holy war. Ask them if it is true. They are working together." Her dark eyes continued to blaze threateningly at O'Flaherty. "He's a CIA spy, setting a trap for our new leader. Search Ahmed and Yussef's possessions; see for yourselves," she continued to yell. "Ask them why their bombing attempt failed. I will tell you why," she spat. "Because they saw a chance to enjoy the pleasures of the corrupt West. They abandoned the jihad. They are betraying us."

Bedlam erupted throughout the room. Everyone was yelling. Insults were hurled at her. There were shouts for a search of the brothers' belongings. Once again, al-Amin demanded silence. "Search them and their possessions," ordered Hasan. "We will soon find out if this Western jihadi is lying." He scowled viciously at Daniela.

Hasan considered the evidence that the search had unearthed. A bundle of high denomination euros had been found among Ahmed's belongings; a scuffed well-used credit card had been found when they'd searched Yussef's clothes. It had been issued in his name by a bank in Damascus.

The brothers loudly protested their innocence. Hasan gave them both a chance to speak.

"It is part of the money I was given in Spain—that she gave me, to help me escape," shouted Ahmed.

"She is evil," protested Yussef, agreeing with his brother. "She must have slipped the credit card into the pocket of my robe when she first arrived. I swear that I have never seen it before."

Daniela watched as Hasan walked behind the table and spoke quietly to al-Amin—receiving a nod of assent. He took the gun that the leader slid across the table to him and approached Daniela. Challenging her, he pointed to O'Flaherty. "You have denounced him as a spy. Very well. Now you must kill him—and them also." He pointed to Ahmed and Yussef, then handed the gun to her.

Without hesitation, she grabbed it and levelled it at O'Flaherty's head, squeezing the trigger several times. There was no sound . . . except the rapid clicking of the firing pin into an empty chamber.

She had been tricked.

Seeing now that the magazine had been removed, she threw the gun to the ground with a stream of vicious swear words. Turning, she snatched the gun lodged in Hasan's corded belt. Taking aim again at O'Flaherty's forehead, she pulled the trigger without hesitation. But Hasan had been quick to recover. As she aimed at O'Flaherty, he grabbed her arm, reaching for the gun. It was too late. The explosion echoed throughout the room. Grazing the side of the American's head, the bullet buried itself in the roof. Blood streaming down his ear, O'Flaherty fell backwards—his tall frame crumpling heavily to the floor.

Hasan had wrenched the gun from Daniela hands. She seemed to have reverted to being a wild animal. Hunched forwards and fists up, like a kick-boxer circling her quarry, she lunged forward and kicked O'Flaherty's shoulder. She spat at the bleeding form on the floor, her saliva landing on his straggling red beard. "He's a spy. Kill him," she continued to yell.

An angry guard pointed his automatic at her head.

"No!" ordered al-Amin.

His single command was enough.

~~~

Hasan seemed elated.

"You are fortunate," he said to Daniela. "The money you promised has been received. Al-Amin now wishes to arrange shipment of the gold from Spain. All of it. Seven hundred and ninety-seven gold bars," he sneered. "Another good-omen number. Your precision intrigues him. He wishes to meet with you again—to hear your recommendations for the transfer. I will inform you when. In the meantime, enjoy the splendours of the desert—from your room.

"The red-haired infidel. You were not successful in killing him; your shooting skills are poor. He has a graze, nothing more. We will make sure you do not get such a chance again. You should leave war and weapons to the men. Your place is at home—in the bedroom."

Daniela was relieved but not surprised by the news. O'Flaherty had moved his head at the instant she'd squeezed the trigger aiming at the roof. For a terrible moment, she thought that the bullet might have hit him. Hasan's intervention had almost killed the American.

Her plan was still in place, but they would need a lot of luck.

214

Girl With a Vengeance

Sattam brought tea.

This time, Daniela had a chance to speak with him—even though he remained painfully shy. Out of earshot from the women, she praised him for being a great soldier. It made him smile. She was able to ask some questions about his family, and smiled frequently to relax and encourage him. He was slow to understand but happy and enthusiastic. The sparkling gemstone bracelet she was wearing seem to fascinate him. It was a cheap piece of costume jewellery—the type of thing a tourist might pick up in her travels. She'd received it from her doppelganger at the hotel.

"Will you do something for me?" she asked. "I'm hungry. I want a piece of fruit. Anything. But you must not tell anyone; it's just a secret between us," she added, giving him a wink.

He laughed.

"Sattam, you must hide it inside your gown—like this." She showed him. "You give it to me; then I will give this to you." She held out a small coin. He nodded but looked again at the bracelet on her wrist, and his fingers played with its bright colours and shiny glass shapes. It was what he really wanted—but she knew that already.

Ten minutes later, he was back. Closing the door behind him, he shuffled over to her. He took a lemon from underneath his gown, and his face lit up as she handed him the coin.

"Don't show it to anyone. Hide it. "It's our secret."

He nodded his understanding to the beautiful lady.

O'Flaherty was painfully aware of the bandage bound tightly around his head, above his ear.

He couldn't move to check it—Hasan had made sure he was tied up and tightly bound by tape to a chair. His wound was still seeping.

Although it felt a little better than it had earlier, he still had a throbbing headache. He'd been astonished when Daniela had attacked him. It was totally unexpected, and at first, he hadn't understood what she was trying to do. Only afterwards had he been able to figure it out. She was putting on a spectacular act for al-Amin's benefit.

That was Daniela. She liked to seize the initiative and control events. Whatever plans their captors had in store for them before he'd arrived, she had defined the agenda that followed. In the process, she'd shown herself to be a rabid zealot—willing to kill any infidel for the cause. It had been a masterful performance.

In retrospect, he thought, the empty gun must have been planned between Hasan and al-Amin as a test of her loyalty. Daniela couldn't have known—not for sure—that it had an empty magazine. Not until she grabbed it. Firing directly at him had been a calculated risk on her part. When she'd snatched the second gun, the test had nearly gone awry. If they'd had any concerns before about her loyalty to the jihad, he doubted that they still lingered after her second attack and attempt to kill him. He'd been convinced by her charade; almost certainly, they would have been too. The shot had barely missed him; it had been a very close call.

They were both still alive, and now he was aware of the urgent need to authorise the final stage of the attack. Langley would be waiting for his signal. The squadron's aircraft would be in the air already, but the raid wouldn't start until he gave the final attack order. As a result of the fracas with Daniela, he'd been confined to his quarters under guard—a security measure imposed by Hasan. With his hands and feet immobile, there was no way to reach the army truck he'd stolen and retrieve the radio phone hidden under the driver's seat. So near and yet so far, he muttered to himself. Time was ticking away.

He hoped that Daniela had an ace card up her sleeve.

Daniela had a visit from Jamal. He looked stressed.

"We'll be moving from here soon," he told her, looking at his watch. "It's too risky for us to stay. We will travel tonight in small groups, using different routes to avoid attracting attention. I'm worried about your safety, Daniela. Now that the Cyprus money has been received, I do not think they will allow you to come with us." He shifted his metal cane and sat close to her, looking deeply troubled. "You have kept your side of the bargain; you are delivering the money to us, as you promised. Al-Amin is impressed with your skills, but Hasan does not trust you. You are a Western infidel. Therefore, they will not rely on you. I have proposed that they should allow you to return to Spain—to assist with the transfer of the gold to our people there. It is a lot of money—worth more to them than your life, I have to say. Hasan opposes it. He thinks that Ahmed and Yussef can go there and retrieve it. Personally, I do not think so.

"I have argued with them. You have been effective for us as a courier—several times now. You know how to move freely between countries. I have told them we should trust you, yet they are stubborn." Then he smiled a little, his eyes brightening. "Al-Amin thinks it could work. Of course, if that is our leader's decision, Hasan will not argue. It is our only chance to save you. Al-Amin will see you one more time before we leave—to discuss the gold. That is your chance to convince him. He respects your intellect. You must think of a convincing plan to retrieve the gold, Daniela. A plan in which you yourself will play a vital part. So that they will not kill you."

Daniela dared not ask about O'Flaherty, but her mind was on what would happen to them once al-Amin and his entourage moved from the village to their new location. O'Flaherty was in danger; she was in even more dire straits. Left behind, they would be killed by the villagers. Their bodies would be buried deep under the fields, leaving no evidence.

Jamal's face had become troubled again. "I wish I could do more to deliver you to safety, Daniela. We have come a long way together—only to arrive at this." He gestured to the outside. "I am sorry."

Daniela leaned over and kissed him. "I am a survivor, Jamal, just as you are. We could have been killed many times, you and I. Yet, we are still here. *Inshallah*, I will be able to able to survive one more time. You must carry on with the jihad. With the money, you can do some of the things we have talked about many times—for the people. I will take my chances."

He shook his head and looked tearful. "I will speak again to al-Amin. I will beg him to support your safe return to Spain."

She was quiet for a moment, as Jamal looked fondly at her, his eyes brimming with emotion. "Jamal, if I fail," she began, wiping the moisture collecting in his eyes. "If I fail, there is one thing I wish not to experience. I do not want them to rape me. You understand what I am saying . . . what I am asking?"

His tears continued, yet he nodded his understanding. Reaching into his robe, he took out a handgun and, out of sight of the guards, slid it to her. "Only for that one emergency," he whispered. "I wish to spare you that pain. Do not carry it with you, Daniela. Hide it until you need it. Be careful—it is small but it kicks like a camel."

She laughed. "I cannot carry it, Jamal. They search me regularly. Maybe, with luck, I will not need it. Thank you." She held his hand tightly. "*Inshallah*, it will not be necessary. We have much more work to do together—many things to achieve. Much more living to do."

When he was gone, she examined the gun closely. It wasn't Jamal's own gun. He must have procured it especially for her—not wanting her to suffer. She was familiar with the model—a 9 mm Glock slimline G-43 subcompact. With its slender shape and short handgrip, it was a woman's gun—light and easy to conceal. She checked the magazine. It was full: six live rounds. Nothing in the firing chamber. The slide was smooth and worked perfectly. A nice weight.

Pausing for a moment, she thought through her plan. Crouching next to the bed, she explored the wooden slats under the mattress with her fingers. Moments later, the slim magazine was secured between the bed boards. Looking around for another hiding place, also close to the stone floor, she jammed the unloaded gun behind a wooden dresser pressed closely against the wall. When needed, she figured it would take her only a few seconds to retrieve the items.

In the meantime, they would be safe from the prying eyes of the women and the guards.

Breaking Camp

O'Flaherty listened; he recognised the sounds. They were getting ready to break camp.

He couldn't see his watch; his hands were tied behind his back. He guessed it was around 1400 hours. They'd be leaving within the hour, ninety minutes at the most. The Navy SEAL raid had to be confirmed soon or it would be aborted. Straining and then releasing his wrist muscles, he tried again to loosen the thick tape. His feet were tied to the chair. He'd half expected that his friend Nazih might have found a way to visit or get a message to him. Maybe even help him. It wasn't a good sign. No one had told him anything since he'd had his headwound bandaged; that was hours ago. He revised his plan, based on a best guess of what might happen.

If he could just get to the stolen army truck, he could hold them off while he made radio contact. Trouble was, he didn't know where in the village they were storing the vehicle—or even if it was still there. Plan B, he thought, would be to grab someone's cell phone and hope he could make outside contact. He'd assessed his guards' capabilities hours ago. Only two. Experienced guerrillas—but he'd have the element of surprise. If he was able to make the call, his next priority would be to find Daniela. Then figure a way to get them both out before the Navy SEALs arrived. Control's instructions were clear:

219

locate and capture. They didn't want him or Daniela anywhere near the drop zone. The risk of causing casualties from friendly fire would slow them down. It was when mistakes were made.

O'Flaherty knew he mustn't allow al-Amin to get on the move. Orders were orders, and that gave him very little time. He'd had his own plans—before Daniela had pretended to kill him. Her unexpected actions had knocked him out of action.

Now he was helpless—and he resented it.

What the hell was she up to?

Sattam had hidden the coin in his special place.

Several precious things were stored there. It was a place his mother had never discovered; it was his secret. The beautiful lady had given him a coin for his collection. He liked her. Very much. As soon as she'd told him, he'd known what she had meant. He must hide it. Not tell anyone.

Every day, when he was not doing errands, he retreated to his stash. Wrapped in a cloth, hidden in a cavity in the wall, it remained undiscovered. Today, he brought it out and carefully counted the pieces. Everything was in order, and he was content.

His mother, Noor, was calling him. He liked her name; he had heard his father say it. Noor. Noor. He laughed and ran into the kitchen. "More tea, Sattam. They want more tea," his mother fussed. When it was ready, she placed it on the tray.

He took it to the men. But he was thinking about the beautiful lady—and the sparkling colours on her bracelet.

Knowing that the soldiers would be leaving soon, the village women looking after Daniela were fidgety and anxious. They had not been told what to do with her. Their nervous concern was shared by her guards—local men whose darting eyes revealed that they were terrified of their al-Qaeda visitors.

Apart from the execution of the Mukhabarat spy, there had been no violence in their village since al-Amin and his soldiers arrived. In the old days, there had been terrible atrocities. Now the villagers just wanted to rebuild their lives and get on with things.

The girl prisoner had eaten little, asking only for tea.

The women called for Sattam—and soon he appeared, lurching side-to-side as his uneven legs propelled him forwards. As always, his pink tongue was hanging outside his mouth as he struggled for breath. He nodded his understanding of their instructions and made the laborious journey back to his mother's kitchen. Soon, he returned with Daniela's tea. The three women, speaking in whispers, could not decide what they should do after the soldiers left. Huddled closely together, they waved him past the guards into Daniela's room.

She was relieved to see him. "How is my soldier?" she asked. He grinned as he put the saucer and glass on her table; he hadn't spilled a drop. "Shall we share another secret?" she asked. "I have something more for you to hide."

He pointed to her sparkling bracelet. "This?" she asked. He nodded eagerly. He'd been thinking about it all day. "Then it must be a special secret," she whispered. "Can you do that?"

His face became radiant with innocent pleasure; he would not tell anyone. He would be brave like his father and brother.

She showed him the unloaded gun and how to hide it behind his back—under his robes.

Not long afterwards, her guards pulled her from the room.

She limped—her right foot bound tightly with the bandage that Jamal had given her. Searching her at the entrance to al-Amin quarters, his guards left little to the imagination, taking perverted delight in exploring her private parts.

Inside, Hasan was preoccupied with packing. He appeared jittery and paid scant attention to her. Al-Amin was sitting behind his table, looking deep in thought as he stared at the gold ingot in his hands. Limping towards him, she bent into a slight bow and lowered her head.

With a cursory glance, he indicated for her to sit on the floor. "The gold," he asked brusquely. "It was difficult to move?"

She nodded, rubbing at the pain in her bandaged foot. It was rapid movement that he did not see. Within seconds, she had slipped the loaded magazine wedged underneath the bandage into the pocket of her gown.

Facing al-Amin, she recalled the precise numbers she'd rehearsed and replied to his question in a clear voice. "Emir, there are seven hundred and ninety-seven bars. On average, each weighs a fraction over 12.47 kilos; therefore . . ."

"Nine thousand, nine hundred and forty-one kilos." Frowning, he supplied the answer rounded to the nearest prime number.

Daniela's startled look revealed that she was impressed; inwardly, she was pleased that he had not missed its significance: her plan of engagement seemed to be working. "Far more weight than most passenger trucks can carry," she continued. "A special vehicle will be necessary, able to carry ten tonnes of cargo."

"You used such a vehicle to move them?" he asked.

"An old Humvee. Reinforced for the rough Spanish terrain. But we did not have to drive far. For a longer distance, Emir, a cargo plane will be needed—something small and powerful. There is a private airfield close to where the gold is hidden. A pilot could file flight plans for a domestic journey to the Spanish coast, perhaps under the guise of a wealthy citizen travelling on vacation. Refuelling at the secondary stop could provide the pilot with a flexible range of destinations. Those details could be decided at the last minute. The critical part of the operation would be the first stage—removal of the gold bars from the garage where they are hidden."

"You have a plan for that too?" he asked sharply.

She wondered if it was sarcasm. Had she been too assertive? But the supreme leader had asked a question, and she must answer. "A cargo weighing ten tonnes reduces the options, Emir. I was trying to anticipate the obstacles to transporting the gold."

For a moment or two, he stroked his beard and seemed to be considering some issues. They could hear the revving engines of convoy vehicles outside, preparing for the journey. Daniela smelled gasoline and diesel—probably drivers filling their tanks, she thought. Now she was worried. There wasn't much time, and she must delay their departure as long as possible. She must get him alone.

"Al-Andalus," he said with finality. "It must be recovered—and returned to Islam."

Daniela was astonished. That was a subject requiring a long discussion, not now. Many more urgent issues were at hand. She had to think quickly—to encourage his thought process. "Emir," she answered, "Mustapha often said that al-Andalus is merely on loan to the Christians." It was a bold line. Yet, being a little cheeky—amusing, while avoiding being insolent—had often worked for her in the company of men. It showed spirit and passion. She was not sure if she'd said the right thing. "Surely, that is one of the things for which the faithful fight? Just as the Hagia Sofia has been returned to its true purpose as a mosque. With the help of the infidels' money, these things are possible."

Hasan passed through the room, collecting a few belongings. He looked at al-Amin and glanced at his watch. "There is not much time, Emir." His voice was respectful.

"There is always time," the leader snapped, "when important issues must be decided."

At that moment, Daniela knew that her fate hung in the balance. She needed the gun. Where was Sattam? She desperately needed a weapon, and time was not on her side. On impulse, she improvised. Her throat felt dry. She licked her lips, and wiped them with the back of her hand.

Al-Amin observed her discomfort. "You are thirsty?" He clicked his fingers. "Send for tea," he ordered offhandedly. Hasan hurried from the room.

"I wish to serve the jihad, Emir," she said, frantic to keep his attention on the gold. Sattam would bring the tea . . . and the means to kill al-Amin. She was aware that she was gabbling. Her hands were shaking. "The West has much money but is weak and corrupt. I can assist the cause. There are many like me who also will serve, if they are instructed properly." She looked carefully for his reactions. This is the time I must convince him, she counselled herself. It was her only chance. The moment she had waited for.

"I will do anything you require," she heard herself say—and wished she could think of something less banal. Falling silent, Daniela intuitively did what she'd always been able to do superbly well—put herself in the place of the other person and imagine what they must be thinking. He's made up his mind about what to do with you. Your fate is already decided, she warned herself. "What is it you wish me to do, Emir?" she asked. "I can help bring money to you." It wasn't original, but she knew it was the strongest card she could play. "A courier to bring riches from the West." My God, I'm sounding desperate, she thought. If he considered her only as a courier, she was doomed. She must take charge of the conversation and influence his thinking.

"Mustapha's people can help us, Emir." The inspired thought came from nowhere: I must remind him that I am here because of Mustapha . . . because of my uncle, Raphael Robles.

Al-Amin said nothing.

Was he being indecisive? He was infuriatingly hard to predict, so difficult to engage. What was he thinking? Daniela felt panic rising in her gut—aware that she was a mere woman, knowing she could only go so far in voicing her recommendations. To speak out of turn would be a grievous error. For any woman to do so would be a mistake; for a female Western jihadist, it could be fatal.

Then a stroke of luck. For no reason she was able to discern, he ordered his guards to leave the room. They looked confused and unsure. As his permanent escort, it was their solemn duty to remain close by his side at all times, ready to defend him—if necessary, at the cost of their own lives. His tone was commanding. "Wait outside," he ordered sternly.

Reluctantly, they shuffled towards the door. One of them gave a side-eye to Daniela. It was a resentful glare that said he would cut her into little strips if she were not pleasing. But her eyes were downcast, as they must be, and she did not see his look of intense hatred.

At that moment, the door opened and Sattam entered nervously carrying his tray of glasses of tea. Closely behind him came Hasan. "I will deal with this," al-Amin ordered loudly. "Leave us."

Hasan began to protest.

"Leave!" al-Amin commanded angrily. "Have the car ready. We will depart on our journey soon enough." Sattam seemed confused by all the shouting. "Go away," al-Amin instructed. He sounded increasingly irritable, she thought. There was no saying what he would do if he became angry. Hasan obeyed.

"Allow the boy to serve the tea, please, Emir," begged Daniela. From the distance came a faint roll of thunder. "The weather is changing," she said, moving to where the boy was waiting with his tray. "Thank you, Sattam." She slipped the sparkling bracelet from her arm and gave it to the boy. His eyes widened, and he sat down to play with the multi-coloured glass.

She rubbed his back in a gesture of affection. From under his robe, she retrieved the empty gun and inserted the magazine concealed in her hand. It was a cumbersome but necessary additional step: Daniela had known she could not take the risk of the boy playing with a loaded gun.

Moments later, she bowed in front of al-Amin, offering him tea. Walking behind him, she pressed the loaded gun to his head. It felt strange in her hand. Too light in weight. Something was wrong. Instinctively, she'd known that someone had tampered with it, perhaps removing its firing mechanism. Now fully committed, she must follow through.

Al-Amin was seated with his hands on the table, next to the gold ingot. He seemed surprised, saying nothing at first. A smile slowly formed. "Impeccable," he muttered. "I was not expecting that. Now you think you wish to kill me?"

Daniela saw that he was not afraid. His hands began to drift from the table. She detected the slow furtive movement and ordered him to move his hands forward, palms down—outstretched. He was forced to splay his arms wide to the edges of the table. For him, physically, it was an awkward and uncomfortable position.

Seconds passed.

"You are not a killer," he said, straining his thick neck upwards. "If you were, by now you would have done it. In our culture, we do not have conversations with our victims before we kill them. I know that you will not shoot that gun, Daniela."

"You are wrong, Emir. I want you to have a few more seconds of life. More time than you gave my parents—and my brother—before you killed them."

His eyes widened, and he read her face. "Spain," he said quickly.

"Yes." She almost choked her words. "Atocha—11 March 2004; the day you killed my family. I know that you ordered the attack."

He shrugged. "It is war." For him, it was not a callous dismissal but a statement of reality.

Rolling thunder in the distance seemed to be coming closer, yet it was more than just the weather. Suddenly, the air was being chopped by the determined pulsating vibration of powerful rotors. Daniela knew that the Navy SEALs were arriving. O'Flaherty had done his job. It was not the result she'd planned, but capturing al-Amin alive was an outcome she would have to accept. Second best—because somebody had tampered with the gun.

"Retribution, Daniela?" al-Amin interrupted her thoughts. He sounded defiant and unapologetic. Despite his predicament, he was still very much in command. A raised eyebrow indicated a challenge. "Do you have the courage to shoot me?" he scoffed, attempting to provoke her.

Outside, there was a loud volley of semi-automatic shots. Return fire answered immediately. The noise of intense gunfire confirmed that a major raid was underway. Explosions of stun grenades shook the building. In the growing darkness of early evening, powerful hand-held searchlights pierced the gloom, projecting an almost blinding light into the room. Then came the flashes of exploding percussion bombs. Angry bursts of semi-automatic fire; more shouting. The sounds of people panicking: men yelling, village women screaming. Then the intense whiteness of a magnesium flare just above their building bathed the room in a ghostly artificial light.

Behind his thick glasses, al-Amin's dark eyes were heavy-lidded, giving nothing away. She knew that his brain was razor sharp and agile. He would have assessed his situation—knowing now that he was about to be captured. The one vital piece of information he did not possess was that the gun she was pointing at him had been rendered useless. There was no time at present for her to figure out how, or why. The stark reality was that she had come all this way to kill him, but now she could not.

227

Battering rams were being used to breach doors—as troops checked and cleared each building. More semi-automatic gunfire. They were getting closer now, almost outside. Another flashbang. She and al-Amin instinctively ducked their heads as an explosion above them showered debris from the roof—creating a light fog of dust. More shouts emerged from outside; shorter bursts of rapid fire now. Resistance was weakening.

The attackers were outside the door.

Al-Amin began to stand up. He wants me to shoot him, she thought—trying not to glance at her impotent gun, focused only on the threat it posed. It was evident that the prospect of being captured did not appeal to him. If he had been wearing a suicide vest, she knew he would have detonated it already. The explosion would have ripped them to shreds.

With gritted teeth, standing over him, she forced him to remain seated. The barrel of Jamal's gun pressed hard into his forehead. She'd been trained well and kept him fully in her line of sight. Not once did she allow her wild, wide eyes to waver from his good eye. Time slowed. Her mind was crystal clear; she knew what she must do. It was a battle of wills. She forced herself to stare at him, aware that her vicious look of revenge was her only remaining weapon—stubbornly refusing to admit to herself that, in truth, she was powerless against him.

Fleeting thoughts of Alejandro returning from his interview at the Madrid private school intruded. As clear as yesterday, she could see her young brother sitting innocently on the train entering Atocha station. The image made her grimace, and she forced it away. Clenching her teeth tightly together, she tightened her grip on the gun—squeezing the trigger part way to its firing position. Just one more small motion. Wanting to, yet she knew it was futile.

Al-Amin's good eye still glared provokingly at her—his squint eye now wandered independently. His downturned mouth sneeringly mocked her, and because she could do nothing about it, she detested him even more. His confident self-assurance further inflamed the intense hatred of him that had consumed most of her young life.

Behind her, the door was being forced open.

She had no time left. This was it.

But the men entering the room were not Navy SEALs. They were Hasan, Mohammed, and Nazih—weapons drawn, ready to protect their leader. Suddenly, there were shots. She saw Mohammed fall towards her, a bullet through his back into his heart. Commotion outside. A Syrian Army soldier in full combat gear burst into the room. Another shot, and Nazih fell dead. Startled, the young boy Sattam made a sudden movement. The soldier, spooked, turned and levelled his gun. "No," Daniela screamed, running to throw herself over the young boy. "He's a child."

Another gunshot. Not realising she'd been shot, she felt warm blood pulsing from her. It came in powerful spurts.

The bullet that tore through Daniela's neck failed to sever her carotid artery, but it ripped out a piece of flesh the thickness of a man's finger. Landing heavily, she was dimly aware that she must protect Sattam—protect the child with her body.

Then she lost consciousness.

Trapped

He had not been able to send a signal to his command centre at al-Tanf.

Hearing helicopters incoming at a distance, O'Flaherty knew that their mission had failed. They were not the Navy SEALs descending upon the village.

Now in extreme danger, he tried to break the back of his chair—struggling to free his ankles and arms from the thick tape strapped tightly around him. Straining with all his considerable strength, he still couldn't loosen it. There was gunfire, closer now than before. He was helpless. This was not how it was supposed to be. Not what he'd planned. Cursing loudly, he shouted for help. No response. His guards were no longer there. He was on his own, and he laughed bitterly.

Then, a voice came from the door—from behind his head.

He felt the tape being cut away. "It's the Syrian Army," said his rescuer. "They've captured al-Amin and Daniela. We have to get out of here . . . now!"

There was no time to argue. At least he was free, thought O'Flaherty.

"She was shot, badly wounded. Maybe the medical corps can save her life, I don't know," he heard his rescuer say. "They were taken to a helicopter—under heavy guard."

Hearing this, O'Flaherty turned and looked in the direction he'd heard the aircraft land. His rescuer thrust an automatic and several clips into his hands, shaking his head vigorously. "She's captured and unconscious on a stretcher," he yelled. "You can't help her, Michael."

At his debriefings, O'Flaherty retold the events that followed. He described how he and his rescuer knew that any attempt to save the hostages would be futile. They had to withdraw immediately. But retreat to where? Moments later, he said, the issue was decided for them. Their attempt at conversation was drowned out by bursts of automatic weapon fire aimed at them. They returned fire, and O'Flaherty pointed to the window. They went through it in seconds, landing in a narrow passageway below. Behind them, moments later, the wall of the room was blown outwards by a grenade.

O'Flaherty told his debriefers how they'd caught sight of Jamal and his driver. The pair was trapped in a shoot-out with a small contingent of Syrian Army assault troops. Crawling, sheltered by a stone wall, they were soon alongside their comrades. Jamal had given them a grateful glance—pointing to three enemy positions. It was flat ground, O'Flaherty told them, but the enemy had a superior position in elevation.

One of them was a sniper, Jamal had yelled. The marksman was keeping them pinned down. There would not be much time before enemy support troops arrived. O'Flaherty knew that Jamal was unable to move quickly. "Where's the car, Salman?" he'd shouted to the young driver as a burst of gunfire punched bullets into a stone wall above their heads. A metre away lay the body of a regime soldier shot earlier by Jamal. It had caught his attention, said O'Flaherty, because two unused percussion grenades were hanging from the dead soldier's belt. It was an opportunity for escape. Leaning over towards Jamal, O'Flaherty had picked up his metal cane. Using the inadequate protection of the wall, he'd crawled as close as he could to the dead soldier.

On a count of three, the others had sprayed their attackers with a barrage of gunfire, forcing them to take cover. It had been enough time for O'Flaherty to snag the dead soldier's belt using Jamal's cane. Under a hail of bullets, he'd dragged the body close enough to detach the grenades, then signal to his comrades. They'd nodded and crouched for cover behind the wall, knowing that the grenades' percussion waves would be deafening. O'Flaherty, lying on his back, had lobbed one and then the other at the Syrian government soldiers. Two resounding explosions had shaken the wall sheltering them. Shots from their opponents ceased. Still cautious, O'Flaherty—with a feat of strength his comrades hadn't witnessed before—had hoisted the dead regime soldier's head and shoulders above the wall. The sniper's bullet went through the dead soldier's forehead.

A second later, one of Jamal's bullets passed through the sniper's brain.

Now they had just moments to make their escape.

From his days as a SEAL, O'Flaherty knew all about "locate and capture" missions. Earlier, he'd detected the rotor beats of a third aircraft. He knew that two of the attack helicopters would already be ferrying al-Amin back to home base: one transporting its priceless payload; the other ready to provide cover fire. Special forces from the third helicopter would finish off the remaining resistance in the village. Then they would mount a sweep-up operation, taking out stragglers. If they spotted Jamal's car speeding from the battleground, a single well-aimed air-to-ground missile would destroy them all.

Luck was on their side, he told them at his debriefing. Salman was already behind the wheel, engine revving. Minutes later, Jamal safely inside, it had moved at fast speed in the direction of Ibrahim's farm.

News of the battle raging at the village had already reached Ibrahim. He knew it was where his former commander had arranged an important meeting. He'd also heard that three Syrian Army Special Forces helicopters had mounted an attack on the village. Under his orders, several of his men had taken up defensive locations manning the two surface-to-air MANPADS he'd acquired months earlier from a source in Iraq—traded for a sizable shipment of narcotics. He knew that the missile launchers would even up the odds. Seeing the dust of Jamal's vehicle travelling fast towards him, Ibrahim ordered his pilot to start up his helicopter. Abandoning the farm and his drug operations had become necessary. A strategic withdrawal was needed; he could come back for his inventory later. His men would scatter to the wind.

Salman braked Jamal's vehicle to an unsteady stop. Seeing the preparations underway, Jamal blurted his thanks to Ibrahim. His comrade seemed unfazed. They would fly the helicopter over the border into Iraq where the infrequent border patrols knew him well. Ibrahim's frequent trips had a foundation in commerce that was valuable to both sides. His distribution network inside Iraq was well lubricated with incentives. The Iraqi border authorities—when they found out—would look the other way in return for the promise of a generous cross-border shipment. There was just one problem: there were too many passengers. Ibrahim ordered his pilot to get out. "He'll be okay," he announced. "He has family nearby who can shelter him. I can fly this thing. Get in, quickly."

His passengers looked dubious. Ibrahim's poor piloting skills were legendary, O'Flaherty told his debriefers. "They were wasting precious time, so I put my hand on my rescuer's shoulder and said to him, 'You saved me, my friend. Now it's my turn. For the cause, it is vital we get Jamal to safety. You know what to do. I'll take the car and abandon it if they get too close.'"

Ibrahim had frowned but nodded at the wisdom of the red-haired infidel's proposal. "We don't have much time," he'd said. Urged on by a stream of foul language from Ibrahim, O'Flaherty's rescuer quickly took the fourth seat.

"Who was your rescuer?" they'd asked at his debriefings.

"It was Nazih who rescued me," O'Flaherty had answered. "I'm incredibly grateful to my old friend."

O'Flaherty retold the story of his escape several times—until he almost believed it too. It wasn't true. Nazih had been shot in the back, much earlier. He was dead seconds before Daniela had received the bullet in her neck.

Someone else had rescued O'Flaherty.

But he was never going to tell them who.

Within the hour, Ibrahim's pilot landed their helicopter at an isolated settlement on Iraq's western border with Syria. The place was well protected. He was a well-known visitor and part-time resident. They were assured of safety there. Jamal had received a minor flesh wound in the gun battle at the village but ignored it—demanding instead to find out their leader's fate. It was a huge setback for their plans—and for al-Qaeda's rebirth in Mesopotamia.

Reporting the capture of al-Amin to the few members of High Command still remaining in Peshawar had become Jamal's most urgent priority. In response, he received orders to remain where they were and await further instructions. While their pilot looked after refuelling, Jamal questioned everyone—taking the opportunity to find out what had happened. He was certain they'd been betrayed. The raid must have been directed by an informer on the ground, or by someone nearby who was monitoring their evacuation plans. He'd thought at once of the two Westerners—immediately suspecting them. But he'd struggled to understand how either could have been responsible: Daniela had been seriously injured and might be dead; the red-haired jihadist had narrowly escaped being killed in the gunfight—and had helped save his life. Neither of them would have any reason to assist the Syrian regime; it was incomprehensible.

He and Hasan agreed that there must be a traitor inside the camp—one of their own people.

Jamal reverted to type. He ignored the pain and setbacks of the recent past. His pain was not just physical: his best friend, Mohammed, had been killed in the village. So, too, he'd been informed, had many of his platoon comrades—men long dedicated to the cause, including Nazih, their imam Ali, and the faithful little mechanic Mahmood. Their deaths caused him intense anguish; after all, it was he who had called them back into the service of the jihad. So much waste of such good men.

With fierce resolve, once again he became the fearless combat soldier of old. His men witnessed the change and were thankful for it. Al-Amin had been captured by the Syrian Army. Everyone knew what that meant. But, for now, Jamal was filling the gap. He was decisive and tireless. While the group waited for orders, he assessed his battle position critically, deciding how to consolidate his remaining men within the area under his command. Despite casualties, he was confident that enough men had survived to form a viable counter-attack force.

Ibrahim had changed too. He was keen to rejoin his former comrades and consolidate his resources under Jamal's command. Hasan was subdued and contrite; regretful that he had not been able to protect al-Amin. Now he spent his time with Jamal, willing to be subservient to the older man, helping him re-establish a base that would allow al-Qaeda to secure the region—to reassemble the band of brothers. At least those who had survived.

It took more than a full day for O'Flaherty to complete his journey to al-Tanf airbase. He'd made good progress getting away from Ibrahim's farm but soon had to abandon the car to avoid being detected.

Initially on foot, then hitching rides, he threaded his way southwest through regime-held territory towards the deconfliction-zone border with Jordan. The most dangerous part of his journey occurred close to the airbase itself. He was confronted by armed rebels, who questioned his story. He was in luck. A former member of Jamal's brigade recognised his distinctive hair and tall frame. Vouched for, he was given water and food, and allowed to continue his journey towards the Jordanian border.

O'Flaherty knew that US patrols constantly policed the M2 Highway close to the airbase. But he was worried about being shot if he flagged one down. Anticipating the American soldiers' trigger-happy reaction if he approached them looking like a jihadi, O'Flaherty took two precautions that probably saved his life. He stripped naked to show that he was unarmed and not wearing a suicide vest. Then, holding his bare arms high in the air, he stepped onto the road to flag down an approaching US military police vehicle.

To the astonishment of the heavily armed American troops, he sang "The Star-Spangled Banner."

At the top of his voice.

CHAPTER 10
Damascus: Daniela

From the deep wound in her neck and intense fatigue, Daniela knew she'd been near death.

She was not aware that a skilled Syrian Army surgeon on board the helicopter had saved her life. It had been a close thing. Then she'd spent several days heavily guarded in an intensive care unit—somewhere in Damascus, she guessed later. Her doctors and nurses were tight-lipped, and scared.

Interrogations began as soon as she was able to talk—which was difficult. A large section of her mouth was swollen after two neck operations. Her tongue was numb and one side of her face felt paralysed. Her doctors said she would recover but needed an extended period of rest. Their opinions were summarily dismissed by the Mukhabarat security forces, who were impatient and condescending.

Daniela played the game. She drifted in and out of consciousness, both real and contrived. They'd responded unsympathetically, ordering medications that kept her awake and talkative.

She was disciplined in her resistance but lost track of what she'd told them.

Voices in the room roused Daniela from her drowsy state.

The Mukhabarat Pair again, she thought. The man did most of the shouting and threatening. A younger woman followed his lead; she seemed more perceptive and intelligent. A classic good cop/bad cop set-up, Daniela guessed. She was wary—knowing they'd have a bagful of cross-examination tricks and would use a full range of interrogation chemicals. It was just a matter of time.

The man re-opened his questioning. "Tell us again who you were working with—give us his name," he demanded.

"We want to go easy on you; you still have your life ahead of you," purred the woman. "It would be a pity if you were to lose your good looks."

"The American you were with, what is his name?" barked the man. "It is him we want, not you. Yours was a minor role; we are happy to release you."

"You will be free to go," said the woman.

"Just tell us his name; that's all we need," the man lied.

"There is someone here from Spain waiting to take you back home to your family," the woman continued the charade. "With nice clean clothes." She glanced at Daniela's unflattering hospital garb. "This does not suit you. You are young and beautiful. We will give you all you want—and your freedom—if you help us."

Recalling her line-of-defence interrogation training, Daniela forced herself to visualise a person she knew—someone who had nothing to do with the mission. She fixed her attention on her swimming instructor at university. Concentrating on him, she wanted him to be at the front of her mind when the chemical injections loosened her tongue. It was a standard technique to protect vital names. She had banished O'Flaherty and Jamal from her thoughts. Colonel Scott, Bill Yates, and Antonio too. She had to protect them. Place them beyond recall.

It wouldn't stop her captors, yet it would make it harder for them. Maybe for her, too, but that was less important. Determined to protect her mission, she resolved yet again to give them nothing. She began to fantasise about her swimming instructor—focus on his handsome face, his lithe body, his powerful swimming stroke that hardly rippled the water. His sexy voice. Anything to keep her thoughts away from those close to her.

What mission? There had been no mission. It was all just a mistake.

She was just a tourist.

※

Several days after her capture, things changed. Woken by her guards, she was dragged to the usual hard metal chair and her wrists and ankles bound with again sturdy plastic tie-downs. The Mukhabarat Pair failed to appear. Instead, there was a new voice.

"Hello Daniela," he said, entering the room from behind her. His tone was laced with self-confidence and sarcasm. "How is Spain's top undercover agent today?"

Hasan!

Was she imagining things? It was Hasan, she was certain—here in Damascus. Stepping in front of her, dressed handsomely in casual Western clothes, he stood there with a confident smile, confirming that this wasn't another cruel interrogation technique. Hasan had been al-Amin's personal aide. She'd imagined that he'd been either killed or captured at the village. Obviously, he wasn't a captive; he was very much the captor. But in the enemy camp! It could mean only one thing: he'd been working for the Syrian Army Special Forces all along.

Of course, it all made sense now. It must have been Hasan who had alerted them—making sure they'd reach the target before the Navy SEALs. There was no other plausible conclusion. He was a Syrian spy planted alongside al-Amin. How had he done it? She was amazed. In spite of her weakened state, Daniela managed a smile. "Congratulations, Hasan. You fooled us all."

Her compliment pleased him, and he was generous in his response. "Your scheme," he said, "it was a good attempt on your part. You were quite convincing: al-Amin believed you."

"But you didn't?" asked Daniela, playing to his vanity.

"Of course not," he replied, without providing any explanation. "Anyway, your mission failed. Instead, we have al-Amin in custody. How is your neck wound?" he asked, shifting the subject. "I'm told it was quite serious. Our surgeon on board the helicopter saved your life. After plastic surgery, it will be a small scar—to remind you of your foolishness. You were an important field agent, yet you seem to have an unfortunate habit of going off script—and rescuing children."

"I don't understand," she lied.

He laughed. "You received your wound to save the boy's life. That was perhaps understandable. Yet, months ago, you sacrificed your whole mission simply to rescue a stupid child from the streets of Barcelona. After that, we knew everything. We watched each move you made. Al-Amin and his men knew nothing, of course. They were so busy watching you and your American friend that they forgot to look over their shoulders and be vigilant for the real enemy—us. Never send a woman to do a man's work," he gloated. "You're too emotional."

"I'm impressed," said Daniela, ignoring his jibe. "How did you manage to get al-Amin to trust you? That was very well done. You convinced his men too."

"Ha! You think you can make me talk?" sneered Hasan. "More tricks! It is not why I came here."

For a moment, she worried if he intended to assault her—to finish what he'd started in the village. It seemed unlikely; there had been something about that encounter that had not been quite right. It had puzzled her. His strength was far superior to hers. If he'd wanted to, he could have raped her, but for some reason, he hadn't pursued his advantage. Then Jamal and the others had burst into the room and saved her. It was odd. Now, it seemed, Hasan had some other objective, she thought. What was it?

"How would you like your freedom?" he asked. "How would you like to go back to Spain?"

She said nothing.

"I'm surprised, Daniela. We thought it would appeal to you—and there is not much effort involved for you. An easy task. We will make a trade. One-for-one." He paused, his mouth distorting into a threatening sneer.

"We want your lover; we want Jamal."

Hasan's words encouraged Daniela. He had supplied vital intel and inadvertently provided her with a stronger bargaining position. Maybe it could help save her life. His demand for an exchange—herself for Jamal—was absurd. Yet, it told her that Jamal was not a captive of the Syrian regime. Perhaps he was a captive of the regime's enemies? If so, who? The West? Had Michael O'Flaherty survived the raid and escaped? Perhaps Jamal too? Potentially good news, but still a lot of unanswered questions.

"Jamal is not for sale," she said dismissively.

He slapped her face hard. "Don't be insolent, Daniela."

Blood dribble down the corner of her mouth. Licking it, she swallowed hard. She had underestimated his masculine pride—his macho self-image. He stood up abruptly and left the room. Moments later, her heart sank as the Mukhabarat Pair entered and she was dragged back to her cell.

Two very painful hours later, she passed out.

She was dragged into the same room where she'd had her previous encounter with Hasan.

He continued talking as if there had been no pause in their conversation. "We want Jamal," he repeated.

She was bloodied from the torture that she'd endured, yet managed to find the strength to respond. "I do not know where he is."

"Of course, you don't. We didn't expect that you would. I want to know how you communicate with him. What message boards do you use on the darknet, Daniela?"

She had prepared her reaction and jerked her head up in surprise. Hasan saw it and smiled in triumph. "Ah, I thought so. It would be the only possible way. And, of course, you will have various codewords to communicate unwritten messages and warnings. I wish to know them all, please. You will write them down—and no tricks, Daniela. You have not yet felt the intense pain that we can inflict on your beautiful body."

Threateningly, Hasan put his face within centimetres of hers.

"No tricks, Daniela. You understand?"

Langley: Deputy Director

The mission's failure was being covered up.

Denial from the Oval Office.

Project Catalyst had been an unauthorised covert maverick initiative, huffed the president sitting imperiously behind his desk at the White House. Fake news. Heads would roll.

Lieutenant Commander Michael O'Flaherty was in the hot seat at the mission's debriefing facility at Langley. He'd been flown home hours after he'd arrived at al-Tanf. He looked strained and despondent, thought the deputy director. She glanced around the table. A stern-faced retired brigadier general from the Department of Defence glared at the others. Her section director—also a former military man—sat next to him, his face impassive and unforgiving. O'Flaherty, dressed in civvies, sat alongside Colonel Scott, whose face seemed a masterpiece of control but with enough undisguised excitement in his eyes to confirm his message: "I told you so."

For an hour, O'Flaherty had been speaking. He'd been interrupted only by questions allowed for clarity. A rapid-fire interrogation had followed. During it, the deputy noted that Colonel Scott sat back and gloated. She could deal with him later, she thought. For now, they had an allied officer in captivity, imprisoned—their intelligence on the ground informed them—by the Mukhabarat in Damascus.

"We failed in our primary mission to capture al-Amin. I have to remind y'all this is now an exercise in damage control," snarled the Department of Defence brigadier general, his southern drawl in full flight. "There'll be an internal inquiry, of course. However, the president wants this operation shut down—now. By which I mean, it never existed. Am I clear?"

"There are elements of it that are outside our control, sir," said the director. "Our allied officer in captivity, for example."

The deputy director could read the brigadier general's face. She guessed that his personal view was that Daniela Balmes would have to take her chances—that she was a pawn in the wider scheme of things. Yet, he seemed smart enough not to allow such thoughts to escape past the necessary filters of high command.

"We will do our best to get her repatriated, of course," he responded with narrowed eyes. "But we don't even know the extent of her injuries—or if she's still alive. In the meantime, her connection with us cannot be acknowledged.

"That's an order."

Thirty minutes later, in the privacy of her office, the deputy director looked enquiringly at O'Flaherty.

He was sitting across the desk from her, his long legs sprawled across the carpet. As he often did when he was thinking hard, he rubbed the sides of his head vigorously with his fingertips. His unmanaged mane of red hair stuck out incongruously. His efforts to tidy up his unkempt field agent appearance—one better suited to the Langley office culture—had been largely unsuccessful. "I don't think I impressed them," he said.

"They're in a foul mood," she conceded. "It's disappointing. The fundamentals underlying the mission were good. You and Officer Balmes executed according to plan. It was a first-class performance—except that the Syrians were onto us. They beat us to al-Amin and captured him. Not your fault, Michael. Even so, no one in Washington is happy about it. They don't want to be associated with a failed operation. No surprise there; it's not our culture. We like to win."

Although despondent, O'Flaherty seemed unfazed by the talk of failure. There seemed to be something more pressing on his mind, she thought. "Daniela," he began, but she stopped him short.

"Don't even think it, Michael. The chance of getting approval for a covert raid to rescue her from Damascus is a non-starter. We'll have to rely on the diplomatic route."

"That's a tough nut to crack, ma'am," he shot back explosively. "We can't even get this administration to admit that the mission took place—and that she's a captive in a hostile country."

Occaquan: Waterfront Café

It was Saturday morning, and the smell of sausages sizzling on the grill made O'Flaherty feel hungry.

Ducking his head under a low wooden rafter, he spotted his host and slid into the window-side table. "Morning, sir," he greeted the brigadier general.

"Breakfast," exclaimed the senior man. "My mother always said it's the best and most important meal of the day, Lieutenant Commander. How was your drive down?"

They small-talked for a time while their meals were brought from the kitchen and the waitress deposited a fresh pot of steaming coffee on the wood slab table. The tables either side of them were empty, O'Flaherty noted.

"I'm known here, and they do that for me." The brigadier general smiled. "They probably think everything I talk about is top secret," he added with a laugh. "I like this place; it has a lot of old-world charm. Best breakfasts east of the Mississippi too. Care to take a walk?" he invited while paying the bill and adding a generous tip.

Minutes later, they found themselves alone on the old wood jetty jutting out at an angle into the river. "I wanted to check with you off the record, Lieutenant Commander. I know you have your hands full on this mission. You did well to deliver our target into the hands of the Syrian government. Job number one done. Congratulations. How's our boy on the inside?"

O'Flaherty shielded his mouth with his hand. "Krystal is still well embedded, sir. He's been credited in Damascus with contributing significantly to the success of their raid. I think he'll be an invaluable long-term asset for us—as we planned."

"Who's being blamed for the security leak?" asked the brigadier general. He took a cigar from his pocket and slid it from its aluminium casing. Slicing the end, he lit it—producing successive clouds of blue smoke. "The leak that ostensibly allowed the Syrians to snatch al-Amin from under our nose?" he added for clarity.

"That'll come out at the enquiry, sir," replied O'Flaherty. "It was a big and complex operation involving a lot of people. It may not have been a leak on our side. Possibly just a combination of things. Either way, we achieved our purpose."

"Officially, this is not a military operation," the brigadier general reminded him. "No disrespect to the CIA, but this is well beyond their remit. Sad to say, today's civilian agencies are rife with careless talk."

"I agree, sir. It was always our plan to close it off—once the target was delivered."

"No snags likely to impede our Phase Two, then?" asked the brigadier general.

"No, sir. We didn't anticipate that the Spanish officer, Daniela Balmes, would be badly injured and captured. That damage can be contained. We kept her out of the loop deliberately; she knows nothing about Phase Two, so there's nothing she can reveal under interrogation."

The brigadier general nodded and tapped cigar ash into the water. "Still need-to-know, eh? That's vital, Lieutenant Commander. I don't want anyone hearing about Krystal any more than is absolutely essential. You know that better than anyone. If any cracks develop, I want you to take care of them personally. Is that understood? Just as I said to y'all the other day, the president wants Operation Catalyst shut down and buried as soon as possible. Of course, he doesn't know all the details about Phase Two, you understand? Now, is there anything I should know before we proceed?" He looked O'Flaherty directly in the eye, testing the strength of the lieutenant commander's resolve.

"I'll take care of everything, sir. Phase Two is good to go."

Cheltenham: GCHQ

"They're out for blood, James," observed the section chief.

"Yours," he added ruefully. Examining a snagged fingernail, he shook his fingers. "Damned painful."

"Hopefully, I can handle it, sir," replied Garwood.

"On the face of it, the mission failed. You're in for heavy fire from the committee this morning, James. If it doesn't go well, I'll have to step in. Fingers crossed that won't be necessary. You know what these bloody secretaries of state can be like—trying to prove themselves, always after their ministers' jobs. Thompson isn't bad, but he's a stickler for detail.

"New rules from here on in," noted Garwood without any real passion. He glanced through the thermally efficient, bullet-proofed, triple-glazed windows onto the lush Cotswolds landscape. A heavy rain squall was heading in from the Irish Sea, and his thoughts drifted to the race card for the meeting at Cheltenham that weekend. The going might be wet, he thought.

"New rules, exactly!" the section chief continued. "The next phase is strictly QT, James. Every additional person in the loop adds to the operational risks. Even O'Flaherty's boss, the deputy director, doesn't know about Krystal. So, today, you'll have to rely on receiving support from the few remaining cool heads. You'll receive only tacit support from MI6; they have to be extremely careful how they assist you. If the financial oversight people get a sniff of a cover-up or a whisper of the billions we and the others have wagered on covert ops, they'll scream for an internal investigation. Not good for anyone, James. Not good at all. How is O'Flaherty managing with Washington, by the way?"

"They're still looking for scapegoats, sir. Michael is in the line of fire. If he becomes the target, friends will have to step in."

"I'd tread very carefully if I were you," said the section chief. He glanced at his watch and stood up. "Good luck handling this morning's onslaught. We can talk again afterwards.

"I'll make a reservation for us at my country club."

Madrid

Glum faces around the table told the story. Project Catalyst had failed.

Daniela had been seriously wounded and captured—arrested as a terrorist spy by the Syrian government. The extent of her injuries was unknown. Making it even worse, not a word was emerging from any government about the capture of al-Amin. Nothing. Complete silence.

"We've made urgent diplomatic approaches to Damascus, of course," said Claudia, occupying the top seat. "They haven't confirmed or denied they've arrested a Spanish national. We're continuing to press them, and the Russians too. The Americans haven't said a word. It seems that the White House wants the whole thing to just go away. The Brits are in touch with us, but they don't seem to be any more successful than we are in communicating with Damascus—the Syrian government refuses to comment."

"What's Lieutenant Commander O'Flaherty telling us?" asked Diego. "I mean, he was able to get out safely through al-Tanf."

"We haven't had access to him," replied Claudia. "I think he's been muzzled. Immediately after the raid, we were informed that Colonel Scott flew to Langley on a US Air Force jet. Except for the intel about the capture of Daniela Balmes, there hasn't been a word from him. Usually, communications between the allies would be jamming the encrypted lines. This time, the silence is scary. I'm surprised the Americans didn't have a game plan for this contingency. Maybe they did." She gave them a cynical look. "It looks like the Oval Office is defining events now. Our prime minister has been briefed, but Washington hasn't returned his calls."

"I think it's a mess," intervened an older man sitting alongside Claudia. He was dressed in a dark suit and wore the tie of the Academia General Militar. He glared at her sternly. "Like all of us, I'm concerned for the well-being of our officer, Daniela Balmes. Until we obtain the cooperation of the Syrian government, however, it seems we can't do much more than keep pressing them for an answer. If she's still alive, we want her back in Spain as quickly as possible. Then we'll be able to hear her version of what happened—how the operation went wrong. If she's dead, we must repatriate her body; that's just as urgent. In the meantime, Spain has collaborated in a very elaborate scheme—dreamed up by the Americans—so that they can locate and capture al-Amin—just as they did with bin Laden.

"It's become clear now they were beaten to the target by Syrian Army Special Forces," he continued. "In the process, we—ourselves—have put our officer at extreme risk. We have allowed the huge fortune in laundered money formerly in our possession—from Aladdin's

Cave—to be transferred to al-Qaeda. Meanwhile, our American allies are ignoring us." His face coloured. "If word of this screw-up gets into the public domain, our government is finished. We'll have no credibility—not a leg to stand on." He stared at Claudia. "I want to know what your plans are to contain this shambles, Chief Inspector. We need to find out what's going on—make sure we protect the PM and the government."

Claudia seemed unfazed by the senior politician's self-serving outburst. "Sir," she began evenly, "perhaps one piece of good news is that the British were able to freeze the Cyprus money transferred to a clearing bank in Dubai. It's a reputable institution, and they were able to trace the recipient account to a charity controlled by al-Qaeda. There's a US embargo on such transfers, so the money will be returned to us."

He shrugged, seemingly begrudging her that one consolation prize. "My point is still valid."

Diego was annoyed that the Madrid man was being more obstructive than cooperative. It was frustrating. He'd been hoping the senior politician might have been able to provide a few insights into how they could ascertain Officer Balmes' condition and begin the steps necessary to repatriate her. Apart from telling them that the prime minister had summoned the US ambassador, the politician had contributed nothing. Consulting his cell phone and gathering his belongings, he'd just announced that he had to leave.

"Keep me informed, Chief Inspector," the politician instructed Claudia, and walked out of the room—ignoring Diego.

Barcelona: Antonio

Among those most closely linked to Daniela, Antonio was the last to hear about the failure of her mission. He received a secure call from Diego. Just a brief update, not much more. Yet, the Madrid policeman made it clear that the situation was serious; she'd been injured and there was no news coming out of Damascus. *Nada*!

Antonio had been struggling at work. His joint investigation with Diego's team was not making any headway. He was no closer to tracking down who was behind the shooting—the sniper's failed attempt on Daniela's life. Truth was, he admitted to himself, he was growing weary. Playing cat-and-mouse games with Aurelia didn't help. He'd run checks on her friend Louis and found nothing remarkable. Setting aside his personal dislike of the man (or was there an element of jealousy?), he'd found nothing on their records that would justify closer surveillance.

Neither he nor Diego had made any headway in their enquiries about the gold pendants. He had considered hauling in Aurelia for questioning—pressuring her to identify the people behind the unique looking ornaments. But it would be a fishing trip, he admitted. And he could lose any goodwill he'd established with her. Meanwhile, other investigations in his department had become more urgent, so the attempted homicide case file sat on his desk collecting dust. This morning's call from Diego didn't do much more than redirect his thoughts to Daniela. He no longer felt the excitement and lust that had characterized their early days together—in Turkey and Barcelona. He'd become disenchanted and frustrated with her antics.

He recalled their meeting in the underground car park. It was not a moment he was proud of—or could easily rid from his mind. He'd slapped her hard. He'd never done that before, to any woman. When he thought about Daniela, there was still an element of fascination—and a lingering allure. Not sexual any longer, not in the conventional sense. He'd always found his attraction towards her hard to define. The fact was, they'd both moved on. He knew that. Even so, the news of her injuries and incarceration upset him. It brought regrets, and there wasn't a damned thing he could do to help her.

Damascus New Palace: A Week Later

Garwood examined the room again. He'd been ushered into a cavernous reception area—waiting for his appointment with the minister.

He was its only occupant. He'd had nothing else to do for the past half hour but observe the opulent modernistic décor of the Damascus New Palace. It was an austere and echoing creation of its architect—impressive in its vast size but lacking, he felt, the warmth and charm of the old palace in the Ar Rabwah neighbourhood.

They'd left him to stew in the heat of a glass-walled anteroom. The sun streaming through the glass ceiling was merciless. Deliberately, no doubt, there was no shade. The structure seemed to be air-conditioned everywhere, except where he had been asked to wait. Someone must have switched it off. For thirty minutes, he'd been a portrait of patience and decorum. He knew it was a carefully calculated delay by the minister, timed to diplomatic perfection.

Aware that he was being watched by hidden cameras, he knew they'd be examining every detail of his discomfort. No doubt his facial movements and body language were being observed and reported—perhaps even viewed on the surveillance monitors by the minister himself. Garwood had dabbed almost continually at his wet forehead with a linen handkerchief. His underarms were swimming. Doubting that any Russian diplomats would be subjected to such calculated humiliation, he knew better than to react negatively to his treatment. After all, he was taking one for the team.

Eventually, someone arrived and he was escorted from the hothouse into a vast meeting room. In contrast, it was cool and pleasant. Moments later, several aides appeared, followed by the minister himself. The aides drifted away.

"Your Excellency." Garwood bowed uncomfortably. At the last minute, he had slipped his jacket back on—not wishing to display his sweat-stained shirt and saturated underarms.

The minister was cordial. He confined himself to pleasantries and minor diplomatic chit-chat until they had finished the usual ceremonial tea. "Your visit is welcomed, Lord Garwood."

He sounded bored, thought the British aristocrat. There was one compensation: it signalled the start of the formal part of the meeting. "It is a long time since we last met, is it not?"

"Far too long, sir," agreed Garwood. "I bring with me the greetings of the prime minister and the British government."

The minister bowed graciously as he accepted the customary felicitations. "Yet, your government has not been a good friend to our president, I think."

"Not in recent years, Your Excellency, it might be said," conceded his visitor. "That hallowed role is enjoyed by Russia and Iran, it is well known. But the United Kingdom is your good friend. More consistent than others, in fact, in your fight against ISIS and al-Qaeda—and long before."

The minister raised an eyebrow. "That particular claim can be debated, Lord Garwood. For one thing, ISIS is not just our fight. By withdrawing peremptorily from Iraq, the Americans created that monster. As with al-Qaeda today, our fight is yours too. Additionally, we should remember that your country was an architect of Sykes-Picot, a century ago. What good has that done for the Arab world?"

"Along with France, yes, sir, we had that responsibility—historically. Its well-meaning intent ultimately was to support the Arab cause. We were your friends then, as was France. We remain so. London has supported Syria many times—on important issues," Garwood added hastily.

The minister allowed himself a wry smile. "History shows that the purpose of Sykes-Picot was to control the Arab world, not to support it. You and the Americans were interested in our oil. You still are. This time, not to buy it from us but to force us to keep it in the ground—except for emergencies, when you need it."

Garwood knew he could not dispute the minister's summary. He needed to move on and quickly get to his agenda. His host was quicker. "Our president remembers with great fondness his time living and working in London. Also, the first lady, of course. Syrian, yet born in London. A British citizen."

"The president has always been most welcome, Excellency," said Garwood, scrambling. "The first lady is free to travel to the country of her birth whenever she pleases."

"And the president too?" probed the minister. His eyebrows were raised, his head tilted, anticipating the answer and warning against the wrong one.

Garwood nodded. "Yes, of course, Excellency. We remain friends and allies and trust that our desire to continue will be sustained for a very long time. The president will always be most welcome in Great Britain."

"Mmmm, yes, a diplomatic answer, Lord Garwood. It's no surprise, given your pedigree. I know that you have been well-schooled in these things. However, inconstant friends are the scourge of every political leader. You should remind your masters of that." His tone had shifted. He sounded irritated and mildly hostile.

Garwood was aware that he was still on weak ground. He was anxious to avoid engaging the minister on a review of Britain's imperial history in the region.

"These are strange and unexpected overtures, you are making, Lord Garwood. We have heard nothing of the same from your former ambassador. Where is he now?" The minister again raised an eyebrow. Garwood resisted smiling at the minister's slyness. The man was a veteran politician and a well-educated diplomat. He was reminding his guest that, many years earlier, the UK's well-respected ambassador had been recalled at short notice by London—at the start of the hostilities. He'd never returned.

"Can we shortly expect diplomatic recognition of our president by your country, Lord Garwood?" the minister continued to press his advantage.

It was the question that Garwood had hoped to avoid. Such a discussion was well beyond his mandate, and he'd been cautioned against being drawn into that discussion. In anticipation, he'd rehearsed his response. "Excellency, you know the answer to that is well above my pay grade."

"Then what is your mission here, Lord Garwood? Why your request for an urgent meeting here in Damascus? If your purpose is not to pave the way for a resumption of full diplomacy between our countries, then what? What *do* you want?"

"You are astute, Excellency," conceded Garwood. "There are two things . . ."

"Astute?" interrupted the minister, raising his voice. "Astute? We are Arabs. You have been flattering us, beguiling us, for generations. Astute is not the compliment we are seeking. We want the compliment from your country—the diplomatic recognition—that we can pursue our own destiny without interference from the West. We need to start rebuilding. The president would be pleased if your mission here is to discuss investments in our country. Investing in our future alongside us. Those would be the actions of a true friend."

Garwood knew that the minister was delivering prepared remarks. Without doubt, they had been agreed and rehearsed. Agents of the Mukhabarat would be tuned in electronically to their conversation. They would know that Garwood's remit would be to convey the minister's words—and tone—to London. In that respect, the minister would achieve his primary diplomatic purpose from their meeting. He knew, however, that their discussion so far was merely a prelude—a necessary preamble to the dialogue that the minister would be expecting.

"Some more tea?" enquired the minister, satisfied that his master's message had been duly conveyed. Garwood knew that the minister was a firm believer in shuffle diplomacy. Results might take time to achieve. A source at GCHQ had told Garwood that President al-Daser had scheduled a meeting with a Russian military mission for later that week. The Russians would be well aware of Garwood's visit—as would every other country with surveillance and wire taps in and around Damascus. In diplomatic circles, it never harmed to create a little leverage. The mystique of Garwood's diplomatic mission to the palace would enhance the president's bargaining power with the Russians. But long-term capital investment was not why Garwood was here—and he was aware that the minister knew it.

"Excellency," he began, "there is a matter of some delicacy that I would like to address—with your permission." He received an impatient hand flourish from the minister inviting him to continue. So far, their meeting had gone largely as he had expected. Now for the difficult part, he counselled himself. The minister would be expecting a request for something.

"A Spanish national, Minister—a female visitor to your country—has disappeared. We are most anxious to trace her and ensure her well-being." He paused, receiving no response. "Her most recent whereabouts were in north-eastern Syria, we believe."

"What is she doing here?" snapped the minister.

"A tourist with a visa, I believe, sir. On a photography tour of ancient monuments."

"Hah!" exclaimed the minister. His sarcasm echoed across the cavernous chamber. "Hah!" he repeated.

"Perhaps you have heard something, Minister?"

Garwood's question was met by an indifferent shrug. "A photographer?" the minister questioned.

"That's what we understand, Minister. It appears also that she is a serving officer with the Spanish Civil Guard but here on vacation."

"A spy?" stated the minister. It was not a question.

"Perhaps a more delicate mission," ventured Garwood. "Of mutual importance."

"Oh?" queried the minister. "Of mutual importance?"

"We would very much appreciate any news of her." Garwood skirted past the minister's dangling bait.

"How important is this tourist, this Spanish Civil Guard officer, to Great Britain?" asked the minister. "Is she a British national as well? Would it not be more appropriate if an ambassador representing Spain were here to make these representations to us? I confess to being confused, Lord Garwood."

"Your Excellency will be aware of the void that has been created. Regrettably, diplomatic networks between your country and the West have been another casualty of the war—the war we still fight, mutually, against al-Qaeda. Diplomatic channels have yet to be restored. We are most anxious to know if the officer is alive and well."

"I have heard no reports otherwise," offered the minister. "Most information concerning missing foreign nationals is copied to my department. In the absence of any unfortunate news to the contrary, I imagine you can assume she is alive. As for her well-being, I will have to make enquiries."

Playing his part, Garwood absorbed this unexpected, and welcome, piece of information and nodded his thanks. He hesitated before speaking again. "Your Excellency, now that ISIS is largely defeated and peace is being restored, I would anticipate that your government will receive various requests from chargé d'affaires and others—to reconnect, shall we say? Diplomatically, as you are aware, it's a matter of protocol. Many countries have not yet been invited to present their credentials, including our allies in Europe. I thought that, as old friends, you and I might benefit from a candid conversation."

"Protocol," huffed the minister. "Yes, Lord Garwood, you are well versed in that black art. Now, before we conclude this meeting, is there anything else? Something tangible I can take to the president—as a gesture of your country's goodwill?"

"We would be very pleased to accept your guidance on that subject, Excellency. As you might understand, I did not wish to arrive here with the offer of a diplomatic gift that might be interpreted as being presumptuous. One that, well, might not be regarded as fully reflecting the high esteem in which the president is held." Garwood kept a poker face and thought he saw a glimpse of a wry smile on the minister's face.

With the prize he'd sought now assured, the minister offered his hand in a satisfactory goodbye to his visitor. "I expect you will be hearing from us, Lord Garwood. I will check further on your Spanish tourist. Have a pleasant stay here in Syria, although I expect you will want to hasten back home.

"Restoration of diplomatic relations. It is an important task for us—particularly as a prelude to direct foreign investments and infrastructure funding," he added sternly. "As a matter of goodwill. I'm sure you understand.

"Good day, sir."

The Pentagon: Section 9

"Your intention is still the same, sir?"

"Inform the president only hours beforehand? Yes, that remains my intention, gentlemen," said the brigadier general. "At that point, we can spin the story that despite the failure of Project Catalyst, we are still capable of scoring a few spectacular touchdowns. But hold off saying anything about our man in the field. You never know what this administration is going to tweet. Krystal is a long-term deep undercover asset. We've invested heavily, and we have to protect him.

"Is there anything else I need to know?" he asked and saw the look that passed between the section chief and O'Flaherty. "What?"

"Officer Balmes, sir . . . Felix." O'Flaherty took the lead. "We think we can rescue her. Krystal has let us know that she's recovering well. We know where she is. Bringing her back alive would be very acceptable to our side, to Spain and the Brits. It would support our agenda."

They talked over the plan that O'Flaherty outlined. Finally, the brigadier general made a decision. "Okay, arrange it through your deputy director. She doesn't have to know anything about Krystal. I'll handle the president personally . . . if that's ever possible.

"It will be covert, and we can't offer you a lot of support.

"Bring her home, Lieutenant Commander."

Damascus

O'Flaherty sat opposite two men.

The windowless room in the Damascus suburb was like an underground bunker—featureless and sealed off from the outside. Poorly vented by a free-standing air-conditioning unit, the air was hot and stale. The room smelled of male perspiration and rancid coffee.

None of them seemed overly concerned. Standing near a wall covered in maps and satellite images, a young British special forces captain in shirtsleeves was pointing out the location of exits to a Syrian government building. "If you have to revert to Plan B, sir, try to make your way here. One of my men, disguised as a street vendor, has scouted the outside. Uniformed police usually are posted in pairs, here and here." He tapped the map. "My man spotted several plainclothes. That's no surprise; it's well-guarded.

"Now, if you could stand up, sir, we'll need to take several measurements—to make sure the PSD uniform fits you." He glanced at

O'Flaherty's tall, muscular frame. "We are adding some rank—giving you authority to move freely around the building. Forging your security pass, too, based on one we borrowed yesterday. What's your choice of handgun?" he asked a moment later. "It will have to fit into the Syrians' standard issue uniformed officer holster."

O'Flaherty glanced at his section chief. Both men smiled at the British officer's attention to detail.

"We've scheduled your entry to the building for just before 1600 hours, sir," he continued. "In the heat of the afternoon, their security officials tend to get a bit tired and sloppy. Before your chauffeured car draws up outside, one of our IT people will hack into a secretary's appointment files—on the floor where we believe Daniela is being held. We will confirm just beforehand. You will have a bona fide appointment with a senior official—arranged through the offices of the Revolutionary Guard. So, your visit there will be legit.

"The entrance to the roof and helipad has two guards," he added. "It faces west, so typically they shelter inside from the afternoon heat. We have an operative on the maintenance staff who will render them unconscious just before you get to the roof. Hence, that step won't delay your escape. We were worried about the possibility of snipers on nearby buildings, but the PSD building is three floors higher than the nearest one—and we'll have sharpshooters on board our rescue aircraft, sir. Any questions?"

"If I think of any, I'll ask." O'Flaherty smiled. "Good job of planning, Captain. Thank you."

"One last thing, sir," he answered. "I'll be heading up our unit in the approach helicopter. Don't be fooled by its markings—the boys will be doing a special paint job overnight. It will look like a genuine Syrian security forces aircraft. When you see me get out on the roof, you and your asset must sprint for the cargo doors. Leave the rest to us.

"If the aircraft doesn't arrive on schedule, assume that something has gone wrong. Go back inside the building and follow Plan B out onto the street. That's why I recommend you don't activate the fire alarms until you're certain of your exit route." He saluted, and prepared himself to go back out onto the street. "Cheerio, sir. Get a good night's rest. We'll message you with final details tomorrow. If all goes well, we'll have you and your asset out of the country by 1700 hours."

"Just in time for a nice cool imported beer at the officers mess."

The Brits had sent a signal to O'Flaherty confirming that Daniela was being confined in rooms on the fifth floor of the seven-storey PSD building. "We think she has a female guard with her at all times," the note said. "The best we can do is provide you with several M84 flashbangs and smoke grenades. Our maintenance man will place them in a cloth sack inside the rubbish bin in the men's washroom. Normally, the door is locked; he'll make sure the lock isn't functioning. It's to your right as you emerge from the elevators on the fifth floor. Everything is on schedule. Your driver, Ali, will be waiting for you inside your underground car park."

At 1530 hours, along with the section chief, O'Flaherty emerged in full uniform as a PSD colonel. His insignias indicated that he was member of the much-feared Sabre Squadron. It was a feature cleverly added to his uniform by the Brits, to expedite his passage through the building's security systems. Walking down the stairs to the underground car park, they climbed into the black chauffeur-driven limousine.

"Ready for this?" asked the chief.

"I am. Just hoping they aren't." O'Flaherty grinned.

On the street, as the vehicle threaded its way past a disorganised shamble of road works, he began to play his part. He'd rehearsed it numerous times already. The Brits were efficient. He could trust them to carry out their tasks on time and with precision. He was expected to deliver his part. In his mind, he'd split his journey to the fifth floor into three segments. Each had to be executed perfectly.

Already thinking about the first segment, he assumed the attitude of a PSD colonel—authoritative and impatient. He doubted that his passage to the elevators would pose any problem. His arrival would cause a panicked scramble among the ground floor flunkies. Stopping at the security screen to identify himself, his appointment would be quickly confirmed and his progress to the next segment unimpeded.

It was the unknowns on the fifth floor that he was most concerned about. Their intel sources were good, but there was always a chance that her captors had moved Daniela. Coming up empty-handed was not a prospect he relished. He felt he'd let Daniela down once already on this mission; he didn't intend to repeat it.

With the afternoon traffic, their journey was slow. In many respects, Damascus was back to normal after the wars. But there were signs everywhere of its destructive aftermath. Before the rebel forces had been suppressed, they'd shelled the city. Mortar damage was widespread, yet a surprising number of buildings seemed untouched by the conflicts. From visits years earlier, he recalled the busy sidewalks and the noise of daily commerce. Today, there was a noticeable absence of the throngs of tourists who'd once moved freely through the Old City—frequenting its charming shops, restaurants, and bars. Without them, much of the exciting buzz had gone.

"Five minutes ETA," said the chief, glancing out of the side window. "Traffic's heavy today."

His phone rang.

The chief barked at their driver to turn left at the next intersection—away from their destination. "We've been ordered to stand down," he said to O'Flaherty. His voice was terse and angry. "Orders from the White House."

"Dammit," exploded O'Flaherty. "What are they doing?" As they headed back to their operations centre, he shook his head. In thirty minutes, all going well, they could have retrieved their asset. Daniela could have been released from Syrian captivity and been safely on her way home.

Not for the first time, O'Flaherty cursed the chain of command.

What the hell was going on inside Washington these days?

Langley: CIA Section 9

The brigadier general with the southern twang was chewing gum.

"All right, all right. It's time to set the ball rolling," he said to a beefy, muscular man behind the desk. "Let's up the ante on these bastards. Show the sons-of-bitches who's in charge.

"Authorise the raids."

Al-Qaeda Retaliates

News of the kidnapping raids was first published online, by the Qatari news channel *Al Jazeera*.

Three abductions had been carried out simultaneously in broad daylight—in three capital cities: Damascus, Baghdad, and Beirut. Headshot photos of the three senior military captives, each against a backdrop of the newspaper's previous-day edition, showed them grim-faced and dishevelled. The headline read: "Our Holy War Continues." There was no mention of the capture of al-Amin a month earlier by Syria's elite forces. Nothing was said of his whereabouts. Even so, al-Qaeda's message was clear.

In the office of the deputy director in Langley, a small group was reviewing the news of the al-Qaeda abductions. "You have to admit that it's impressive. Weeks ago, al-Amin was captured by al-Daser," said a senior analyst. "You'd think al-Qaeda would still be reeling from the shock. Yet, they're able to mount a significant counterattack. We were expecting something—but not this. It has to be the work of their high command. It's all the more significant because it's so well coordinated. Precisely timed. Simultaneous political strikes against three capital cities in the Shia Crescent."

"It's an escalation of the conflict," agreed the deputy director, "although al-Qaeda hasn't claimed responsibility yet. That's unusual in the circumstances." She frowned. "I'd have expected they'd be gloating over their success by now. They've been able to pull off a slick operation and coordinate the ensuing global publicity more effectively than the best spin doctors we have here in Washington."

In a chair, at the back of the room, Michael O'Flaherty sat silently and looked morose. Yet, closer attention to his alert and intelligent features might have revealed that he was far from being gloomy. He knew all about the kidnappings. Returning from his aborted mission to rescue Daniela, he'd learned that his raid on the PSD building had to be called off because it had been eclipsed by other events. Section 9 had brought forward its timetable for the three abductions that would be carried out in al-Qaeda's name.

The brigadier general had taken him aside to explain. "We have to get al-Daser's attention on several more pressing matters, Lieutenant Commander.

"Repatriating the girl will have to wait."

CHAPTER 11
Xavi

The lack of any fresh information about Caterina's missing brother was concerning him.

Despite their efforts, there'd been no news for weeks. The team he'd put together was beginning to tire. Nothing obvious, but he could tell from their now less-than-regular briefings that their dedication was waning. Xavi tried to breathe new energy into their efforts, without much success.

He admitted his failure to Pilar.

"Maybe I shouldn't have raised her hopes," Xavi conceded.

Caterina seemed content enough. At least, she hadn't been visibly disappointed when he'd last talked to her. In other ways, her life seemed to be moving along. She had university exams coming up, she'd told him. Her personal life seemed to be keeping her busy too. Pilar and Xavi had kept regular contact with her. Occasionally, she dropped around to see their kids—sometimes babysitting for them.

She still asked about Antonio and, one day, took Xavi aside. Her young face was bright, but she seemed embarrassed about what she wanted to say. "When is he coming back to Barcelona?" Her eyes betrayed an excitement. "When he does, can you arrange for us to get together?" she begged.

Xavi continued to brief Antonio on the status of the missing persons investigation. His colleague and friend appeared attentive. He seemed concerned about Caterina, but other duties were keeping him away from the office—forcing him to spend a lot of time in Madrid. Then, early one morning, a surprise email arrived. Noting the time at which it'd been sent, Xavi realised that Antonio must have been working during the night, thinking about Caterina's brother. He'd come up with a promising idea. A bit off the wall, but that was typical of Toni's creative thinking, he told Pilar.

Explaining Antonio's idea to the chief, Xavi was pleased with his response. The Mossos chief was receiving positive comments from Madrid about the work Antonio was doing on his special assignment with Diego. He was happy to give the go ahead. "It's a bit unusual," the chief commented. "Typical of Antonio's unconventional ideas. Anyway, nothing else is working, so let's give it a try. Are you sure it's not going to upset the girl?"

With authority to proceed, Xavi handled the situation carefully. Caterina didn't seem at all upset. Delighted with Antonio's idea, she provided several excellent quality photos of the various pieces of furniture her brother had made. "Lorenzo has a unique style," she agreed. "His designs and marquetry stand out."

Within days, the furniture that Caterina had offered for sale online had attracted several potential buyers. She'd been smart. Caterina and Pilar agreed it would be best to price the items high—to keep away bargain hunters. Pilar insisted that, to protect Caterina, they should buy a prepaid phone and use it solely to take calls on the listing. "I'll handle the enquiries," she offered.

Her urgent call to Xavi that morning came during a meeting he was having with the chief. She was breathless. It was the first real breakthrough they'd had in the missing person case. "A buyer from Florence has one of Lorenzo's pieces," gushed Pilar. "It was carved very recently. The buyer bought it locally and wants more. Oh, Xavi! This could mean that he's alive. In Italy, for goodness' sake. Let's pray it's true."

Xavi was more circumspect.

"You have contact details for the buyer?" he asked his excitable wife.

Lorenzo

Within three hours, overnight bag in hand, Xavi had boarded a Vueling flight to Peretola Airport. That afternoon, he met the buyer of the furniture and established where the woman had acquired the beautifully intricate hardwood bench with its impressive marquetry. He called Pilar to let her know but cautioned her to restrain her excitement—until they knew for certain. Xavi tried to rein in his own elation.

The furniture buyer was a professional in the trade, graceful and helpful. She agreed with Xavi—the smell of the wood and unhardened polish of the piece she'd purchased indicated that it had been finished very recently. She had an idea where, she told him. Together, they visited a small cooperative workshop in the *mobili antichi* district, not far from the Basilica di Santo Spirito.

Xavi was grateful for her assistance. A native Italian speaker, she also spoke Spanish and several other languages. Hearing the story, she soon caught the excitement. "He's an amazing craftsman: a master."

Inside the workshop, a woodworker, with a padded hammer and glistening sharp metal chisel in hand, directed them to a small alcove at the back. It seemed to Xavi that, in those few moments, they had exited the modern world and time-warped back to the old Florence of Medici master craftsmen. They might just as easily have been working on the timber doors for the cathedral of Santa Maria del Fiore. Threading their way past partly assembled pieces of art, the aromatic smells of seasoned wood and stain were intense. Large slithers of fresh shavings lay curled amidst the sawdust. Craftsmen—bent lovingly over their work benches—gave rapt, critical attention to the works being fashioned with their skilled hands. It was evident to Xavi this was an ancient temple of creativity. Few sounds were audible except hushed voices and the abrasive chafing of timbers by artisans and wood grains being polished to perfection by devoted apprentices. There wasn't an electrically powered tool within the hallowed atrium.

It was an amazing place of work, thought Xavi, resolving to take a few photos before they left. For now, however, their eyes were on the solitary figure of a bearded man. Almost like a surgeon, he was absorbed with insetting an intricate pattern of exotic veneers into pencil-thin channels surgically cut into a piece of astonishing beauty. "Lorenzo?" asked Xavi quietly, not wanting to interrupt the master's concentration.

The bearded man looked up and smiled pleasantly, then returned to his work.

"We call him Luigi," said a nearby woodworker. "He's very quiet and prefers to keep to himself." Pointing to the skylight above the bench where Lorenzo was sitting, he continued. "He likes natural light. It's amazing. He's a genius. He spends hours examining the grain and subtleties of the wood before he starts work on it. What an amazing eye, he has. Such gifted hands.

"We have no idea where he comes from—but we love having him here.

"He inspires the rest of us."

They were gentle with Lorenzo; each of them in turn tried to coax him to leave—to return home.

He smiled agreeably as they talked, but clearly had no knowledge of who he was or how he'd arrived there. One thing was clear: he did not want to move from his sanctuary. It was a dilemma for Xavi. Devoid of ideas, he turned to the furniture buyer. "Bianca?" he asked.

"You have photographs, the ones you showed me, of the other pieces he created," she observed, flicking her long hair over her shoulders. She took the phone he'd offered, which was opened to his gallery.

"Luigi," she said to Lorenzo. "*Un momento per favore.*"

Girl With a Vengeance

As soon as Lorenzo's eyes saw the photos of the pieces he'd created, his eyes brightened. He looked closely at them, then at Bianca, then back at the pieces, enlarging the image to study the detail. He nodded. The pleasure etched on his face was that of a child. They conversed in Italian. It was mostly Bianca who spoke while he listened with an occasional brief question.

"He says they are his pieces," she explained to Xavi. "He remembers creating them. Regrettably, he cannot recall the circumstances. He knows nothing of his life before he came here. He does not remember having a sister. I am sorry. Perhaps you could speak to him in Spanish or Catalan?" she invited. "It might trigger a memory."

Xavi recalled something. It was a photograph that Pilar had taken of them at Easter—with Caterina and the kids. He texted his wife and, moments later, showed Bianca the image she'd sent. "This is his sister." He pointed out. "Wait, I will enlarge it for him."

Shown the photo, Lorenzo smiled vacantly.

"It does not trigger any response, as you can see," she said. "I am not an expert, of course, but I think you will need the assistance of a professional—to help return his memory to him. I'm sorry, I wish I could be of more help. I am not a doctor, yet I suggest it may be wrong to move him from here. Clearly, he is content with his work. Creating more trauma for him might cause a reaction. That is just my advice, Xavi. You must decide."

He nodded. "Certainly, we cannot move him against his will. That would offend my colleagues here in the Carabinieri and might be unlawful. We must proceed by the rules. But at least we have found him—and for that, we are immensely grateful to you, señora."

"If you wish," she offered, "while you make the appropriate arrangements, I can visit him every day, to make sure that he is well. Also, that way, I can find out more about his life here—where he is living. If perhaps he has a friend . . ." She looked at Xavi with a raised eyebrow. "Perhaps that friend is a benefactor. Perhaps not. As a policeman, you

267

will need to know these things, of course. It would be a tragedy for his family if he is spooked and runs away—if we lose him again. I can make a few phone calls to explain the situation to a friend I have in the police—if that would help you, Xavi? In the meantime, with his condition, I think it unwise to let him far from our sight. One never knows what is going on up here." She tapped her head. "Now it is almost time for a glass of wine before dinner. They will be finishing here soon; it is the Italian way. After the work, the relaxation. For you, too, in Spain . . . I think.

"My friend, the policeman, he has some influence. He is a friend of my late husband. After you two have spoken, I invite you for dinner. And Lorenzo, of course. He must come too. I will ask him—we will talk about the furniture he loves so much. Also, I will ask him for permission to take his photograph. You will need that for identification and other purposes."

Xavi was impressed with Bianca's cool efficiency. He'd worked through a plan in his mind on the flight into Florence. But until he'd confirmed Lorenzo's identity—matching it to the photos that Caterina had supplied—and found out what was going on, there was little else he could do. Now this gracious and generous Italian lady was stepping in and making the kinds of arrangements he needed to make. She was gentle and highly organised. Elegant and beautiful.

He'd have to identify himself to the Italian authorities if he intended to take Caterina's brother back to Barcelona. As a Spanish police officer, a thousand kilometres away from home turf, he had no more jurisdictional rights in Italy than the average citizen. Given Lorenzo's medical condition, it was inevitable that the repatriation process would take some time. There were decisions that Caterina and her family would have to take. His role as investigator, his job here, was coming to a close. It was time to hand over responsibility to others.

Out of pure generosity, Bianca was stepping in to help. She seemed to understand that Lorenzo, suffering from amnesia, was a flight risk.

He might find the sudden attention too much—and unsettling. She'd offered a clever solution, and her friend in the Florence police force would assist—when necessary—in a more official capacity.

Xavi called Antonio, asking how he wanted to proceed. The most important thing was that the missing person had been found safe and well; he was aware it was not always the outcome. That alone was a reason for celebration. He would call Caterina and give her the good news. He had a hunch that she'd jump on the next plane—to be reunited with Lorenzo.

There was a lot more to be done yet.

Thanks to luck and some very nice people, it had been a successful journey.

The Café

Antonio was having coffee with Diego in a small café in Madrid. He was airing his concerns about their investigation into the sniper's attempt, a year earlier, to kill Daniela.

"There's something we're missing, Diego. Something big. We've been focusing our attention on searching for the sniper. Yet, there are so many other loose ends on this case. So many things we haven't been able to explain. Not just about her but about al-Qaeda cells here in Spain. You've told me that neither Claudia nor you believe you've caught the ringleader yet. A powerful person is helping them. Daniela was getting close—maybe that's why the sniper was ordered to kill her. Maybe not. We don't know."

Diego nodded his agreement but said nothing. He seemed to be aware that Antonio was about to launch into one of his famous investigative inspirations. He remained quiet as his colleague hoisted himself to his feet and paced up and down the deserted café floor.

"We could tackle it from a different viewpoint," suggested the Mossos detective, sitting back at their table. "Ask ourselves what outstanding issues we're still dealing with—the ones we don't have answers for. See if there are any common themes, any patterns. Something we've missed."

"Why not, I suppose?" Diego didn't sound convinced.

"I'll give you the first question—one we haven't been able to answer," Antonio began. "It was a long time ago in Ceuta when we were removed from the David Casals homicide investigation. The Civil Guard brigadier stripped us of every iota of information we had about the case; then he sidelined us. Obviously, he'd received orders from someone high up in the chain of command in Madrid. Did you ever identify who that person was?"

Diego shook his head. "When I got back to my office, the file had already been sealed. Like you, I was locked out of the case. I couldn't get near it. Later, when the intel about the al-Qaeda bombing attempt in Barcelona became the big news, and when Raphael Robles' cover was blown, the file was completely erased. I couldn't even enquire about it. But I could ask Claudia to revisit it, using her Army and Civil Guard connections. I'd love to have a shot at getting even with that brigadier—and interrogate *him*.

"Before you ask, Antonio, I'd say the next big unanswered question is about Raphael Robles," he continued. "What I mean is that, at GEO, we still haven't squeezed him dry of information. Not just that, but we haven't really been able to get through to him yet. He's still cocky and confident."

"Another outstanding issue is the sniper," Antonio added. "We now know who he is—but not who gave him his orders. That's on me to find out. I'll give it high priority."

"Numbers four and five are the cold case murders of Francisco Rioja and the builder," said Diego. "So far, we've associated those with Luis, the chauffeur—we've assumed that he killed them. But did someone else have a motive to kill Rioja? It happened about the time I interrogated the condesa—when she blew open her husband's cover and denounced him as a traitor. He died shortly afterwards from a heart attack."

A waitress emerged and hovered nearby; they ordered fresh espressos.

"It's interesting how many of these unanswered questions involve the condesa, isn't it," observed Antonio. "She's a common element in at least half of them. That doesn't make her guilty of anything; it's just a detective's observation."

Diego watched as Antonio stood up and continued to pace the room. He'd seen his Mossos friend like this before and knew better than to interrupt him. It was DI Antonio Valls doing what he did best—thinking laterally. After a few minutes, he returned to the table with a glint in his eye.

"Indulge me in a silly game," he said, and reached for a paper napkin. "I'm going to write down a name—and not show it to you. Then I'm going to pitch you on a new scenario. After that, you write down the name that comes to you. Let's see if our deductive powers get us anywhere."

Out of Diego's sight, he scribbled a name and hid it. "Here's my pitch," he began. "Just a few minutes ago, looking at the loose ends in this case, we agreed that the condesa was a player in most of them. But neither you nor I—nor Claudia, apparently—think she's guilty of anything more than a few episodes of infidelity with the Russian Pavel. She's not the terrorist mastermind we're looking for." Antonio's eyes were now bright and anticipating. "What if it's not the condesa but someone very close to her? It would have to be someone who also was trusted by her husband, Carlos. Someone who is, or was, close to Raphael Robles and who knew what he was up to. A person in a position of influence—who, right now, is trying his or her best to remain above the fray. I think it's someone the condesa knows well—but doesn't suspect.

"Ok, Diego, who comes to mind?"

Seconds later, two upturned paper napkins displayed a single name—Felipe.

"Shit," said Diego. "He's never even come up on our radar. It makes so much sense—he's been involved every step of the way. We've never even thought it necessary to check into his background. He's a lawyer; it's routine for those guys to be present everywhere."

"Let me give you his collaborator's name," proposed Antonio, "cynical bastard that I am."

He slid the paper napkin over to Diego.

"Holy shit," Diego exploded. "You can't mean . . ."

"Yes, Robles," confirmed Antonio. "If you check out Felipe's background, my guess is that he and Robles are connected a long way back in time. You may have to investigate their history at school and university. Think of it: two well-educated, intelligent people, probably idealists from the very beginning. Neither is married—although, by itself, that means nothing. They could be gay lovers. But if we work with the theory that Robles is bisexual—based on his history of abusing Daniela—we may have the fresh lead we badly need in our investigation."

Antonio continued talking. "We could bring Felipe in for questioning, but we don't have any obvious grounds for doing so. He's a lawyer; he knows his rights. If he's the terrorist mastermind, we need to nail him with good old-fashioned conclusive evidence. A deep background check on him is the first step."

Antonio's words were lost. Diego was already out of the door, speaking into his cell phone and heading back to GEO Headquarters. Antonio guessed that, very soon, his friend and Claudia would be putting their heads together.

Then he received a text from Diego. It said simply: *"Claudia has additional information that she couldn't share before. She has issued an arrest warrant for Felipe. A Red Alert."*

Antonio knew that if they'd found evidence that Felipe was the terrorist mastermind, they'd make damned sure they swept up every fish they could catch—in a massive counterterrorist dragnet. That was a job for the federal authorities. He had other leads to follow. Aurelia and her sniper brother were among them. Louis, too . . . and the grandee. There were a few additional pieces of the puzzle still missing, but he had a feeling they were involved somehow, and the net was closing around them too.

He just regretted that there wasn't something more substantial he could do to help Daniela.

Despite everything, he still couldn't quite let go.

Aurelia

Antonio needed a breakthrough—something that would get them to the next level.

It came by chance later that afternoon, and it came from Aurelia. He knew immediately that something was wrong. Over the phone, her voice sounded strained and she was breathing heavily. "He's here," she said. "At least he was. My brother was here, Antonio. You told me to tell you immediately."

"Where?"

"My apartment, but he's left already. Just a few minutes ago. The thing is, I think he's going to kill someone."

"Are you in danger?" His voice was concerned.

"No, I'm fine. He wouldn't threaten me. It's someone else he wants."

"Do you know who?" Antonio asked, trying to anticipate where her brother was heading.

"He didn't say, but he was talking about someone he needed to get even with. The person who'd given the instructions for the sniping incident he was dragged into. He said he'd found out that the intended victim was innocent. He'd been set up to carry out the killing—by someone with a lot of influence and power. He was fixating about it and is determined to hunt the person down. He told me about another incident, when he was in Afghanistan with the army. I'm sure he's suffering from something serious. Severe stress, at least. He needs help, Antonio."

"Does he have a gun?"

"Yes, it's in a sports bag that he brought with him into my apartment. He showed it to me. It's a high-powered hunting rifle, disassembled into parts. He had a handgun too. In his belt. He didn't threaten me, but he was really angry. He scared me. I begged him not to throw his life away and told him that I want to help him recover. That seemed to calm him down for a time, but he started to ramble again about his target. Then he left."

"How long was he there with you?" he asked.

"About two hours."

As she was talking, Antonio was texting instructions for Xavi to issue an APB. He was fairly certain that Dampierre would be heading for Madrid. That gave the roadside patrols a good chance of intercepting him en route. Yet something was nagging at him. Why would Aurelia's brother have taken his sports bag into her apartment? Maybe he didn't want to risk leaving the bag in his vehicle—where it could be stolen. Or maybe it was because he didn't have a vehicle.

"Aurelia, can you get your car keys?" he asked, anticipating the worst.

She came back a few moments later. "They're missing. They were by the front door—I think he took them, and my car."

It confirmed Antonio's hunch. Meanwhile, he'd been texting instructions on his phone and checking his watch—calculating the driving time to Madrid. "Your licence plate. I'm going to need that—and make, model, and colour.

"We may be able to intercept him, if we're lucky."

Reports were coming in, based on CCTV footage, showing that Aurelia's car was travelling east, towards the French border, not in the direction of Madrid. Then he received a call: the driver had been stopped and apprehended.

"Send me a photo," instructed Antonio, already suspecting something was wrong. "That's not him," he said when the image arrived on his phone. "He's created a decoy." Glancing at his watch, he calculated that it had been over three hours since Dampierre had left Aurelia's apartment. The decoy had lost them valuable time. Antonio knew that the fastest Renfe AVE high-speed train from Barcelona to Madrid had a journey time of two-and-a-half hours. It would have been a tight timetable, but Dampierre could have made the journey—and arrived in Madrid already.

Minutes later, he received a phone call from a sergeant commanding their mobile units. The driver of Aurelia's vehicle had a plausible explanation. He'd told the sergeant he'd been hired to drive the vehicle to a drop-off point in Gerona. The description he gave of the vehicle's owner matched that of the fugitive. Worse yet, the vehicle pickup had been at Barcelona Sants train station—the departure point for high-speed trains to Madrid.

An hour later, Diego called. Surveillance footage confirmed that Dampierre had a reserved first-class seat and had arrived unchallenged in Madrid, carrying a sports bag. "We have a sniper loose in the city, Antonio.

"And we don't have any idea of his target."

News of a police incident at the Royal Palace reached Antonio that evening.

Diego had called him. "We arrested Felipe this afternoon. I've been incredibly busy interrogating him. We haven't had much time or the resources to track down the missing sniper—concentrating our efforts instead on Felipe's links with al-Qaeda. We should have paid closer attention."

He sounds defensive and apologetic, thought Antonio, wondering what was coming next.

"I'm calling to tell you that the grandee . . . the Duke of Valladolid died this evening. He fell, or was pushed, from his apartment window. We don't know yet if it was murder or suicide. Claudia's been dealing with the Royal Household for the past several hours. The news is breaking; you can imagine that the media will be all over it. Sorry, Antonio, we have no further intel on Jules Dampierre, or his whereabouts." He rang off.

Antonio set aside some work on a separate investigation he was doing for the chief. Like Diego's team, his squad was already fully stretched. There was only so much they could do with the available resources. Even so, tracking down the sniper had become a personal priority. A question continued to nag at him: Who had given Dampierre his instructions? Both he and Diego had concluded that, most likely, it would be someone in the Royal Guard. Yet, when he'd been interviewed, the sniper's former commanding officer clearly knew nothing of his recent activities. They hadn't been in contact for some time, he'd said. Other enquiries supported his claim. They'd checked with his army buddies and superior officers without success. The line of enquiry had gone cold.

Once again, Antonio was stumped. He was working at his office when Diego called again.

"Potentially an important break, Antonio," said his Madrid colleague. "Our community patrols received a call from someone who used to know the sniper. Actually, the call was from his wife. She's quite distressed. They received a visit from Dampierre—not long ago. The man was trying to downplay it, but we're hauling him in for questioning. We're also applying for a search warrant. I suspect we might find weapons inside his house—legitimate licenced firearms . . . and maybe some illegal ones. Here's the thing: from what we know so far, this guy may be a small-scale arms dealer. He hasn't opened up yet. Our people will get him to talk."

"I'll keep you informed."

Diego called off.

Madrid: Serious Crimes Unit

Diego was sitting in, as an observer.

He was watching with considerable interest the real-time video of a man being interviewed in the next room. The interviewers were well into their questions.

"So, you admit knowing Jules Dampierre—from your army days. He visited you today asking some questions?" barked a middle-aged female interrogator. Her hostile demeanour indicated that her take-no-prisoners attitude was probably the nicer side of her intimidating personality. "Tell us again why he was visiting you—and what questions he asked." Her raised eyebrows suggested she was not convinced he'd been fully forthcoming. Examining a thin file that a uniformed officer had just delivered to her, she cautioned him. "Oh, and before you answer, I should tell you that, issued with a search warrant, we've found a substantial stash of illegal weapons and ammunition at your house."

"Sir?" she prompted when he said nothing.

"I want my lawyer; I have the right to legal representation," the man fired back.

She laughed. It wasn't a pretty sound. "That's not how this works, sir. You've been watching too many movies. Demanding to see your lawyer is a privilege reserved for regular criminals. You're facing charges under terrorism laws. Special rules. So, I'll ask you again, why was he was visiting you—and what questions did he ask? What did he want from you? If you don't answer—and truthfully—we'll bring in the heavies." Shifting her considerable mass that overflowed her chair, she looked at him enquiringly. Her male partner, sitting alongside at the table, flashed a warning to him. His look said, "I'd cooperate if I were you."

Time ticked away. The interrogators seemed to have endless patience.

"Okay, but I need a deal," he said eventually.

"Duly noted," said the woman, clearly not interested in negotiating any details. She passed the file folder over to her partner, giving him a knowing and triumphant look.

Diego was impressed. The female officer had used her resources to good effect. The man began his statement: "I was Lieutenant Dampierre's controller on the day he was given his assignment to assassinate the target. I received my instructions from a minister in the government—I'll tell you who in a few minutes. We'd been recruited by a special forces unit, so everything we did was legitimate. You can't put me in jail for that."

He paused and looked at the woman, but she said nothing and let him talk. "Lieutenant Dampierre only had a small opening—a short window of time to make the kill. He could have taken the shot, but someone in the line of command kept delaying. Eventually, I was instructed to order him to abort his mission. But, almost simultaneously, I was told to wait, and then the order to proceed came."

"The order to abort; who issued that?" demanded the woman.

"The government minister," replied the man, giving her the minister's full name.

"Who did he report to?" she pursued.

"We were told not to discuss that information with anyone," he replied.

The woman got to her feet and stood behind him. She pointed over his shoulder at the mirrored glass observation window. "You see that? Behind that glass is a very powerful man. He's watching you and he's much more powerful than the special forces you talk about. Now, I don't want to upset that powerful man behind the glass. Yet, it seems that is precisely what you want me to do. So, I'll ask you one more time. Who overrode the minister's order to abort the mission? Who was it?"

The man looked terrified, glancing back and forth between the woman and the mirrored glass. "The order came from a senior Civil Guard officer in Madrid. They have jurisdiction over the elected government in military matters; they had the override."

"Name?" demanded the woman, becoming exasperated. She was not expecting the answer she heard.

"Colonel Claudia Ramirez," blurted the man. "She gave the order for Lieutenant Dampierre to proceed with his mission and eliminate Officer Daniela Balmes. That was the question the lieutenant asked me today, and I gave him the answer I just gave you."

In the next room, with his face now pressed close to the mirrored glass, Diego almost fell off his chair.

Claudia looked up when Diego walked into her office, followed by several armed officers.

Seeing the grim determination etched into his face, she immediately understood. Rubbing her forehead, she breathed an audible sigh. "I hear you've arrested the sniper—Jules Dampierre," she said. "I'm grateful for that. He was on his way here to kill me. Now you know why.

"I've been waiting for this, Diego," she added. "You've come to arrest me, haven't you!"

"You're too good a detective not to have figured it out."

Antonio couldn't recall a time when he'd heard Diego sound so defeated—devoid of all energy. His colleague had just finished telling him about Claudia's arrest and the charges.

"I was there in Istanbul," said Antonio after a pause. "I thought that the Civil Guard commandant who'd come to repatriate Daniela was one of the rudest and most intolerant officers I'd ever met. Looking back, I guess he was doing his job—the best way he could. When I met Claudia, I had no idea that he was her father. They're so different. I guess they had one thing in common. Both of them were convinced that Daniela was a double agent. Claudia was determined that Daniela had to be stopped despite the minister's command to halt the assassination attempt. She and her father had to stop the transfer of the money Daniela had stolen. They had to stop it going to al-Qaeda to fund a massive increase in terrorism. It's such a tragedy. She was doing what she thought was right."

"Claudia broke the law," said Diego, his voice flat. "She didn't have authorisation from her superiors in the Civil Guard. She went outside the chain of command—something she'd never done before in her whole career. Just one mistake—and only because she didn't know. None of us did—not at that time. Even when we found out about Daniela's assignment, we couldn't tell you, Antonio. You weren't in the need-to-know loop."

"Well, Claudia did try to put things right—after she found out," said Antonio. "Credit to her for that. She did everything she could to help support Daniela's mission. Don't take it too personally, my friend. You weren't at fault."

"None of us were, really," said Diego. "Even so, Daniela had an almost impossible assignment. Both of us made it more difficult for her.

"I don't know how that girl managed to survive—against such huge odds."

CHAPTER 12
Mossos Headquarters: William

He wanted to help.

So, William turned to where his skills were abundant and exceptional—cyber sleuthing. His efforts would have to be unofficial. His boss needed results. That meant he'd have to be resourceful and quick, and very careful. Kiko would be a genius addition to his research efforts, he thought. He'd met her in the Mossos IT department. They'd dated and became inseparable. It was such a familiar relationship now that he'd almost forgotten her Spanish name. Besides, she preferred Kiko. It had an edge, she said.

"What is it that we don't know?" she asked that evening at his apartment.

With the assistance of some recreational drugs, they were already on the same wavelength. He was able to reply at the level she'd pitched her question. "You're asking who's at the top of the chain of command—the person to whom everything goes? The chief honcho? The commander-in-chief? The single most important, best-informed person we have to hack?"

She nodded.

It was evident to William that she'd already reached her own conclusions. "I need to go online," he replied with a grin. "This particular incursion is going to be a first for me, Kiko. Obviously, you're up for it."

Over the next half hour, they deftly dodged through cyber landmines, firewalls, and security screens. Rejected as a malicious attacker numerous times, Kiko took a fresh route and eventually found a revolving door in a personal interest application favoured by the target. William added an auto-translation filter. Minutes later, undetected, they gained access to the personal files of the ultimate authority—the person who, at that moment, was in control of Daniela's fate. They watched in excitement and awe as he made keystrokes in real time.

They were in.

Waiting patiently until he signed out, they went to work exploring. It was now well past midnight. On the heels of their searches, the ravenous cyber worms that Kiko introduced instantaneously consumed all evidence of their activities—eliminating everything, leaving no trace behind. Eventually, they stumbled onto several private communication files, gasped at the contents, downloaded them, and exited.

"Who can we give them to?" asked Kiko, unsure of what William had in mind as a next step.

He was equivocating. He admitted that he hadn't given it much thought. The intel they'd downloaded was dynamite—highly credible and revealing but obtained illegally. That didn't matter, he explained to Kiko. They weren't seeking evidence to be used in a court of law. In the right hands, this information was politically devastating.

But who could they trust?

Antonio was sleeping when William called. They took a taxi to his apartment. It was 0200 hours, and Barcelona was still vibrating with its boundless energy. "Holy shit, guys," said Antonio, several times.

"Do you know what to do with it, boss?" asked William.

Kiko watched in nervous anticipation. It was the first time she'd met the legendary Inspector Valls. Would he cooperate? She needn't have worried. Antonio was already speed-dialling Madrid.

"You guys go home," he mouthed, as the call went through. "Good work, and thanks."

"Diego?" he said loudly. "It's Antonio. "You'd better be awake for this.

"I can't tell you who it was, but a reliable source just hacked into President al-Daser's personal computer."

Pablo

"You haven't met Pablo yet," said Diego, not waiting for an answer from Antonio.

"He's taken over from Claudia here at GEO 60. He's seen the files you sent me. By background, he's CNI," he added. "If we can bring him on side—convince him that your idea can work—he'll help us. I've arranged for a meeting." Diego knocked on the CNI man's door. "By the way, he's impressed with all the work you've been doing for us. Full of praise."

"Hola Antonio," said Pablo, greeting the Mossos homicide squad officer like a long-lost friend, along with a strong embrace. "It's been a long time."

Antonio grinned. "A nice surprise for me too. You're an important man now, Pablo."

"You haven't done badly yourself, Antonio."

Diego looked mystified. "Antonio and I were roommates at the Academy," Pablo explained. "We haven't seen each other for years. Come and sit down, Toni. Diego has briefed me on your idea, I like it. More importantly, I think it could work.

"We just have to get the PM's support."

Flying Kites

It was February, and a windy Sunday in Barcelona. Unseasonably warm.

Hot Saharan winds had airlifted tonnes of sand across the Mediterranean, settling deposits of golden-brown desert dust across the city—on cars, outdoor café tables, and the Juliette balconies of Ciutat Vella. Children playing on the street thought it was magical and fun—tracing their initials and drawing Cupid hearts. The girls, daring and giggling, embarrassed the boys by carving shy admirer's admissions of everlasting love. Parents, seizing the opportunity, caught the spirit of the moment and herded their boisterous broods to the park or waterfront—carrying beach mats and long neglected kites rescued from the dusty cupboard by the front door.

Antonio, who was in town for the weekend, had just received a call from Pilar and Xavi. "Want to join us and the kids?" they asked. "We've invited a few of the others as well. Bring a jacket. It's forecast to be much cooler by this evening."

Commuting back and forth to Madrid had taken a toll on him. He knew he needed to get out more and take work less seriously. Since Aurelia's brother had been taken into custody, he and she had hardly spoken. Adding to the sombre mood, Claudia's arrest had depressed everyone. He'd never known Diego to be so withdrawn. It got worse. There had been no further news of Daniela. He'd heard through mutual friends that Maria had become engaged and admitted to himself that, in a way, he felt relieved. He'd treated her very badly in the last several months of their relationship. Hearing that she was very much in love with the new man in her life, he felt less guilty—although not a little jealous.

He felt older. Wearing glasses, prescribed by his reproachful eye doctor—who had scolded him, saying they were long overdue—he felt self-conscious. He'd rushed his decision and hadn't made a good choice of the frame. Now he looked older as well. The sole highlight of his recent existence had been Xavi's success in locating Caterina's brother. He was happy for her. His dejected mood was the outcome of all the other things getting him down. The idea of some fresh air was appealing. Besides, he got along well with Xavi and Pilar's kids. It would be fun to get out and relax for a time. Gratefully accepting their invitation, he felt a pleasant but unexplainable sense of apprehension.

Hours later on the warm soft sand of the beach, with the strings of several soaring kites in his hands, he towered above his friends' clutch of five youngsters—trying his best to keep his balance as they stood on his feet and grabbed hold of his legs. He laughed in a way he hadn't for a long time. It really was enjoyable and, he admitted, gave a different meaning to life.

Caterina arrived—alone. Without quite knowing why, Antonio gave way to an impulse and kissed her with a flourish that would earn the envy of the most romantic of paramours. It was natural, eager, and long-lasting. By the time it was over, they received the appreciative applause and wolf whistles of everyone standing nearby. The applause continued insistently until the couple re-engaged for a second even longer round. Pilar snuck a photograph of them; she thought that Toni had never looked so happy.

Just when they'd nearly given up all hope for him.

———

Two evenings later, Antonio arrived nervously at Caterina's apartment. He was fully armed.

Not with a gun but a small, soft red leather box. Taking out the diamond ring, he proposed to her on bended knee in her kitchen. She had no hesitation. They made love and both declared they'd never felt so happy.

Caterina had a surprise for him too. "I hope you want kids." She giggled nervously. "Because I'm already three months. I thought I'd be showing more by now."

Antonio was very late for work the next day—and deliriously happy.

The Condesa

Sitting in the living room of her home in La Moraleja, the condesa thought about the call she'd just received.

Two officers from the security services were on their way to talk to her. They had a special request—a highly sensitive and confidential matter. She knew Detective Inspector Diego Abaya from GEO 60 and liked the man. She had not heard before of the Civil Guard ranking officer who had identified himself as Lieutenant Colonel Pablo Delgado.

It sounded serious. Defensively, she became anxious that their visit might be connected to Felipe's arrest. She hadn't been told much after he'd been taken into custody. She'd been cautioned again under the Official Secrets Act and interviewed numerous times by the security services. Dreading this new visit, she wondered if some additional, potentially awful, information had come to light about her husband, Carlos. He and Felipe had been very close for so many years.

Felipe had betrayed her. After Carlos's death, she had trusted the family lawyer with all her personal affairs, her innermost thoughts. She'd been devastated when they'd told her about his arrest. After the events a year ago at the lodge, and her discovery of the treacherous plot devised by the general and Carlos, her confidence had been shattered. For months, she'd been working hard to restore Carlos's good name. Was this visit a prelude to yet another set of ghastly revelations?

Hortensia showed the two officers into the condesa's soundproofed office. Her greeting was polite but curt. Straightaway, she noticed that they seemed defensive, and that made her curious.

Diego took the lead. As he outlined the purpose of their visit, she managed to hide her surprise and sense of relief. They were here to ask a favour, not to grill her about Felipe. She listened carefully and quickly transitioned her thinking to focus on their request.

"We are under strict constraints, Condesa," said Pablo, awkwardly. "Clearly, there are many aspects of this initiative that we are prohibited from discussing. Despite your former senior status and security clearance within the government, I apologise that we are not permitted to be more forthcoming." He passed her several of the documents that Diego had received from Antonio.

"I won't ask how you obtained these files," she said after reading and handing them back. "However, I'm not entirely unsympathetic to the idea. One question before I talk to the prime minister: Are you sure that all the normal diplomatic channels have been explored? I mean, from my experience in government, it's not always evident to everyone what's happening behind the scenes."

Pablo looked pained. "Diplomatic cooperation usually is the most appropriate—and, invariably, the most effective—route to obtain the release and repatriation of our nationals." He stopped and gestured towards Diego. "What my officer is telling us is that in Daniela's case, our combined initiatives so far have fallen between the cracks. It's a stalemate; nothing is happening. That's why we are proposing an unofficial Spanish initiative."

The condesa's intelligent eyes were bright and sparkling. "Those documents, Lieutenant Colonel, will give the prime minister the political leverage he needs to get a repatriation deal with Damascus. He may not need to use them—just having the information may be enough. There's a significant political win here for the government—if we are successful. It's a shrewd thought process."

Pausing, the condesa was aware that she could seize the moment and advance her own agenda. Her earlier wary and defensive thoughts about Carlos and Felipe had been swept away in an instant. To make such as request, the country's top security forces must trust her. It was a profound realisation . . . and a huge relief.

"I agree that the downside risks are limited, and I have the advantage of knowing the background in this case," she said eventually.

"I'm prepared to take it up with the PM immediately. I will put my full efforts behind it."

"You have my complete and heartfelt backing. Let's do it."

Damascus: Tishreen Palace

The condesa was driven to the old palace by a uniformed driver, escorted by a young and physically powerful armed bodyguard. Undoubtedly, he was a Mukhabarat undercover officer, she thought. The limousine flew a national flag pennant. Heavily weaponed police escorted them on a cavalcade of noisy motorbikes.

She'd had dinner alone at her hotel in the central district. The atmosphere in the upper floor dining room overlooking the Barada River was subdued. Outside, the evening call to prayers echoed loudly across the city. Recorded voices of the imams resonated from the minarets demanding unequivocal participation of all believers. They instilled a feeling of collective orderliness that she respected and, in some ways, envied. It was strangely calming, she thought.

Despite the obvious war damage elsewhere, this section of Damascus remained vibrant, bustling, and confident. Dark-shaded windows in the limousine meant that she saw little along the journey. Just a blur of lights and glimpses of people on the streets and buildings—many of whose history stretched back several thousand years. Damascus had always been at the epicentre of world events.

A lady walked towards her—arm outstretched in greeting.

"Your journey, Condesa?" she asked. "It was not too demanding?"

"Thank you for seeing me at this hour," she replied, aware it was late evening and that the lady was close to the focus of power in the country.

Soon they were sitting alone in a small drawing room, its upholstered chairs plush and the ambience relaxing. Architecturally, it was magnificent, she'd noted, as she'd followed her hostess into the room. Quite Ottoman in its décor.

"The president . . . he is a good man," said the woman, speaking with poise and dignity. "Obviously, he is preoccupied with the recent hostage takings. He asked me to greet you."

"You are both very gracious," replied the condesa.

The woman nodded, still appraising her visitor.

The condesa was impressed. The woman spoke fluent Spanish and clearly was well-educated. She lapsed occasionally into English, to better express what she intended to say. When she did, she had a cultured accent that seemed to originate from the South of England. London private schooling, perhaps, the condesa guessed.

"I understand that you are strongly favoured as a future candidate for prime minister in Spain. That would be a first, would it not?"

The condesa shrugged. It was not a dismissive gesture, more of a modest acknowledgment.

"Setting aside for a moment your mission here tonight," her elegant host continued, "I am wondering if perhaps we might briefly discuss the future. Wars are terrible. We may have disagreements about the rights and wrongs, yet in the perspective of millennia of history, differences tend to become blurred."

The condesa stiffened. Not if you are the victim of a bullet or an IED or chemical attack, she thought, but said nothing—mindful of her purpose in coming here. She had no wish to alienate her hostess. Simply to ensure Daniela's safety and take her back to Spain. As a politician, practised in the ways of the legislative chambers of the Cortes Generales, she had a strong sense of when to stand and fight a battle and when to withdraw to fight another day.

"Nothing ever is one sided," she acknowledged neutrally. "Here, in what we in the West refer to geographically and politically as the Middle East, you know that better than most."

The woman picked up on the theme. "Our region is complicated. As a female, you understand that. We face many constraints that do not hinder you in the West. Well, I say that, but you have your own sets of obstacles in pursuing the espoused Western democratic creed of what is right and wrong. It is a high bar for all of us to attain—indeed to aspire."

Her hostess was being civilised, and the condesa doubted she had the right to lecture her on matters of state. "It is late evening, and I do not wish to impose upon you and your family's time . . ." she began to say.

The woman gently brushed aside her concern. "It is important for both of us—for our countries. I have checked personally. Officer Daniela Balmes is fully recovered and healthy. She received a bullet wound in her neck, but our surgery was successful. Cosmetic care will remove the superficial traces, although not perhaps the deep trauma she has been through. You may be surprised by what occurred, although I do not expect you wish to comment on the incident."

Holding her face without expression, the condesa was aware that this powerful woman would know all about the raid at the village during which al-Amin had been captured, and Daniela too. If the woman was going to berate her or make a demand, now would be the time. Lord Garwood had been unable to break the impasse over the negotiations for Daniela's release. Talking to her host, the condesa sensed she could do better.

She was aware that the recent hostage takings by al-Qaeda would bring focus to the discussion. The woman, by nature, did not seem to be confrontational, she thought. She was hard-line, yes, but not adversarial. The condesa was grateful that she was being treated cordially and with respect. Yet her guard was up. She'd read a widely circulated *Vogue* article from years earlier. She knew that her host was exceptionally intelligent and could be quite convincing.

As if reading her thoughts, the woman smiled. "Our ability to know what is taking place within our own country should not surprise you, Condesa. After all, we have a sophisticated intelligence network. More effective than most, I think. It is a combination of advanced modern technologies and good old-fashioned sleuthing. At school in England, I enjoyed reading Sherlock Holmes. His disciplined observation was supported by careful and systematic deduction. Above all, as we do today, he relied on a consistent flow of reliable information."

It was obvious to the condesa that she was referring to the legendary skills of the Mukhabarat. Days earlier, however, they had not been effective enough to prevent the hostage-taking of one of their most senior military officers. She said nothing in reply.

"You're a practising Catholic?" the woman continued before the condesa could respond. "I respect your faith. My family's background is Sunni; my beliefs are Ba'athist. We have a few differences of view with other Muslims; yet we hope to become reconciled over time. Also, with other faiths. It is not an easy task, as your history in Spain attests—the Inquisition, dealing with the aftermath of al-Andalus. These reconciliations are not immediate; it is the nature of things. Sometimes, they are barbarous and cruel. Rarely, as you say, are they one-sided."

The condesa did not wish to engage in a debate. It was neither the time, nor her role. "Officer Balmes?" she asked gently.

"My . . . the president . . . has no objections to her being released," said the woman without hesitation. "Unconditionally. She is free to leave at any time. Now, if you wish."

"Your gesture is compassionate and generous," said the condesa, trying to hide her surprise and delight. "Thank you." She meant it genuinely, recognising that it was a huge concession by Damascus. Yet, her instincts told her there was something not being said. She recalled the last-minute instructions she'd received in Madrid from the prime minister.

"May I ask, ma'am," the condesa began. Her tone was diplomatic, as she proceeded to reveal her prime minister's olive branch. "Would the president be willing to allow his foreign minister to receive our ambassador—to discuss possible resumption of diplomatic relations?

However, I must be frank with you," she added hurriedly, "there would be strict conditions regarding human rights. Spain and many other countries have been extremely concerned." She left the rest unsaid.

The answer she received was heralded by a look of concern from the woman. "Five years ago, we were on our knees—nearly beaten by ISIS and other forces pitched against us. The caliphate was our enemy, and yours too . . . the Coalition's. We were crippled by two wars: the war against terrorism and the civil war. Sometimes, it seemed in those long dark days that there would be no future for peace in Syria. Fortunately, that is now mostly past us—for the moment. Yet, we are left poor and impoverished.

"We are anxious to rebuild, Condesa," she continued. "Yet, it must not be at the price of reparations that would be even more crippling. Please recognise that fact. There must be no misunderstanding." She leaned forwards in her chair. "The Syrian refugee problem, as it is described in the West, is a horrible tragedy. It is awful. Much of it could not be avoided. Do you think that we wanted to lose our youth to the world—our families, our doctors, and our scientists? Why would we deliberately drive away future generations of our people so desperately needed for rebuilding our country? The answer is that we didn't, and we don't. We already have lost so much.

"We know that enlightened policies of human rights must be part of the healing process throughout our country," she continued passionately. "Meanwhile, to protect those who have survived, we need to rebuild and soon. We fear the risk of a famine; we worry about further violence and unrest. Yes, we will be anxious to negotiate diplomatic understandings—but not on unilateral terms."

The condesa was aware that nothing more on the subject should be said that day. She nodded her understanding, conveying a silent acknowledgment that the woman's message would be conveyed directly to Spain's prime minister, and beyond.

"Al-Amin?" she ventured.

The woman delayed her reply. "Nothing about the capture and imprisonment of al-Amin has been disclosed by our government. In the president's view, nothing needs to be said." She paused. "His interrogation is ongoing, and we are anxious to share any pertinent information with our allies."

The condesa knew that this was her moment to pitch the prime minister's request. "Resumption of diplomatic relations would bring other issues into context," she began, but the woman was already well ahead of her.

"Such as extradition treaties?" she enquired. "You would require al-Amin's extradition to Spain—to face the crimes committed at Atocha?"

The condesa nodded and reminded herself not to underestimate her host. "If I may?" she asked and opened her bag—taking out a photograph. "This is Raphael Robles, a former senior policeman and, perversely, head of al-Qaeda in Spain. He's in jail in Spain and will identify al-Amin as the principal architect of the Atocha train station massacre."

Glancing at the photograph, the woman said, "Ah yes, the man you call Mustapha. We know about him, of course. Not from Officer Balmes—she merely confirmed it. Our security services had been monitoring him for some time—before you arrested him."

The condesa was adept at controlling her body language but inwardly was taken by surprise.

"I cannot predict what the president's response would be to such a request," said the woman. "My own view, however, is that he would not support a showcase trial of al-Amin in Spain or anywhere else. As a country of empathetic people, we Syrians feel deeply for the loss of life from the Atocha tragedy. It was truly horrible. Ghastly.

"The president is dedicated to a mission of peace," she continued. "In this region, it is a long-term vision and the journey will not be easy. It is time for the West—and others—to realise that the solutions to our regional problems must be allowed to emerge from here—in this country and others. In short, we value the West as an ally and as an investor—but we will not support its continuing presence or any future interventions as a military power. Jumping in and out of our country, whenever the mood takes you, has to stop.

"Looking into the future, al-Qaeda has the opportunity to transform itself. Instead of remaining as a terrorist group, it can become part of the peace process," she added. "Maybe it will; maybe not. At present, such an outcome is unwelcome speculation to many. Things may turn out very differently. Yet, agreeing to al-Amin's extradition—and inevitably a showcase trail in the West—would be counterproductive to the interests of this region. The president believes that, as a league of Arab and geographically allied nations, we can work it out for ourselves. Even if mistakes are made in the process."

There was silence in the room.

"More tea?" she asked eventually, receiving a polite decline.

"I don't wish to delay you. It's late," said the condesa.

"Of course. You and Officer Balmes will wish to leave as soon as possible. I understand." The woman lingered for a moment, seeming to want to end the meeting on an appropriate note. "Daniela certainly is a remarkable young woman. She has experienced much in her young life."

Rising from her intricately embroidered armchair, the woman offered a firm handshake to her departing guest. Her eye contact was direct and unflinching. "I wish there were more women in the world like her."

"Like us."

Langley: A Friend Calls

Levi Morstadt, veteran of Mossad Collections in Tel-Aviv, was on the phone to O'Flaherty.

The Israeli had just given him a summary of the condesa's conversation at the Tishreen Palace. In addition, he was now passing along the news that—at that very moment—the condesa was walking down the palace steps with a tired but grateful Daniela alongside her. "No attribution please, Michael," he said, relishing the significant role he was about to play in world affairs. "She wasn't wired, and we didn't let her know we'd be listening in. Just don't ask how we eavesdropped. Even you guys won't be told how we did it. We have to keep some technology secrets, my friend."

Michael O'Flaherty silently acknowledged to himself that the news of Daniela's release was an incredible relief. He listened as Levi continued excitedly. "Both ladies will be escorted straight through airport security and customs and will go immediately to their waiting aircraft. Their captain is talking to air traffic control right now; it looks to us like it's all systems go. The Syrian president himself and the first lady have given the green light. Permission has been given for the condesa's Ejército del Aire jet to leave Syria. The skipper has filed flight plans to Torrejón Air Base in Madrid. Israeli jets will shadow the Spanish aircraft's flight across our air space. We're assuming you'll take over from there. Can you confirm that, Michael?

"Flight time is about five hours," he added. "You'll already have done the math. That's an ETA of 1500 hours in Washington. Just enough time for your president to make a press announcement that the Syrians have nabbed a high-value al-Qaeda operative—and have him in custody. Your president can announce that Syrian Special Forces captured him, with American and Russian collaboration. You can leave Israel out of the loop on this occasion. My advice, Michael," he continued, "you'd better add the Ruskies to the credits or they'll get pissed off.

"I know you're not a spin doctor, my friend," Levi continued, "but we see this as a win-win, as you Americans like to call it. A win for the region and for the Middle East peace process. For your president as well—in a vital election year. Yes, of course, it will help Israel too." He continued dispensing his advice. "Your president's people will want to confirm all of this with Damascus first. Coordinate the announcement worldwide; you've got the gist of it. A verbatim copy of the recorded conversation that took place at the Tishreen Palace tonight is en route to your usual drop box. Along with some video too. It will help you guys authenticate the event and save time. Call me when you want to take me for lunch, Michael." He rang off.

Five minutes later, O'Flaherty knocked on the door of the deputy director. "Enter," she instructed. Standing in front of her, O'Flaherty delivered the news. "It's been authenticated, ma'am," he assured her.

Moments later, she was talking directly to the Oval Office. The foreign secretary and NSA chief of staff were in the room, listening in as the gloating president took her call on the speaker phone. Alongside him, the White House press secretary quickly grasped the full significance of the news. Her nimble fingers were already keyboarding a first draft of prepared remarks for the president to consider. She knew that, as usual, he'd probably just stand at the podium, hold them in his hand, and ad-lib his announcement to the world. He always did. Most likely, he'd tweet as well.

Her efforts were redundant. The president's wily foreign secretary had already drafted a highly confidential press announcement for the president—he'd done so a week before al-Qaeda's hostage takings in the three Middle Eastern capitals. The lowly press secretary didn't know it, but the raid had been a shared secret between Section 9, the president, and a select few members of his inner circle. Elite sections of the United States national intelligence services had once again flexed the collective muscles of their covert capabilities.

The press secretary quickly realised that her efforts had been eclipsed. The game had been stacked since the start. Clearly, there was another agenda at play. This wasn't just the president's work; she suspected that other very powerful people were directing events.

She suppressed a gasp. It was a heartfelt gut reaction. A whisper of a deep-state cancer in the world's most powerful democracy? No, it couldn't be. Could it?

The wily foreign secretary's only concern was just what—and how much—the US administration would have to offer in concessions to the Syrian government for it to agree with Washington's terms and conditions. The staged hostage-taking had badly rattled Damascus. He reflected with some satisfaction that the price might not be as high as the presidential inner circle had estimated. Overall, it mattered little.

The president, always an opportunist, had acted immediately on the new developments. As far as he was concerned, he could dismiss any inconvenient truths as fake news. He was already stabbing at the button on his red scramble phone to Moscow.

There was another deal to be done.

Welcome Home

Daniela's debriefing at the Torrejón Air Base was finally over.

After a thorough medical exam, the interrogation had taken three hours. It wasn't as strenuous as she had expected. A Civil Guard colonel had been toughest on her. In response, she'd simply described the key events and left out the things she couldn't explain—the unanswered questions gnawing at her. There were too many of them, and some things had happened recently that just didn't make sense. Well, not unless you were highly cynical and had a very suspicious mind—and that exactly described her mental state at that moment.

"We will need to talk to you again, Daniela," Diego had said quietly to her at the end of the debriefing. His voice was kind and considerate, she thought. There was no hint of criticism; no suggestion of failure. Just establishing the facts. If anyone blamed her for the mission's failure, she certainly didn't detect it. Overall, they couldn't have been nicer. It was clear that they were proud of the way she had conducted herself. They were in awe of her ability to survive under unbelievable pressure and—against all odds—come back alive.

It occurred to her that the Americans might not be so understanding. That confrontation was yet to occur—and she needed to be well prepared for it. She was convinced that they hadn't told her everything. Something was going on in Washington that they weren't revealing.

One thing was for sure. She might be home and relatively safe among friends, but she knew that her mission was far from over. The game was still afoot. What concerned her most was that it was a dangerous game of cat and mouse.

A vicious and unscrupulous cat.

And she was the tiny mouse.

CHAPTER 13
Langley: Deputy Director's Office

Their smiles conveyed their relief.

"She's home," said the delighted deputy to the team assembled in her office. "Well done, everyone."

O'Flaherty shared his boss's sense of reassurance, even though he thought that her congratulatory message to the team sounded more motivational than reflective of reality. It had been the Spanish government that had negotiated Daniela's release, achieving something that the US administration either couldn't or didn't want to do. He stayed behind as the others returned to their desks.

"You'll want to get over there and check on her, Michael," said the deputy. "She's been through an incredible level of stress for a long time. We owe her a great debt of gratitude.

"What a remarkable young woman."

Flight to Madrid

O'Flaherty knew he had to get there quickly; he couldn't afford to delay.

There was too much at risk. Daniela was safely back in Spain, and she would be subject to ongoing interrogations. The Spanish authorities would be carrying out post mortem reviews—their own investigations into what had gone wrong, trying to determine why Project Catalyst had failed. For Section 9 in Washington, it was all about damage control, the Department of Defence brigadier general had told him. They had to be in the driver's seat, able to set the agenda and direct the outcomes.

Before leaving for the airbase, O'Flaherty had read Daniela's debriefing statement—taken when she'd arrived at Torrejón. He'd read the condesa's statement too. Neither had said anything that contradicted his account of events. He'd re-read Daniela's account several times—knowing she was quite capable of sanitising her story. What she hadn't said was as important as what she'd told them.

Now, saddled into a web seat of the half-empty US Army KC-135 station hopper flight that would arrive in Madrid in around twelve hours' time, he thought through the implications of her account—what she'd said happened at al-Amin's village hideout. It seemed to him that she'd left out a lot of details, and that worried him.

He cursed his luck. The 135 was the only military flight available at short notice. He'd flown in them before and knew from experience to come prepared. Military personnel knew they had to layer up to counteract the aircraft belly's unevenly ventilated conditions. Too cold in parts; too hot in others. The 135 wasn't as bad as some other aircraft he'd experienced during missions. It wasn't as restrictive as some of the smaller airframes that offered only a shared urinal and honeypot. On those long journeys, the toilet arrangements were grossly unpleasant. Resigning himself to the situation, he pulled the zip on his travel gear tightly around his neck, folded his arms, and settled in for a long and uncomfortable overnight journey to Europe.

Unable to sleep, O'Flaherty's hyperactive brain forced him to review what he knew—and speculate on what Daniela didn't know. She'd been incarcerated and most likely told very little while locked away. Unless someone in Madrid had briefed her, she wouldn't know much about what had been happening—outside Syria—since she'd been captured at al-Amin's village. It was unbelievable: the raid had been two months ago now.

In captivity in Damascus, Daniela would have found out that al-Amin was in Syrian hands. She wouldn't know anything about his own activities—that, during the raid, he'd escaped from the village along with Jamal. She wouldn't know that he'd tried to rescue her from the prison in Damascus. She wouldn't know about the reprisals—the US-staged retaliation, carried out in the name of al-Qaeda, against the Syrian Special Forces' capture and detention of al-Amin. And she wouldn't know about the hostages they'd taken. Most importantly, she wouldn't know about Hasan and his covert role. That was the main risk that worried him.

O'Flaherty was aware that there were some pieces of intel, and some news items, that he shouldn't share with her. Not yet. Officially, she was still under active interrogation—despite her soft-soap handling by Spanish authorities at Torrejón. They were smart; they'd know they had to adhere to the debriefing protocols. He could be confident that they wouldn't have given anything away. It wasn't that they didn't trust their own officer; it was merely standard procedure after a mission. The interrogators' job was to glean the facts of where she'd been, what she'd seen and heard and said—without being influenced by intel gratuitously being fed to her.

When he met Daniela in Madrid, he could dig deeper—and certainly intended to do so.

Months earlier, soon after the raid on al-Amin's village, after his escape to al-Tanf, he'd been subject to the same debriefing protocols—interrogations just like hers. He'd told the CIA debriefing team most of the story of what had happened. He was the only one, from the West at least, who'd been there to witness it first-hand. There was no one to corroborate or dispute his testimony. Except Daniela, of course. It had been a tough interrogation, but his account had been accepted. The victors always write the history, he'd reassured himself privately. He just needed to talk to Daniela. Was there anything she would contradict?

His thoughts drifted to the condesa. In many ways, she'd been an inspired choice. The Spanish prime minister had been prudent and insightful. Against the odds, they had achieved an inside edge in diplomatic communications with Damascus. He wasn't sure how. Historically, the Spanish hadn't been particularly well-connected in the region. Normally, O'Flaherty felt comfortable that there wasn't much he didn't know about what was going on—in and around Damascus. Somehow, this time, the CIA had missed it.

Right now, Daniela was an unknown factor—and she had a mind of her own. There were several other things he needed to take care of in Europe—dangerous loose ends. His journey was well-timed, he reflected, as the rhythmic hum of the KC-135's engines finally lulled him to sleep.

Safe House

Daniela woke up in a sweat.

She woke to the ringing of church bells—the sound of Christianity. And a buzz on the intercom. Feeling disorientated, she recalled vaguely that she was in a safe house—somewhere in Madrid. It didn't matter where; she was home. Sleep and take some downtime, they'd said. Glancing at a clock, she saw it was well into the afternoon. The intercom buzzed insistently.

"Daniela!" Unmistakably, the voice was Michael O'Flaherty's. "I have your favourite beverage," he shouted. "A nice carajillo—fresh from down the street. What do I need for your security guard to let me in the gate—a password or something?"

He knocked at her door moments later. Hesitating to open it, she breathed in deeply and studied his image on the video intercom. She'd recognise his red hair anywhere—except that, to her surprise, it was now closely cropped. He looked and sounded different. Finally, unlocking the door, she stepped aside and let him in—noticing his compact travel bag.

He grinned. "US Army flight; I arrived an hour ago. Came right here. You have a tough security detail surrounding this place. Fortunately, they were expecting me; I was cleared through. Hey, you look wonderful." He pulled her towards him and gave her a hug. Then he saw the scar from her neck wound. "Holy smokes! I heard about that. I read your debriefing statement too. We can catch up on each other's news in a minute. How are you feeling? You've been through an incredible ordeal, Daniela."

"A little tired to be honest, Michael. At least we both made it out." She smiled and searched his face—needing his opinion. Not of how she looked but for a clue. Had she screwed up? She'd had her chance to help capture al-Amin and failed. But Michael was giving nothing away—not even the ghost of a look of recrimination. He just seemed delighted to see her. Maybe she was imagining the questions gnawing at her?

Breaking free, she walked to the kitchen. "They haven't allowed me a phone or a laptop, and there's no TV here. But they've stocked the fridge; it's jammed full. Do you want a glass of wine or something?"

He shook his head. "Have you slept much, since getting back?"

"Surprisingly, yes," she answered. "How long are you staying in Madrid?" she added. "I expect you want to hear from me what happened?"

"No rush," he said. "Take your time."

"You should fill me in too. I wondered if you'd got out all right. How did you escape? What happened to Jamal and the others? Are they still alive?" She came and stood close to him, as if not wanting to be overheard. "Did I screw up, Michael?"

He'd been expecting the question and had his answer ready. "There was a leak. The Syrians knew about us all along. It wasn't your fault, Daniela."

303

"Three years, almost. That's what it took us, Michael. Three years to get close to him—to bring him down."

"We got that part right," he replied. "No shame. As tough as it is on us personally, we have to get over it and move on. We'll find out eventually where the leak came from. That's someone else's job now." He paused. "I flew over as soon as I could, to see if you're okay."

Reaching out, he squeezed her shoulder reassuringly. "Do you want to walk me through what happened?"

O'Flaherty had left Daniela's safe house and gone downtown to check in at his hotel.

Before his visit, she'd been tired and run-down. Now she felt exhausted after giving her account of events and answering his questions. He'd been gentle but insistent. She'd had lots of questions for him too—it hadn't been a one-way street when it came to those, but it was very one-sided when it came to answers, she thought. As lacking in energy as she was, Daniela pulled herself together and made another full-octane coffee. Things still didn't add up. She knew he was holding back; there were important things O'Flaherty wasn't telling her.

Her questions needed answers, and she needed help. People she could trust. Recalling the phone number she'd been given, Daniela called the condesa.

La Moraleja

"Can we talk?" asked Daniela.

An hour later, they were seated opposite each other in the security of the condesa's study at La Moraleja. "I'm not sure where to begin," said Daniela.

"Something's wrong?" probed her host. "It's safe, Daniela—between these four walls, nothing is being recorded. You can speak freely."

Daniela took a long drink of chilled water. "I think my mission was a set-up," she began. "I think it was set up from the beginning. Honestly, I'm not trying to blame someone else because it didn't meet its objectives. I think it was set up to fail."

"By whom?" asked the condesa. "And why?" Her frown was etched deeply into her elegant forehead. When she'd received Daniela's call, she'd been concerned—on several levels. There had been a cautionary note in the medical examiner's observation notes that the girl was exhibiting signs of extreme stress and exhaustion. PTSD had been mentioned. She and Deputy Inspector Diego Abaya had discussed Daniela's condition outside the interview room at Torrejón Air Base. Diego had reassured her that, in his opinion, Daniela was very much in control of her emotions. Her answers to the debriefing questions had been clear and articulate.

"I think it was set up to fail—by the Americans," Daniela continued. "This is really going to sound weird."

The condesa shook her head. "Nothing could surprise me." She paused. "Daniela, if you're wondering if you can trust me, I'd be happy to arrange for you to speak to someone in authority who can help. Have you talked to DI Diego Abaya about this? We can arrange it, if you'd feel more comfortable? Antonio, if you'd like? But there's a question I must ask: Is your life in danger? Do you feel that your life is threatened?"

Daniela shook her head. "I don't know. I'm not even sure about the concerns I have. A lot of it's circumstantial. I don't want to sound paranoid or make excuses for having failed my mission."

As the girl was speaking, the condesa had a flashback to the traumatic events at the lodge—involving Carlos and the coup attempt by the general. She understood very well the position that Daniela was in. The girl didn't know who to trust. Something very important was bothering her. The claim about a set-up—if it was true—needed to be handled by the proper authorities. When they'd met at the palace in Damascus, the girl had said very little. She was exhausted. On the flight back to Madrid, she'd slept most of the way. On the orders of the prime minister, there had been no discussion of her mission. The condesa knew her job. The PM's and security forces' instructions had been precise: "Negotiate her release and, if you can, bring her home safely. Don't discuss anything with her." Now it was different: the girl was home and she'd been debriefed. They could talk.

An hour ago, when the condesa had agreed to Daniela's request to meet, it had been a judgement call on her part. The girl trusted her—enough to seek her help. The condesa knew that her handling of the situation would come under scrutiny. That didn't bother her. She wasn't without power and influence, and she had a shrewd idea that something significant was in play. Daniela's phone call—and request for help—had come as a surprise. The condesa wasn't naïve, and she'd had her own experiences of the conflicts between Spain's security forces. She was wary of the Civil Guard too. Over the past few years, she'd learned a few things about who she could, and couldn't, trust.

The condesa made up her mind. She'd rely on her gut instincts. "Daniela, I want to help you," she said. "It's obvious from what you've told me that there's another agenda at work. Maybe something of international importance. I'm a civilian and, as you know, a former minister of the government. I've taken the oath of secrecy. You can trust me. I'll stand by you, and help. I promise." She paused and squeezed the girl's hand. They were icy cold. "Whatever it is that's worrying you—we have to find answers. We have to get help from people we can trust—who *you* can trust—people in authority who can take the appropriate actions. I'll tell you what I propose, and see what you think of my plan. Is that okay?"

Daniela nodded. Her face was drained of colour; she looked thin and stressed.

The condesa smiled reassuringly and held the girl's hands to warm them. "I think the first thing we have to do is to protect you. Make sure you're safe. Then we have to shift the huge burden of responsibility you've been carrying. You've been shouldering too much. How you've done it, I have no idea. You really are a remarkable person, Daniela. Incredibly strong—and brave. Now that you're back among friends, we can help you.

"DI Diego Abaya is your official liaison officer. If you trust him—as I do—I suggest we call and ask him to come here. While he's on his way, I think it would be wise for you to tell me all about it—and we should record it, just in case.

Over the next hour, Daniela presented her thinking to the condesa.

Then Diego arrived.

O'Flaherty's Report

Returning to his hotel—a tastefully renovated old heritage building in Madrid's downtown area—O'Flaherty composed his report to the deputy director.

He was careful to be factual and objective. Daniela had carried out her mission in exemplary fashion. Astonishingly, against the odds, she had reached the target. They'd been betrayed, and she had nearly lost her life in the process. She'd been incarcerated and tortured. With her early history of childhood trauma and subsequent abuse, the cumulative impact was more hardship than most humans could endure. She was a remarkable young woman and a brilliant operative. A natural and intuitive espionage agent. He quoted the medical examiner at Torrejón, who'd added a cautionary note to his findings. The doctor had referred to Daniela's extended period of detention in Damascus by the Mukhabarat—and concluded that she was exhibiting signs of chronic traumatic stress.

O'Flaherty revealed something that he'd known for some time but had excluded from his earlier reports when she'd been screened for admission into the agency. While living with Raphael Robles, she'd become pregnant. Abortions had just become legal in Spain, but a stigma remained. Robles had arranged a procedure privately; it had not gone well. There was doubt if Daniela would ever again be able to have children of her own.

In his summary, O'Flaherty said that Daniela needed an extended period of rest—and therapy. He concluded that a final decision would the prerogative of the Spanish authorities. However, he recommended that Officer Daniela Balmes should be retired from operational duties with the agency, with full compensation—receiving medical and financial support to enable her transition back into the workforce.

It would be best if she were retrained for less stressful duties—in a civilian occupation.

Barcelona Train Journey

The tall, muscular man who boarded the non-stop express train from Madrid's Atocha station to Barcelona early next morning looked around the carriage to locate his tourist-class seat.

Stuffing his well-used backpack into the overhead rack, he settled down to sleep. On schedule, the journey would take less than three hours. He was lucky; the summer tourist rush had not yet begun and the train was half empty. With a dark wig and fashionable, coloured glasses, O'Flaherty looked like a typical budget traveller. Despite his height, there would be minimal risk of being remembered, he figured. A hoodie shielded his face, hiding it from the train's security cameras. Later that day, he would make the return journey in much the same way—but with a change of disguise.

Exiting at Barcelona Sants station, he caught a taxi to a local hostel. It was a budget establishment and he had no intention of going inside. Paying off his driver, he lingered for a few moments before strolling up the busy street. Already close to noon, the day was getting warm. Stripping off his hoodie, he stuffed it into his backpack and hailed a second taxi—this time, travelling close to his intended destination in a pleasant suburban neighbourhood.

It would be a surprise visit.

"Hello Bill," said O'Flaherty.

"Michael!"

Opening his front door, Bill Yates seemed surprised—although his surveillance cameras should have forewarned him, thought his visitor. "Sorry to disturb." With a grin, O'Flaherty handed him a bottle of Kentucky Reserve. "I heard you'd retired, Bill. Sorry I missed your going-away party."

"Come in," said Bill, admiring the gift. "Nice thought, Michael—thank you. An unexpected pleasure. I didn't know you were coming into town. Mind you, I haven't been in touch with the office as much recently." He looked at his clothes. "Excuse my appearance. Gardening today. Roses are budding nicely. Come on through." He stepped aside to let his visitor in. "Bit untidy I'm afraid, ol' buddy. Bachelor household and all." He placed his gloves and secateurs on the kitchen table. "Nice choice," he said, looking again at the rye. "Put your backpack over there. How much time do you have?"

"My flight just got in," lied O'Flaherty. "I need to talk to you confidentially—about Krystal. Better here than at the office. Shop talk. Need-to-know classified stuff—the usual drill." He glanced around the room. "Your place is looking nice, Bill. It's been a few years since I visited." He saw the framed photos and, alongside, a small vase of fresh red roses. "Is it hard . . . without Carol?" he asked "She was a lovely lady."

"It changes your life, Michael." He breathed in deeply. "Hey, can I offer you a drink?"

"One of those would be nice." O'Flaherty chuckled, pointing at the gift bottle. "No ice, no water, Bill. I think we both deserve it, don't you? Oh, and a glass of water, please. I'm dehydrated from the flight."

Bill returned a few minutes later with two cut-glass tumblers of the rye and some water. "Cheers," he said, as they clinked.

O'Flaherty's mobile sounded. "Sorry," he said, putting down his untasted rye. He spent a few minutes keying in some data before resuming their conversation. "Thing is, Bill, I want to talk to you about the Russian business. Our communications with Alexei in Latakia." He downed half the water in a single gulp. "Wow, I needed that," he said, finally picking up his glass of rye, noting that his colleague was already well into his. "Tidying up loose ends, Bill. We all worked hard on that job. Yourself included." He walked to the open French window. "Beautiful garden. Your pride and joy?" Closing it, he drew the heavy curtains across and returned to his chair. "Sorry, do you mind? It's a bit bright on my eyes."

"The Russians, Bill," he said again a few moments later. "They're constantly trying to compromise our field officers. That's why we carry out random screening audits. Station chiefs like you are high up on their list. All intel is filtered through the local command centre. You know all of this, of course."

"What are you saying?" asked his host. "I'm not being accused of something, am I, Michael?" He laughed, but then half-choked as he saw O'Flaherty's narrowed eyes and impassive stare. He took a nervous gulp of his drink.

"The Russians made a play for the money that Daniela secured at the Cyprus bank. But I think you know that, don't you, Bill? Our old friend Alexei and his boss decided to supplement their pensions. You were my point guy with him, Bill. You handled all the communications. I checked some of your emails; you became very free with some sensitive intel."

"I was trying to assist Daniela," said Bill. "In Latakia, she needed their help."

O'Flaherty shrugged. He didn't seem convinced. "Thing is, Bill, I know that Daniela gave you the access code for the bank safety deposit box in Cyprus; she told me. You passed it along."

Bill shook his head. "The emails, yes. Not the passcode. I didn't give that to anyone."

"Anyway, it was a risky move on your part—and theirs," continued O'Flaherty, ignoring his plea. "Unfortunately for them, the Brits had the bank covered 24/7. Their entrepreneurship backfired. GRU found out, and they don't like freelancers. With our president and his Russian connections, you'd be surprised how much overt cooperation goes on between ourselves and the Kremlin. Two great former empires struggling to adapt to their inevitable decline."

"Michael, I didn't. It's not true," Yates protested loudly and started to get to his feet, but O'Flaherty interrupted.

"It's not just that, Bill. It's the other things you know about—Krystal, he's too valuable. I can't take a chance. You've become too much of a risk."

His host slumped back in his seat and examined his drink.

O'Flaherty shook his head. "I wouldn't contaminate a beautiful rye like that, Bill. Go ahead and enjoy it. My orders are to take you in—back to the States. Leave everything as it is, please, including your devices. In prison, you can have your personal stuff brought to you. For now, just leave it for the professionals to go through."

Bill's eyelids seemed heavy. He looked tired, listless, and sleepy. He looked again at his drink. "Michael, I didn't reveal anything to anyone. I promise you, I didn't. Not the passcode. Honestly. I wouldn't do that." The glass slipped out of his fingers and rested on his lap.

"Sorry, Bill, I lied. Just like you lied to us," said O'Flaherty, staying seated. His tone sounded harsh.

Considering his next moves, he stood up. Putting on a pair of coated plastic gloves, he went to the kitchen sink. There, he decanted his untouched glass of rye back into the nearly full bottle and replaced it in his backpack. Taking out an identical bottle containing a few measures of unadulterated rye, he went back to Bill Yates' body and

311

transferred his host's fingerprints onto the bottle, positioning it on the side table alongside him. From a thick, zipped plastic bag, he removed a smaller bag with traces of crystals—fragments of the poison he'd administered moments ago. Transferring his host's finger and thumb prints onto the bag, randomly this time, he left it on the side table.

Washing the glasses they'd used, he placed them inside his backpack. Filling the sink with hot water, soap, and chlorine from under the sink, he flushed the pipes thoroughly. It was a pity, really, thought O'Flaherty. Bill's job was unspectacular. He'd been a popular fixture at Barcelona Control. A dependable fixer. No one had ever questioned his loyalty; it was just assumed.

He checked the cupboard and adjusted the layout—to suggest that only one glass had been taken out. Re-opening the lounge curtains, he wiped down the surfaces he'd touched. Removing the disk from the surveillance system, he checked the room. Finishing touches, he thought. Taking one of the framed photographs of his victim's wife, he repeated the fingerprinting process and placed it flat against Bill's lifeless body. It looked like the grief-stricken man had ended his own life. No suicide note, but that meant nothing. O'Flaherty didn't care if forensics found faint traces of his DNA. His explanation—if one were ever needed—would be that he'd visited the house several times previously.

Glancing at his watch, he saw that there was plenty of time to get rid of the evidence in his backpack en route—with time to change into a new disguise and catch his train back to Madrid. Then he would check out of his hotel and get a taxi to Torrejón Air Base, where a USAF Gulfstream was flying in from Washington to collect him.

Mission accomplished, and with the time change, he'd be back home by late evening.

Bill Yates's body might have lain there for days had it not been for a thoughtful neighbour.

She liked Bill . . . very much. Also living alone, she often cooked his evening meals. Her shocking discovery was reported immediately to the Mossos. His address came up on their system as having diplomatic status, and Antonio's Homicide Squad was alerted. Xavi was on duty when the suicide was reported. His instincts told him to call Antonio. "According to our records, the victim is connected to the commercial section of the American consulate here in Barcelona; I thought you'd want to know, amigo."

Antonio said he would be there in thirty minutes. He called Diego. "Can you take a closer look?" the Madrid policeman asked. "See if there's anything suspicious. I can't tell you much at this stage, but it could be connected to the work Daniela was doing. There's a backstory to what's been going on, and I think she'll need our protection."

Xavi's unmarked car pulled up outside the victim's house. Arriving shortly after him, Antonio was pleased to see that the squaddie attending the scene had followed instructions precisely. The place was taped off, and no one allowed inside. Minimal disturbance protocols had been observed. Walking the scene inside the house, he and Xavi observed what they'd expected. Presuming that the suicide had been staged, they looked beyond the obvious—but found nothing. "If it's what Diego suspects," noted Antonio, "it was done by a professional. There's absolutely nothing out of place. There aren't even any signs it's been sanitised. I don't think we're going to find anything in here. We have time of death at around 1300 hours today, so let's concentrate on finding videos of anyone who approached the house or has been seen in the neighbourhood."

"The surveillance equipment has been deactivated," said Xavi. "No disk."

"That could be explained," said Antonio. "The victim retired recently. It was probably the embassy's property. Being government, they'd want their equipment back. The victim, himself, might have disabled it. If the killer knew the system, any surveillance tapes would have been removed as a precaution. It points to someone who worked with the victim. Certainly not a random break-in and burglary. Nothing valuable seems to have been taken."

"No luck on surveillance tapes in the neighbourhood, so far," said Xavi several hours later. "I've got extra people on the job; they're going door-to-door. We haven't got an opinion on cause of death yet. If it was a homicide, the killer certainly paid scrupulous attention to detail."

Antonio had called Diego several times and, later that day, phoned again to provide an update. "The best guess we can make, assuming it is homicide, is that the killer was a pro. It was targeted. No sign of break-in. He or she knew the victim and was familiar with his routines. It might have been someone connected with his work, but we don't have any substantiation for that at the moment. No indications of foul play. Quite the opposite. We're going to have to rely on investigations external to the house.

"We have this on highest priority, Diego.

"If there's any evidence to be found, we'll find it."

Diego

His run-in with Colonel Scott months earlier hadn't endeared Diego to the man.

Yet, Diego knew he had to take action over what Daniela had told him at the condesa's house in La Moraleja. Now, with the news of Bill Yates's apparent suicide, a much more urgent but clearer picture was emerging—and it pointed to Michael O'Flaherty's involvement. If Diego intended to inform the CIA of his concerns, he knew he'd have to proceed through the proper chain of command—and Colonel Scott was the American's immediate superior. The mere thought of it left a bad taste in his mouth.

On board the USS *Bataan*, Diego hadn't had much interaction with James Garwood. The English peer seemed to be in O'Flaherty's pocket, and the two seemed as tight as a well marinated wooden bung hammered into an oak barrel. The special relationship at work again. He speculated for a few minutes: Could he rely on the Brit to keep any discussions between them confidential, and if so, what help could Diego expect from him? Undecided, he texted Pablo and asked for an urgent meeting.

"It's too risky," declared his boss. "If what Daniela has told you is true, there's another very significant agenda at work, and we don't know who has their fingers in the pie. But we do have confidential access to the CIA's organisational structure from our own files and the CNI. I have a friend there, Diego. I'll give him a call and check the lay of the land . . . before we commit ourselves."

Several hours later, Diego received a call from his boss and was given the information he needed. "Lieutenant Commander O'Flaherty is on special duties. Currently, he reports to the deputy director of the Europe and Middle East Special Operations Section. CIA talk for covert activities," said Pablo. "The deputy is a long-term CIA officer, Helen Hunter—solid as a rock, according to my source.

"Here's the politics, Diego, and it may help us decide how to proceed. Helen Hunter is a civilian, by which I mean she doesn't have allegiance to the American military. Colonel Scott *is* former military; so is Helen's boss, the director of the section. So is Lieutenant Commander O'Flaherty—he's Navy, as we know. And he's also connected to a little-known department of the Department of Defence called Section 9. By definition, that's military also."

Pablo paused to give Diego time to absorb the implications. "If Daniela is correct, and there's another agenda at work here, it's being run by the military, not by the CIA. The CIA reports to the president and the cabinet. The US military reports to the secretary of defence, and ultimately to the president. But, as we've seen in the past, that gives them a lot of power. Do you remember General Alexander Haig's bizarre 'I'm in control' claim during the Reagan era?

"We have a parallel situation organisationally here in Spain. In GEO, as part of the National Police, we're civilians. Our Civil Guard is closer to being military; they see themselves as the ultimate guardians of our country's security. What I can tell you is that if the Americans have a dark secret and they're running a deep covert op—overriding Project Catalyst—it's being run by the military, not the CIA."

"That's what Daniela told us," said Diego, his face taut with concern. "If the US military has embedded a deep covert operation within ours, they certainly haven't told us about it. Daniela claims that her operation was used as a decoy for the Syrian military to capture al-Amin, or at least orchestrate his capture by the Syrians. She's adamant that, looking back at it, her mission was a set-up from the beginning. I'm beginning to think she's right."

Diego breathed in before continuing. "And that means there is only one person within the CIA we can reasonably trust in this instance. The deputy director of the covert section that Lieutenant Commander O'Flaherty has been seconded to for Project Catalyst."

"Helen Hunter," said Pablo, finishing off his thought process.

Pentagon Section 9: A Visit

Deputy Director Helen Hunter was escorted to the head of Section 9's office.

"Helen." He beamed. "A pleasure. Come and sit down. You don't visit us nearly often enough."

"I'll come straight to the point, sir." She watched as the brigadier general patted his suit jacket pockets.

"Too used to my military uniform," he said. "Wearing a business suit doesn't come naturally after all these years. No pockets." He laughed. Going to his desk, he picked up his glasses. "How can I help?"

"Project Catalyst," she began, "was it a decoy?"

He looked mystified. "What do you mean, a decoy? A decoy for what?"

"That's what I'm asking, sir. What else have you got going on?"

"You're going to have to be more specific, Helen," he drawled. "You know I can't comment on military initiatives. Now, I can see you're upset. Sit down and tell me what's on your mind." He leaned over his desk and switched his phones to mute.

Fifteen minutes later, during which his face had remained impassive and uncompromising, the brigadier general leaned back in his chair. "From what I'm hearing, Helen, this theory of yours relies almost completely on the statements of a field officer who has just recently been released from an extended period of incarceration in Damascus. She's undoubtedly a very brave young woman, but through the grapevine, I've heard that she's suffering from a severe case of PTSD. She needs treatment and help, I understand.

"As for the suicide of one of our former diplomatic service officers in Barcelona, you have offered me no evidence that the officer's death was anything more than an unfortunate event. He'd recently lost his wife. So, you can see why I'm having difficulty supporting your assessment. I'm sorry, but I'm going to have to ask you to refrain from discussing this subject. That's an order," he added. "If you want me to formalise it, I'll talk to your director personally."

He stood up. "Now is there anything else you want to say?"

"No, sir," she replied. "Except that I'd like to put something on record. I believe that what's in play is a covert operation within a covert operation. Our allied officer Daniela Balmes may be suffering from PTSD, but she has been with us every step of the way—and I believe that she has assessed the situation correctly.

"Project Catalyst was designed as a decoy from the beginning."

Deputy Director Helen Hunter left the Pentagon building.

The head of Section 9 watched from his prestigious corner window as she strode vigorously across the visitors' car park, slamming the door as she got into her compact EV.

"Oops," he said aloud, patting his suit pockets for a fresh cigar. "This might need damage control."

Madrid: Torrejón Air Base

He had passed through check-in and military security—and was seated in the almost deserted departure lounge. The facility was cavernous and had seen better days. Outside, the screech of recently airborne F18s cut through the quietness of the Madrid evening.

"Your aircraft will be landing shortly, Lieutenant Commander," said an orderly, with a salute. His uniform jacket bore the emblem of the Grupo 45 VIP Lounge personnel. "May I get you anything while you wait?"

O'Flaherty didn't feel thirsty and knew they would feed him during the flight to Washington. He shook his head and went back to reviewing some non-classified material on his laptop. It was hard to concentrate. Recent events haunted him. Still, they'd been necessary, he reminded himself—national security.

"Hello Michael." He heard her voice behind him. Must be losing my edge, he thought. He hadn't even heard her footsteps. That was Daniela—she moved everywhere like a phantom.

"Hi! Come to see me off?" he asked, his senses already alerting him. "Quick trip. Sorry, didn't have time to say goodbye." Involuntarily, his eyes strayed to his mobile lying on the plastic tabletop. Yes, he could have phoned her, he thought. He looked up. "I can call the waiter?" he asked, but she shook her head. Neither of them thought it was a social meeting.

"Michael, you didn't tell me everything. You didn't tell me about Hasan. You didn't tell me that what I was doing—all those three years—was a set-up. It was just a decoy for the real operation you're involved in."

O'Flaherty said nothing while he rapidly recalibrated the implications. Despite everything, he'd underestimated her. During their meeting at the safe house, she'd given no indication that she knew. How much else did she know? He looked beyond her across the departure lounge; she was alone. No sign of any reinforcements. Anyway, he'd be out of here shortly.

"What do you want, Daniela?" he asked, moving into attack mode. Take care of everything, the brigadier general had directed.

Her raised eyebrows and questioning look told him that she had a lot more to say. She didn't look wired, but he couldn't take a chance.

"Let's take a walk outside," he invited, picking up his travel bag.

Daniela followed him through the doors to the asphalt strip running alongside the low-rise pre-fabricated administration buildings.

At this time of the evening, only a few essential personnel seemed to be on duty. Many of the office and services buildings were in darkness. In the distance, portable lights shone brightly, illuminating a Spanish military cargo plane being offloaded by forklift operators. A steady green light from the darkened control tower to an incoming aircraft indicated that it was cleared to land. She could barely see the inside of the dimmed tower and the shadowy silhouettes of air traffic controllers.

"How did you know?" he snapped.

"How did I know?" she repeated his question. "I didn't, not until quite late. When too many things didn't add up, I started to question various events." She turned to face him and saw no evidence of surprise. Rather, it was a look of irritation—with an insinuation that she was being insubordinate. She'd never seen that look from him before. "When Yussef and I were captured in Latakia, I wondered why the Russians were so cooperative. I explained that away, figuring you had arranged it. Then on the limousine drive with you in Turkey, I asked you about the role the Russians were playing. You told me that sometimes our political interests and theirs are aligned. That we both want al-Qaeda to be defeated—for al-Amin to be apprehended. That was okay, too, except that I fell asleep very quickly. I wondered about that afterwards. A sleeping pill in my drink? I was tired, but not that tired. You just didn't want to answer my questions, Michael.

"None of that became significant until we both deployed to Syria—when we were in al-Amin's camp. Hasan's animosity towards me was convincing at first. He was terrifying. When he tried to rape me, I knew that wasn't real. It was an act—I could tell. Women can. Then, later, he behaved strangely just before the raid by the Syrian Army special forces. He was nervous, as if he was expecting something to happen. At the time, al-Amin was questioning me about the location of the gold in Spain. I thought that Hasan would remain very close to him—not allowing a Western infidel, a woman, to get near. After all, it was al-Amin—their supreme leader—and he'd dismissed his guards. But Hasan didn't seem overly concerned about his leader. That was when I first started to think something was going on . . . something I didn't know about and couldn't control.

"When the young kid, Sattam, brought in the tea, Hasan followed him in. He'd been coming in and out like an anxious parent," Daniela continued. "Earlier, I'd shown Sattam how to hide the gun that Jamal had given me. When I went over to help the boy, I retrieved the gun from under his robe. As a reward, I gave him my coloured bracelet, as we'd agreed. He was mesmerised by the coloured glass. I wanted the boy to leave, to get to safety, but Hasan had left the room and secured the door. At that moment, there were just three of us in the room. I knew what I had to do."

"We always knew what you *really* intended to do," interrupted O'Flaherty. "You planned to kill al-Amin. Your orders were to capture him alive—not assassinate him in revenge for the death of your family at Atocha. We didn't trust you. We were onto you from the start, Daniela. That's why Hasan searched the boy and disabled the gun—to stop it working. It was convenient for Hasan's plans for you to hold al-Amin at gunpoint—to keep him positioned exactly where he wanted him."

"Well, your plan worked. I was familiar with Jamal's Glock, its weight," said Daniela. "So, when I took it from Sattam, I knew right away that somehow it had been disabled—the weight was wrong. It could only have been Hasan."

"Al-Amin didn't know that," said O'Flaherty. "You had the drop on him and you got him talking. That was being recorded—Hasan made sure of it. He'd hidden a bug on al-Amin's desk."

"Confessing to the Atocha bombings, Michael? I don't think that was Hasan's purpose."

"No?" asked O'Flaherty; his tone was mocking and his callousness took her aback.

"I think Hasan was outside the door listening to our conversation," she replied quickly. "He had to control the exact timing of the raid and the capture of al-Amin. At that time, I was thinking he was on our side; it was the only explanation that made sense. Hasan had probably disposed of al-Amin's personal guards. They were long dead by then. Standing in front of al-Amin, I had no option but to play my part and carry through with my threat on his life—even though I knew the gun wasn't working."

"Al-Amin wasn't armed. No gun, no knife," said O'Flaherty. "You weren't in any danger, Daniela. It was a contained situation. Hasan had control of it. Full control."

They had walked past several darkened buildings and saw the white landing lights of an incoming heavy military aircraft switch on in the distance. Its powerful engines revved high as the aircraft lowered its landing gear and prepared for final approach. The sound almost drowned out their voices, yet O'Flaherty didn't seem to notice.

Daniela picked up the story. "Hasan was just awaiting the arrival of the Marines, I thought. But you and he were following your special agenda—you both made sure that it was the Syrians who arrived first and captured al-Amin alive. Meanwhile, my guess is that you found some reason to delay calling in the Navy SEALs for their final approach to the village."

Daniela paused. "But something went wrong, didn't it, Michael? The Syrian Special Forces squaddies—a lot of them—burst into the room. No doubt Hasan had shown them where we were. They went straight for al-Amin, intent on apprehending him. One of them saw the young child, Sattam, put his hand in his pocket and maybe thought he was reaching for a weapon. That's when I leaped onto the child, to protect him—with Jamal's empty gun still in my hand. That was stupid of me; I should have thrown it away."

Involuntarily, she stopped walking and rubbed her neck with her hand. "My guess is that you were so concerned about my rapid loss of blood, you ordered Hasan to get me immediate emergency treatment from the Syrian Army medics on board the attack helicopters. I'm glad you did; otherwise, I wouldn't be alive today. I owe you my life, Michael.

"But it meant a change of plan, didn't it? You and Hasan had to adapt quickly. Hasan probably ordered the Syrian Army attack commander to fly me to hospital—maybe on the same aircraft as al-Amin, that's just a guess. I became another high-value hostage for the al-Daser regime.

"You and Hasan escaped exactly the way you explained at your debriefings, except for a few changed details. I read your debriefing statements—Diego gave them to me. You told them that your long-time buddy Nazih rescued you from the room where you'd been tied up. He cut the tape binding you, and you escaped—meeting up with Jamal, actually helping Jamal and the others who were pinned down by sniper fire. That encounter was a bit of luck. You fled to a nearby farm, where you convinced Jamal to fly to the safety of the Iraqi border in his friend's helicopter. You used his vehicle to get part way back to al-Tanf. That was true, at least. Problem is, Michael, it was Hasan—not Nazih—who had rescued you. Nazih and Mohammed were killed earlier in the shooting. Hasan did it—I was there in the room. I saw him fire his gun. I don't know who shot me; I was trying to shield the young boy. Really, it doesn't matter anyway."

They'd reached the fenced end of a row of darkened buildings and had to turn back. For a moment, the screech of reverse thrusts from the military cargo plane braking awkwardly on the runway blocked out all sound. O'Flaherty hesitated and Daniela's defences kicked in. She knew what he was capable of—what he could do, if pushed. She wondered where Diego was at that moment.

"The important question is this: Why did you want to lie to me about your friend Nazih, who was already dead?" she asked as they slowly retraced their steps to the departure area. "I'll tell you why, Michael. It was because you had been colluding all along with Hasan—he's your CIA sleeper agent—currently embedded within the Mukhabarat. You didn't want to draw anyone's attention to Hasan's true undercover role.

"Hasan needed to be seen by Jamal and his men in the act of fleeing from the village. That was after al-Amin had been captured. It was a vital part of his cover story—so that he could retain operational credibility within al-Qaeda. After that, he returned home to Damascus. Because of his success in directing the raid, Hasan is now a hero within the Mukhabarat. He's earned himself a key part of the decision-making about what happens to al-Amin. That was your brainwave, Michael.

You intended all along to make sure that al-Daser's troops captured al-Amin and that the Navy SEALs did not. You wanted to make sure that al-Qaeda knew their new leader was in Syrian government hands—so that reprisals would be directed at Damascus, not at the United States.

"Clever idea, that, by the way," she continued. "You'd already figured out that when Damascus inevitably ran to their friends—the Russians—for help in retaliating against al-Qaeda, the war on terrorism would escalate. The US would have a valid reason to re-engage militarily in the region—dragging the unwilling Coalition unwittingly with them. I'm fairly certain that isn't official US policy. Maybe even the president doesn't know. Maybe you and your friends in the military have set him up to fail. Just guessing," she added.

"American voters have voted several times now to stay out of Middle East conflicts," Daniela continued. "But it's what your real boss, the brigadier general—and the military—wants, isn't it? Bypass Congress. Set up a deep state within the republic. Re-engage directly through the Executive Branch. Give Russia a reason to escalate its military presence in the region—hence their cooperation. Both countries can sell more weapons and technology in the process. The old imperialistic mantra: instigate instability—and keep feeding it."

O'Flaherty was shaking his head. He almost seemed to be mocking her, she thought. "That's all supposition, Daniela. Besides, we were operational. Decisions had to be made on the spur of the moment. It's for the greater good." He paused. "I don't want to diminish your efforts. You were superb—every step of the way. Immaculate. No one else could have done what you did. But you and I are both inconsequential in the wider picture. I'll admit it: the real objective always was to establish Hasan as a deep undercover officer. We've done that now, and Project Catalyst has to be dismantled. You're too much of a professional to fight against it.

"It was our only way of getting back. How do you think we knew about al-Amin? We knew about him because Osama bin Laden told us. That's one of the reasons why we kept him alive after Abbottabad. We didn't kill him; he died later. We gave him an honourable burial, a Muslim burial—a warrior's burial—near the Khyber Pass that he loved so much. We are not animals, Daniela. We are just playing by the same devoid-of-rules terrorism warfare that our enemies engage in. We have to protect our country and our people. That's our job."

"Well, you're right there, Michael. Anyway, I can't prove anything. My account of what went on in Syria is in conflict with the official version that you've put in place. Again, very clever of you, actually. I'm viewed as damaged goods. Suffering from PTSD. That's the way this will go down, won't it? You've discredited the only person who could give evidence against you."

"Evidence of what?" he asked, his voice tinged with barely suppressed anger. "I'm not being charged with anything. I'm still operational, Daniela. You're not. You did your part and you've been stood down. Get over it. Accept the reality and move on. It is for the greater good. Just remember that," he shouted after her as she began to walk away. "We're not winning the war against terrorism, Daniela. Not the way we've been playing it. You know that."

"You're not wrong there," she replied with a harshness in her voice. A regret, almost. A note of resignation.

"Dammit, Daniela," he said angrily. "We're in this together, you and I."

A smaller aircraft had landed, which Daniela guessed from its USAF markings was the Gulfstream arriving from Washington to pick him up. He'd also observed its arrival. They watched as it moved from the active runway through the connecting lanes towards them. She thought he seemed relieved at the prospect of going home.

Behind them, the Gulfstream was being guided into its parking position by ground control staff. As its engines shut down, refuellers

325

moved into position and attached the grounding cable. O'Flaherty looked at his watch. "They're going to turn around and depart immediately. Well, I'm glad you're safe, Daniela. And I mean that genuinely." His voice trailed off as he recognised the man walking briskly towards them from the terminal.

"Detective Inspector Abaya," he said as Diego arrived at where they were standing.

"Lieutenant Commander O'Flaherty," Diego replied brusquely. "I want to talk to you about the death of your former colleague, Mr. Bill Yates. Can you tell me, sir, where you were between 1000 hours and 1600 hours today?"

"Why would I have to do that?" shot back O'Flaherty. He gesticulated over his shoulder at the parked Gulfstream, where the refuelling was in progress. "I'm leaving shortly. I'm an American government senior security officer, as you know. You don't have the authority to detain me." He looked at Daniela with accusing eyes. His aggressive demeanour was accusative. It said that he thought she was responsible for Diego's arrival.

It didn't seem to faze Daniela. "You killed Bill Yates," she said. "You killed him to protect your special mission. That was why he died—you were worried that he was no longer reliable, that he'd become a security risk. You thought he'd betrayed us, Michael. He didn't. Bill was innocent. You thought he'd conspired with the Russians—with Alexei—to snatch the money from the Cyprus bank. He didn't. How can I be so certain? Because he couldn't have. I told you that I'd given Bill the passcode to the safety deposit box. It's true. I did give him a passcode, but it wasn't the right number. For my own security, I gave Bill a bogus number. I had to.

"Don't you see?" she continued earnestly. "I couldn't risk giving the real passcode to anyone but al-Amin. My life depended on it; so did our operation. The money had to be there when al-Amin's people turned up at the Cyprus bank to withdraw it. That was the only way I could earn his complete trust and have a chance to do what I had to do."

She watched as O'Flaherty's eyes narrowed, and he breathed in deeply. There was no way he was going to admit anything, she thought. He'd circled the wagons, and she was on the outside. After all they'd been through together, they may as well be strangers, she thought.

But there was one final thing left to say.

"It's not the fact that you deceived me, Michael, that you used me for your own purposes. It's not even the horrendous waste of time and resources you've put us all through. Between allies, that's bad enough. Let's put all that aside for a moment. Here's the thing. You've bet the farm on embedding Hasan deep undercover. It's a hell of a bet, Michael—and it's a mistake. Hasan can't be trusted; he's a double agent. He's not working for us—he's a Syrian Mukhabarat agent. Not just pretending to be, he actually is—he works for them. They embedded him into the West.

"He's playing you, Michael," she added. "And it gives me no satisfaction to tell you that. I know that Hasan was behind the failed attempt to withdraw the money from Cyprus. He had to do it before al-Amin's people got there. That's why he created the set-up at the village. He pretended to try to rape me, but I knew that wasn't what he wanted. He had me in a stranglehold; he coerced the passcode out of me. But I scrambled the number and gave him a bogus code.

"You probably don't believe me, do you? Well, earlier today, Diego talked to your friend James Garwood. The Brits have Hasan's accomplices in custody. The passcode I gave Hasan matched the number they used to try withdrawing the money. It's the smoking gun, Michael. You can't trust Hasan. It was pure greed on his part. By doing what he did, he put our mission—and my life—directly at risk."

She stared at O'Flaherty. "This new covert operation—it's your mission, not mine. But we are allies, at the end of the day." She gestured towards Diego. "Almost for sure, he and I will be ordered by our superiors to say nothing. For us, too, ironically, your mission is vital to our national security. The thing is, I don't think you'll be welcomed back to Spain after the deception you've masterminded. Not just that. Bill Yates was an innocent man, Michael. You could have shared your suspicions about him. Trusted me. Instead, you made a fatal error. He didn't need to die."

In the background, behind O'Flaherty, at the top of the steps leading to the Gulfstream, a silhouette appeared. Daniela and Diego turned to walk back to the terminal.

"I don't have to answer to you," shouted O'Flaherty angrily. "Or to him." He gestured towards Diego. "He's got nothing. It's all circumstantial. I don't have to answer to either of you."

"No, you don't. But you do have to answer to *her*," said Daniela, turning and pointing to the top of the steps where Deputy Director Helen Hunter was waiting.

Diego had already walked back to the terminal. Daniela hesitated momentarily before following him. For a moment, there was a sadness in her eyes, but it soon hardened.

She continued to walk away. "Goodbye, Michael."

"Good luck."

EPILOGUE
Diego

At GEO Headquarters, there's a spiral-bound notebook.

We found it several years ago, at the time we arrested Raphael Robles and charged him with treason and other crimes. It's one of several items of official evidence locked in ultra-secure storage. For me, it stands out as a reminder of how this whole thing started—how I became involved in what, at the time, seemed to be a routine homicide investigation in Barcelona. One that led right to the top of al-Qaeda's leadership, involving several additional deaths and resulting in the arrest of some very prominent and influential people.

The notebook is the kind that every student uses for jotting down reminders and recording homework assignments. Handwritten and anonymous, it's mostly blank pages. Penned in red ink, in a young girl's neat handwriting, the words reveal what the author was thinking at the time—her state of mind. It's an alphabetical list of the people who died at the scene of the 11 March 2004 massacre at Atocha train station.

I don't know what was going through Daniela's head when she wrote it. Her name isn't on the front cover, but we don't need a handwriting expert for confirmation. We know it's hers. Beneath the one hundred and ninety-three names of the confirmed and named dead, she had added her only sibling and her parents:

Alejandro Balmes
Mum
Dad

Not her parents' names but what they were to her. Simply, Mum and Dad. Sometime later, she'd added her own name in black ink—the only person on the list still alive. I think about that notebook a lot.

They say that from evil can come good. I'll leave it to others to argue that point. In my work as a policeman, I deal with evil in its many forms every day of my life. The only good that I've seen doesn't emerge from evil. Sometimes, good thrives despite it. Daniela's young life was like that.

Lieutenant Commander Michael O'Flaherty returned to the United States. Despite the criminal charges he might ordinarily have faced in Spain, he took up full duties as a senior officer with Section 9. On orders from our prime minister, the Civil Guard seized and destroyed all documents and files relating to him—and to Hasan. It's not his real name, of course. He may still be embedded somewhere deep undercover. O'Flaherty is a clever man and astute. My guess is that he found a way to turn Hasan.

He was right when he said we are not winning the war against terrorism. That's why the activities of frontline spies remain vital. It's a murky occupation, full of deceit and dubious loyalties. Trust is like a veneer of very thin ice covering a village pond on a warm spring day.

The condesa played a significant role in repatriating Daniela. She's back in government as a senior minister. It's rumoured that the PM will step down before the next election, setting in motion a leadership vote within the governing party. The condesa is the people's favourite to succeed him. She's an exceptional woman—an inspiring leader of the new Spain.

Antonio remains with the Mossos in Barcelona, where he and Caterina are raising their young daughter. It's no surprise that Xavi and Pilar are her godparents or that another child is on the way. They all meet regularly at the same Catalan restaurant they've frequented for decades. Occasionally, Zineb and I join them—along with Antonio's sister, Isabel, her partner, Julia, his parents, and his granddad. It's an anniversary of sorts. We can't talk about the case, but there's always a note of sadness. Each of us share a deep respect for those who'd fought hard for their beliefs and made the ultimate sacrifice.

We heard through intelligence sources that, in Syria, Jamal returned to his former profession as a surgeon. He continues as a strong and highly respected advocate of political and economic stability for the region. He's a senior representative in the ongoing regional peace talks. Daniela still wears the blue sapphire brooch he gave her.

When the outcome of Claudia's behind-doors court martial was announced, we received a wonderful surprise. The military judge presiding found that, based on the information available to her at the time, Claudia was acting lawfully in her position within the Civil Guard. The judge found that her actions in ordering the sniper to proceed were reasonable under the circumstances—she had no knowledge that Daniela was working in a deep undercover role. Daniela gave evidence as a witness in her support. Claudia was reinstated as head of GEO 60, where she continues today.

At Claudia's invitation, Daniela joined our group and works as an intelligence officer—with certain special remits. In contrast to the depressed mood that prevailed after Raphael Robles was arrested and imprisoned, spirits today are high again within our team. We have an outstanding reputation. Each year, a long list of enthusiastic and well-qualified candidates from a wide variety of backgrounds—and countries—apply to join us. Thanks to Claudia's strategic initiatives, our relationship with Spain's autonomous enforcement and security forces is collaborative, effective—and widely admired.

Since joining GEO 60, Daniela has been involved in some sensitive and challenging missions. That's nothing new for her. She's beautiful, smart, and determined. As a field agent, she's a natural.

That girl from Barcelona is one tough cookie.

For news on more books from Peter Woodbridge, visit:
PETERWOODBRIDGE.COM

Follow Peter at:
facebook.com/PeterWoodbridgeAuthor
instagram.com/peterwoodbridgeauthor

BEARWOOD
PUBLISHING